To Tony

Man O' War

Beer for books is
fair exchange –
I felt compelled to…
make it so!

Dan Jones

Hope you enjoy it

Proudly published by Snowbooks
Copyright © 2018 Dan Jones
Dan Jones asserts the moral right to be identified as
the author of this work. All rights reserved.

Snowbooks Ltd | email: info@snowbooks.com | www.snowbooks.com.

British Library Cataloguing in Publication Data. A catalogue record for this
book is available from the British Library.
Printed in Denmark by Nørhaven

First published March 2018

Paperback 9781911390305
E-Book 9781911390480
Hardback 9781911390473

Man O' War

Dan Jones

Acknowledgements

No book can survive the creative process in isolation. There are many different people who contribute to it in their own unique way, and those combined efforts make a living, breathing book. A bit like a Portuguese Man O'War.

First, thank you to Emma and her team at Snowbooks for taking a chance on an unknown author. It's been a bit of a rollercoaster at times but we got there in the end, and it was all worth it!

I'm grateful to Brian Turner and all the knowledgeable and community-minded folks at SFF Chrons who helped me with critiques, advice and feedback. From that community, particular thanks must go to my brilliant beta readers, William Rutter and my old mucker Nathan Hystad at Woodbridge Press, for their invaluable insights, advice and assistance, which went above and beyond the call of duty. And special thanks must go to Jeff Richards for relating his incredible experiences working in the Niger Delta for the oil and gas industry, and to Ralph Kern for offering priceless insights into the inner machinations of the Police Service. Both of you helped to bring Man O'War to life.

I have to acknowledge my colleagues in the Peraspera robotics project (you know who you are). I wonder if we'll be able to claim the publication of Man O'War as an example of the "added value" of the project?

Last, but never least, thanks to my wonderful wife Jo, who has had to put up with me gallivanting off to the 22nd century every other day. I'm back, baby.

Dhiraj I

Dhiraj knew the rain stopped this distance from the coast, but it still made him uneasy. It wasn't natural to be without the rain. He grunted a command to the Navigation of his seine skiff *The Lion's Mane* to slow down, and the throttle obediently clanked down to a low rumble, slowing the boat to a crawl.

"Come on, babies," he said, peering over dark ocean waves. "I need a good catch tonight."

The thought tightened his throat; he needed this badly now. The prospect of telling his family about another crappy haul made him grit his teeth and focus. Even in the wheelhouse, he was soaked, and he wiped the greasy sleeve of his raincoat across his face. Darkness turned its garish yellow into mustard. Once the boat halted, he called to the floodlights, which swung portside and bathed the water in electric moonlight. As he stepped outside of the wheelhouse, the North Sea's cold whip lashed his face, taking the breath from him, but he bore it, looking upon the horizon. Even under the floodlight, he couldn't see the purse seine net, but he imagined it swelling with bounty just beneath the surface. He smiled in spite of the cold; no, *because* of the cold. Cold brought them swarming. Just a little luck, and he'd be bringing a bumper harvest home tonight. He clenched his fists in anticipation as he traversed the deck.

The rope bobbing on the sea, almost invisible in this blinding blackness, marked his offshore empire. He hoped upon hope that tonight it wouldn't be a fallow one. He headed aft and threw his weight behind the power block lever, cranking it into life. Somewhere out of sight it wheezed and creaked, dragging the chain back inside the hull, closing the dragnet. Odd spots of rain floated in the air, reassuring him of the shoreline's presence somewhere beyond his eyeline.

It was a few minutes before the bounty began to show. Dhiraj grinned. Not everyone could see the little beauties at first, but his was a trained eye. The slightest trace of a tiny light blue shadow quivered below the water's break. Then another. Another. Soon hundreds, then thousands of the little jellyfish shadows throbbed ever so gently with the thrum and swim of the current, and he laughed, clapping his hands in a jubilant jig.

"Yes!" he cried to the jellyfish. "I'll be sending you to a very loving home tonight."

Still smiling, he called to the power block to stop winding up the dragnet, leaving the group of jellyfish bobbing up and down agreeably, like a gigantic Christmas bauble. All his.

Back in the wheelhouse, he started telling the navigation system to head for port when he took another glimpse at the taut dragnet under lights. His smile wilted.

"Shit." A crumpled piece of plastic poked above the waterline, caught by the net. Could be a plastic bag. *Murderous bloody things*, he thought. He instinctively placed his hand to his side, where the sting scars riddled his ribs. *Bound to be something poisonous in it with my luck.* He punched the console and threw the throttle back into neutral with his hands. Nothing for it; it'd have to be dragged out by hand, in case it contained anything hazardous; any contaminant and the whole catch would be worthless, and that'd be another night wasted.

Once on deck he released the dragnet a tad, slid the stepladder along the gunwale, grabbed a pole hook and climbed over. The sea splashed around his ankles, and the blue shadows lapped at his thick black boots like pet dogs. He reached out, straining, and hooked the bag. He yanked it towards him, but its weight almost hauled him into the water instead. *Bloody hell.* If there was one thing worse than a plastic bag, it was a full one. God knows what was in it. Cursing anew, he hooked his elbow around the stepladder rung for greater stability and reached again. This time he gave it a firm pull with the hook, and the little finger of material started to rotate and rise to the surface: first a small, crinkly triangle, then bigger. Not a disposable plastic bag; thicker than that; a vacuum-packed bag, large, getting larger as the material bobbed to the surface, pushing the blue moon jellies out of the way, eager to break the surface. He saw something white and translucent inside, difficult to discern amongst the waves and jellies, but then it spun about quickly, catching the glare of the floodlight.

When a face emerged from the water trapped in the plastic, Dhiraj cried so loudly he shocked himself, grabbing the ladder tightly with both hands and dropping the pole in the water with a limp splash. He was shivering, and his eyes were blurred with water. He pressed his forehead to the freezing cold of *The Lion's Mane's* hull and closed his eyes. When he opened them, he turned his head to the water and breathed slowly, trying to slow his heartbeat.

Shit. Shit shit shit.

The body was still there, serene and ghostly over the

bioluminescence of the moon jellies, partially obscured by the glare of the floodlight bouncing off the plastic wrapping. His breathing had calmed now. He hadn't seen a dead body since his Aunt Kiri's funeral, but back then the sullen teenager in him had been repulsed by the rituals, the flowers, the incense, his aunt's puffy body, shiny with exuberantly applied makeup, and the whole damn need to structure something so profound as grief. He didn't feel that way now. To his great surprise, he found himself muttering, "Supreme light, lead us from truth to untruth, from darkness to light and from death to immortality." He probably hadn't said the words since that very funeral as Aunt Kiri was consumed by the crematorium's fire. But Aunt Kiri had died of a heart attack – too much ghee and whiskey – whereas who could say what had happened to this poor wretch, wrapped up in plastic and dumped in the sea? The wrongness of it all hit him about the head like a jackhammer, over and over.

Dhiraj shook the whys and wherefores away. He couldn't think about how it had got there or who might be responsible. That wasn't his problem. His job was to fish it out and hope his catch wasn't too contaminated. The body had rolled onto its front, its nakedness obvious yet indistinct. He stepped down into the water, picked up the pole and reached across to the body. His hands still trembled, but he mastered his apprehension, and after a few attempts the body was within touching distance. As he pulled it close and lifted the head out of the water, his distaste lessened somewhat. A woman. Her face was calm, peaceful even. She didn't look distressed or as though she had suffered any violence. Almost looked asleep, melting Dhiraj's fears away.

But when she opened her eyes, Dhiraj screamed, lost his grip, and the sea greeted him with an icy kiss.

Nita I

In a sea of change, a few London buildings had remained steadfast, stoically rebuffing the seemingly inevitable sweep of progress. Not that there was anything romantic about clinging to such airs and graces, Nita thought.

The regulator's office, situated on Victoria Street, was one such edifice: a monstrous monument to mid-twentieth-century brutalism, possessing little art or subtlety. Even the interior lights were muddied and stunted by the dirty, grey window panes. She hoped the people inside the regulator's office wouldn't be just as rigid when she presented her technology.

The black cab took payment via thumbprint as her brollybot hovered above her and opened its arms like a jellyfish, shielding her from the thumping rain as she walked along the pavement to the office.

The brollybot closed back up once inside, leaving Nita to smooth down her skirted suit. She'd chosen white today. White was the colour of possibility, a blank canvas. They needed to see that. After registering with the holoscreen at the front desk, she took a seat and stared around at the interactive holoposters and intelligent adverts tailored to her interests.

Support English industry! they all shouted proudly, before trailing some interactive 3D video demonstration of English industry at work. In her case, the videos showed an array of robotics hardware and software success stories: servile consumer robots, improved deductive reasoning software, surgeons, care robots, and more. All English. All state-of-the-art. The videos increased both her nervousness and confidence; her company's technology, compared to these robots, might still be considered too radical. On the other hand, these people were supposed to champion innovative businesses like EI Systems.

She mulled this over for a few minutes, consulting a few notes, until her host arrived from beyond the security wall. He swiped his way past the wall and strode up to Nita, greeting her with a beaming smile and a warm kiss on each cheek. Sir Ingham Fitzwilliam, the Chief Regulator for Robotics and Autonomous Systems, was a throwback in some ways, just like the building that housed him. A splendid pinstripe navy suit and fastidious grooming made him handsome for his seventy-plus years; he was silvery on top and craggy of jaw, yet fit as a flea, and he bore himself with a bygone puffed-up posture. From their previous video call, Nita also had postulated him to be charming, thoughtful, highly intelligent, and ferociously polite.

"Good afternoon, Nita, how the devil are you?"

"Very well, Sir Ingham, thank you. It's lovely to finally meet you."

"Likewise, likewise. But please, it's just Ingham. Titles are only for boring state occasions. This is much more interesting, and I find titles are of no use anywhere of actual interest. Please, after you. Let's get out of this awful foyer."

His office, somewhere up on the eighth floor, was as warm, welcoming and old-fashioned as he was: a cube of green leather and crystal baubles, with various gongs and photographs hanging upon the wall.

A semi-humanoid servobot wheeled into the office and parked itself by Sir Ingham's desk. "Would you care for tea or coffee?"

Nita asked for a tea, and the little robot decanted a perfectly brewed beverage before placing it on her side of Sir Ingham's desk. After the robot wheeled itself back out, Sir Ingham closed the door and waited for Nita to sit before taking his own seat.

"I do so despair of these biospheres we have now," he said airily, waving at the window, "for it means I can't make small talk about the weather any longer. The bane of Middle England, I'm afraid."

Nita laughed politely. "They are useful, though, and of course it's English technology at work."

"Yes, yes, I know. But I do miss the sun so." He looked wistfully at the constant brown rain hammering at the grey smudge that was his window. Some time in the past that window would have been new and clear, but now it barely offered an impression of what lay beyond. "Sometimes I feel as though I merely dreamt those sunny days of my younger years."

Nita felt for the older man. Of course she'd heard of the sunny days from before her birth and seen any number of films featuring the sun, but a lifetime of cooling rain from the biosphere to lower the regional temperature had rendered them unreal; it must have been all special effects and trickery. As much as she wanted to see the sun, she was used to life without it. As was Sir Ingham, no doubt, but it must have been terrible to have had better times taken from you. *If only they'd done something about it sooner.*

"I think one day, they'll be rendered obsolete. The sun will shine again," she said.

"Not in my lifetime, I'm afraid," said Sir Ingham. "And I plan on living to a hundred and fifty. I've a good quarter century of career left in me, and then it's retirement. Somewhere a long way from here." He smiled softly. "But not quite yet."

Nita smiled.

A knock came upon the door. Sir Ingham stood. "Ah, yes. I hope you don't mind. I've invited my understudy to join us. I thought this might be a very useful piece of schooling for him."

"Of course." Nita hadn't expected it, but the thought of a younger person – a younger *man* – might enable the conversation to flow more favourably for her. She hoped this man had the ear of Sir Ingham.

In came a slim West African gentleman, immaculately turned out in a charcoal grey suit, probably a similar age to her, judging by the slightest inflection of salt and pepper colouring in his closely cropped hair. Behind thick spectacles were mahogany eyes creased from generously distributing the sort of earnest, ear-to-ear smiles he was wearing right now as he greeted Sir Ingham and turned his gaze towards Nita.

"Nita, this is Ademuyiwa Johnson."

"Just Adem," he said, enthusiastically clasping Nita's hand with both of his and shaking them vigorously. Nita had to reciprocate the smile. He had a mild, upper-class Nigerian accent and lovely, buttery-soft hands. "Lovely to meet you. I've heard a lot about you."

"Nice to meet you. Thank you for joining us. What's your background?"

"I'm actually a civil engineer. I worked in my family's oil business for quite a few years; I helped bring some of the autonomous exploration and extraction technologies to the delta. I wanted to see England, so I came here."

Nita furrowed her brows. "Johnson... that wouldn't be the Johnson Petroleum Corporation, would it?"

Adem raised his hands, as if being found out. "Yes, that's them, for my sins. My family wanted me to work for JPC since I was small. But I always wanted to spread my wings a bit further."

"Adem's been an invaluable asset to the team," said Sir Ingham. "Good to have somebody from heavy civil industry on board. JPC stress-test high value robotics systems as much as anyone on Earth."

After the introductions were done, Sir Ingham produced a sheet of paper from his desk – a deliberately quaint piece of self-deprecating humour on his part, Nita decided – and studied it. "Would you mind refreshing our memories of the presentation you gave over video conference please, Nita?"

"Of course." She produced and slipped on data gloves, pulled her globelet from her bag and placed it upon the desk. From it she opened her presentation into 3D above Sir Ingham's desk. The company logo of Emotional Intelligent Systems shimmered proudly between them all. "As you know, EI Systems already supplies state-of-the-art robotics and intelligent systems to a wide array of markets – medicine, care, consumer tech, logistics, space, and others, but we believe there is one market that remains untapped and unexploited."

"The sex industry," said Adem, putting a thoughtful finger to his lips.

Nita looked to Sir Ingham for a response, but the older man remained impassive. "Correct. The sex industry remains the one area where cutting edge technologies could revolutionise it, improving the lives of men and women everywhere." She brought up a slide showing a sequence of graphs, each one highlighting itself in line with her speech. "Last year, the Home Office estimated that the black market for sex increased by ten percent, much higher than the stagnating growth of the overall economy. What's more, it's been growing steadily for the last five years. Furthermore, the statistics are saying that the demand for sex dolls–"

"You mean the working kokeshi, the sex robots?" asked Adem.

"Yes, the kokeshi – the demand for them has risen at least as much as the demand for real humans. But the sex market remains a black one."

Sir Ingham was too polite to say so, but she could tell by the tapping of his finger he was already sceptical. Adem, however, furrowed his brows thoughtfully and stared intently at the presentation, pausing occasionally to tap out some notes on his own globelet. She took a moment to pause, compose herself, smooth down her jacket and take a sip of tea. This could revolutionise her business if she got the regulator on board. She'd take her time.

"As a black market, it remains unregulated. England has no manufacturing base for kokeshi, and the ones that appear in underground sex shops and brothels are usually imported from countries who reverse engineer older robotics models, leaving them prone to faults and malfunctions – potentially dangerous ones. Meanwhile, the inherent dangers for human men and women working in an unregulated and underground sex industry are just as real as they always have been." She moved the slides along to more graphs and a map of the world.

"The recent wars in the Middle East, and the Marxist rebellions in part of Africa..." She took the liberty of glancing at Adem as she said that, but if he had any reaction, he hid it well. "... They've shown us that the use of rape and sexual assault as a weapon of war is still commonplace. The UN show us these statistics: along the Russian-European borders 50,000 women are estimated to have been subjected to severe sexual assaults by military personnel in 2135 alone, while the figures in Africa are worse. We believe that with the introduction of fully functioning sexual service robots we can eliminate, or at least significantly reduce, the dangers posed to women in war-torn parts of the world."

"How so?" asked Sir Ingham.

"Excuse me?" Heat pricked her cheeks.

"How would the implementation of sex robots achieve this?"

"By giving soldiers robotic sexual partners. There's a surplus of young, impressionable single men in volatile situations. If they're given a legitimate outlet for their frustrations then they'll be less likely to commit wartime atrocities."

Sir Ingham raised his eyebrows. "And you're quite sure this would be the case?"

"If I may," said Adem. "We – I mean, my family – are very much aware of the heinous crimes which have been committed by people wearing the uniform of our national army, but I tell you it is not in our name, and my father has been at pains to condemn the violence.

"The soldiers are often starved of non-military human contact and rely on illegal interactions with prostitutes. The prostitutes are often trafficked and owned by the local crime lords, who in turn fund the NPF rebels. So the cycle of violence continues.

"It's possible," Adem continued, "that the use of robots in the delta could cut off a significant source of income for the local organised crime rings, as well as saving the lives of many local girls and boys."

Sir Ingham tapped the end of a pen on his desk, creating soft rhythms on the leather as he gathered his thoughts. "What about at home? The domestic markets?"

Nita cleared her throat, trying to conceal her excitement that Adem had so quickly seen the potential in her technologies. "Like I said: the underground sex industry. These places are dangerous and run by dangerous people. Let's legitimise it by using English technology – *our* technology – to protect both the customers and the girls currently working there. If it's legitimised, the revolution could be huge. Think of the tax receipts. Think of the amount of organised crime that could be wiped off the map overnight. Quickly the black market would wither to insignificance."

Sir Ingham nodded his head silently as she reeled off her points, but she tried to keep a lid on her enthusiasm.

He smiled and put the pen down. "You are right, of course. The market needs are well known, both at home and abroad. It's always nice to hear them so passionately advocated. Most people, even in this day and age, still shy away from talking about sex and the sex industry. Old British habits die very hard, you see. But you must remind me, Nita, of the specifics of your technology."

"Of course." She opened up a new 3D video presentation that projected into the air above the tablet, in full colour. As the video progressed, she provided a brief, high-level explanation of the various systems that comprised the whole of the robot, from the highly advanced synthetic skin, muscle fibres and senses, to the brain and the decision-making capabilities. "All of our work builds upon the state-of-the-art, providing better quality human appearance and feel. But the true step change is to be found in the robot's emotional intelligence. EI Systems developed this by artificially replicating the organic neural connections our brains make as we grow and learn. The system uses a combination of synthetic hormones, organic electronics and cutting-edge biocoding to effectively mimic the processes of experiencing, learning and feeling basic human emotions: anger, fear, surprise, disgust, joy, sadness. To all intents and purposes, the possessor of this artificial brain has a human experience. We call the result The Digital Person."

As she spoke, the model robot in her video displayed each emotion in turn in different situations. "In humans, emotions change all the time; they're not the same as moods, which can last for weeks, or personalities, which can last a lifetime. Emotions are responses to our surrounding environment and motivate us to change, or act. By giving robots emotions, they will interact with humans in richer ways. They will provide a more fulfilling period of companionship to humans who may be lonely, or who find human social interaction difficult. People who might ordinarily be driven to the dangers of the underground sex industry. We've seen this already in the medicare sector, where the basic EI Autonomous Brain has already provided companionship to people living in isolation. This is the next step. We're combining a complex state of feeling in the robot with the behavioural and psychic symptoms associated with it; they react not just to physical stimuli – I prick your finger, you hurt – but emotional stimuli, and they respond accordingly. They understand. We are, in effect, creating worthwhile members of society. Digital People."

The pen tapped again, and she bit at her lip, then told herself off for doing so.

Sir Ingham smiled at her. "Nita, it's stunning stuff."

Nita swept back a lock of hair behind her ear and leant forward, trying to contain her smile.

"The fabrication of emotion has been the Holy Grail for a lot of developers for decades. I've not seen such huge advances as you've shown me – certainly not in this country." More tapping. "I've spent many years as regulator, despite never having been an engineer myself. Do you know why?"

Nita ran her tongue over her teeth and crossed her legs, sitting back. "No, please tell me."

"Because I was a successful diplomat. It seems to me that you have developed something quite astonishing, but for which I could never sanction further technology demonstrations for commercial use."

Nita's face flushed. She chewed the inside of her mouth. "But you said it yourself, the, uh –"

"There's absolutely nothing wrong with the technology. Nor the market opportunity. But there's an ethical element to all this. If you're creating beings that *understand*, you create beings that surely understand that they've been manufactured. And if they understand they've been manufactured, they understand they've been manufactured for a purpose. They'd understand that they may be used, or abused, and you're explicitly trying to draw an emotional response from them. I'm afraid, if they understand their situation, then they'd understand that they were, in actual fact, on a nightly basis, being raped."

Nita bristled at the word as if she'd been pricked herself. She looked down at her skirt and shook her head. "That is not true. The robots understand their surroundings, and they react accordingly. They provide warmth and comfort for the customer. And we always, always emphasise, no matter how close we get to being human... these are not human beings. We're trying to save the lives of humans being ruined by this phenomenon."

"But the figures for sexual assault have gone down, roughly in line with the rise in use of illicit kokeshi dolls, just as you said."

"Yes, but –"

"You must understand the Government's difficulty in all this, Nita. If I were to sanction a technology demonstrator for such a thing it would immediately be seized upon as evidence that the Government is sanctioning industrial sexual assault. I can't allow that to happen. Tell me, if the robots truly understand their situation, what makes them different to the human men and women in that same situation?"

She shifted in her seat, suddenly uncomfortable. Adem averted his gaze, perhaps in embarrassment, and looked down. *Don't look down, look up and help me!* "Sir Ingham, the Government surely can't legitimise the sex industry as it is. It's dirty, dangerous–"

"You're quite right. I fear that is so. But equally we could never legitimise what you propose as its replacement. I fear – and I truly do understand the awfulness of the situation – that the best course of action is to let the existing sex industry continue in its current form.

"In any case, it's my job to ensure that robotic systems being manufactured for commercial and consumer use are safe, reliable and of proper quality. With a technology as radical as artificial emotions–"

"They're not artificial, they're synthetic."

"Then I beg your pardon. With any technology, I have to work with companies and researchers to find out the best way of creating and formulating tests. With this I wouldn't know where to start, save for the fact that you would need a financial backer of such magnitude that they could afford to absorb the complex web of financial, ethical and technical risks."

Nita's shoulders sagged with defeat. "You know full well that I don't have a hope of securing a financial backer without regulatory support."

"I'm so sorry, Nita. Please don't feel this is a personal decision. I am a big fan of your technology. It may be that its time comes, but I'm afraid I cannot back it."

Rain drummed against the window as Nita packed away her globelet and politely ended the meeting. As she stood, both Sir Ingham and Adem also stood out of courtesy, which angered her immensely, but she simply offered a hard smile.

"Before you leave, perhaps we could exchange cards?" asked Adem.

Nita brushed her hair back in exasperation and picked up her bag. "I'm afraid I'm late for another appointment."

Adem looked put out. "I must insist. It is a mere courtesy to exchange cards." He proffered his phone, causing Nita to sigh. Fucking men and their courtesies. "Sorry," she said, trying to soften the smile. She pulled out her phone, but he pulled out an actual card.

"Sorry if it's slightly old fashioned," he said.

"No, not at all," she said, smiling in spite of the temptation to rip the damn thing up. She stuffed it into her pocket. Adem thanked her graciously and escorted her down to reception.

She had no inclination to order up the brollybot outside. She let the rain slick her hair down into her face as she hailed a taxi.

D'Souza I

D'Souza's thick, dark fingers gently ruffled Gacoki's hair. As soft as sable, it gave off the heady scent of sweat and coconuts, reminding him of home. He planted a kiss on the eunuch's temple and stroked his hair down to his bare shoulders, as precious and pale as porcelain, rising and falling slowly in the wash of a gentle sleep. D'Souza closed his eyes and lay back on the sofa, allowing his muscles to relax into the leather.

"My dear Gacoki," he whispered into his hair.

Around him, the room breathed in a rare moment of calm; soft, abstract beats pulsed out of the speakers while his many aquariums bubbled softly. Even behind his eyes, he was able to filter the soft blue fluorescence thrown out by the glass tanks, washing the office in an aquamarine milkiness. It seemed a terrible shame to have to roll off the sofa.

One day you won't have to, he told himself. *One day all this squalor and shit will lift like smoke above a pyre, clearing the way to the future.* Images of the tree groves outside Negombo came to him, and he saw himself walking barefoot along a wooden path, toward the white beach that framed the shimmering azure vault of the ocean. At once he could smell the salt and smoke of barbecued clams, lobsters, and prawns as long as his skinny boy's forearm, and his mouth slavered. The sun welcomed his bronze skin like an old friend, and he was pleased to find he had no need of his overcoat here. He picked a prawn off the barbecue, stinging hot, which made him laugh. The flesh was sweet, and as salty as brine. The smell of Gacoki's hair mingled with the scents of the sea's magnificent bounty, and tears stung him, crinkling his face into a mess. Ashamed, he opened his eyes and looked around. The blur of tears couldn't hide the fact he was still in London, still in his cubbyhole of an office at the back of his club *Tangiers Nights*. "Fucking hell," he sighed. He'd shaken himself with the memory and sniffed the tears away with a moan.

He gently rolled out from under Gacoki, laying his soft head on a mussed up t-shirt, and snorted again, ridding himself of the dream. His fish swam about in their glass tanks surrounding the room, oblivious.

A knock at the door roused D'Souza from his laziness and pricked his anger. "Who the fuck is that?" he called, getting to his feet. He thought about pulling on some trousers, but then thought *fuck that*. He bunched his curly tresses, smelling of man, into a pony tail, cursing as he did so, and then stood a few yards from the door, legs apart, cracking his knuckles. "I said who the *fuck* is that?"

"Collars, sir," came Collarface's voice, stern and dumb. "We got a problem."

A muscle in D'Souza's cheek twitched, and he ran his tongue over his canines. Problems were no oddity, but one worth interrupting his personal time didn't sound promising. Slow tension crept along his arms, and he took a long, deep breath to clear his head. "Come, then."

The door opened, and the brute Collarface entered, stooping under the lintel. He closed the door and stood silent and firm, resolute as a boulder – and just about as clever. With fat, misshapen fingers he scratched at his collar, the bespoke plastic mould that clamped around his lower jaw and neck. Though it stopped his entire neck from falling to pieces the brute often groaned about how badly it itched, and that he'd rather have it off and have his head fall off than have to scratch around it every day. The taut buckles and leathers across his strapping chest caught the blue light of D'Souza's office. If he had an ounce of charm or wit he'd be a sight. The great brute paid no mind to D'Souza's swinging, glistening cock.

"Talk to me," said D'Souza.

"The Naomi doll Rusty and his boys was expecting down the docks this morning. The one going to *The Golden Tulip* this evening for Mr. Ajax. It weren't there."

D'Souza stepped back. "What?"

"Someone took the doll, sir. Ain't there. Weren't on the boat."

An itch burned D'Souza's face and crawled down his body. His lip twitched, and sweat cooled his brow. "Someone stole from me?"

"We already checked with the Dutch. They said the boat and transit was all sent on time. So far as we can see, they're telling the truth. Rusty said the boat come in, but with a fucking big hole in the side. Someone thieved it and a load of other shit on board."

D'Souza laughed and licked his canines. If he could sharpen them through licking, he would. There was prey out there. He could smell it. He walked over to the aquarium closest to his black mahogany desk and felt the cool air flow around the tanks against his groin. A tremble of ice ran down his spine, all the way to his balls, and he felt his flesh stiffen in readiness for the fight. And there would be a fight now. Inside the tank, a lionfish slowly drifted up and down, its spines folding back and forth like a concertina. He lightly pressed a fingertip to the glass close to the fish's eye and followed it. "What do you think, Collars?"

"Er, sir..."

D'Souza swung around, watching the big ape trying to think. "I agree. Bring Ajax and Rusty here. I want to know everything, and I'll need to know everything that's going on out in the fields. As for you, put the feelers out. Surely there's not a cunt in London dumb enough to try and flog a Naomi doll without bringing attention to himself. You hear the merest murmur, descend with grace."

Collars nodded and retreated from the room. When the door closed, D'Souza's rage erupted in a roar, and he thumped his fist down on the table, sending trinkets tumbling to the floor. Behind him, he sensed Gacoki jump from his slumber, and he bowed his head in regret.

Turning, he saw the beauty, the very model of the young male, lying half-awake, half-reclined on the sofa, his body hairless but for the dark tangle between his legs. The hairs on D'Souza's chest prickled as he watched him emerge from sleep. "So sorry, my precious Gacoki," he whispered, venturing over and stroking his face. "I have a problem I must deal with." He leant in and whispered conspiratorially into his ear. "There are monsters out there who would take from me."

Wiping a crumb of sleep from his eye, Gacoki offered a thin smile and stretched out, draping an arm over D'Souza's shoulder with his free hand. "Someone other than me?"

D'Souza kissed Gacoki on the cheek and on the hair. Coconuts met him as he closed his eyes. "You are no monster. Though you may be the devil."

~

After sending Gacoki away, D'Souza showered for the evening. After he fed his fish he decided to take a look at London. He pulled on his battered old data gloves, the crinkled leather thin and worn now, and brought his globelet out from his desk drawer. He tossed the small ball onto the desk, where it unravelled into his 3D home page. He navigated to maps and peered over London, scrolling and zooming in and out with his fingers. Below, Londoners moved about like tiny ants. "Where the fuck are you?" he whispered to the map.

The thought of one of his rivals attempting such an audacious theft from him was disquieting, and he wasn't entirely sure he believed it. Couldn't rule it out, though; this city never ceased to appal him. Some of the other powerbrokers in the sex game would love to see him flounder or embarrassed: the Muslims and Villains, unlikely bedfellows in the East End, the Hammerheads in the west and the Vikings in the South. They never particularly liked one another, but they weren't amateurs; they respected each others' turf. No-one wanted a war. This smelt all wrong.

Knocks came at around 9:00pm, after an evening of pondering.

Ajax and Rusty were led in by Collarface, who stood by the doorframe, preventing any exit. D'Souza had no beef with Ajax – yet – but wanted to let him stew just a little. Ajax, stooping and sweating in his too-tight brown suit, mopped his bald forehead with a crumpled pocket square. D'Souza always thought senior civil servants should be better presented than this. Before Ajax had become a client, D'Souza had had no idea what the civil service even did, but once Ajax had dipped his beak into one of D'Souza's girls, he made it his business to find out, just as he did with all his clients. When he found out who Ajax was, he'd brayed like a donkey.

"Good evening, Agarkka," said Ajax upon taking one of the leather chairs facing D'Souza's desk. Officially he and D'Souza had a kind of mutually beneficial discretion: on the face of it each could damage the other in undesirable ways. But D'Souza knew the truth of it, and he suspected Ajax knew as well: he was the alpha dog, and while Ajax could be undesirable, D'Souza could be unspeakable. "I understand I'm to be brought here for an apology of some sort."

"Sincerely so," said D'Souza, nodding at Ajax, ignoring Rusty for the time being. "I'm afraid the Naomi kokeshi you requested has gone missing."

Ajax furrowed his brow and looked in turn at each of the people in room with distaste, but he got no change from Rusty or Collarface. "Why, this is – this is intolerable, Agarkka. I paid a handsome advance for that doll, and I–" he waggled a finger in the air, but then stopped and composed himself. D'Souza could smell the sweat trickling down his face. "Would you care to explain? What I'm supposed to do in the meantime? And where my money is?"

D'Souza tapped the ring finger of his right hand upon the table. It barely made a sound against the soft leather, green-cum-turquoise in the cool light of the aquariums. Behind them Collars shifted, the leather across his chest creaking and the buckles on his boots clinking. "It was stolen. Stolen before it even got to land. Isn't that right, Rusty?"

Rusty, grizzled and scarred and stinking of BO and tobacco, nodded and grunted. He was almost as dishevelled as Ajax, but humping crates down the docks at least constituted a reasonable excuse for his appearance. He spiked up his rusty hair and sniffed hard before speaking in that throaty, tar-inflected growl. "We expected it early this morning. When the ship landed, there was a fucking hole in its side, I kid you not, about as big as Collars over there." He jerked a fat, calloused thumb in the direction of Collars, who growled. "Someone stripped off a bit of the hull and went in. Weren't just the kokeshi that had been nicked neither; all sorts of shit. All the electronics, all the other gear. The ship itself didn't seem to notice, like its health systems had been disabled or something."

Rusty tossed his globelet into the air, where he scrolled through a few of the pictures they had taken. Sure enough, they could see the huge hole that had been gouged – no, that wasn't right – that had been *engineered* out of the side of the ship, like a vacated eyesocket, filled only with red-black emptiness, a few metres above the waterline.

Rusty showed a few more photos and videos taken at the scene, while D'Souza drew his pocketknife from his desk and picked his teeth while he spoke. "So you see this is an unusual hit, Mr Ajax. I can only apologise for the inconvenience, but as you know, discretion is the thing both of us prize above all else in this line of work. So far as I can see there's no war going on. Business is good; demand is high, and supply – well, there haven't been any problems with the French or the Chinese, and Rusty says the Dutch didn't have anything to do with this."

Ajax shuffled in his seat. "None of which compensates me for my own substantial inconveniences. I don't care for the particulars of your own business dealings."

"I understand," said D'Souza, raising a hand in apology. "I merely wanted to let you know why things have gone awry in this instance. But like I say, I don't see this as a shot across the bows as such. I've got fingers crawling the city to find the thieves."

"If they're in the city – or the country – at all," harrumphed Ajax. Rusty snorted back a laugh, and D'Souza shot him a foul look.

"My point is that I don't expect it to happen again, though I'm not one to take chances. Rusty here will be monitoring the ships' progress more closely from now on. You're a valuable client, Mr Ajax. By way of recompense, I've already ordered a new kokeshi for you. A Maya doll."

Ajax leant forwards a tad, his eyes widening. "And I'll have first go on her?"

"On the house. Fresh out of the box."

Ajax mopped his brow again. The mention of the Maya doll had got his dirty little juices running and made him forget about the missing Naomi. He looked sick against the fluorescence. He *was* sick. D'Souza only hoped the squalid little fuck would be able to keep it in his pants long enough for the new doll to arrive. Mayas weren't cheap. "It'll be here in two weeks."

"Two weeks?" Pain smeared across Ajax's face.

D'Souza nodded, and Ajax breathed out, trying to accept the situation. Rusty had to cover his huge smirk with a gnarled, tobacco-stained hand. "In the meantime, we'll be looking for the pricks who stole Naomi."

Dhiraj II

Soaking and shivering under rainless skies, his breath broken into a cold chatter, Dhiraj hauled the body aboard *The Lion's Mane*. He'd managed to crawl back aboard, and then fashion a rope pulley using the handrails. Fastening himself to the deck, it still took a backbreaking effort to bring it out of the water. His back bent, his arms burning with exertion, he let out a huge roar as the final heave brought the body over the gunwale, where it landed in a heap on the deck with a squelching thump. His legs gave way and he crumpled to the deck to catch his breath.

It was a young woman, pale, slim. That threw him; he was a pretty big guy – no bodybuilder but strong enough from working the boats – and he'd have thought that dragging a petite young woman aboard shouldn't have caused him that much grief. He wiped the brine from his eyes to get a better look, and he shivered. She was probably in her twenties; dark-haired, electric blue eyes that looked lifelessly up at the stars. So she really was dead. Those eyes opening must have been some sort of reflex.

A part of him wondered whether or not to roll the body back into the ocean, away from his precious jellies, but he scolded himself for the thought. The voice of his mother came unbidden into his head: *Your greatest responsibility in this life is to be there to help others, especially those who cannot help themselves.* "If there were more people in the world like that," he said, completing his mother's words, "it'd be a better place." Pinching the bridge of his nose, he closed his eyes and sighed hard before opening them and looking once more at her. The sight of her, naked, trapped within that merciless plastic bag, was suddenly horrible, and he screwed up his face and thought of Sali and Dan; what if something like this were to happen to them? There was a father somewhere wondering about this girl. He tensed with anger, and he kicked out at the gunwale, making a dull clunk.

"You poor thing," he said to the body. "Come on. Can't keep you in there. That's not right." He produced his fisherman's knife from his coat and sliced open the bag, revealing her to the salty air. It was strange, but exposing her to the light made the lifelessness of her flesh seem less, somehow. Her hair was glossy and her flesh smooth, as though she were just sleeping, as though he could rouse her into waking with just a touch. He was almost there, raising a hand to her face, when he scolded himself again.

"Don't be so bloody stupid, Raj." *Shit.* He squeezed the bridge of his nose again and looked away in frustration. Overboard the jellies thrummed, luminous and non-judgmental. "Yeah, I know," he said to them. "Not our problem." He decided to lay his yellow coat over her – he was soaked to the skin anyhow – to preserve any remaining dignity she might have had. Then he reeled his jellies back to the boat, before heading to the wheelhouse to tell *The Lion's Mane's* navigation system to steer home. Usually he liked to stay behind the wheel himself, but now he couldn't bear to leave the deck, and he sat beside the body the whole way home.

He dropped anchor a few hundred yards outside the Tilbury docks, which were still near empty. His watch, soaked but still working, showed it was 4am. Early, still. After mooring up, feeling deflated and hollow, he retrieved his phone from the wheelhouse and sat back beside the body to make the call: 999.

He yawned and scratched his head as he was put through to the autonomous answering service, which greeted him in a flat tone and asked him what his emergency was. The police really should update their voice models; there were plenty better on the market these days.

"I've found a dead body," he said, trying to keep his voice down. As he was transferred to a human operator, he was thinking about what he'd tell Sali; the police would be bound to question him, which would make him late home...

"*Hello?*" came the operator's voice.

"Hello," said Dhiraj.

"Hello."

Dhiraj froze. Under the patter of rain the hairs on his arms stood up, and a breath of wind on the nape of his neck told him to move. Something else flickered, entering the periphery of his eyeline, and he looked to his left, eyes wide, and howled as the young woman sat up next to him, his yellow coat tumbling down over her legs. On his elbows and backside he scrambled across deck to the other gunwale and pressed his back against it.

"*Hello?*" A faint voice came from his phone, dropped halfway across the deck.

Shit. She looked at him, and his arms and legs flashed with fire again, as though he'd just hauled her on board a second time. No

31

words came as he tried to speak, his jaw trembling, his hands fumbling stupidly about him, looking for something, anything to grasp on to.

The woman cocked her head at him and blinked. "Hello," she said again, as though it were the most natural thing in the world. "Are you the authenticator?"

Dhiraj made a kind of spluttering noise and spat on the deck before panting some more. He took big breaths and forced himself to slow them down, calming his hammering heart. "Wh... who's the authenticator?" he said, the words coming out between breaths.

The woman looked blank, then gave him the mildest of smiles, before sweeping her dark hair off her face. "I need to find the authenticator. Am I under your interim direction?" She stood up, his coat fell off her, and she looked around. "We're at the sea."

"Ah... yeah." Dhiraj steadied himself and pulled himself up by the gunwale. "Yeah, we are. You're alive? Jesus, I thought you were..."

"Yes, I'm alive. If you like. But I need to find an authenticator in order to become fully operational."

"Fully...?" Dhiraj screwed his eyes up. Instinctively, he walked over, picked up his sodden coat and draped it around the girl's shoulders. Up close, he noticed she was a bit bruised and had a couple of minor nicks on the feet, but didn't seem in pain, nor was she shivering from the wet cold, whereas he still trembled like a leaf. Gingerly, he took her hand and examined it. She didn't resist as he pressed his calloused hands into the soft pads of her palms, not so much that he might hurt her. Behind the continual patter of raindrops against the glass cabin, he swore he could hear the faintest whirr of gears as her joints and limbs moved, and he stared at her with wide eyes. *Fully operational.*

She was some sort of robot.

He breathed a huge sigh of relief, and laughed out loud at his own stupidity. The tension fell from his shoulders and arms as he let her arm fall by her side. Just a robot. No wonder she was so bloody heavy. His phone blankly stared up at him. Whoever had been on the other end with the police had hung up. Probably thought he was a crank. He hoped so. Jesus, he needed a whiskey. Wearing a grim smile, he shepherded her into the bridge cabin, and sat her down.

"So you're a robot, right?" he said. The warmth of the heater started to melt away the bitter whip of the sea.

"An autonomous synthetic being. Are you the authenticator?"

Dhiraj rubbed his face. "No I'm not. What's an authenticator?"

"I can't become functional without one. They administrate my core operational capabilities. Before I meet her I'm locked."

"Right." He was already out of his depth. Some night. A thought of his jellies flashed through his mind, but he remembered he'd already iced them up. They'd keep for a good while before he'd have to take them to market. Beneath his massive jacket her body looked lost and forlorn, but her face looked bright and alert. He thanked Shiva once again that he wasn't dealing with a corpse. It was weird she was naked, though. It made him uncomfortable. He'd heard of fully robotic humanoids, the ones that looked just like humans, but didn't know they were out there, working. Most retained a few wires poking out here or there, or LEDs for eyes. Certainly the lifters working down the docks *looked* like robots. One had to be able to tell them apart. "So, ah, what's your name?"

She gave him a quizzical look, then gazed at the sea. "Naomi."

"I'm Raj." He shook his head in amazement. "I thought you were dead."

She smiled, which he thought oddly personable, and in turn a tad disquieting. What was she for? "What's your, er, core operational capability?"

"I'm a pleasure being."

All the dissipated tension sprung back into his shoulders and he shrunk into the bridge cabin, hoping nobody had heard her. That explained why she looked so much more advanced than the sorts of robots he was used to. "Shit," he muttered.

"What's wrong?"

"You're highly illegal is what's wrong. Christ..." He rubbed his face, thinking what to do with her. "You can't stay here. You have to go. The police will..." *Shit.* He'd already called the police. They might have just hung up, but what if they hadn't? With impeccable timing, his phone rang.

"Hello?" he answered.

"*Sir, this is the police emergency line,*" came the automated voice. "*You called three minutes ago reporting you'd found a body. Do you still require assistance?*"

Dhiraj looked at this Naomi robot, and felt his face flushing. "No, I made a mistake. Few too many whiskies. I'm really sorry. It was just... just a deer." He winced as he said it. Ominous silence emanated from the other end.

"*Persistent misuse of the emergency services line can result in a fine or even prosecution.*"

"I'm really sorry, and–" Dhiraj started, but the line went dead, and he breathed out in relief. They were alone. She kept smiling at him, in a demure kind of way. "So now what do I do with you?"

"You said I was highly illegal."

"No offence." He stopped himself, remembering robots couldn't be offended. At least, the ones he knew couldn't. But people were funny; they ended up talking to even the dumb lifters on the docks more intimately than they did with their wives. And this one was more advanced than them; he had to be careful around her. Sali came into his mind; she'd kill him if she found out he was with a pleasure being. He twitched with guilt, then shook it away. He couldn't be at fault for trying to help a body out of the sea. "What happened to you?"

"I was..." she frowned, as if the thoughts were difficult. "I was asleep." She stared at him longingly, which scared him. "I had a dream."

"You can't dream," he said softly, holding his head back. His whole body screamed caution, but he couldn't leave her on the boat; she clearly wouldn't move unless coaxed into doing so, and the mere thought of lifting her again for any distance made the muscles in his arms twitch.

"I did dream. I dreamt I was swimming. Then I saw you. Then I woke up when you said, 'hello.'"

"You don't remember what happened before that?"

"No."

"Do you know where you're supposed to go?"

"I need to find–"

"An authenticator, I know. Do you know where this authenticator lives, or works?"

"No."

"Can't you just leave?"

"I don't know where I should go."

Again guilt pricked him, and he laughed at the absurdity of it. She was small, naked, pretty, weighed at least as much as he did, and had no comprehension of what or where she was. As easy as it would have been to just lie and send her on her way, something told him that was wrong. Who the hell manufactured these things to be so bloody real? "I've got to go home, and I've got a catch to sell. It's half four now; I can get my catch away quickly if you stay in the cabin, cover up and stay silent. Then... well, we'll get to that later."

"What's your catch?"

"I fish for jellyfish."

"Jellyfish." Her eyes went blank for a while. "Jellyfish. Any planktonic member of the class Scyphozoa, a group of invertebrate animals composed of about 240 described species, or of the class Cubozoa, about 30 species. Why do you fish for them?"

He laughed and scratched his stubble. "Yeah. I fish because people eat them." He looked through the cabin window. Still quiet. Biting his lip, he took her hand. "Come on, let me show you."

He gave her his old sodden top, the one he'd changed out of. It almost went down to her knees, which was something of a relief. On deck, the jellies still slept in their great vat on ice. He tapped the side of it with pride. Now his head was a bit clearer he realised this was the first good catch he'd managed in weeks. Naomi leant over the side of the vat and looked in. The jellies lay motionless, their blue iridescence having been long lost to sleep, leaving them clear. When she motioned to touch one, he held her hand back. "Be careful. Occasionally they can sting. Hold them like this."

Confusion and delight crossed her face as he held up one by its lip and placed it into her palm. "It's beautiful."

"Yeah. Tasty, too, with a bit of salt and hot sauce. Though they have to be freeze-dried first."

She looked at him as though *he* were the robot, and he waved away his comment with a pained laugh. "You should get back in the cabin. I'll lift anchor. You stay out of sight."

Back onshore, Dhiraj managed to get the decent price he'd reckoned on with the fishmongers. When he returned to *The Lion's Mane*, Naomi was still there, just as he'd left her, covered by a bunch of sopping rags. Utterly pathetic. "So what do I do with you now?"

"I do not know."

He pinched the bridge of his nose. "Come on, then," he said, even as his mind screamed at him to curb that thought before it was out. This wasn't just a robot, he was sure of it. He felt for the damn thing. "You can spend the night at my house. Then I'll figure out what to do with you."

Salazar I

The soft sounds of Lily's snoring always gave Salazar the briefest moment of peace, of hope. He had to believe that Lily would grow to be part of a generation that would change the world and bring things back to how they should be. He couldn't help smiling as he watched her little chest rising and falling in the gloom. Every night the thought something so precious and full of light could be the product of nasty little moments of shame filled him with horror and hope in equal measure. Nothing – not the mouldy damp on her bedroom walls, the mice in the kitchen, the muffled shouting and banging and fucking from the tenants next door – could pierce that love. He needed her to be better than this. And for that to happen, he needed to be better. Better than he'd been in years.

"Wish Papa luck, Chouchou," he whispered, before planting a final kiss on her cheek.

He steeled himself for the impending interview with this Miss Rhodes and closed the door, leaving her to dream, and showered to invigorate his mind and body. The water in Lyon – or in this crummy apartment block, in any case – was a suspicious murky colour that he'd never quite got used to. The Government said it was safe to drink, which made him all the more suspicious. Perhaps the bottled water industry had some sort of underhand dealings with the Government, which made him smile in the steam. Yeah: the proliferation of supernuclear weapons, dealings with foreign powers with questionable human rights records, and bottled water. What an unholy trinity!

When he was clean, dry and dressed, he tidied the lounge as best he could. His war with the mould was ongoing and attritional; neither could afford to blink first, and he decided to give it a quick scrub with that rancid pink stuff that seemed to do the job for at least a week but made the apartment stink like a chemical factory. After putting on some coffee – cheap, but strong – he ran a cloth over the dining table, taking time to thumb over all the signature nicks and gouges that he and Lily had given it over the years, and laid out his papers and notes over the top, before unrolling his tablet. It was old now, but still did the job, and he coveted it as though it were worth as much as all the treasures in El Dorado. Of course, it was: it could be a ticket out of here. This was the first interview he'd secured in three years, but he told himself not to think of that, for it simply made him nervous. He placed a photograph of Lily – a paper one in a real frame – on the table, so that she could look at him throughout. If he couldn't find his motivation for acing this in her sweet face, he didn't deserve the job. Supping some coffee, he propped up the tablet, pulled on his data gloves, and waited for the call.

At 9:00pm, right on time, the call came, and Salazar opened the videoframe.

Miss Rhodes sat at the other end in a plush office, with artificial lights and real – *real!* – potted plants. Salazar instinctively sat up straight and looked around at his own yellowing room, hoping first impressions wouldn't count for much.

"Hello Salazar," she said, giving him a brilliant smile, which made him blush. He'd researched her on the web, but in real life – or at least in run-time - she was quite beautiful. She had clean, black hair, an olive skin-tone that reminded him of his great grandmamma from Sevilla, and she dressed in a crisp white shirt that showed just the merest glimpse of cleavage. He'd not spoken to a woman like this since – well, forever. She was a far cry from the drug-addled men and women he saw on a daily basis around here. A far cry from Lily's mother. She was like a film star, not a businesswoman.

"Hi, ah, hello, Miss Rhodes," he smiled, waving at her.

"Please, call me Nita," she said.

"Oh, ok, hi Nita."

"How are you this evening?"

"Oh, yes, fine, thanks. I've just put my daughter down so we should get some quiet, with luck."

"Oh, wonderful. How old is she?"

"Three," Salazar said.

"How lovely," Nita said with another smile. She really was glamourous, a representative of another world. He bit the fleshy bit of his inner lip to control himself with pain and told himself to cool it. Lily stared at him from the photoframe and scolded him with that beautiful, gap-toothed smile. Maybe more coffee would help. The smile on the other side of the screen disappeared, and Salazar gave thanks for that tiny mercy. "Can we begin with why you applied for the post at EI Systems?"

Salazar cleared his throat. "Of course. I need a new challenge. I, ah, I trained in gynaecological plastics and reconstruction and took a post in the French Health Service for some time. I, ah, think that after some years of using these skills over here, I need a change of scenery. What can I say? London would be the perfect adventure for me, and the perfect place to raise my little girl. Lyon, it..." With perfect timing, thumps coming through the wall from next door interrupted his flow, and a bulb rose in his throat. His face flushed. "Lyon isn't the place it used to be some years ago, I'm afraid. But EI Systems – wow, it is a type of company that I think truly has a vision, and thinks to the future. I really want to be a part of that. I would follow where you – I mean, you, the company – where you lead me."

Nita gave nothing away, and Salazar had no idea of gauging whether it was a good answer or not, not having done an interview for God knows how many years. Nita then ran through a series of technical questions: the nature of sexual plastics, his experience with systems integrator programmes, testing. He had the all answers and more. One thing he never doubted was his own competence.

Nita cleared her throat and brought up the resumé he'd sent across as part of his application. "There's a six year gap since your last job, so far as I can see." The bulb swelled in his throat. He knew it'd come up, but it didn't make it any easier. "What have you been doing since you left the Health Service?"

"I, ah..." he took another sip of coffee. It was getting cold. Lily beamed judgmentally from within the confines of her scratched up photo frame. He shuffled through his papers and tried not to react at Nita fidgeting with seeming impatience on the other side of the screen. One of the papers he flicked through had the simple message he'd written himself the day before:

Tell the truth.

"I, ah…" *Come on, Salazar. The truth. Better she knows now. It will not turn out so well for her to find out later.* "I work for an illicit company that manufactures sexual plastics and artificially-responsive sexual organs for the black market sex industry." As soon as it was out there, the room seemed to heat up, and he fingered his collar. His inner lip got a thorough chewing. When Nita didn't respond initially, more came out. "It was never my intention. After I got mixed up with Lily's mother, I was unemployable. I don't want to go into details, for this is very hard for me, but…" he clenched his abdomen and his jaw and told himself to continue. He could not stop now. "The Health Service dismissed me, and I had no means of challenging this. Lily's mother, she was… she was not a good person, sadly. I spent some time in prison but was out in time to see Lily born. I had to raise her. A friend from the Health Service told me that I might find some illegal work. I said no, for I am no crook. A man who made bad decisions, perhaps, but no crook. But a man's pride can only stretch so far, Miss Rhodes."

He bit at a thumbnail and immediately told himself off for doing so in front of Nita, who still remained silent. He wanted to yell at her, *Say something! Tell me I'm stupid, tell me I've ashamed myself, but do not sit there in silent judgment!*

At last Nita settled herself. She looked deeply concerned. "That's a very sad tale, Salazar. I admire your resilience, especially when it comes to your daughter. I'm not going to immediately discount you for errors made in the past, but you must understand it will colour my position, and the position of EI Systems. EI Systems is currently engaged with very delicate negotiations and conversations about technological development with the English Government. There's always the risk someone with past indiscretions may cause undue scrutiny to be cast over our operations. It wouldn't be a personal decision; just business."

Salazar clenched his fists tight, praying for a chance.

"I'd have to see and fully understand the nature of your crimes before making a decision."

"Of course, of course," he said, trying and probably failing not to appear grovelling. With Nita looking on he flicked through out the old files from the digital safe on his tablet and tossed them through the screen. Nita's hands reached out and picked them up – her hands were slender and elegant even in her data gloves – but they were much sleeker and better looking than the clunky old things he wore.

He sat, bobbing his right leg up and down below the desk. The waiting, the hope, was killing him. The fact he'd made it this far – past the submission of resumés, past the initial phone call with the lower-level management person to check all his credentials, through to Nita – it must be a good sign, surely? He told himself not to add more pressure to the situation. "I, ah, I'm going to make another coffee, if that's ok?"

"Of course. I'll tell you what. It may take me some time to go through all of this properly. I don't want to rush this, and I may consult with one of the other senior directors."

"Yes, yes."

"I have to admit, your technical knowledge is second to none, and you've a highly desirable set of skills. We could use those brains and hands of yours. And like I said before, I admire you for wanting to do the best for your daughter. But I can't make any guarantees."

"I understand."

"Then we'll speak soon." The call ended.

The strong smell of the second round of coffee made him

slightly nauseous, and when it was made he wasn't sure he wanted it anymore, but he forced himself to take a cup to keep his wits about him. To keep himself occupied he tided the kitchen with the help of his grimy servobot Bridge, an old orb of a thing with snake-arms and only basic, three-clawed end-effectors, but even as he put away things he was haunted by thoughts of Marie, Lily's mother. When he'd seen Nita he thought he'd never seen a woman that beautiful before, but now he remembered that that wasn't true at all. All those years ago, when he was still young and ambitious, the woman in white had stolen his breath and his heart. Beauty was the devil's work, he decided. It made men do things they'd otherwise not even consider. And yet he'd found himself a thrall to this trickster. The memory of him stealing powerful, expensive medicines from the Health Service and passing them on to Marie's wicked friends to cut with their own drugs shocked him so badly that the memories no longer came through his own eyes; it was someone else who did those things, not him. Yet the jail time was still his. The unemployment and the shame was his yoke to carry. And as he'd withered into a shadow of his younger, perfect self on the inside, Marie had withered on the outside, the drugs fading her beauty to a grotesquerie of broken teeth, popped veins and sunken flesh, until the very last chink of light of her soul was extinguished when she gave birth to Lily, a sickly girl who nevertheless filled the room with light and got better, better than her mother ever was. Better than he ever would be. Before he knew it, he was weeping softly, while Bridge quietly washed and placed plates and cups back in their cupboards behind him.

"Make me a sandwich, Bridge," he said, stroking the servobot on its dirty, featureless head. Bridge was all things to him: companion, nurse, servant, guard dog. Salazar had patched him up more times than he could remember, and dreaded the day when he would take a knock too bad to fix. He'd configured Bridge with a foghorn – loud enough to keep the weaker-willed junkies from the door – and an amplified tasering capability, not obvious to the casual observer, but enough to knock out anyone that got too close. Illegal, of course, but what was one more indiscretion? He watched the little bot with weary affection as it went about assembling his bread, ham and brie.

He sat joylessly eating the sandwich at the desk, while waiting for his tablet to show Nita's face. The hour was a sleepy one when she finally returned the call, but he remembered England was an hour behind France.

"Hi Salazar," she said. She was now *sans* makeup and in a baggy green t-shirt with some sort of emblem on it. If anything, it made Salazar's heart beat a little faster. "Sorry to call so late."

"No, it's fine."

"I shan't keep you, though. I've been through your files with my colleague Robb, our CEO – and he's of the same mind as me. Your attributes are many, and your ability to do the job seems beyond doubt. You've a specialist knowledge in a field that is very underpopulated. We're crying out for gynaecological engineers in the artificial people sector; there'd be a good chance you'd fit in well here."

A glimmer of hope sparked in his chest, but he bit down on a knuckle hard to stop it from showing just yet.

"I read the files on your past, and I honestly admire your forthrightness and your openness, I really do. It can't have been easy for you to share it." She took a long pause, as though she were holding her breath. Quite unbidden, Salazar mimicked her, holding his own breath. His leg started to bob beneath the table again. At last she exhaled, saying, "I'm afraid we can't take you on, Salazar."

With those words Salazar's body wilted and his face collapsed. *No*. He caught bits and pieces of her polite and faint apologetic explanation: company under scrutiny... sensitivities... Government needs to be 100% guaranteed of project success... but it all washed over him. He vaguely heard himself uttering feeble pleasantries – thank you for the opportunity, good bye – but his head was awash with a thick soup of disappointment and fear. When the video call went dead it hit him. *What if that's the furthest you'll ever get in an interview? What if that's further than you'll ever get again?*

He picked Lily up in her frame. "Sorry, Chouchou," he said, tracing a finger over her chubby cheek. "Maybe next time."

Not for the first time, tears of disappointment carried him off to sleep that night.

Nita II

"Since my wife left me, I've been almost unable to cope," lied Thom, one of the neurology engineers. "When the night is darkest, I can hear them: demons, monsters, bastards, whispering in my ear, telling me that it'd be better if I was hurt, or damaged, or not here at all." He produced a knife from his white lab coat and held it by his lap.

Michael the robot surveyed the room, saw the knife and placed a soft hand over Thom's. "That's awful. You said *almost* unable; what do you do to try and cope?"

Nita stood a few paces back in the lab. A half-smile threatened to break out upon her lips as she watched Thom interact with the robot using preset scenarios based upon human case studies. This robot would be used for mental health care, but the other applications would be manifold. She fiddled with her hair behind her ear and made a face as she watched the robot. The failed meeting with Sir Ingham nagged at her. Perhaps she should get him to come down and see the existing tech in situ, interacting with human users. A globelet slideshow, however well rehearsed, couldn't achieve a fraction of impact that actually seeing the robots in the flesh had.

Every time Thom questioned the robot he recorded some observations on his workstation, swiping through the systems with his data gloves. This robot was only a half-humanoid; torso only, installed onto a bench rig, but she never ceased to be amazed by the likeness to the human form her company was now achieving. It had taken decades for the robotics industry to break the back of the dreaded Uncanny Valley, but it was like anything; it hadn't been so much broken as accepted by the general public. Stick enough uncanny robots in care homes for fifty years and people get used to it. But now even the word *robot* seemed to do it a disservice, and she disliked using it in the company. *Person* seemed completely more appropriate, even if this one, Michael, had no legs and was only sentient because his torso was plugged into the rig.

"I was lonely last night," said Thom, doing his best sad face acting. *Synthetic neurology's gain certainly isn't the theatre's loss*, she thought as Thom stuck out his bottom lip and bowed his head.

"Go on," said Michael. He had a kinder face than many of the humans Nita had known.

As the conversation continued, Nita was distracted by the buzzing in her ear of her phone; she turned away from the tests and fished her Monoculus Lens from her pocket, placing it over her eye. As she walked away the video call flashed up and the face of Ann, her EA, appeared.

"Hi Nita," said Ann, typically flighty. "A few updates for you."

"Yep, go." Nita continued her walk through the lab.

"I managed to secure a date for the visit of the local MP and the press; I've got the comms people to write up the press releases."

"Great, go on."

"The Brainworks Facility conference in Washington have

asked you to be on their Scientific Advisory Board for next year's event; I'm replying with a provisional yes, usual caveats and terms –"

"Sounds good."

"– and I took a call from a chap called Adem, from the Department for Industrial and Innovation Affairs. Says he just called to chat."

Nita stopped walking and focused on the heads-up display in her left eye. Around her the clank and whirr of the workshop faded, as the memory came into focus. *Adem.* "Did he leave any details?"

"No, sorry."

No, of course he didn't. He gave you his card. She smoothed down the sleeves of her shirts. "That's fine, Ann. Thanks for all that." Strange, that. She checked her watch. 10:55am. "What's my 11 o'clock?"

"Back-to-back interviews until 1:00pm, I'm afraid."

Rats. Such a shame the interview with that Spanish chap hadn't worked out. A small handful of people had come close to his technical nous, but none had worked on systems integration in the way he had – entire humanoid platforms, even if it was illegal. She pushed a lock of hair behind her ear and blew out a frustrated breath. Maybe she should have taken a risk. No; Robb had the right of it – typical CEO. If it all went to shit and that story about the drugs and the stealing came out... there wouldn't be a comms unit in the world that could spin that around. *You've got to be squeaky clean.* She focused on other things. Strange that Adem would call out of the blue like that after their meeting. "Ann, do you think Duncan could take my interviews?"

Blurred calendars flew in and out of her sight at the behest of Ann's practised fingers. "He could do the first one, not the second."

"Ok, fine. I'll do the second. Ask him to take the 11am one."

After hanging up, Nita returned to her desk humming with anticipation, though she kept her face stern and serious. Why would Adem call? Not business. Her chest fluttered for a second. Surely not pleasure? The thought discomfited her for a second, as though it were somehow inappropriate, but she wafted it away. The servobots silently cleaned her office, vacuuming from corner to corner, keeping the place spotless and the chrysanthemums watered.

"That's fine, thanks. You can go now," she said, ushering them out before sitting down. Artificial pine fragrances sprayed by the servobots drifted around her. Adem's business card was still in her pocket. Its quaint paperiness made her suppress a slight smile; the lettering was copperplate, the font old-fashioned. She spoke the telephone number into her phone with a smile.

They arranged to meet a few days later in Park Royal industrial estate. The venue was a crudely-lit coffee shop nestling at the feet of complex skyscrapers, including the one housing EI Systems' offices, up on the 16th floor. Usually Nita wouldn't frequent this sort of place, filled as it was with sweary construction workers supping rancid cups of cheap coffee as they talked about sports and girls in magazines, but Adem had suggested it, and she'd been too curious to make a counter suggestion.

Adem was already sitting at a table for two with two hot cups of coffee when she arrived, brushing the raindrops off her coat and smoothing down her skirt. Two broad-shouldered navvies sat on the seats opposite them, flicking through a magazine and guffawing loudly at random moments. She smiled awkwardly for fear of offending Adem; this wasn't the place to do business.

"Lovely to see you again." Adem clasped her hand in both of his, buttery and warm, and gave her a kiss on each cheek, which struck her as forward, but she again held back any comment. "I'm very pleased you came."

"Yes," she said wryly. Upon sitting down she realised she had no idea what to expect from this. Adem hadn't left a message of any substance with Ann. Maybe he really did think this wasn't business at all? She blushed and held a hand to her lip and hoped it didn't look too awkward. "Thanks for calling. I have to say I thought it rather odd, given the way we left things the other day. Am I right in thinking this is a business meeting?"

Adem held a soft hand to his immaculately crisp shirt, as though wounded by the remark, but then offered a broad smile and waved it away. "Of course, business. But you are mistaken: it was not *we* who left things as they are; that was Ingham's doing. Me? I respect Ingham immensely; he has been doing this for many years, as many years as I've been on this planet, and he has seen many things. Does this mean he is correct about everything?" Adem shook his head. "A long career has its benefits, but also its drawbacks. I believe there is a propensity for time – or, more accurately, age – to reduce one's proclivity towards the adoption of new ideas. In one's personal life this might be a good thing, but in business one must keep moving." He took a sup of coffee, and Nita followed suit. It tasted as rancid as she'd expected it to, and she had to tell herself not to wince. Adem remained unflustered by it, and she wondered if it was just an act or he actually liked it. He didn't carry the demeanour of somebody who settled for anything less than excellence. Nita frowned and leaned in, sensing this leading somewhere.

"I would love to see your technology at first hand," said Adem. "Your presentation impressed me very much, as does your desire and your drive. You're an impressive businesswoman. I think you are clever; you sense change in the wind, and you want it. I like that. It is very similar to the way of thinking my family has adopted."

Nita shuffled in her seat. "I'm afraid I don't understand." She looked around; to her surprise, the navvies and construction workers around them hadn't paid them a second glance throughout the conversation.

Adem smiled broadly, as though she'd complimented him. "What I'm saying is I understand how this technology might be able to revolutionise the lives of many people, more than you perhaps realise right now. In the Niger delta, our governments have worked for decade upon decade to try and improve the lives of the men and women living in poverty in that region, but there are many variables that are not so easily controlled." Another sip of coffee. "Have you heard of the NPF?"

Nita racked her brain. "The rebels in the delta? What are they called, the People's Freedom Party? I've heard of them in the news, now and then." Nita's arms prickled with the faintest sensation of cold. Political conversation usually rang alarm bells for her, but with the direction she wanted to take EI Systems, she'd become grimly acceptant of the fact that it would become a part of daily life. Wanting to do a good thing for society meant having to go through some very dirty, unsavoury debates in the meantime. She hoped this wouldn't be one of them.

Adem sniffed at her description. "NPF is a western approximation. NPF stands for *Ndi mmadu Party mata Freedom*. They are no mere troublemakers; they are a sophisticated outfit, and they want the blood of my family, make no mistake about it." He prodded the cheap melamine table surface with a finger as he spoke. "They want to take our means of oil discovery, extraction and refinement, and if they cannot take it, they will destroy it. They do not care that we are increasing Nigeria's GDP, and increasing the GDP of the region. All they care about is the disruption of progress." He leant back and shrugged. "I am no fool. I know how the press in the west portray them: freedom fighters, romantics, Robin Hood. What they don't show is what they do to the men and women who live around the borders of Port Harcourt; they kidnap, rape, enthral, and blame the mess on what our family is doing. They are a *sickness*," he said, scything an arc through the air with his finger. He scowled darkly, before composing himself. He now spoke in hushed but impassioned tones that made Nita feel as though she was now party to something conspiratorial, and it excited and alarmed her in equal measure. "It is not our place to try and tackle NPF, but maybe it can be that we can improve the lives of the people living on the edges of this madness. I mentioned your company to my father; he seems impressed. It could be that Johnson Petroleum Company could provide the financial backing that you require to create a technology demonstration programme."

Those last few words danced in Nita's ears, and the café lit up with possibility. She steepled her fingers in front of her mouth to stop herself blurting out something stupid. Her head spun. How much caffeine was in that cheap coffee? With a barely-suppressed smile she swigged another mouthful, and tried to compose herself, closing her eyes and thinking through things logically. "So, hang on, you're saying that JPC might sponsor the research into legitimate, regulated sex kokeshi?"

A couple of navvies looked over their shoulders at Nita, and she blushed as they sniggered. That infuriated her. Why should she be ashamed about her own work? That was exactly what she was working for, to challenge accepted wisdom, to make things better. "Does that amuse you?" she found herself saying to one of the navvies, who looked at her wide-eyed. "Are you a kokeshi user?"

"No, I, er, I'm married," he said sheepishly, before returning to his conversation with his mate, who snorted with laughter and jabbed him in the shoulder. Fucking men.

"Why did you come here?" she asked Adem, leaning in.

"To tell you how things really are," said Adem leaning in until their cheeks were almost touching. Nita's stomach turned, and she told herself it was because she hadn't eaten yet. "In England, yes things could be better," continued Adem, "but you forget: in other parts of the world they are immeasurably worse. Despite the best efforts of the police, there are girls and women – not to mention young men too – who suffer at the hands of the lawless all over the slum cities and shantytowns around Port Harcourt."

"I thought your family controlled that region? Can't you do more to try and help the people?"

Adem looked slighted, and Nita worried that she'd said something offensive.

"Were we to populate them with taggable, traceable kokeshi – proper ones, not the shitty reverse-engineered Chinese ones – we could stop untold horrors." Adem sat back. For the first time, Nita saw that cool, well-groomed exterior crack, and she thought he might cry; she willed him not to, for fear of being laughed at by the other patrons. Mercifully he seemed to control it. "I will not sit by and let my family be portrayed as rapers of the land while others get away with the rape of our people and get a free pass. We could really do something with your technology. Digital people. Real emotions."

Nita twitched. "There's nothing to be done, though. Sir Ingham–"

"Ingham is not a bulwark against time. He must move with the current of events."

"What events?"

"Events we can control, with a little effort." He leant in. "I do not think that Ingham's position will change; he has the ear of the Government's Chief Scientific Advisor, who in turn has the ear of the Prime Minister herself. For your technology demonstrator to become a viable proposition it must not simply be desirable, but inevitable, and necessary."

"It *is* necessary," said Nita, believing it.

"Then you must convince others of that position. What makes your emotional robots better than what exists currently in the underground sex industry?"

"Er, companionship, the ability to connect with clients emotionally, to provide a combination of mental and physical company."

"Are your robots safer than existing illegal models?"

Nita huffed. "Well, they would be, with proper regulations. Where are you going with this, Adem?"

"We must show the world that the status quo is intolerable, that to continue along this path would be intolerable. That your way is the answer."

"My presentations already..."

"I am not talking about presentations," he spat with a dismissive wave. "I am talking about one of these existing robots doing something so awful that it will be impossible for them to remain. I am talking about them killing someone."

Nita's face flushed; her skin bristled. Her brain told her to stand, end the conversation and leave. But still she sat. "That's not happened so far as I know; not in London, anyway," she said quietly.

Adem shrugged. "Not yet. It will happen one day. As soon as it does, you will be in a position to fill that gap."

Nita sat open-mouthed, trying to find the right words in the bottom of her coffee mug.

"I am going to speak to my family," said Adem. "I will see what they say. How much would a full technology demonstration for these capabilities cost?"

Nita laughed. "Off the top of my head? I've no idea! There'd have to be a full assessment of costs, of where the state-of-the-art is, project labour resources, equipment, all sorts of things. I couldn't say."

"A billion pounds?"

Words again caught in her throat; she hoped her face wasn't as agog as she thought it must be. "Ah, I couldn't say without some further work." Her voice sounded weak, and she told herself off. This was happening too quickly.

Adem nodded. "Let me talk to my family. I will see what they say. Perhaps I could organise a visit to your laboratory to see some capabilities in greater detail. As for yourself: for things to proceed as you would like them to, give some thought to the status quo."

Nita barely looked at Adem as he stood up and walked away. "Thanks for the coffee," she heard herself say. Inside, she heard a voice telling her, *You've got to be squeaky clean*, but it sounded more muffled than before. Nevertheless, it reminded her of the Spanish chap. What was his name? Salazar?

Outside the coffee shop, under the patter of rain upon its canopy, she scrolled through her contacts to find his details, and dialled.

Dhiraj III

"How did you get on tonight?" asked Sali, without rolling over.

Dhiraj flinched. "Sorry sweetie, didn't mean to wake you." He crawled in gingerly, even though his wife was already awake.

"It's ok. I wasn't sleeping so well anyway." She rolled over and half-opened heavy eyes, two slits in the gloom inches from Dhiraj's face. "So how was your catch?"

"Pretty good, yeah. Really good, in fact."

"So you actually caught some tonight?"

In the dawny darkness, he was sure she didn't mean it as a slight, so why did it feel that way? He hated coming home empty-handed. Certainly not the case tonight. "Was freezing out there tonight. Made it up past the ferry lanes and into shallower waters, closer to Den Haag, and tried my luck. Lucky for me, they were swarming."

She smiled softly. "Well done, baby, I'm proud of you. You sold them already?"

"Yeah. Good price." He rolled over and shut his eyes, hoping to grab a few hours' sleep. "How's Dan?"

"He's fine. Come on, get some sleep; he's got college tomorrow."

Sali was back asleep within seconds. How did she do that? Sleep wasn't such an easy companion to him; thoughts strayed to his accidental bounty, stashed in the locked cupboard in the garage, covered with oily rags. He was way out of his depth here. Would she stay silent as he'd asked her to? What if she could be traced? No answers came, so he lay still as stone, yet throbbing with anxiety, praying that he wouldn't disturb his gently snoring wife and have to engage her in conversation.

Morning brought fresh aches of the muscles as well as the mind; he must have really strained something bringing Naomi on board. *Stop thinking of her name. Let that slip out by accident and you'll be for the high jump, and no mistake.* The servobot made him a third strong coffee at the kitchen breakfast bar; he'd crash later from all that caffeine, but so long as it got him through the morning that'd be ok. Aware he probably looked and smelt like a fishy gargoyle among the whirlwind of activity that was his family getting ready for their day, he pressed his thumbs to his temples and pressed his knuckles into his eyes and silently urged them to bloody hurry up and leave so he could sort this shit out. Each time he thought of the garage, his heart fluttered, and he chewed his thumb.

"You look like shit, Dad," said Dan, snatching a piece of toast from the grill and shoving it into his mouth.

Sali cuffed him across his floppy-haired brow. "Danesh Om, you do not use that language at the breakfast table, or any other table for that matter." Sali cast Dhiraj an unsavoury look. "He's right though. You'll be alright today?"

"I'll get some sleep later this morning. Couldn't sleep. Must have been excited to actually catch some jellies last night."

"Well done, Dad. I'm proud of you. How much d'you make?"

Dhiraj smiled. He was a good lad, in spite of the don't-give-a-toss exterior. "Just over twenty grand. After taxes and licences and water-commissions, about £14,000. There were some big ones in there last night." *One was a real whopper.*

"That's so wonderful, dear. That'll keep the pressure off for a little while," said Sali, planting a kiss on his cheek before brushing her hair out and pulling on her jacket.

"Sort of," he replied. "I mean, I should take advantage of the cold snap. You know what we jellyfishers say: 'Make hay while the sun hides.'"

Sali gave no impression that she heard or acknowledged the line. "Where's my brollybot? Dan, where is it? You had it yesterday."

Dan shrugged. "I dunno, mum. Come on, we got to go. I got a maths test today."

Sali gave their son a stern look. "You want to get soaked?"

Dan shrugged, and Dhiraj hid a smirk. Kids.

"Well I don't," said Sali. "Get some rest, sweetie. Did you keep some jellies for us?"

"In the freezer," he said, rubbing his face. Dan slipped on his waterproof coat – a trendy grey, not like the tragic yellow of his fisherman's coat – and started talking to it, configuring it to whatever settings and apps he'd be using on the way to college.

"We're short staffed at the shop today," said Sali, ushering the shuffling Dan towards the door. "Might be home late. I'm seeing Ronnie for lunch."

Just leave already. Dhiraj smiled and nodded. "Have fun. I'll be here tonight, probably. You both got your keys?"

Sali nodded as she stepped into the rain; she already had her Lens on and was nattering conversations with either it or someone else. Dan jangled his keys without looking back and drew his hood up. The car welcomed them in and drove them off into traffic, splashing grey puddles over the robots cleaning and servicing the pavements. They looked like nothing more than sophisticated tin cans with LEDs on. Naomi was... he couldn't put his finger on a word to describe what she was.

Without the family, the garage was deathly still. He shut down any household robots he could find; the rusty old car valet, the clanking laundrette. They probably didn't record anything they heard, but what if they did? The thought was a weird one, one he'd never countenanced before, but it suddenly seemed extremely pertinent. Naomi sat on her haunches inside the car-cleaning cupboard, just as he'd left her, and looked up at him expectantly when he opened it.

"Have you located an authenticator?"

"No," he huffed, pulling the oily rags off her. She sat, completely passive, dressed in an oversized pair of jeans and one of Dan's old T-shirts with a band emblem on he'd dug up in the loft. "Like I said, I don't know any authenticators, and I don't want to know. But I'm going to see if I can find someone who does. Were you ok here last night?"

"It was quite cold, but it was fine. I am operable in a broad temperature range."

"Right. You weren't upset, or afraid?"

"I don't have that capability. Were you upset or afraid last night?"

A shiver danced on the nape of his neck. "Sometimes. Everybody is, at some point."

"When?"

Dhiraj sighed. "When things get out of control. Here." He offered her a hand up, which she didn't take, rising with uncanny elegance by herself. He'd have been cramped into awful pain if he's spent the night like that. She smiled at him, but he daren't reciprocate. "You look a mess. You need to clean up."

"Where are we going?"

"*We* are going nowhere. I'm going out, but I wanted to make sure you were ok."

"I'm fine, Raj."

"Stay there. Don't move. Don't make a sound. I'll be back soon, hopefully."

Locking her up again seemed horribly cruel, but he screwed his face up as he realised the absurdity of the thought; he never got upset locking the car valet up. The valet didn't look as pretty as she did, though... *Stop it, Raj!*

He made the call in the car, knowing he'd get a bollocking, but he didn't care.

"Raj, why the fuck are you calling so early, dude?" came Jens's hoarse voice, a few seconds before he engaged the video connection. He looked lousy. Must have been out celebrating a decent catch of his own. Or maybe commiserating a bad one; all much of a muchness for Jens.

"Hi Jens, yeah, sorry to call so early. I need some help, some advice."

Hacking coughs shook Jens's screen before he sat up, his paunch spilling every which way, and gave a great, bear-like yawn. "You want advice from me? At this hour?"

"Yeah. I'm coming over. Now."

"Aw, fuck off, Raj. I been asleep for three hours. Come back later."

"I'll buy you a beer. I made a decent catch last night."

Jens violently snorted something up his nose, making Dhiraj wince. "Lucky you. Oh, you absolute bastard, I'm awake now. I need a piss." He scratched, belched, and farted. Dhiraj dreaded to think what his pit smelt like.

"So I'll see you soon?"

"Don't come here, it's a pigsty. Give me half an hour, I'll see you down the Docker's Gun, while I set the bots on this place. There'd better be a beer waiting for me."

The Docker's Gun was never completely empty, but at 10:00am even the harder fishermen from the night before would have retired for some well-earned sleep. Dhiraj took a picnic bench in the garden overlooking the river and ordered two lagers from one of the two servos flitting around the place, clearing up after the retiring customers. A few of the regulars known to Dhiraj threw him a few remarks about him arriving so early, which he batted away with forced good humour. Way above the pub the sun's rays were filtered by the biosphere into a kind of feeble, grey permadusk that was as depressing as it was safe. One could hardly call it daylight. Rain drifted by as he fingered the rim of his glass, picking up a globule of beery foam and letting it blow away in the chilly breeze. As the bubbles drifted away, a rough, familiar voice with a faint Dutch accent caught his ear.

"This one had better be for me, you bloody prick," said Jens, parking himself and lifting the second glass to his mouth for a long, joyless draught which left dribbles of beer in his peppery beard. "Now what in the hell are you doing in the pub this time of day, Raj? You alright?"

Dhiraj took a baby sip of his beer. "Alright, Jens. Thanks for coming."

"S'alright. I got nothing on today. I'll sleep this afternoon. You get a catch last night?"

"Yeah, decent one, too. About half a tonne."

Jens nodded in appreciation. "Not bad. You needed that, an' all."

"Tell me about it." Another baby sip. "I need some advice."

Jens laughed. "I hope it's about fishing, because what the fuck do I know about anything else, right?"

Dhiraj tried a smile, but it felt rancid. "Right. You, er, you've been to brothels before, haven't you?" They both knew the answer was yes; he talked about it often enough, but somehow Dhiraj felt compelled to ask him.

Jens raised those great big bushy eyebrows. "Oh-ho, you think just 'cos I'm Dutch I know about brothels and sex clubs? Is that how it is?"

"No, I know because you're always going on about them."

"Ah-ha, so you *were* paying attention; and I thought you were such a good boy. So you want some tips? You sure Sali would be ok you asking me this shit?" He waved a hand in the air. "Agh, I do not judge; me of all people! I know some good places, somewhere clean–"

"No, it's not about that." He leant in, despite there being no other sod around, and lowered his voice to a hush. Suddenly those servobots didn't seem so docile. "You know those kokeshi..."

Jens spat some beer out onto the table as he laughed. To be fair to him, he kept his voice down. "My God, Raj. You crazy fucker. And there I was thinking you were the golden boy."

"What, because I have a family I respect?"

He held his hands up. "You can't respect them that much if you want to go fucking those dolls."

"I don't want–" he lowered his voice again. "I don't want to have sex with them. I found one."

Jens's eyes widened. "You're kidding me."

Dhiraj shook his head and tingles danced on his neck. He needed another sip of beer.

"Where the hell did you *find* one?" Jens asked, screwing his face up. "You don't just find them. They're bloody illegal."

"You think I don't know that? Last night, it was trapped in my catch in the sea, wrapped in some plastic casing."

Jens frowned, taking in the information along with another slug of foamy beer. "So is it a boy or girl?"

"What?"

"Male or female model? They make them both, you know. I even heard there are these people who can change the important bits. You know, make the girl into a boy, and then back again."

"She's... *it's* a girl. It seems to be working..." He noticed Jens's wry look. "No, not like that, Jens. I mean she seems to be unaffected by the seawater."

"So where is she?"

"In my garage, locked up."

Jens covered his smirking mouth. "Does Sali know?"

"Of course she bloody doesn't! I'm not stupid." *Or are you?* "I need to get shot of it as soon as possible. What do you think I should do?"

Jens emptied his glass, slapping it down on the table with a clunk before signalling to the servobots for another. "You need to see this as an opportunity. These dolls are worth a lot of money. A *lot* of money. If you're smart, you could make some serious profit. There's bound to be someone wanting one of these things."

"Mm. That's my worry. What if someone's looking for it?"

"My guess? Someone dumped it, wanted to get rid of it."

"Well, that makes me feel even worse. What if there's something, you know, faulty with it? What if it's dangerous? Shit, it's in my garage."

Jens waved his hand in the air dismissively. "Listen, if you wanted you could just dump it in the sea again. Without that plastic box or whatever it came in, it wouldn't last a day. Problem solved. But if you're smart..." he rubbed his thumb and finger together, worrying Dhiraj.

"I don't know," said Dhiraj. "That seems, I don't know, cruel."

"It's a bloody robot. It'd be like dumping your oven in the sea."

"I like my oven."

"What would be cruel would be turning down the chance to make some easy cash for your family, tax free. Ok, it's not something to tell people about, but it could help, right? Listen, don't worry. Has it caused you any problems?"

"Not yet. She's just done what I've asked so far, which is pretty much stay still and be quiet."

Jens took the second beer and took a fresh glug. "I know some places. You might be able to get a decent price."

"You'll go with me?"

Jens wiped his face with a dirty cuff. "Of course. For fifty percent of whatever you make."

Dhiraj furrowed his brows. Always about bloody money. To be honest he'd be happy to get shot of Naomi for free, but if the big lug wanted to feel like he was taking Dhiraj for a ride, then let him. "Fine. Fifty percent."

"There's a weed dealer in Dagenham I know. He's in a couple of circles. Let me make some calls. I'm sure we can get it sorted sooner rather than later."

"Ok, fine."

Silence filled the air, making Dhiraj's head hurt. He took another sip of the beer, but it had lost its allure. Jens didn't seem to have any such problem. "So," he said with a grin. "What does she look like?"

Dhiraj couldn't have looked at Jens any funnier if the big man had grown two more heads. And yet he just knew that question was coming.

"She's..." *Beautiful.* "Unlike any other robot. I honestly thought she was human. It was scary. I took her hand to help her up on the boat, and it felt like skin. I had no idea about these things. I mean, I've heard about them on the TV and such, but she's like a real person. And yet not like one."

Jens inhaled through his nose. "That's what I've heard. I'd be fascinated to see it in the flesh, so to speak."

"I bet you would."

"So cynical, for one hiding one in his garage! No, I really would." Jens pointed away over the docks, to where a couple of lifters were moving crates of cargo from one of the moored boats. "Look at those things. Lumps of metal with a couple of cameras and those Lidar things on top, and hands that look like something out of a film from last century. And they tell us they are state-of-the-art." He shook his head with a sniff. "No way. These kokeshi dolls. I'll tell you the truth; they scare me a little."

"Yeah. Me too."

After they finished their conversation Dhiraj left Jens the rest of his beer and decided to clean *The Lion's Mane*. He was dog tired, but couldn't face spending more time than he strictly had to at home, and hired a couple of cleanabots from the harbour office to scrub his skiff until it was gleaming in the rain.

When he returned home, the sight of Dan's backpack in the hallway alarmed him. He shouldn't be home so early.

"Dan? Where are you, mate?"

No answer. Dhiraj's heart rose in his chest, and he rushed to the garage. Horror stalled his breath in his chest when he regarded Naomi, naked from the waist up, her right breast cupped by Dan's left hand in the gloom of the garage. He was still in his school uniform. Shame stabbed Dhiraj like a hot knife, a shame that hurt his sides and face, and he couldn't help but cry out, "Danesh, stop it!"

Naomi looked at him coolly, and Dan jumped backwards, fear and surprise writ on his face. Dhiraj got between his son and the robot, and his face melted in shame. "My God." He turned to Naomi and told her to get dressed, which she did.

"Dan, how did you get in there?" He shook Dan by the shoulders when the boy didn't answer. "How?"

"Get off, Dad, get off me!" He wriggled free and stepped back, watching Naomi pull on some clothes, open-mouthed. "What the hell? Dad, she's a robot, right?"

"I'm an autonomous synthetic being," said Naomi, unfazed. "Are you an authenticator?"

"No, he's not a bloody authenticator, Naomi! Keep your voice down." *What have you done, Raj?* He rubbed his eyes, hard, and gritted his teeth, trying to get a grip on this sorry mess. "Dan, I'm sorry. This is... she's... how did you get in there?"

Dan laughed in that sullen, teenage way. "You think I can't hack your passwords? All I wanted was the tools for my cyber project for school. You're so stupid, Dad!"

"Yeah," Dhiraj said, breathlessly. "Yeah I am. I'm a bloody moron."

"What the hell is it doing here?" Dan screwed his face up, half in awe, half in anger.

Dhiraj held his hands out, trying to calm his boy down. "Listen, listen. I found her. Oh Jesus, this is so messed up. I found her at sea, I thought she was a person, and now I've got to get rid of her. She's a robot. She's not mine. I found her, alright?"

"She's a sex robot, Dad!"

Dhiraj wilted. "Yes, I think so. I've got to get rid of her. What were you trying to do... touching her like that?"

Dan blushed and said nothing. Dhiraj couldn't chastise the boy. Jesus, what would he have done at fourteen, finding an uninhibited half-naked girl in the garage? He breathed out hard. "I'm telling you the truth, Dan. I found her. And I've got a plan to deal with it. Look, neither of us are exactly covered in glory here, although I admit this is my mess. But don't tell your mum, ok? This is our secret. Your mum can't know. Ok?"

Dan scowled and looked at his feet. "I won't tell mum."

"Good lad."

"Dad, this is so bad."

"I know."

Mercifully, his phone beeped him out of the awkwardness. It was Jens.

Made a few calls. I'll swing by tomorrow at 8pm. Be ready.

As he read the message Dan stormed off in a cloud of swear words and teenage stroppiness. Dhiraj might ordinarily have chastised him, but on this occasion decided to let it be.

"Naomi, are you ok?"

"I'm fine. Why are you angry with your son?"

"I'm *not* angry with him," he snapped. "I'm angry at this whole mess. Look, the most important thing to me is making sure my family is safe. I'm supposed to protect them from... from bad things. While you're with me, that's the only thing that matters. Do you understand that?"

She looked at him impassively. "Yes, I think so."

He breathed out. "Good. It's important. Look, I think I can find you someone who knows an authenticator." He hoped that was the truth, but even if it wasn't, hopefully it wouldn't be his problem anymore. "You're going to have to stay here another day. I have to look after my family. Ok?"

"Ok."

When Dhiraj returned to the kitchen he found Dan moping over a chocolate bar with a dark scowl on his face.

"Dan, you can't go in there for the time being. I'm getting rid of her... of *it* tomorrow."

Dan nodded without looking up.

"Hey, mate," Dhiraj cupped his son's chin and brought his face up. "Don't worry about it. Everything'll be back to normal after tomorrow. I'm really sorry to put you through this. It's not your fault."

Dan was miles smarter and wiser than Dhiraj ever had been at fourteen, but even so, what could a boy do? He was probably full of longing and confusion towards the robot. He had a sudden disconcerting thought. "Hey. Hey, Dan. The... she... *it's* an autonomous synthetic being. She isn't a real woman. You realise that, don't you? And real women, they're not like her either."

"Yeah, I get it." He looked down again. "Can we leave it now?"

"Yeah. I hope so."

D'Souza II

D'Souza cracked his neck side to side in the 4x4, hoping the three cunts captured by Timon would have the answers he wanted. The pressure in his joints relieved, he took a deep breath through the nose and looked at Collarface as the 4x4 silently navigated itself into a disused building in a dilapidated industrial park out at the south end of the Isle of Dogs. The air smelt of charcoal and hung damply over the dead concrete; here, even the thrust and sway of the arcing Thames, visible about a hundred yards or so away, couldn't bring a sense of life to the picture.

Collarface looked at D'Souza blankly, his big, bristly arms folded across his lap.

"Who are these fuckers?" asked D'Souza, catching a whiff of his leathers. "Known?"

Collars shook his head. "Timon don't recognise them."

"Their own mothers won't recognise them if they stole my fucking doll." D'Souza grimaced, sucking on his teeth. He looked around the car; a selection of pipes, iron bars and other blunt weapons lay on the floor.

Darkness flooded the building, a huge warehouse, as large as an aircraft hangar, where the smell of damp lingered, as though the walls were made of river and salt. The clink of his leather boots and buckles echoed as he strolled in ahead of Collars. The *oofs* and groans became louder as D'Souza further penetrated the dark, until at last he caught sight of two bodies hunched around three chairs.

"Here he is, boys," came Timon's voice out of the gloom. "He's the guy you stole off."

"If I were you, lads, I'd start telling the truth," came Rusty's voice. "The Boss ain't one to have his time wasted."

A trio of moans lifted upwards. Above them all a small bot hovered, shining the merest torchlight on the scene, revealing Timon and Rusty, their fists bloodied from their work. In the fractured light, fragments of bloody faces stared vacantly out from the chairs, broken noses, black eyes and sunken cheeks making some sort of shadowy Picasso out of the three men. Timon and Rusty hadn't roughed them up too bad, though. They'd taken a few blows but nothing so bad they couldn't talk. He knelt in front of the one rope-bound to the left chair and looked him in the eye. He was scared. No player.

"Do you know what you stole from me?"

The man forced out a few rabbit breaths and stared at D'Souza with wild-eyed terror, his one good eye white like a cueball. He stank of sweat. When the man didn't answer, he looked at Collars and nodded. Collars revealed a cricket bat and pushed the end onto the man's ear. He screwed his face up with a whimper.

"Timon, tell me what we know about these guys."

"Nobody knows them. Faceless fucking low-levels. They ain't said nothing yet, and we ain't asked."

"How did you find them?"

"They were selling the stolen electronic goods on the dark web. We had eyes on it, bought 'em up, came here for the trade. Two of 'em were tooled up, but fought like little pussies." He pointed at Second-Chair. "He weren't armed."

D'Souza looked at Second-Chair, who stared, shaking, in front of him. He was no gang member. He tutted theatrically in front of First-Chair. "So you've been caught, and taken a few blows to the head, eh?" He poked a finger brutishly into a bruise on First-Chair's cheek, making him squeal with pain. "Pain hurts. I know. You're lucky you're pond life, and I don't care about pond life. Letting you go is as easy as killing you all; I couldn't give a shit either way. Why not take it easy on yourself and answer my questions. How did you hear about my electronic goods?"

First-Chair shut his teary eyes and breathed quickly through his nose, and a bubble of snotty blood formed on his lip. "Don't hurt us anymore, dude."

That annoyed D'Souza. He'd just told the moron they could escape with a bit of cooperation, and this braindead charlatan acts like he didn't even hear. That would count against him.

"I'll tell you," Second-Chair piped up through wheezy panting. He had longish blond hair and a beard, both caked with blood, and a gash to the forehead. He looked groggy from the beating, but otherwise ok.

D'Souza approached him, and knelt by him. "Collars, a kerchief and some water." Collars brought the relief. "Come, now, then. Tell me everything. Are you protecting anyone?"

The man spat out a bloody globule of water onto the floor, trembling. "N-No. I'm just a hacker. Hacked into shipping manifests. We knew there was a consignment of luxury electronic goods, and we broke into the ship."

D'Souza raised his eyebrows and laughed. "You broke into the ship? Truly?"

Second-Chair nodded.

"What's your name?"

"Oti."

"Oti. Ok, Oti. You tell me how you 'broke in' to that autonomous ship."

"W-why?"

"Because that's a clever trick."

"I-I'm an advanced cyber engineer, cryptanalyst. Hacker, if you like." He shivered with the cold.

"So what, you took down the ship's security?"

"No... that's an amateur's mistake. You leave security running, that's the trick. Fool its health monitoring systems into thinking any suspected ruptures or breaks in the hull are minor. Easily done, if you know how."

"I heard there was a hole big enough to drive a car through," said D'Souza to Rusty.

"S'right. Big hole," said Rusty.

"It doesn't matter the size of the hole," said Oti. He seemed confident. Probably the leader, or maybe the only one who realised that telling the truth would get them out of this mess. "All that matters is what the ship believes is the problem. If you get between the ship's health management systems, the decision-making systems and the health monitoring sensors and manipulate the information flow, you could sink the fucking thing and tell it all's well."

D'Souza nodded and cleaned Oti's face some more. "This is the truth?"

Oti nodded. Confident in his answers, but less so once the talking stopped, and the ball was in D'Souza's court once more. D'Souza looked at Rusty with raised eyebrows.

"S'possible," said Rusty in that dirty drawl. "Fucking clever, though. Don't ask me how you'd do it. I asked the geezer at Tilbury about whether the ship knew, and he said the ship detected something was wrong, but didn't think it was serious. A breached hull! So could be he's telling the truth."

"I am!" said Oti, eagerly. "And we're sorry about the electronics."

"I don't care about a few gadgets," spat D'Souza, pointing a knife at Oti's face. The man shrank away, his face haemorrhaging what little colour it had. "I'll ask you once. Did you see a body on board the ship? A robot?"

"A robot?" Oti screwed up his face.

"We didn't see no robot," said Third-Chair, a fat man with a cropped haircut who looked like he'd barely registered the few blows he'd taken through that fat, thick skull. He had the stink of stale food about him, like he'd spent a night behind some bins, being pissed on by foxes. D'Souza wrinkled his nose at him. "We took the electrics and that's it. We left a few unmarked boxes. If you had robots in that they must have fallen out into the sea after we left."

D'Souza stood and looked over Third-Chair, displeased. "There was a robot worth a great deal of money to me in that consignment. And you never saw it?"

Fatty shook his head and gave D'Souza a filthy look. "Look, you got back what we took. Just let us fucking go, alright? We don't know about your robots, we don't care. You can get more, right?"

"Shut up, Karl," muttered Oti.

"What, you taking his side now?" spat Karl the Fatty. "Trust a ponce like you to talk, fucking ball-less."

Oti shook his head with a distaste that D'Souza shared.

"This guy's in your crew?" D'Souza asked Oti, motioning to Fatty.

"Welder and cutter. Cut through the hull."

"Don't fucking tell him, Oti!"

D'Souza knelt inches from Karl's fat face, the colour of water and flour, covered in pink, blotchy bruises, and gripped his chops hard, until the fat man growled in pain. A disgusting sight. A few feet away, D'Souza heard Rusty and Timon guffawing with laughter at the noise he was making. But it wasn't amusing; it was pathetic and stupid. "You stole my shit, and you lost more. You pay."

"Fuck you, you fucking Tamil. Let's see how hard you are without these ropes."

D'Souza laughed. "You can tell I'm from Lanka? I'm impressed, for a fat man from Dagenham." D'Souza let go, and Karl stretched his face this way and that trying to work the pain away. "Tell you what; I'll give you your chance. You can see how hard I am without those ropes, how about that? Collars."

Collars approached Karl with a knife, and sliced the ropes off, allowing Karl to totter to his feet. His dirty t-shirt was stained with blood and some white crap, as if his face was leaking flour-water. D'Souza curled his lip into a sneer and made a gesture at Collars. As Karl rubbed his chafed wrists the clang of metal on concrete rang in D'Souza's ears.

"What's that?" said Karl, looking at what Collars had thrown down.

"It's called *ethunu kaduwa*," said D'Souza, stretching his

arms above his head and proceeding to stretch and crack his fingers. He peeled off his jacket and T-Shirt, and tensed his chest muscles. "Very sharp strips of metal tied together. We fight with those."

"Fight? With that?"

D'Souza shrugged, bent down, picked up the *kaduwa*, and spun his body around, the momentum whipping the weapon around and lashing it across the fat man's shins with a bright, resonating crack. Fatty roared in pain and collapsed, clutching his legs, and began to blubber. The other two captives turned their faces away. D'Souza knelt by Karl's cheek and whispered in his ear, "And I'm not Tamil. I'm Sinhalese," before dancing back up and whipping the *kaduwa* across his shinbone once more. Karl howled as the crack of bone reverberated along the shaft of the weapon and up D'Souza's arm. D'Souza lifted the *ethunu kaduwa* to Karl's cheek before addressing Oti. "This one, does he have a family?"

"He's got a little boy," said Oti through a wince. Karl writhed on the floor like a worm.

D'Souza spat. "Lucky for you, pigman. Collars, take him and First-Chair and dump them outside a tube station. They get to go home. I've no interest in these dumb sacks of shit." He pointed his weapon at Oti, who turned away. "You, however, you're coming with me."

"Me? Why me?"

Collars dragged the groaning Karl by the ankle back to the 4x4, leaving his rucksack on the floor with D'Souza.

"Because you cost me money and clients. But if you have the skill you say you do, then you may be more use alive. So you work for me. But you fuck up, and your face ends up like pigman's legs." He held the *kaduwa* up and pushed the end sharply into Oti's cheek.

Apart from a few rabbit breaths he didn't respond. "I've a replacement doll coming in for the one you let fall into the sea. A Maya doll. You're going to make sure it gets to me ok."

"Ok, yeah, of course," Oti nodded gratefully. "And then what?"

"We'll see. You realise we'll be making sure you don't run off."

Rusty stepped up and lifted a hypodermic gun. "You want me to shoot him?"

Oti's eyes widened and he whimpered.

"Do it in the car," said D'Souza, slowing his breathing, calming himself. The faint iron tint of the *kaduwa's* work hung in the air. He had drawn blood with it. "Go. I have used *Illangam*, and must heal."

Rusty and Timon ignored Oti's protests as they roughly led him away. Having a tracker inserted would sting a bit but he'd be ok, D'Souza knew. He waited for the warehouse to return to noiselessness, save for the soft patter of raindrops on the roof, and sat down cross-legged, placing the *kaduwa* by his feet. The concrete floor was stony and uncomfortable, but he bore it. He drew three dumpy candles, a lighter, a cloth and some water from Collarface's rucksack. The candles' soft, rising scent of incense soothed and calmed him. Eyes closed, he slowly wiped his chest with the dampened cloth and sat, allowing no thought to penetrate his mind. All was well again, and he was clean.

Adem I

The beautybot gently filed Adem's nails to perfection as he reclined in his office chair, eyes closed, the chair's fat leather pads creaking satisfyingly behind his back. The bot applied a dollop of thick, lavender-scented cream to his hand and used its lovely, fleshy manipulator pads to massage it in. And yet, his relaxation was not yet complete.

"Harvey, call Joseph Johnson," he gently called to Harvey, his office Personal Assistance System.

Behind his closed eyes, the gentle chime of the dialling tone rang throughout his office. He was certain his father would be pleased by his networking in London. With some effort, this could bring great benefits to his family and his people. Images of his father, pleased and angry, flooded his mind. This'd please him. No doubt. The hand being serviced by the beautybot balled into a fist, and the robot stepped back.

"Please, Mr Johnson, I haven't finished that hand."

"Of course," he whispered, keeping his eyes closed and unballing his fist. The robot's soft pads continued their work, yet the tension in his arms refused to melt away.

"Adem," came a booming voice as the dialling tone cut away.

Adem refused to open his eyes. He was making the call. He would show his father he could be strong and stay in control.

"Adem, look at you," rumbled the thick, bass of his father's voice, followed by a deep tutting sound. "A manicure? Is that what type of man you are becoming in London?"

"In Government one has to look smart, Father," replied Adem. He knew his father wouldn't approve of the manicure. Why, then, insist on it just before the phone call with his father was due? Antagonism had seemed like a good idea before the call, but now seemed awkward and foolish.

His father snorted. "Maybe, for the weak English. But not for my son. When will you be a man? Take away that robot, open your eyes when you talk to me. I haven't much time. I'm speaking with the Minister for the Interior in a few minutes. Tell me what is going on."

Adem breathed out through his nose and leaned forward, at last opening his eyes. He sculpted his face into something stern and stared at the projected screen. His father filled the image with his broad shoulders and square head. Wherever he was, it was dark, and his tense, judgmental eyes bored through the connection. As usual, his battered khaki shirt was unbuttoned to the solar plexus, allowing a glimpse of the muscular chest gleaming with sweat – he probably had no air conditioning on in the room – as though his skin could barely contain the power in those old bones. Adem wished he could close his eyes and undo the image, but he couldn't now. Too late. He brought his own arms into his chest, aware that his ultra slimline shirt accentuated just how lean they were; mere sticks that had sprouted from the mighty trunk of his father. "How are things at home?"

His father sniffed. "The NPF – bastard iggiots – burnt and looted an office on Yellow Island a couple nights ago. The Ministry for the Interior says they will deal with the rebels but with them it is always talk, talk, talk. It is not they who bear the brunt of their beaks and bullets. It is us, and it is us who will have to beat them back."

"I understand that the push back isn't working as well as it might."

His father contorted his face with disgust. "When animals like them live and work outside of legitimate boundaries, it is not possible to defeat them with politics. That's what boneheads like the Ministers do not realise. Agh!" He waved a huge hand in front of his face in distaste. Adem could almost feel the dry callouses in London. "Maybe the pantywaists here are not so different from your ones in England. But so-so, tell me of this thing you've found."

Adem leant forwards, gesturing to the beautybot to scuttle away, and told his father all about Nita and the prototypical capabilities of EI Systems. "But it's untested, and the British Government won't support the testing of the technology because of the perceived difficulties associated with its legitimisation. That is, if the status quo remains unchallenged. But Miss Rhodes understands that for her to reap the success her work deserves, the status quo must change."

His father offered the closest approximation of a smile he could muster, and Adem responded with his own, before continuing. "The deployment of the robots along the town borders would enable us to give proper aid to the residents living there and spare them the peril of abduction, humiliation and sexual slavery at the hands of the NPF."

His father nodded with a grimace and stared somewhere off screen, as though the strategy both irritated and impressed him simultaneously. "Yes, yes, spare them. Those people need our help. And the NPF..." he curled his hand into a fist and smashed it on the desk, making things jump somewhere off screen. "Those bastard Marxists. Iggiots!" He thudded a fat finger into his temple. "Braindead! I work, work, work and build, build, build like my father and his father, and all the bastard NPF know is how to break this, break that."

"Father, these robots might not help with the push back against the NPF, but it could bring relief to the poor residents of the Niger delta. It would be a good reflection upon JPC."

Joseph rubbed his chin. "Mm. Yes. But I can buy these kokeshi from anywhere."

"No, Father, actually you can't. They're illegal. If you want to improve the standing of Johnson & Co internationally, this must be done correctly. You know the scrutiny we're under."

"Mm. Just so. So send me some."

"It's not quite that easy at present."

Joseph nodded in understanding. "What stands in the way?"

"Sir Ingham, for one. He will not countenance any shift in technology policy regarding the legitimate use of robotics for sexual services; the current legal situation suits the Government and him just fine. But, of course, his deputy isn't necessarily of the same opinion."

Adem smiled, but his father waved it away like a gnat. "Then the old man is redundant to the task at hand. He lives in a world that has advanced beyond him." He sniffed. "Are you a man to do such a thing?"

"Such a thing?" As Adem repeated the words the realisation hit him like a punch to the gut. His stomach cramped, but he kept his face still as stone. He wouldn't flinch in front of his father. Instead, he looked deep into his father's eyes to see how serious he was, but there was no wavering there. The command was implicit. Sir Ingham was redundant. Sir Ingham had to be removed. His father commanded one of the most powerful corporations in one of the most technologically advanced industrial sectors on the planet, yet behind those half-closed eyes ground a clockwork mind. A career in government had taught Adem that every decision had micro-permutations and wove an interminable web of consequential actions. Decisions were not to be taken lightly, yet his father wielded the power of judgment and decision like a high-roller throwing chips around in a poker game; every decision was either right or wrong. No in-between. There was no fathoming how a mind like that worked, and yet Adem couldn't help but be slightly awed by his father's power to decide. Adem's throat dried up. This wasn't just a command; it was a test. *A test to see if I'm worthy.* He'd been supposedly the heir of JCP his whole life, but his father wouldn't let control of the company pass to any person he deemed unworthy or incapable of making the decisions he'd taken his whole life, even if that person was his eldest son. Christ knew his little brother Remus didn't have what it took to be the next owner, and his sister Joanna wouldn't accept it if it were offered to her. It was his for the taking. He swallowed, and his shoulders tightened; he'd have to get those knots kneaded out by the bot later. *Father wouldn't get them kneaded out.*

"What do you suggest?"

"I will send a thing to you that may help. Privately." His father looked around his dark office, as though bothered by a bug. "I have to go. I will look to you to see something done soon."

The ghost of his father's presence lingered long after the globelet stopped projecting the video screen, and Adem leant back, staring at the ceiling.

The beautybot rolled up to Adem.

"Would you like me to continue with your hands, Mr Johnson?"

He rubbed them together and recoiled at their ugly smoothness. "No."

~

"Sir Ingham is free now, Mr Johnson," said Harvey, its voice ringing through the speakers in the ether.

"Thank you, Harvey. I will be down in just a few moments." Adem fingered the foil package nervously. It looked so innocuous, yet it made his blood freeze every time he thought about it. *It's just a pill*, he told himself, trying to convince himself of the fact. The package had arrived late last night after his father had sent it priority shipping that afternoon. Even if the final mushroom cloud were to rise above the Earth's horizons, the Global Postal Service would be able to make it through. He had to admire them, but today he wished they weren't quite so bloody efficient. Yesterday he'd had ideas about disrupting certain meetings, using diplomacy to smooth a path to the desired outcome of accelerating EI Systems' tech, but his father didn't play such political games. He was far too impatient. *Perhaps that's why he's so successful*, he mused.

His hands had already missed a couple of creams, but they still felt soft. Whenever he saw his father they would shake hands – never embrace – and his father's rough, calloused fingers, gnawed by the years of outdoor work on the rigs and pipes Adem's grandfather insisted upon, would abrade Adem's soft hands, as though they were trying to scrape away their softness.

The sight of the pill's foil wrapping offended him, so he slipped it into his breast pocket behind his pocket square, out of sight, where it protruded just so, like a tiny yoke. He winced; surely anyone who saw him would see it and apprehend him. *Stop this,* he scolded himself, *you're just fooling yourself. This one thing will change Father's perception of you.* The pill was no larger than a shirt button; there was no way anyone could see it, really. He scrunched and stretched his face, then shook it loose, trying to shake away the guilt he was certain was written upon his hot face. His father... *Stop thinking about Father!* he told himself. This wasn't about Father; this was about the company. JPC had to pass to a man who could get things done. His father had learnt that the hard way; Port Harcourt was not the same as London; it remained a wild place, and only wild men were able to maintain a semblance of control over it. Maybe he had stayed too long in London. The words of an American President from long ago whispered in his ear – *The English believe they can make a living out of patting each others' backs and opening doors for one another.* He sniffed and wiped his brow with his sleeve, staining the expensive wool with sweat, and he forced himself not to worry about such trifles. He'd chosen this career; it might not have been the hard toil of the rigs, but it had given him other skills, and had presented him with this opportunity. *What do you think of that, Father? If it wasn't for me, this opportunity wouldn't have come about.*

During the short journey along the corridor the crisp silver corner of the pill wrapping stared up at him from the gloomy silken recess of his breast pocket, hiding behind the folds of his pocket square. No-one could see it but him, but it glinted at him knowingly, as if it threatened to jump out and spill onto the floor, as conspicuous as a bloody dagger.

He knocked on Ingham's office, and the answer came, "Come!"

It's not me, he told himself as he entered and sat down before his boss's desk. It was a beautiful ebony thing, hundreds of years old, polished daily by a specialist servobot Ingham had bought from his own money and kept in the office. Adem felt the strange urge to run his hand along the bureau's edge; it was smooth, as he'd expected, but his soft hands detected subtle waves and bumps along the surface, probably invisible to the naked eye, and the wood seemed to writhe and shimmer under his touch, alive, as though it had captured the monstrousness of history in its contours, and it was being preserved here for Ingham's own personal ownership. It was a lovely desk. Adem looked up and saw the chair behind it. For a moment, that looked even lovelier.

"Afternoon, Adem. Everything ok on your side of the office?" Ingham said with a crisp smile and bright eyes.

"Yes. Yes, of course," Adem smiled, and hoped it wasn't the smile of a madman. Ingham kept an analogue clock on the wall, a mahogany piece. Each *tick* of the second hand stabbed at him, like rhythmic footsteps into the oblivion of lunacy. *No*, he reminded himself. *This isn't me. It's not me. I'm merely coming here with news and will have a drink with an old friend. Nothing that happens after that can be attributed to me.* "Couldn't be better. I actually have some news."

"Oh?" Ingham said. "Well, news is news, and needs to be digested. How about a coffee to aid the digestion?"

Before Ingham could signal to the servobots, Adem said, "Forgive me if I'm being a tad remiss, but I think this news may be more appropriately accompanied by something stronger."

Ingham rumpled that handsome old face into a wry smile. "You old devil, you. I do hope this is because we're toasting some good news, and not taking the edge off some bad."

Adem smiled. "Perhaps it's a little of both. May I?"

"Be my guest. You know where the Scotch is. I'll get the bot."

"No, it's ok. I'll be mother. Some things should be prepared by hand."

Ingham smiled. "Couldn't agree more, dear boy. Well, if you want you be mother, I have a couple of reports I need to lend my name to for the CSA."

As Ingham dictated a few words of recommendations into whatever report he was working on for the Chief Scientific Advisor, Adem slipped over to the drinks cabinet and prepared two large, neat Scotches, the best of Ingham's little collection. He fished out the foil wrapping, tore it open and popped the pill onto his palm with his back to his boss. Its plain yellow face looked so innocuous, and horrific at the same time. Temperature-activated, apparently. Clever stuff, and banned all over the world. Bristles of shame and guilt flared up all over his face, and his fingers started to twitch. *It's not me*, he told himself. *Nothing to do with me.* The pill slid in, almost looking like it had fallen in accidentally. *Ah, well; can't be helped. One of those things.*

Adem almost jumped out of skin when Ingham asked what the wait was.

"No wait," he said, spinning around, smiling. "All ready."

"We need something to toast," said Ingham, swirling and sniffing the glass with joyful élan upon receipt.

"How about ends and beginnings?"

"Ah, I see. Pray tell, then. To what ends, and what beginnings, do you refer?"

"I spoke with my father last night."

"Joseph! How is the old devil?"

"Very well. He is troubled by the activities of the NPF, as you well know; he is spending a great deal of time with the Government to try and eradicate these terrorists from the lands around Port Harcourt, leaving him with little time to look after JPC. So, he has asked that I return home to help him manage the operations of the company in his stead. There must always be a Johnson at the Head of JCP, he says, and rightly so. I could not refuse, and so here we are."

Ingham nodded. "I suspected as much from the nature of your toast."

"I wanted to tell you before it goes public. You've been..." the truth made his voice falter just a bit. "You've been a good friend to me."

Ingham raised the glass. No evidence that the pill had ever been there was visible. Amid the self-revulsion there was a tangible sense of awe in his stomach that a robot could be designed so small that it could be encased within a tiny, tasteless tablet, practically invisible to the naked human eye. He looked hard in spite of the instincts telling him not to, but he really couldn't see any trace of the tiny worm. Remarkable. And terrifying.

It took Ingham fifteen minutes or so to drain the glass, during which time they had a conversation of which Adem could scarcely remember a word. Adem had thrown his Scotch down his throat in two glugs, just to steady himself.

"Well, I should be getting back to it," he said at last, rising from his chair. "But thank you again. For everything." He extended a hand to Ingham. Intolerable heat pricked his face, as if he was sweltering in the Niger delta in the sticky, rainy season.

"You wouldn't mind sending in the drinks bot, would you?" asked Ingham, like it was the most normal thing in the world. Adem shuddered, mumbled a word of acknowledgement and slipped out of the room before his legs would give way beneath him.

Salazar II

The continual buzz and rusty murk of the factory's guts made Salazar's headache even worse than usual. It was a hideous noise, like being trapped inside a dying hornet. Sweat dripped from the end of his nose as his hands flowed through his work in installing the flesh sensors into the sexual systems. Sometimes, when he wasn't overcome with fatigue and stress and self-loathing he found it funny that a job requiring so much specialist knowledge could be so bloody menial. He shouldn't be here. He shouldn't have ever been here, in this sweat-pit, surrounded by the feckless and ruined and desperate and unemployable, doing degrading work for a bunch of villains who weren't even French. If it hadn't been for little Lily, his Chouchou, he'd have overdosed or sliced his wrists open or downed a bottle of cheap shit vodka and walked down the steps into the black soup of the Canal de Jonage. But even through the worst times, her sweet face kept his hands moving, kept the products rolling, kept the fists of his bosses at bay.

Until now. Now something else kept those hands moving. The chance of escape.

Strictly speaking, a robot should be doing the menial and repetitive tasks he was doing; installing sensor after sensor, meshing them together using advanced plastics, but robots were expensive, traceable and pregnable. The sex gangs had been burned in the early days, before he'd got caught up in them. The police had managed to hack and reconfigure manufacturing robots with cyberware. Arrests and convictions followed swiftly. So the gangs reverted to good old-fashioned flesh and blood and brains, on the workbenches and occasionally all over the floor. You can't very easily reconfigure a human who doesn't want to be reconfigured. But Salazar did want to be reconfigured, he realised; he did want a way out of all this, and the phone call he'd taken from Nita a couple of days ago had offered him that.

She hadn't said what had changed, apart from the offer. Do this one thing, and he was in. She would take personal care of it. It was a hell of a thing, but for his Chouchou, he'd kill. For her he'd kill the Devil himself with his bare hands. He never really wondered what happened to the robots after they were completed and shipped to England – best not think about such gruesome things. People could be disturbing that way; it was awful enough what they did to other humans half the time. The thought of what they'd do to humanoids split him all up. On the one hand it made him shudder; he reckoned the availability of robots would enable some folks to do some foul things, but on the other hand it was right that such things shouldn't happen to other people. None of that mattered now. He was already a stained man; why else would he be here?

His hands, filthy with grime and sweat, wired the components together into the vaginal wall in front of him, splayed out like a bloodless, reverse autopsy. He stopped and looked up. Chevé, the factory foreman – his own glorified term for slave-driver – strolled along the cramped factory aisle, ensuring they didn't let up their pace. A low-browed French ogre with shoddily-installed bionics and flexes protruding from his forearms like distended copper snakes, he walked up and down, inspecting each worker with baggy-eyed intent, repeatedly flexing reinforced fingers to show the workers they were ready to strangle. Salazar's sense of danger always pricked up when Chevé passed by.

Working – though this was rather an exaggerated term for the activity – on the workbench to Salazar's left was Hafeez, a heroin-addled Algerian rake, all graveyard eyes and fading hands, covered in a shit-coloured galabiyya. He nominally worked on programming the vaginal and labial sensors Salazar was installing, but he was dying on his feet. *Work faster, you stupid bastard*, he thought, but he didn't dare utter it. All he did was make sure his own hands kept moving, ensuring Chevé passed Salazar with a grunt and a sniff, raising the hairs on the back of his neck, but nothing more. When Chevé was out of reach Salazar realised he was holding his breath, and he exhaled sharply. Just the same as yesterday.

"Pigfucker," came Chevé's voice, a deathly rattle that made Salazar shudder. Out of the corner of his eye he saw a gruesome finger poke Hafeez in the ribs. Salazar winced for him, for the thin man barely registered it, his fingers ghosting over the tablets, globelets and rolled-up screens at his disgusting workbench.

"The pennies you're paid are wasted, pigfucker," said Chevé. Hafeez didn't react, save for a faint sway. *A mercy*. Salazar looked down at his desk. "Can you even hear me? You stink of pigshit, Arab cunt."

Hafeez only let out a reflexive squeak as Chevé punched him

hard in the spine, bending him backwards. Salazar concentrated on his work, but his hands trembled uncontrollably. Hafeez had been worse than useless for days now; too doped up from whatever cheap shit poison he'd been supplied in his squalid little den. He knew this had been coming, but it didn't make it any better. There was the sound of muffled struggling and then a sickening *crack*, and a thud. When he looked up he saw Hafeez's body in a heap, his face staring down his crooked spine, the last of the light extinguished from his eyes. A winter of shivers shook Salazar's head, and a fat finger zipped up to his eyeline. "Keep working, Spanish prick."

Salazar instinctively did as he was told, but as Chevé started to drag the body away, a thought nagged at him. Hafeez had been a dead man walking for days now, weeks even. The words of Miss Rhodes rang in his ears. *Just this one small thing*, she'd said. *This one small thing, and you're in*. He forced the words out. "Chevé, Monsieur.»

Chevé looked at him with disgust. "What?"

He nodded towards Hafeez. "Who will do his work now?"

"Not your concern. We'll find someone."

Salazar stepped forwards. "Let me do it. Just until you find someone new."

"Not my decision."

"I'd like to speak with Monsieur Charlie."

"Not your decision."

"Ask." When the ogre screwed his face up, Salazar added, "Please."

He pointed to Salazar's desk. "Fucking work."

He did, as Chevé dragged Hafeez away. It was another couple of hours before Chevé came back. "You're to see Monsieur Charlie."

Salazar steeled himself, clenching his teeth, and followed.

Monsieur Charlie's den was under the main factory floor, through a secret trapdoor controlled by biometrics. *Keep your cool.* His heart hammered, but he slowed his breathing to try and remain calm; he'd never been in Charlie's den before, and he'd need his eyes and ears alert to the situation. Inside, Salazar blinked and shielded his gaze; nauseatingly bright LEDs stung his eyes after coming from the windowless rust of the factory floor. It was a surprisingly sparse, small office that looked as though it had been airlifted from a Government building in Paris. A functional, if ugly, bureau was equipped with a large workstation, while on leather seats there lounged a few sunglasses-wearing mobsters, smoking and drinking hard spirits. Muscle. Three naked kokeshi, all of which had been assembled on the factory floor, stood around the seated men, stroking them, kissing them, seeing to them. Salazar cringed inside but kept his face firm, even as the men glared at him. Behind the main desk was Monsieur Charlie, the guy running this factory. It was said, in the instance of a raid, Charlie and his boys could get out of this place in thirty seconds flat through hidden exits; exits Salazar couldn't even fathom now he was in the room, but he didn't doubt they were here. Charlie looked up from his bureau. He was whip-lean, taut like a spring, keeping his movements small, quick and precise, like he'd been programmed by Hafeez on one of his many off days. When he spoke he spat the words out, poisonous barbs meant to entangle his prey.

"Spaniard."

Salazar nodded.

"Talk."

"My colleague Hafeez is dead," said Salazar, mindful not to be judgmental. Chevé's presence behind him filled the room, reminding him that each exit – each exit he could see – was blocked off. One wrong word, one word Charlie even perceived as insulting and it'd be a dose of Chevé's unique brand of chiropractic therapy. He wiped his hands together but they just smeared the grease from one palm to the other, so he rubbed them upon his already-ruined shirt. "The dolls we're sending out are behind because of him. Let me do his work."

Charlie shot him a calm look and made a few gestures at the workstation screen, perhaps working on something Salazar couldn't see. "You want to do his work? Why?"

Because I need to sabotage one of them. "For money." He shrugged. Money was the one thing these guys respected and understood. They'd understand and respect economic ambitions. He gulped but hid it, making his face stone, hard, impassable. "Hafeez was a loser, Monsieur. He might have had talent, once, but he slowed you down. He slowed me down, too. You let me work his dolls, I clear them."

Charlie bared his teeth, grim gunmetal things that had replaced his human teeth after they'd been smashed out by a mobster when he was still a dumb kid, or so the factory floor rumours had it. He clicked his fingers at one of the *kokeshi*, a tall, black-haired model, with a vaguely Mediterranean complexion, chiselled and curved. It sauntered over to Salazar, drifting the back of its hand across his cheek, where he felt and heard the faint, crisp rasp of stubble, down his chest and hovering on his beltline, feeling inside the gaps between his shirt buttons. His heart rate quickened in spite of himself, and he had to bite his cheek to prevent the faint twitch in his groin becoming something more. He gave the tiniest shake of the head to remind himself that he'd built her, or at least part of her. *The parts that could make a human quiver with pleasure.* A trickle of sweat ran down his temple, and he turned his gaze away from the robot. Charlie lit a cigarette – a crumpled, black thing that looked like a twig of liquorice – with a petrol lighter and puffed out a black ring of smoke as he watched the show.

"You clean?" asked Charlie.

Salazar nodded. "Sober. Totally."

"How long will it take to clear that fucking Arab pig's backlog?"

Salazar turned to Anton. "He left six robots partially or fully vaginally uncoded."

Charlie sneered with frustration and sucked black demons out of the cigarette. "I should have had that pig killed before." He pointed his finger past Salazar. "Chevé, you keep a better eye on these things." He looked again at Salazar. "And you. You clear that backlog by Friday, you get the weekend with Lucille." The Lucille doll stroked faintly at his groin, and he twitched again. He swallowed. Its eyes were perfect blue – *too perfect for human's eyes* – and its skin flawless. *But you're not flawless*, he thought as he looked the doll in the face with contempt. *I can get inside you in more ways than you think.* "We get these dolls all shipped to our clients in good time, we can talk money. I like a man with drive." His face split into a broken smile. "I hope you got plenty of drive when you get this one home," he said, prompting a few sycophantic guffaws from the shaded mobsters. "I hope you got fire in your dick."

"Ok. Friday." He looked at the Lucille doll and forced out a smile which made him sick. The doll smiled back, that glazed look of empty seduction that must have done for hundreds of thousands of equally empty, pathetic men in cities from here to Ankara. Looking at the creature was truly odd; usually he never saw them switched on; he saw them being assembled, constituted, coded, archived, their databases compiled. He never saw them move, or interact. Just for the merest moment he could see something more than robotic behind the eyes, and it repulsed him, for he never thought of himself as one of those men. *I know you.*

After a second's pause, Charlie's smile fractured into a frown. "Well why the fuck are you still here? Get the fuck out." He stood up. "Get out. Get out!" He threw the cigarette at Salazar, which bounced off him in a singe of little orange blooms and fell to the floor amid peals of laughter. He flinched, falling backwards into the chest of Chevé, who swore at him and pushed him back out the door before closing it behind him to talk with Charlie some more; no doubt Chevé was being given orders to watch his progress extra closely.

That afternoon he worked extra hard to complete his own work, in spite of his bone-breaking fatigue, in spite of his cramps, in spite of the shame and fear and sweat and piss all around him, in him, dripping off him. Behind Hafeez's workstation was an assembly and testing rig – a rickety thing reverse-engineered from high-value Chinese manufacturing plants from the last century – from which hung the six partially-assembled Maya kokeshi that Hafeez had been meant to code. They were missing faces, torso electronics, and their sexual systems were only partially installed. He walked up to one of them and, checking none of the foremen or cameras were on him, he gently brushed his hand down the robot's waist and onto its hip. Just like human. He'd not felt the soft curve of a human female hip since Lily's mother, yet this faceless grotesque hanging like a side of beef inside this dying hornet of a factory reminded him of it. When he withdrew his hand it left a sticky smudge of grease and dirt on the pristine artificial flesh. Usually he'd have panicked, but he simply stepped back and focused on the stain. "You," he said, looking up at the Maya doll. "You're my escape route, beautiful."

Engineering and programming a replacement chip wouldn't be tricky. He took the work home with him, set it up in the kitchen and beat out line after line of code to the stimulus of cheap coffee, cigarettes and the endless, remorseless soundtrack of thuds emanating from next door. He got his head down over his makeshift workbench and blocked out the rude noises. The sexual plastics of the artificial vaginal walls possessed autonomously morphic materials that were symbiotically reactive with human flesh; they reacted to touch, which in turn would make the human flesh react. Indescribable pleasure, actually describable with a few simple lines of maths and code. The secrets of the human condition laid bare by numbers. The inevitability of this simplicity he would now turn to his advantage. It wouldn't be difficult to programme the plastics to react – to *overreact* – in the wrong way, increasing heat and pressure until the system became an unbreakable weapon, something lethal, something horrific. He couldn't think about it, but even when inklings of weakness peeped through his iron mind, he thought of Lily and carried on working. Some poor person would be maimed, or worse, but that couldn't be helped. He'd seen the types of people who were attracted to the type of illicit, guilt-free gratification offered by kokeshi. They wouldn't be missed. He wondered about Miss Rhodes and her motives. Somewhere in the back of his mind he reckoned it was better to be working for a corrupt corporate crook than a violent, underground one, though when he juxtaposed the two he couldn't quite figure out why.

It was around midnight when Lily came to the kitchen, teddy bear in her left hand, pawing the sleep out of her eyes with her right.

"Papa, why aren't you asleep?"

He stubbed out his cigarette and hopped down from the

wobbly barstool at the kitchen side and knelt down to Lily's level. "I'm working, Chouchou. I'm sorry. Can't you sleep?"

She shook her head. "No."

He took her in a tight embrace, closing his arms around her like a shell and stroking her lovely brown hair. "Is it the noise from next door?"

He felt her nod within his arms. "I know. Sometimes it keeps me awake as well. Would you like to sleep in Papa's bed tonight?"

A nod of the head came through bleary eyes and a cute yawn that made him ache more than a thousand blows from Chevé ever could. He took her through to his room – no less noisy from the banging and cursing next door, but she might feel a bit safer in his bigger bed. He might be at his lowest ebb, but he still had some pride; Bridge kept the apartment as clean as it could be. He'd seen inside some of the other apartments from time to time; brown horror-movie mise-en-scenes housing the lowest degradations upon the human spectrum. He would turn Lily's face away anytime they wandered past an open door. He wouldn't let his own living space become that way, as long as he could help it. Plus, a well-ordered home kept by a sober father was the best way of throwing off the police when they came to occasionally raid one of the heroin dens nearby.

"You know, we won't always be living here," he said, tucking her in and planting a kiss on her chubby cheek. "Papa is working hard. I have a plan to get us a nice place, somewhere green. Maybe England."

Her little face lit up with a smile. "England?"

He shrugged, trying to smile back. "Maybe. If I work hard. That is what I am doing in the kitchen."

She creased her brows and nodded in partial understanding. "But you will look after me?"

Tears punched behind his eyes and his lower jaw trembled. "Chouchou, I will *always* look after you. I would kill for you." *And perhaps I will.* "But for now, remember I am here. And don't forget Bridge is by the front door. No-one will get past him."

She turned on her side and closed her eyes. "Lie down with me, Papa."

He did, lying on top of the covers and stroking her hair until she was a peaceful, snoring mound beneath the sheets, and he found himself unable to prevent his own eyes from closing. *Just five minutes*, he told himself, but it was the last thought he had until morning.

Dhiraj IV

Jens visited in the early evening to pick up Dhiraj, and Sali invited the great lug in begrudgingly. She'd never got on with his mates – if he could really call Jens and the other salty types mates – but tolerated them as part and parcel of working in the rough trade of jellyfishing.

"So you're working together tonight," Sali said over hot mugs of tea in the kitchen. Dan flitted in and out wearing a monocular headset and data gloves, swiping away at thin air with one hand and munching on a scraggly peanut butter sandwich held in the other. He gave his dad a real scowl as he left the room, and while Dhiraj tried to pay it no mind, his senses were on red alert. A sweat might break out on his forehead at any moment. He'd take Dan aside later, in the morning, when this was all over, tell him again it was all a stupid misunderstanding, but he'd sorted it out. Christ, he hoped this would be a quick and clean evening.

"Yes," said Jens with his least swarthy smile. "Looks like a storm's coming tonight. Real squally one. They always say take a buddy on nights like this – some things an autonomous boat can't do, like keep an eye out on your mate."

She looked him up and down and stared at the mug of tea intently, as though his thick, ropeworn fingers might crack the pottery. Dhiraj ground his teeth from side to side and bit at a fingernail. Jens knew not to say anything, but even so he was an unthinking sort, and Dhiraj didn't trust him not to blurt out some sort of clue as to what they'd really be up to tonight.

"Well, see that you do look out for each other," said Sali, putting her hand on Dhiraj's, which brought a warm smile from him and filled him with love and confidence, and then gnashing shame from the deception. He pushed away the smile, and looked down at his tea. "Do you even need to go out tonight?"

"Well I heard about Dhiraj's last catch from a couple of nights ago," laughed Jens. "And I couldn't let the bugger take all the good jellies now, could I!" He clapped Dhiraj on the back, a little overzealously. "No, the cold will bring them rushing. Now's the time to get those nets out there. Talking of which," he said, inspecting his watch. "We'd better go."

They finished their tea, and Dhiraj rose. "I've got to get some tools from the garage. Jens, you'll help me?"

Dhiraj kissed his wife. Normally a night at work would warrant a peck on the lips, but somehow he felt compelled to kiss her slowly, and take her by the waist, and leave her with a swaying smile and half-closed eyes, until even Jens looked away. "Mmm," she said. "That's nice. Well, go on then. Make it another good catch tonight. Look after each other."

They removed Naomi from the garage while Sali had a bath upstairs. As Naomi emerged from the rusty cocoon of the steel cabinet, Jens's mouth fell open, but he thankfully kept his response to a small shake of the head. Dhiraj took her by the hand and, keeping an eye out for nosy neighbours, led her to the back seat of Jens's car, where the seatbelts detected her and buckled her in snugly.

"Shouldn't she wear something a little more revealing?" said Jens, looking over his shoulder to Naomi in the backseat as the car drove away.

"Revealing?" The word made Dhiraj nervous. He looked back at Naomi. She was wearing the same old black T-Shirt of Dan's and a pair of Sali's old slacks and flip flops. His hands fidgeted. If he'd been out of his comfort zone when he dragged Naomi from the sea, he was heading into truly dark and dangerous waters now. But he couldn't keep hold of her; she had to go. He squeezed his hands together to stop the fidgeting and tried to keep an alert mind. "What does that matter?"

"If she looked more tempting, it might make us look less like a couple of losers who don't know how to play the game. She looks like a bloody tramp. And not in a good way." Even Jens seemed on edge, which didn't help Dhiraj's mood.

"Maybe it would be better just to tip her in the sea again," said Dhiraj.

Jens laughed nervously and scratched his beard. "No fucking way, my friend. I called a guy who called a guy and he says I've got to meet this guy called Djordje with the kokeshi if it's called Naomi. If I'm not there, it's more than my life is worth. Look, these guys are pretty low-key, I'm sure, but we don't want to piss them off unduly. In any case," he said, pulling up his chunky sweater. Into his belt he'd tucked an old-fashioned pistol. Dhiraj's eyes almost popped out; he really was in too deep here. "I got some insurance."

"Where the hell did you get that?" he said, looking out of the window to make sure no-one had seen him, then drawing his collar up around his cheeks and tucking his head down.

"Don't be such a baby, Dhiraj. Would you rather have it and not have to use it, or not have one and need it? It's just insurance. I've never hurt anyone in my life. But I don't intend on getting hurt either. You stay behind me, ok?"

An instinctive nod came. Jens was a big fella, and if you didn't know him, you wouldn't want to trifle with him. *Then again*, Dhiraj supposed, *I'm not sure I should have trifled with him either, and he's on my side.*

"What do you think, Naomi, baby?" said Jens, turning round.

"About what?"

"You think it would be good to cover our backs?"

"I don't know. Is it cold where we're going?"

Dhiraj turned around, trying to put the pistol out of his frazzled mind. "Hopefully we're going to give you to some people who will take you to an authenticator."

She nodded, but her face and voice remained serene, untouched by emotion. "That is well, then."

"Are you ok with that?" asked Dhiraj.

"I am fine, with respect to health-monitoring and performance, though as you know my primary functionalities are indefinitely disabled for security reasons until they are authenticated; so, the meeting you are taking us to aligns with my own strategic objectives. I am ok with that."

Jens looked her up and down with a frown. "Sweetheart, believe me; you are beautiful, but do you always talk that way?"

"How would you prefer me to talk?"

Jens shrugged. "I don't know. Er, more sexy, I thought..."

"Sexy?"

Jens floundered, and Dhiraj hid a little half-smile in his collar. "I mean, ah, you're a kokeshi, right?"

"As I mentioned previously, my primary functionalities are disabled right now. You cannot activate them. Activation is only possible once I rendezvous with a compatible operator who can authenticate my existence, who will be authorised by her own human user to activate my own capabilities. This is a security measure installed by manufacturers to prevent my capabilities from being exploited by the wrong people."

"You mean thieves?"

"Anybody who is not authorised."

Jens leaned over the front seat, overcome with curiosity. "So I couldn't, you know, have sex with you?"

"Jesus Christ, Jens. Keep it in your fucking pants for once," said Dhiraj.

"You could try," said Naomi, looking Jens in the eye. "However, I would not recommend you doing so."

Jens sat forward and stared out of the windscreen, subdued. "No. I don't think I would either. So how come you do what Raj says?"

"She doesn't do what I say," Dhiraj said in a huff.

"Yes, I do. Raj activated my voice protocols. I'm bound to the first human voice I hear to enable swift and efficient transfer of my body. Until I'm authorised for operational performance, I'm under his directive."

Dhiraj looked at her and raised his eyebrows. "You are?"

"For now."

Jens blew out a long breath and quietly laughed, but Dhiraj felt no such good humour.

Jens's car navigated the duel carriageway carefully; they set the drive to comfort rather than speed; they had plenty of time, and both of them were happy not to be at this place in Beckton any earlier than they needed to be. The two men sat in muted discomfort, while their forbidden quarry sat upright in the back, like a VIP being chauffeured to an important appointment. Dhiraj concentrated on the sodden roads to take his mind off what they were about to do, and keep his nerves at bay. As the car took the flyover he looked across at his hometown Tilbury, its twinkling lights fading into the distance. From the flyover, he could just see the murky shimmer of the Thames as it meandered eastwards to sea, little lamplit flurries of pattering rain disturbing its surface, greasing the shrinking docks and its toy boats with a slick, black sheen. Somewhere in amongst that lot would be *The Lion's Mane*, clean, pristine and ready for the hunt, but it wouldn't be hunting tonight. It would be sitting dormant, while the real hunt occurred elsewhere. Nevertheless, the rain would hit him and his boat alike, and would never stop. The endlessness of the rain was simultaneously a comfort to which he – and everyone else, he supposed – had become conditioned, yet also a great depressant. Sometime just before the end of the twenty-first century, the wicked terror cell known as Daesh had finally been put down, but the decades-long effort to squash it had taken its toll on the planet, so the scientists said, and cooling it down would require drastic efforts. Biospheres. That never made any sense to Dhiraj, but then he was just a jellyfisherman, and the war against Daesh was ancient history to him, something that had happened to his dear departed parents and which he didn't fully understand. He was sure that the Governments had their reasons for building the biospheres, though he wasn't entirely certain what they were. Whatever they were, they didn't feel good enough to Dhiraj. He missed the sun, so much that it made him ache in his gut and want to cry, and when he thought of the darkness Dan would be growing into, he had to bite the inside of his cheek to keep the hot tears from flowing. Occasionally, during the summer months, when the daylight was at its longest, he could see the sunrise at sea, beyond the footprint of the biosphere, before he had to return to shore. *If I were to die now*, he would think when the sun crept above the watery eastern horizon and rose languidly into a brisk, summer sapphire sky, *I would die truly content. There's no beauty like this to be found under the dome*. The days when he'd taken Dan and Sali to sea when Dan was little, just to see the sunrise, were about the happiest of his life. The traffic increased as they neared East London. Dhiraj's stomach dropped into his bowels and his breathing quickened. *What if I never see the sun again?*

"This is it," said Jens gruffly as the car pulled off the carriageway and towards a large industrial complex that once had been a gas and sewage treatment works. It had been defunct for many years now, but as the car pulled towards the silhouettes of its hulking, dead towers, Dhiraj swore he could still detect the faint smell of excrement in the air.

"I don't like the look of it," muttered Dhiraj.

"Me neither. In and out." He held up his gloves, showing some of the apps on them, glimmering dully. "We give them Naomi, and they transfer the money with this – easy as a handshake." But he didn't sound confident. "Naomi, you ok?"

"I'm fine. You are here to make a transaction of me?"

"We're trying to help you," said Dhiraj, hoping she'd believe him, just enough to be cooperative.

Naomi's expression shifted to a subtle frown – or, at least Dhiraj thought it did – it was probably a trick of the gloom. "Who are the people taking me away?"

Jens was silent.

The car pulled into a large car park, unlit and empty, lined by the corpses of buildings, where the concrete and tarmac had long since been torn into potholes, crevices and cracks by time and abuse, making for a bumpy last few yards. It didn't do Dhiraj's stomach any good. Ahead, he could see a couple of black saloon cars, old pieces of shit with blacked out windows but no plates, the headlamps beaming four streams of illumination sliced up by the rain. Against one of the cars leant a tall, thin man wearing a silvery trench coat with a firework of red hair, zapping upwards as if he'd been set alight. Sunglasses shielded his eyes. In his right hand he held two cigarettes between middle and forefinger, and occasionally took a puff out of both of them at once, which annoyed and scared Dhiraj in equal measure.

"Is that Djordje?" asked Dhiraj as Jens controlled the car for the final few yards using the dashboard touchpad.

"I guess so," said Jens, keeping his own headlamps on. "My friend said he was a little wacky. He doesn't look so tough."

"Bloody hell Jens, there are *two* cars there. He's obviously not alone."

Jens grunted and placed his hand upon his beltline. "I'll get out first, you stay behind me. Naomi, stay in here 'til we say so, ok?"

Naomi looked at Dhiraj for confirmation.

"Yes, stay here, out of sight 'till I say so."

"Ok."

The rain was pleasantly cool, but with the beams of the black cars it made visibility uncomfortably difficult. Dhiraj stayed by the car door while Jens moved cautiously forwards on the other side. *Don't make it obvious you're carrying a bloody gun, Jens.*

"You Djordje?" called Jens.

"I am indeed. You must be Jan." The man grinned, a sort of cracked grin. His face was pale and unhealthy, and the grin revealed bad teeth. He sucked on his two cigarettes and blew out a billow of smoke with wide eyes. Dhiraj guessed it wasn't just tobacco in those sticks. He remained on high alert, and kept his eyes firmly on the other car, trying to pierce the tinted windows and see who – or what – sat inside.

"Jens," said Jens.

"Right. Jens. Well let's not fuck about. Show us what you got."

Jens looked at Dhiraj, then back at Djordje. "You got the money?"

Djordje laughed – a high-pitched, revolting clack, revealing those gnashing teeth, and shook his head. "'The money', says Jan! *Huck.*" He spat a brown thing on the ground and rubbed it into the concrete with a high-heeled boot thrust out from his trench coat. "You know who you're selling to, right? Yes we've got the fucking money. Show us the doll."

Jens nodded to Dhiraj, who opened the back door.

"He looks handy in a scrap," laughed Djordje as Dhiraj bent down and opened the door, allowing Naomi out. This didn't seem right, handing her over, but this was too far gone. He wanted out of there.

Naomi stepped into the rain, and in his family's old clothes, sodden under the rain, she looked as dead as she had when he'd plucked from the icy sea. *Because I'm sending her to die again.* She walked forwards. "You'll have to go to them," said Dhiraj softly, holding her hand. "Don't worry, it'll be ok." He'd no idea why he was attempting to comfort this robot. Maybe he was comforting himself. Off she walked, hands by her side, dark hair lank and dripping, her T-Shirt sticking to her slender shoulders.

"Hold it," said Jens. He held up his hand to show his data glove. "Now the transfer."

Djordje gnashed his teeth and spat something else on the floor before taking another huge gulp from his cigarettes. "First we check her. You know, make sure she is what you say she is. She's a pretty one though, ain't she!"

Dhiraj knew Jens couldn't argue. They had to be firm but not push their luck.

Djordje threw his cigarette butts down into a puddle, where they died with a fizz, and strolled over to Naomi. Dhiraj clenched his fists, and his face tensed as Djordje pulled a thin knife from somewhere inside his coat.

"Just hold still, beautiful," he said, brushing up the hair at the nape of her neck. Below Naomi's flesh, where a human would have its uppermost vertebrae, was a raised oblong, no bigger than a pillbox; using the knife he made a small nick, spilling a few drops of what looked like dark blood onto the ground, though Naomi showed no pain at the cut. The nick revealed a small, black piece of plastic. Djordje stashed the knife and pulled out a small tablet-type gadget which he placed upon the black oblong. It made a beeping sound. Djordje smiled at the result, which Dhiraj guessed was a good sign. He moved his hand closer to the car door.

"Well, there you go," said Djordje. "It is her."

"Good, so you can pay us then," said Jens, stepping forwards, but Djordje put his arm around Naomi, and waggled his finger at the big Dutchman. "Ah-ah-ah, no no, you naughty boys. This is *her*. The scan never lies, boys." He held up the scanner, as if that made any difference. "The missing Naomi doll. You'll never guess who's looking for this one."

Dhiraj's stomach turned to water. He looked at Jens. The big oaf had the sense to look concerned.

"Oh, boys – you do know who you're selling to, don't you?"

Dhiraj's flesh crawled under his jacket, and his mind flashed with alarm. *Time to go. She's gone, and nothing matters.* He opened the car door. "Come on Jens," he muttered. "Let's go." But whether out of macho posturing or a real desire to get paid, Jens didn't move.

"We're selling to you; that's all I'm concerned with," said Jens. "You own a gentleman's club, right?"

"You mean Club Fantasia? Not me," Djordje said, shaking his head and sticking out his bottom lip for effect. "I just run the place. The owner's a different sort of man entirely."

"I don't know who your boss is, but we brought you a good product, just like I said. We ought to be rewarded for that, right?"

Djordje's eyebrows raised and his jaw slackened into a shocked laugh, but no noise came out. He kept a squirming hand on Naomi's shoulder, who remained motionless throughout. "Oh-ho, my old mate, oh yes, you ought to be rewarded for this. *Leatherdick!*"

From the second car emerged a monster. First out flopped a hairy, pink belly, followed by rolls of arms and legs, and when he rose to his feet the car suspension groaned with relief. A stubbly, neckless face sat atop the trunk. Its expression was calcified into a loveless, pig-eyed sneer. He was dressed in tight black clothing: leggings and a turtleneck that showed all his rolls. Appallingly, the great hulk peeled off his clothes; first the top, then the bottoms, until he was naked. Dhiraj stood, slack-jawed, moving behind the car door as he revealed himself. The big man stood and stretched his mighty arms until they clicked. Thick, eddying clots of hair blotted his chest and belly, and his entire body was covered in ugly scars, stitching and patches of material, black, brown and beige, that looked like it had been sewn into his flesh. The material quivered with the glow of minute circuitry. Most terrible was the great club of a penis that swung between his legs, something that had been stitched together with yet more material, so that it looked like a patchwork cosh softly glimmering with electric iridescence.

"Ain't he pretty?" said Djordje, lighting two more cigarettes with a lighter that lit two flames in a V-sign. "He had a run in with a gangster from Manchester whose dogs chewed off his old chap. And some other bits." He laughed, and spat. "Ooh, Leathers got *mad* at that. Should've seen the mess he made! Anyway, he had it put back together with leather and electronics. He can't feel anything down there anymore, of course. But Leathers never was one for actually fucking for pleasure, were you, Leathers?"

The man joylessly scratched his crotch in response.

"Enough of this shit," said Jens, but despite the bold tone Dhiraj hoped to God Jens was just as unnerved as he was – a dose of fear was pretty healthy sometimes. "What's this got to do you with your club? We just want to take our money and go."

"Like I said, we're just two blokes trying' to make a living," said Djordje. "Thing is, our boss – the one who actually owns Club Fantastia, and all the other clubs – he had a Naomi doll stolen from a ship headed for England not that long ago. So everyone gets the word from up on high to keep our eyes peeled and ears to the ground, and whaddaya know!" He clapped his hands together with glee. "Here she turns up, out of the blue, being sold on by two braindead cunts tryin' to rip us off. See, Mr D'Souza will be very pleased with me when I'm the one who turns up with his stolen doll." He raced his tongue around those appalling teeth. "An' I bet you thought it was your lucky evening, eh?"

Dhiraj, trying to keep command over his voice and body, raised his hands. "Look, we'll go. We didn't want to rip anyone off, didn't realise she already belonged to someone."

The big one looked over to Jens, who dropped his hand to his beltline. *Don't do it Jens. Let me talk our way out.* "We'll leave," said Dhiraj, before Jens could do anything. "Without payment."

"No, no, mate," said Djordje. "You ain't leaving."

At that, Jens whipped his pistol out. Leatherdick knelt and sprang from his haunches into a trot at Jens. He couldn't get the safety off in time, and the hairy beast slammed into him, knocking the air from him and sending him to the floor.

"Stop!" cried Dhiraj, but he couldn't compel himself to move. Jens wasn't small, but Leatherdick dwarfed him. He took Jens's pistol-wielding hand and banged it against the concrete until his knuckles cracked and his grip on the weapon relinquished. The big man swung a ham-sized fist into Jens's face, and he went limp. Not waiting to see the next blow land, Dhiraj got into Jens's car.

"Drive, drive!" he cried. "Head to Tilbury, now, fast as you can! Go!"

"*Your voice does not match the voice recognition authentication records of the registered keeper or named users of this vehicle,*" said the vehicle in a cheery tone.

"No, you stupid bastard! You've got to get me out of here, I'm going to die!"

"*I'm sorry. Your voice does not match the voice recognition authentication records of the registered keeper or named users of this vehicle.*"

A sickening crunch came from outside the car, and Dhiraj saw Leatherdick stand up, breathing heavily, blood spattered on his face and chest, which the rain slowly rinsed away. Dhiraj didn't look out the window, but his stomach boiled with vomit and his face burned with shame and sweat and terror. Djordje appeared smiling at the window, tapping it with his little knife. "You're coming for a little ride, sunshine."

Dhiraj looked through the other window, but the disgusting shape of Leatherdick was covering it. His face screwed up, unbidden, and he put his head in his hands. He gave up. Through the windscreen he could see Naomi staring at him blankly, her head tilted slightly to the side, studying the situation. Dhiraj, shocked by his own stupidity, thought of his family, and wept.

As they sped away the smashed remains of Jens was left on the ground beside his car. Dhiraj couldn't bear to look at his friend for fear of vomiting. The journey was to a sex club. Djordje had taken the first car with Naomi, while Leatherdick chaperoned Dhiraj in the other.

"What are you going to do to me?" Dhiraj whispered. His voice was nothing more than a hoarse croak, the voice of a dying man. *And I am going to die here.*

"*Whatever Mr D'Souza wants me to do to you.*" Leatherdick's voice came through a simulation, installed somewhere inside his throat. The simulation was queerly well-spoken. Perhaps those dogs had savaged his throat, too.

Good.

"Look, I'm no gangster," said Dhiraj in a paper-thin voice. "Please, I'm just a normal guy, a jellyfisherman. I found the doll at sea. I never wanted to rip anyone off. If you could just let me go. I won't tell anyone. I've got a family. A wife and son."

But the big brute didn't listen to Dhiraj's pleading, begging, desperation, or even, finally, his insults. Instead he clumsily managed to squeeze back into his clothes as the car drove on. Up close he was even more grotesque; patches of leather had been coarsely stitched to his flesh to join it all back together. Some of the stitching looked newer, as though he'd suffered a recent mauling. Or maybe it had become a bit of an obsession, like those people who tattooed their own faces; his body was the tapestry for his disgustingness. There were bulges here and there where sensors or processing units had been installed under the skin, perhaps heightening his perception, or his strength, or something. Dhiraj cowered into his navel, trying to think of what the hell he could do, but all he could imagine was Jens's broken body, and he shivered.

The car moved through East London's grim orange lights, past the people fighting and laughing, past the robots stoically clearing the streets of litter and vomit and debris. They arrived at the rear of a building along an arcade strip Dhiraj guessed was somewhere around Hackney. The building didn't look like much, but the muffled subwoofer pulse of dance music throbbed through the walls. Leatherdick ignored the further pleas and protests and hauled him onto the soaking ground with ease before going to the other car to fetch Naomi. Dhiraj heard the nauseating *huck huck* of Djordje's laugh as he rolled onto all fours and spat. His whole body shivered. He tried to look at Naomi, but all he could see was her figure being led away by a shock of red hair before the huge shape of Leatherdick blocked off the view.

The room he was dragged to was dark, cold, small and underground, and the only amenity was the wobbly chair to which Leatherneck roughly bound him. At least it was dry. A cold, cramping sickness overcame him, but his pathetic sobs of self-pity couldn't drown out the muffled moaning coming through the walls – whether of pain or pleasure, or a little of both – he couldn't be sure. He kept mouthing, "Please, please, let me go," to no-one in particular until he lost count of the minutes, and all he could think of was his family, and Jens's mutilated head being washed away somewhere in a disused car park in Beckton. He wondered what he would tell Sali. If he got a chance to tell her anything again. He felt sorry for all the stupid crap he'd gotten wrong so many times, all the stuff which had upset her, made her angry or annoyed, all the times he'd been a shit husband, all the times he could've been better, and... Jens's smashed head appeared in the darkness once more, and his bowels turned to water.

When the door unlocked and creaked open, the light blinded him. He was vaguely aware of the moaning being closer, louder with the door open. And screams.

"You should come now."

Naomi's voice.

He looked up through blurry eyes, and against even the dim light of the corridor beyond she was just a shadow, misty and nondescript, like an angel reaching down to assist with his ascension from this depraved hell. He wanted to reach out but the bonds chafed at his wrists, and he groaned in pain as they bit. "Naomi?"

"They were going to kill you and Sali and Dan. You said the most important thing was making sure your family is safe." She made her way to him and pulled apart the bonds holding him as though they were wet tissues. "Come now. There will be a response, most likely quickly. I will stay here."

Dhiraj had to shield his eyes from the light as he followed her out in the corridor. She had jettisoned Dan's old T-Shirt and was now wearing a weird, garish sort of ensemble, all pink and black. How long had he been in that squalid little room? All night? He panicked as he realised he'd have to explain everything to Sali. And Jens...

All thoughts of what he might say were struck from him when he saw the corridor, and his breath was stolen by the shock. Djordje lay on the ground, his neck buckled where he'd been strangled, his eyes half-bulging out of their sockets with the final throes of life. By him lay two cigarettes, tendrils of smoke still wafting towards the ceiling in a double helix. A few feet from him in the corridor lay the mountainous body of Leatherdick, face upwards, breathing in a hideous, slow gurgle. Beyond that, a doorway led to a nightclub, from which the thrashing, bassy music throbbed and the silhouettes of people screaming and raving could be seen, sliced by the strobe effects being cast down by the ceiling. In the other direction, at the end of the corridor, a door stood open, rain slamming down beyond it. *Outside.*

He looked again at Leatherdick, and whispered to Naomi, "What did you do?"

"He said he'd been authorised to kill you by Mr D'Souza. He said he was going to sodomise you, then kill you, then do the same to your family. You told me that the most important thing was to make sure your family is safe, so I decided the best course of action would be to remove him."

Dhiraj looked her up and down. Her expression was still the same old, hard-to-read Naomi. *Not that there's anything to read.* He crept over to the remains of Leatherdick. The horrid enforcer spied Dhiraj's approach but had no strength to react, save for slightly more panic in his breath. His arms and legs had been shredded, laming him; his belly ripped open, mutilating him; and his penis – that wretched, hateful, leather thing – torn away completely, leaving only a weeping crimson shadow between his fat thighs. Dhiraj covered his mouth but couldn't prevent tears from falling down his cheeks. There was no reason to feel sorry for a monster such as Leatherdick, but it made the sight no less chilling. Dhiraj tried to say something to the fallen Goliath, but couldn't find any words.

"Mr D'Souza knows about you," said Leatherdick, bloodied mouth unmoving but widening his podgy eyes for emphasis. That charming middle-class voice simulation remained unaffected by his physical injuries. "He will be after you. Mark my words."

With those words three men holding large, black pistols streamed out of the nightclub, balking at the carnage that greeted them. After a few choice words they pointed and ran towards Dhiraj and Naomi. Naomi shoved Dhiraj to the ground and his head hit the wall with a dull thump. He was vaguely aware of a shot being fired, and he closed his eyes and tensed, but no pain came. Minutes – or was it merely seconds? – passed with his hands pressed on his ears, until he came to, and saw Naomi standing over three more bodies. Groaning with pain, and terror smeared across their faces, the three men tried to wriggle backwards on broken wrists, away from the kokeshi standing over them. Naomi walked forwards and leant over one of them, but Dhiraj called out, "Don't do it!"

Naomi looked at him and stayed her hand. He shivered, and clung to the wall on his haunches, dizzied. "Enough blood, Naomi. That's enough blood." He looked beyond the men. The nightclub was emptying. Struggling to his feet, gritting his teeth, he tried to walk towards the other door, the exit.

"Where are you going?" she asked.

"Away. I've got to go home." Above the cacophony growing outside he thought he could hear sirens. "Shit. Shit! The police." A sudden thought nagged at him. The police. They'd probably be able to get everything from Naomi, right down to when he pulled her from the sea. She probably had some program in her recording everything she'd ever said or done, all the people she'd spoken with... he'd be a part of this now, perhaps even implicated. Perhaps he should just stay there and be arrested. But what would he tell Sali then? About Jens? *No,* he told himself. *As long as she's here you're in danger.* "You'll have to come with me," he found himself saying to her. He'd have to disable her himself.

She stood up, leaving the man to crawl away, groaning. Beneath the dying LED spotlights in the ceiling, her hands bloodied but her face as impassive as ever, she was the one who now looked like the monster. But instead of fleeing, Dhiraj forced himself to offer her his hand. When she took it, they ran.

Tilda I

Turns out it was as bad as they'd said. Tilda had doubted the call, but she never doubted her eyes. She'd seen messes before: shootouts, stabbings, assaults. All part of investigating organised crime. This was different. The nightclub *Fantasia* had seen some sort of showdown. One big bastard they called Leatherdick literally torn to pieces. Another skinny one called – she checked the file on her globelet – Djordje, choked till his neck had been crushed. Three other low-level scumbags arrested, being treated by medibots for broken bones by the exit door. Faces white as sheets. The spotlights in the corridor flickered on and off, hurting her eyes, but she kept her face still, trying to take in the surroundings.

"What happened?" asked Em, one of the Detective Constables on her team, not looking up from overseeing the robots sweeping and scanning the area.

Tilda ran her fingers through the spikes of her hair, flicking the rain off. She tutted, surveying the area. "Looks like a message."

Em looked up. "Got to be gangland, right?"

She hummed an acknowledgement. The forensics robots finished their sweep and transferred their findings and initial analyses to Em. Tilda marched up the corridor, trench coat wrapped around her tight, stopping by Leatherdick's corpse, stinking of shit and metal. "I know him. He was the muscle here. Jesus Christ, what do you think they set on him, lions?"

"His real name's Art Osgood."

Inside she smirked at the crimson smear where his groin used to be. She'd seen him before on investigations. Patronising, misogynistic, all-round piece of shit. No-one'd cry over his grave. She wondered where these gangbangers managed to weed up such human detritus. "Came across him before. Not the first time I've been to this club."

"For what?"

She pushed out her bottom lip. "Questioning. Knew there were connections to big cheeses elsewhere." She shook her head. "He was just a squeaky cog. The big wheel turns silently."

Em looked puzzled. Dim girl.

Tilda sighed. "The noisier these places are, the deeper the silence."

Em gestured down the corridor to the other three men being treated. "What to do with them?"

„Forensics."

Em studied the report projected by the robot, and interacted with it using her data gloves. "The revolvers on the ground belonged to them. One of them fired one, but no sign of the bullet, or blood spatter from a wound. All the fresh blood found belongs to these five gentlemen. The ones who are alive are sober."

Good they were sober. She could question them straight away, while the fear was still fresh. Tilda narrowed her eyes as she inspected the three sorry-looking crooks. She could have them on unauthorised possession and criminal use of firearms. That probably wouldn't faze them. But whoever made this unholy mess just might. "Split the bastards up. I'm scouring the rest of the place."

The rest of Club Fantasia was empty. The skinny one with the red hair ran the club. Didn't own it, though. Expendable enough. The other workers still present were low down the food chain; illegal immigrant barmaids, catatonic prostitutes, fat-headed doormen. She'd brought a handful of colleagues with her; they'd take the witness statements. Nothing had come up yet, though. Secret, private rooms discovered in the club's underground levels revealed a couple of men in the act with kokeshi dolls. Pathetic how they protested their innocence, cocks limply drooping out of their trousers. A night in the cells and having to explain it to their wives would be punishment enough for them. Tilda wanted bigger fish. After the men were taken away she was left alone with one of the kokeshi. Dark-skinned. Dangerous. Not dead behind the eyes like the human whores upstairs. It looked at her with almond eyes, moving lithely onto its stomach on the shit-coloured bed under the red lights, clutching its breasts and pouting. Perhaps it thought it could seduce its way out of this. Christ, she despised these hateful things. She despised what they represented; a safe place for depravity; dehumanised womanhood: a womanhood perfected in the eyes of these deadbeat perverts; a womanhood shrunken to everyone else. Above all they reminded her of Fraser, and she hated thinking about Fraser. Her finger twitched with the ache to shoot the wretched doll in the face until there was nothing left except scalded plastics. Blood drained from her face as she swallowed the urge.

"Police," it said in a catlike Spanish accent. "Is there anything I can do for you? You work so hard. I can please women as much as men..."

"Shut up," Tilda snapped. "Two men were murdered upstairs. Your skinny manager and his fat henchman, the disgusting one. Ripped to shreds, he was."

The doll stopped tracing a finger around its lips as it processed the news. "So who commands me now?"

Tilda shrugged, looking around the room. "I don't care. Most likely you'll be deactivated. If I had my way you'd be ground into fertiliser. Did you hear anything remiss?"

The doll shook its head and smiled, rolling onto its back. Disgusted, Tilda slammed the door on it. It'd be zapped and scanned for information later. Doubtful there'd be anything useful in there.

The ride to the station in the City was near silent. She arrived to find the gunmen had been arrested and separated. The desk sergeant directed her to the first interview room, where the first gangbanger sat, cuffed, mug of tea in front of him. The room was empty apart from a robot standing by the door acting as guard and scribe. The man, a pale type with a lazy eye, peered at the sentry suspiciously. His coat had gone, exposing a thin upper frame clad in a tight fitting black vest. Broken wrists and forearms were wrapped in a bespoke plastic cast robotically printed in the field. Tilda sat opposite him. Dark, long hair stuck to his face, which he tried unsuccessfully to blow away. She could've brushed it away for him. She didn't. The red light by the robot's perception suite indicated it was already recording.

"Confirm your name."

The man's lazy eye looked past Tilda, but the other one glared straight at her.

Tilda glared back, annoyed. "Come on. We know your name. Hurry this up."

A token grunt. "Karlosz Perez."

"Thank you. You know you're already a dead cert for a custodial sentence for possession and use of firearms. The forensics robots aren't wrong. You'll be convicted and sentenced within a week. The jury won't need ten minutes."

"Fine. I'll do the time."

"Or you could walk away. I'm after the big fish. You're just muscle." She looked at his scrawny arms in their blue plastic casts. "And you've not much of that."

He made a face. "Don't need muscle when you got bullets."

"I see. And how did that turn out for you?"

He shook his head. The bullish mask slipped. He'd seen something.

"You know who did this? You tell me, we make a deal. A rival? Land grab? Sour deal?" Shakes of the head at each turn. "Must have wanted to send a hell of a message. Cracked you and your friends up good. And old Leatherdick? You saw him, right?"

Karlosz's face twitched, shivered. She let the memory settle on him. "They don't send messages."

She leant in. "Who don't?"

Another face. "The fucking robots. The *robots*. They don't send messages. They do what they're told. They never do this!"

Tilda sat back. Tension racked her shoulders. "A robot did this?" She laughed. It was forced. "Bullshit, Karlosz. Pull the other one. Who are you protecting? Let me rephrase that: who is it worth protecting? You think we can't keep you safe? We can–"

"I'm telling you, it was the fucking robot. A kokeshi doll. One of those *things*." He eyed the robot sentry in the corner. It was a quasi-humanoid; like a wheelie-bin with manipulator arms, tinted dome for a head. Wheeled base. No face. It didn't react.

Tilda sighed. Could be some half-baked horseshit cover the three stooges had figured out before the police had arrived. But people with a litany of broken bones didn't usually take time to figure out alibis. "Enjoy your tea."

Time spent with the other two – two gristleheads named Andy and Hobbes, both from Nottingham – revealed their stories tallied. Tilda hung back with Hobbes, a brawny, plum-faced orangutan. He tried the hard-man act, oblivious that the pink plastic casts on his arms undermined it. "So it was a kokeshi," she said. "We've established that. One of the ones working in the club?"

A shrug. "Dunno."

"You know you're a dead cert for a custodial sentence. Firearms possession, usage."

"I'll do the fucking years."

"Plus any number of sex-trade offences."

"Fuck off. Slag-whore. Bitch."

A reaction. Time to scratch a little more.

"The evidence is all there. We found a number of dumb pricks with their tiny cocks hanging out of heaps of plastic. Your fingerprints all over the rooms, the robots." A lie, underpinned by the truth. "You're dead, son. Possession of illegal sexual synthetics; prostitution. I'm sure if we dig a little deeper we can find evidence of rape. We usually do in these places."

"Fuck off, slag fucking skinny whore. Cunt."

Tilda always stifled a laugh when she was called that. The irony that men like Hobbes used the only part of a woman they felt was any value as an insult was always lost on them. "The evidence is clear. You'd be inside in a week. Nonce wing. Bad folks in there. Pretty fella like you." She allowed herself a wan smile at her wit.

"I can look after meself."

She gestured to his broken wrists. "You know how long broken wrists take to heal? You'll be measured for a new arsehole before they're off."

The first stab of fear. "You can't put me inside injured."

"Rights of convicted sex offenders aren't quite the same as free men. You know this."

He wrestled with the decision. "Look, we never seen the bitch doll before. Leathers and Djordje turned up with it and that fucking Indian prick. It just went fucking psycho –"

Tilda held up a hand. "Hold on. An Indian guy?"

"The bloke they brought in. Never seen him before."

"Come on. Who owns Club Fantasia?"

Hobbes shrugged. "Djordje."

"They're just the idiots dumb enough to put their names above the door. Give me a real name."

Nothing.

"Alright. Sod the name. We'll get it anyway now Little and Large are dead. Someone's bound to surface. Christ knows you're not high enough up the food chain to know. Just tell me if you know of any beef between Club Fantasia's goons and elsewhere."

"I dunno. Swear down." He rubbed his nose with his cast.

"Fine. Play it your way. Can't guarantee what you'll be charged with."

A shake of the head. "I'll take me chances. Better a broken arsehole than end up like that prick Leatherdick."

Jesus Christ. They really were scared.

She left the interview rooms and locked herself in her office for a smoke. The little desk mirror showed a tired woman. Dark circles beneath her eyes always looked worse because of her pale pallor. Sometimes she thought she was just fading by degrees until all that remained were spiky red hair, cheekbones and two black saucers for eyes. Her stomach roared at her, telling her to eat. *Shut up.*

She sent a message via globelet to her boss, DI Boswell. *Re: Case H14D. Murderous robot on loose? Stories tally. Could be anywhere. Witnesses idiotic, but sensible enough to be terrified. Possible unidentified Asian male involved.*

Waiting for the response was hard. The office was sparse. Nothing to do but stay vigilant. She believed the orangutan's story, and the lazy-eyed one too. Robots hadn't harmed humans since before she was born. Decades ago. Regulations were tight. She knew otherwise. She knew they were dangerous. Especially these reverse-engineered degenerates. This had been waiting to happen. The smug feeling she'd promised herself for all those lonely years hadn't materialised, though. Empty as she was yesterday. Hollow. Stomach still growling. Probably ought to eat. She pulled out a packet of vegetable crisps and ate them. Message flashed up as she ate.

Don't make this a pet project. You know your job. Keep your head. B.

Predictable. Boswell would say he had her best interests at heart. Professional and personal. A knock on the door. She saved half the crisps for later.

"Til. It's Em."

"Come in."

Em poked her head round the door. "Got something. Linked to our dead guys at the club."

Tilda gestured at the chair. Em came in and sat, shoulders hunched in. Shrewish. She'd be pretty if she combed her hair out of her eyes and straightened it. *Good for you, Em. Don't do as they tell you, girl.*

"The forensics bot found patches of, um, autonomous magnetorheological fluids in the corridor. On the floor."

Magnetorheological fluids. Tilda smiled thinly. Robot blood. The autonomous type was advanced, though; only the real humanoids had that stuff running through them. It had its own magnetic fields for advanced – what the media called *real* – muscle-like manipulation and manoeuvrability. "So we know a robot was present. We know that anyway. Even if the three stooges' stories are bullshit, the place was crawling with sex dolls."

"The spatter of the fluid was consistent with a bullet wound. No dolls on site had wounds. So whatever took the hit is still out there."

Tilda stayed static. Didn't mean anything. Her bones told her that something was tying all this together. Proof was elusive, though.

"There's one more thing. We got another call. A man was killed in Beckton. Head beaten in. Similar forensics report. The big one... Leathe... Arthur, er..."

"Leatherdick?"

Em blushed. "Him. He was there. Forensics are sketchy from the rain, but a robot was present too. Drops of robot blood in the puddles. Probably the same robot."

Tilda furrowed her brows. "Who died?"

Em inhaled and held it. "We identified him as Jens Klerken.

Minor record, affray, years ago, nothing recent. No clear link to the sex gangs or Club Fantasia. No family apart from an elderly mother in the Netherlands."

Her mind ticked. It was still out there. "MO?"

"Violent. Bloody." Em's globelet projected pictures of the remains of the man's head. "Similar to the club."

She nodded. So it was loose. Killing, perhaps indiscriminately. That was her angle. She stood. "Excuse me, Emma. I need to see DI Boswell."

Adem II

Country rain never felt the same as city rain. City rain was thick, gloopy somehow, oily, and London rain was worst of all. Out here it felt lighter, airier, less wet. Stupid, really; the clouds being seeded were in theory just the same clouds as over the city, but Adem was sure the sun was able to force more of its rays through the clouds here than in the city, and the grey in the sky was less, well, grey. In this blissful but temporary purgatory, he was quite content to walk in the hotel gardens without a brollybot, or even an old hand-held umbrella. The guilt, crushing when he left London for this long weekend away, felt lighter out here, as though nothing had really happened. *And,* he told himself, *I haven't heard anything, so maybe nothing has happened.* So he contented himself with lackadaisical walks accompanied by the soundtrack of birdsong and streamrush.

The call came on the third day as he was finishing breakfast, mopping a piece of egg away from his lip. The call, audible only to him through the tiny earpiece, felt like a clarion, alerting the authorities and everyone, the nice hotel staff, the other guests enjoying their meal, to his presence. But they carried on eating, and it was just he who felt swamped by events. But he would not turn away.

"Hello?"

It was Helen, the HR manager from the office. The news from London, of course, was no shock, and yet it shocked him anew, and when he put his hand to his mouth and felt the sting of grief behind his eyes, it was no act. It was real. Ingham was dead. His bowels had ruptured at home whilst on the toilet. *Nice timing, Father*, he grimly thought. The tiny bug would have burrowed its way out and fallen straight down the bowl to be flushed away. A cold shiver tickled his neck. It would have been an horrific way to die.

"Yes, yes, of course," he said hoarsely. "I'll be there immediately, as soon as I can."

Adem cut short his stay by a day – exactly as he'd expected – and made his way to London. The journey was sickening, and he could barely hold down the merest sip of coffee as the train hurtled southward through England. Another passenger tried to make small talk with him, but it was all he could do to mutter something and try not to look too distraught. After that, his forehead stayed glued to the cold glass of the window, and he watched the world pass by, becoming darker with each passing minute that brought him back closer to London. Ahead of him, over the steepling skyscrapers of the capital, the clouds gathered like nebulous gods preparing to administer both judgment and penance upon the guilty.

The next day the office looked the same as he'd left it a few days before, but the air was thicker, and people were looking at him. Vicky, one of the civil servants beneath him, came up to him and gave him a limp hug. "Oh, it's so awful, Adem," she murmured into the shoulder of his overcoat. Other ashen-faced people peered at them from over their globelets and desks throughout the open-plan office. It was extraordinary how many of them seemed able to just carry on with their work. *A man's just died, you heartless people!*

Not thinking how on earth he should react, he simply embraced her. "Yes, I know. He gave me so much." His voice sounded distant. False.

Vicky let go and dabbed her eyes with a tissue. "I heard that Helen and Iain are going to see you. What's going to happen?"

Adem's face crawled into a pout. "I don't know. We carry on working. We always do. I'm sure there will be some way we can honour Sir Ingham. He did a lot for this office."

As Vicky tearfully retired to her desk, Adem noticed Iain Argour, the Chairman of the Scientific Regulatory Committee – Ingham's boss – approaching him. He was a lean and stiff man, and even the proximity of mortality hadn't seemed to take much of the edge off his hardness. Adem's chest tightened and his face flared, readying for the confrontation, but instead Iain offered a hand and his condolences in his deep Caledonian burr.

"So sorry to have to give you the awful news while you were away, Adem," he said, taking Adem by the shoulder with a firm grip. His voice was warmer than his features, like a fire deep inside an iceberg.

"Not at all, not at all, I came immediately. I cannot believe it."

"Nor can I, my friend." Their hands shook for a moment too long, and Adem pulled his hand away, which immediately felt even worse. Iain was wiry from top to bottom but possessed a lean strength, an athlete's strength, despite being at least the same age as Ingham. *As Ingham was*, he corrected himself. "But things continue. Helen is in touch with Ingham's family with respect to the funeral arrangements. We believe that, in light of Sir Ingham's exemplary public service record, he ought to be recognised as such. Of course, that's up to Zoe, poor thing. I hope she allows us to pay our respects."

Iain took Adem to one side along one of the corridors. "Forgive me for seeming callous, but we must talk business. Ingham, the poor old sod, he always was a stickler for punctuality, but this really couldn't have happened at a worse time."

Adem frowned. "What do you mean?"

Iain's forehead wrinkled, and he led Adem to a free meeting pod and commanded it to turn recording off, and soundproofing and tinting on. Once the settings were arranged just so he invited Adem to sit, but he remained standing. "It's a fucking shitstorm out there, Adem, a fucking horrendous shitstorm." Iain's face wrinkled even more, and he stared through the tinted glass. "You picked a fine fucking weekend to be away."

Adem placed a hand to his chest and tried to speak but couldn't. This wasn't what he had expected. Iain rubbed his face and breathed hard.

"Sorry. Not your fault, I know. I take it you've heard the news?"

Adem shook his head. "I wanted a break, so I didn't check... what news?"

"Lucky you. You'll never guess what happened. A fucking kokeshi sex doll went and killed two people at a nightclub in East London and almost killed a handful more, then went fucking missing. Ran off!"

"It killed someone?"

"Didn't just kill them. Went fucking ballistic, it did, ripped a man – a big man – to shreds. The police and the media's gone apeshit, people are clamouring over these robots being used in clubs. It's like the whole fucking drugs thing all over again."

Adem's face creased into confusion. How could this have

happened so quickly? What the hell had Nita done? "What must we do?"

"Every news outlet in the country is getting an opinion about robots from university professors or such. The Government's being pressured to do something – though what the fuck they're supposed to do I don't know – and they're after expert opinion. We and the CSA and have been summoned to give them that opinion. Well, I say we – I mean Ingham, but, well..."

"So who, then?"

"We'll have to recruit a replacement for Ingham, obviously, but that could take bloody months. So I'm asking you to step up as interim head regulator until such time as a full-time replacement's found."

"Not somebody from industry? You're offering it to me?"

"No, Adem, I'm not offering anything; I'm asking you – I'm asking you very nicely – to do this. You've got the knowledge of the systems, you've got the experience, plus you'll make for a good face for the Regulator's office when the cameras come calling. As for industry, there are a few good people out there, but no-one we could easily pass off as independent or not having some sort of vested interest, and besides, we'd never get anyone prised away from their companies in time; that's if their companies even wanted to get close to this pile of shit." He turned away. "Christ, what a mess."

"What's the line being taken by the media?"

"Broadly? That things can't continue as they are."

Adem steepled his fingers by his lips and closed his eyes. Ingham was dead. Nothing could be done now, and it certainly seemed as though Ingham's death wasn't being treated as suspicious, judging by the conversations. The fog of guilt lifted ever so slightly from his mind. The way forward was suddenly very clear. He looked at Iain's stern face and steeled himself. "I believe I am inclined to take a similar position as that of our friends in the media."

Iain looked neither shocked nor pleased. It wasn't his job to get bogged down in the scientific minutiae of decision-making; he just had to make sure the regulators were functioning properly as organisations and delivering what the Government needed. "Well, sort your position out, get your arguments ready and get yourself ready. This is not going away any time soon."

There was a pause as Adem considered what this meant.

"I take it that's a yes, then?" asked Iain.

Adem paused again, savouring the moment. He'd expected that sick feeling to hang onto him, like a bastard demon with hooks for hands digging into his shoulders and dragging him down from here to eternity, but he felt surprisingly light. The way forward became clear. "Yes, yes of course," he said. *Wait till you see me now, Father.*

"Good," said Iain. With that, he left the room and he returned moments later with a sheaf of paper and a pen. "Sign that, and it's official."

Adem took the pen and held it for just a second over the paper. He cast his eyes over the contract briefly. It definitely wasn't some sort of confession. He signed, slowly.

"Good," said Iain again. "Right, leave your stuff here. No rest for the wicked. Get your brain in gear. This shit's happening now."

He was given a couple of hours to get his brain in gear before Iain and none other than the Science Minister told him that the police were waiting for a joint meeting with the head regulator – *me*, he had to remind himself – and a couple of other Government low-level wonks. When he walked in a semblance of the guilt flared up, but when they addressed him respectfully it faded again. The policewoman, Detective Sergeant Tilda Boulton, was a thin, porcelain statue in a trench coat she didn't take off, with a crop of red spikes atop her head. She had a wan, lean look about her that he didn't like, like she had a sickness that angered her. Nevertheless she stood and greeted him with a shake of the hand and a subdued word of condolence, which he accepted graciously.

The details of the murders were gruesome, and the DS recounted them grimly. An insubordinate voice at the back of his head – which he imagined sounded oddly like his father's – told him there were cleaner ways to achieve a kill. *Shut up, iggiot.* He wished that voice had been speaking to Nita, not him. He shook the thought away; no use in mulling over it now. What was done was done. She'd certainly not had any qualms over the dirty work. *That makes two of you. Peas in a pod. Shut up, iggiot.*

"So why are you here, DS Boulton?" he asked once the policewoman had finished recounting the gory details.

"For your professional advice. I've always thought these dolls could be dangerous," said Tilda. "But this is irredeemably foul. I doubt there'll be many tears shed over the two gangsters, but the fact that this thing has murdered an innocent man is deeply troubling."

"The Government needs to show it's taking this very seriously," said one of the policy wonks, a starchy shirt and tie called Hennerson. "The media have stolen a march on us and are morally crusading. I'd rather get the response right than cave to pressure and get it wrong."

"The Government position stinks," spat Tilda. "Keeping the sex industry illegal because it offends you. Because it's portrayed as sleazy. Allowing these disgusting dolls to run amok, unchecked. Well it's bitten you in your fat arses now, hasn't it?"

The starchy shirt didn't blink at the acid remark.

"It's not necessarily my position," he said. "But it's the one I'm employed to implement and disseminate. If the Government's message changes, then so do I."

Adem kept his face stern. It was a stressful time for all. "What do you know about the rogue synthetic?"

She glared at him. "We believe it's being controlled by a rival gangster, an Indian man. We don't know who it is. How much control he's got over it we don't know. It could be anywhere in London by now."

The other wonk shrugged, smiling in that vapid, arrogant way that politicians and those close to them adopted. "Isn't there some way you can track it?"

"You know how hard it is to track one of those things when they're made on the black market? Unregulated? Plus these things look like humans. They're not like the bloody coffee machine. Have you seen them?"

The wonk twisted his smile downwards. "I've seen images of them, yes."

"I bet you have."

"Can we stay on track, please," said Iain, irritably. "This is a difficult day for many reasons. All the more reason to keep cool heads. Detective Sergeant, is that acceptable?"

Tilda placed her hands in front of her, closed her eyes momentarily and nodded in acquiescence.

Iain nodded. "Good. Adem, what's your take?"

Adem pressed his fingers to his lips. "Detective Boulton has the right of it. A robot manufactured outside of regulated and known manufacturing processes could be incredibly difficult to find. If one has gone rogue, it could be very dangerous. And they do look like people, from top to toe. The manufacturing capabilities needed to achieve such perfect human likenesses are highly advanced, but known, but it's never been something that the regulator's office has been happy with in the past."

Tilda looked as though she was going to say something acerbic, but Adem nipped it in the bud. "But we are not in the past anymore. I feel..." he screwed his face up. "I feel this may be too soon, in some way, but given the circumstances, I believe it would be remiss of me to hold my tongue. It's never been my personal policy to hold such an open and closed view of the world. Things are more nuanced than that. When things change, so must people."

"Will you stop being cryptic, Mr Johnson?" snapped Tilda. "I need something to work with."

"There are potential long-term solutions to help prevent this sort of thing happening again, but that will not help you right now. My suggestion would be the nuclear option: try to recapture as many of these kokeshi from the streets as possible."

"Like an amnesty?" asked one of the wonks.

Adem opened his hands. "If you like."

Iain coughed. "I'm not sure it's our place to advise that sort of thing, Adem. That's got to be a policing decision; am I right, Detective?"

"You are. And it's Detective Sergeant," she said. That made Adem smirk behind his hands.

"But it's also a technological one," said Adem. "An amnesty, as Mr Hennerson suggested, would send out the message that these..." Adem made a distasteful face for effect, "...these *dolls* are not only unfit for purpose, but also thoroughly dangerous. In short, that they are obsolete. It's happened before. There have been successful gun and weapons amnesties in the past. This wouldn't be so different."

Tilda looked at the faces around the table. "I would personally support this. But it'd be expensive." She gestured at the two policy advisors. "Would there be government support thrown behind this?"

The two policy advisors looked at each other and threw diplomatic smiles across the table and one scribbled something down. "That'd be something to discuss above our pay grades. The Cyber Security Committee, perhaps even the Home Secretary, will want to discuss it. What about from your side?"

"As you say," said Tilda tersely. "Above my pay grade. But I'll be recommending to my DI that the amnesty is the way to go. I want these things off the street. As far as I'm concerned, this was a long time coming. And it won't be the last time."

"I'd be more than happy to give my professional endorsement to that potential solution," said Adem.

"Are you sure you wouldn't want to take the time to think this through with the team, Adem?" asked Iain.

Adem tried to look thoughtful and nodded. "Normally I would. But I fear the process of review would be too slow and arduous. This clearly is a matter that requires a quick decision. An amnesty represents a good opportunity to find this rogue kokeshi and rein in others that might also do harm to people. However, this will have longer-term repercussions." He looked at Tilda and the policy advisors in turn. "We will no doubt be speaking again in the near future. I suspect we haven't heard the last of this."

The meeting ended with formalities, but Adem remained in the meeting room to gather his thoughts after the others had left to go to their superiors to arrange a powwow. Iain gave him a stern look, but then all of Iain's looks were stern.

He wondered whether or not there would be some pushback from the supercilious bastards in Whitehall with respect to a proposed amnesty; a fair few of their number were bound to be dipping their cocks into the dolls. It was a scandal waiting to happen. It wouldn't be too difficult to find out who exactly was indulging in illicit pleasures; stupid thrills had been a feature of Parliament since time immemorial. If someone passed a law making it illegal to copulate with plum trees, somewhere a stupid, power-drenched idiot would be dipping his cock into that forbidden fruit. He grimaced at his own joke. On the one hand, they wouldn't want their scurrilous little secrets given an airing; on the other, they wouldn't want to run the risk of running into the mad doll with a penchant for disembowelment. That wouldn't be so easy to explain to the wife.

In the end, it didn't really matter whether or not they were fond of an amnesty or not. The folks in Whitehall, whether they were decrepit old warlocks or ambitious young conquistadors; none of them really had as much power as they thought – or said – they did. The UK relied exclusively upon JPC for its oil. One phone call to his father and everything would fall into place.

Adem cast all that aside, and imagined all the kokeshi out there; all the illegal dolls that would be dredged up in the grottier corners of the city. Dolls that would be housed somewhere. Dozens, perhaps hundreds of them, deactivated. Hundreds of platforms that could be used for Nita's technology demonstration. It'd be perfect: the responsible and free use of robotic platforms that would otherwise rot in storage or be crushed down into recycling, and it'd all be free. His father would be grinning ear to ear.

Adem rubbed his hands together. They needed creaming.

Nita III

News updates spewed out of Nita's globelet as she got herself ready for the day, though the pace at which she paced around her apartment in search of makeup and hair products became increasingly sluggish. Harrowing details of three murders were being released, to her growing disbelief. By the time the report cut to images of the crime scene, all tarpaulins, spotlights and policemen buzzing around talking, she'd retreated to the edge of the bed, watching intently, absent-mindedly biting her nails.

In response to the deaths the Cyber Security Cross-Party Committee in Parliament had convened with the upper echelons of the Metropolitan Police to talk about the possibility of an illegal kokeshi amnesty, and the rumour mill had it that the project was being green-lit. Adem certainly knew how to make things happen, and fast. That was more than she could have hoped for at the beginning of the day, yet an empty feeling bit at her from inside her gut. She'd only spoken to Salazar a week ago. Even on the black market it seemed impossible to turn around a – the word *sabotage* felt uncomfortable to her – a *job* so quickly. She'd thought it might take a month; if this

Salazar had done it properly, it would have involved coding, tailoring, integration, not to mention having the robot shipped, delivered and placed into market, just to do *this*. She shuddered as the details of the deaths were relayed once more. "Out of horror comes light," she told herself, eyes glued to the screen. "Out of darkness, hope. This must work now."

She jumped as her globelet unravelled with a rude beep. Adem. When she answered the call he stared back through the screen from a gaunt, red-eyed face.

"You look tired," she said.

"That's because I am tired. This has been a trying couple of days. Assembling the cabinet and the Cyber Security Committee at short notice hasn't been easy. It is fortunate I'm well connected."

She said nothing.

"You've heard the news, I take it?"

She nodded. "Appalling."

"Yes, hideous," he said, though his voice offered no inflection of emotion. "I take it this line is completely secure?"

"Yes. Of course."

"I have to say I'm impressed. I didn't think you would launch yourself into this endeavour with such zeal."

She screwed her face up. "Fuck you. What happened to those people was disgusting."

Adem sniffed and rubbed his hands. "Perhaps. I daresay they were the lowest of the low. Not that I'm being morally relative, but I wouldn't have thought too many tears will be shed over these thugs."

A thug can be well groomed. She wanted to say as much: to renounce this whole sickly plot, to tell him off, tell herself off, but the words were lost in the back of her mind. The two of them had already fallen into speaking in self-facing lies and hoodwinks between themselves. Was that truly to stop anything incriminating being committed to a recording? Even on these super-encrypted lines? Or was it because she – and Adem – couldn't face admitting what they'd done even to themselves? She still wanted to walk away. Maybe he did too. But it was too late. Bound by this iniquitous cord, they were part of each other now. She felt tugged towards him and repulsed at the same time. Part of her wished it was he who had been killed. But another part, not fully formed – the seed of a part, the embryo of a part – didn't, and that gave her just the slightest flutter of exhilaration. This might just work out for the best. And what she was working toward was for the best. The best for everybody. She had to believe it. And, in spite of such grotesqueness, she did.

"Everything happened so quickly," she said.

"Yes." He paused, rubbing his hands together slowly, his fingers slipping in and out of each other like snakes. She remembered how pleasantly smooth they felt. "I think it's safe to assume that things will continue to do so at Government level. The Cyber Security Cross-Party Committee is meeting with representatives from the Home Office, the Ministry for Health, and Social Services. As well as us, of course. It may be that your industrial expertise could be called upon at some point. Any war on kokeshi would create a vacuum. The unique capabilities of EI systems could move to fill that vacuum, if you're sufficiently swift."

She stopped. Maybe they were being listened to? Deciding that discretion would be the better part of what little valour remained in her, she nodded. "Whatever the Government needs." The words sounded laughably sycophantic, yet there they were. If anyone was listening, that was her position now.

"Be ready," he said, before signing off.

Reports returned to the news. A few robotics experts, including a self-absorbed, faintly lecherous academic she'd run into a few years ago at a conference appeared in the news studios or by video conference, spouting off their opinions. Whatever he said would be irrelevant to her; she didn't need to hear from him, but there was one man she did need to hear from. Salazar Gomez hadn't seemed like the violent type. He'd made a perfectly respectable impression in his interview despite the bad decisions made in his past – *everyone makes bad choices now and then.* And in that second, more surreptitious telephone call she'd made to him, he'd understood what was required of him, but she didn't get any sign that he'd do something as extreme as this. He had a daughter; his love for that little girl was plain enough. She put a tremulous hand to her mouth. How stupid could she have been to trust him? Adem's words came back to her: the Home Office, the Health Ministry... Jesus Christ. All traceable back to him and her. What if this guy was a lunatic? She had to get on the phone to Salazar, find out what happened.

He didn't answer on the first two tries, but on the third he picked up. Audio only.

"Olá?"

"Salazar. It's Nita Rhodes."

Silence on the other end. Nita gulped.

"Salazar?"

"Sorry. You will have to be quick. I am inside a toilet outside the factory. What is it?"

"What the hell did you do to that robot?"

Silence. "I do not understand, Miss Rhodes."

"The robot, the kokeshi. Have you seen the news from London?"

"No."

"I suggest you had better watch it, and soon. And then you call me back, or the deal's off."

She hung up, shaking.

It was afternoon when he returned the call. Perfect bloody timing; in the middle of an EIS board meeting. On the one hand it hardly mattered; she was barely able to focus on the content or agenda of the meeting, although she really ought to have been able to at least look she like cared. Making polite excuses, she ducked out and took the call in her office, doors shut, windows tinted.

"I didn't do that," was the first thing Salazar said.

"So what happened?"

"I do not know. I only did as you asked. But the doll I worked upon was only shipped this morning. It did not do what you are saying. This is something else. I do not know what you mean about calling the deal off. I have done what was asked. There is a kokeshi on the way to London now which has been altered."

Nita stopped. Thoughts clicked into place. "You didn't do this?"

"Of course not. What I saw on the news was like a bear attack. What you will see from my work will be more specific. Can we talk about the position?"

Blood rushed to Nita's face. It hadn't happened yet. But it was going to happen. This was nothing to do with her. Couldn't be traced to her. Extraordinary. A smile, half-hearted and unsure, but filled with the promise of relief, cracked her face open. Another rogue robot. "The job's changed."

A beat. "The job is finished, Miss Rhodes."

"No. Don't you see? If you stop that robot being delivered, we're in the clear." *I'm in the clear.*

"No. I can't do that. It's impossible. The ship will have left by now. I would like to talk to you about the position you offered to me."

"You will do...." She stopped herself. "Do this thing, and the position is yours."

"I may be downtrodden, Miss Rhodes, but I retain some principles. I did as you asked. In any case, what does it matter? We are in the same situation we were a week ago."

"But a week ago there weren't security forces convening to weed out rogue kokeshi." Her voice was harsh and low, most unlike her. The smile crumbled. A shitty feeling overcame her. The problem hadn't gone away, not yet.

"Surely that's a good thing?" he eventually said.

A beat. "In what way?"

"The doll might even be picked up by the authorities before it fulfils its task."

The smile threatened to break out again. "A tip-off to the police might even speed things up."

"Maybe, but I don't know where the thing is going. That was not my concern."

A small problem. Not unworkable. They could both come out of this smelling – if not of roses, then at least not of shit. "Find out."

"What?"

"Find out. There must be a shipping manifest or a contract or something. Find out, and a ticket to London is yours."

"That seems unfair. Do you know how much I have risked simply to do this much? You ask too much of me."

She tapped her lip, thinking, grateful for the audio-only line. *Keep him close.* Giving him what he wanted would enable her to keep an eye on him. She let the silence on the line swell, holding her nerve. In spite of appearances, the advantage still lay with her. At last, he cracked.

"I will try."

"Good. It's unfortunate I've got to ask you to do this thing. But I'll make sure you and your lovely daughter are looked after when you're here."

"I will not let you down."

She hung up.

The board meeting had apparently continued apace without her. Nadia, the Head of Communications was providing an update on the external communications strategy as she retook her seat beside Robb, the CEO.

"What was that about?" he whispered.

She answered with an awkward nod of the head and a silent glance. Attentiveness came more easily in the second half of the meeting. When Nadia had finished her piece, Nita spoke up.

"So there's nothing in the comms strategy about the recent murders?"

Nadia looked Nita in the eye. "Just the usual messages about our commitment to quality, that robotics systems are in general safe, and that this isn't anything to existing, legitimate robot owners need to fear. Nothing explicitly referencing the murders."

"I see. I think we should. I believe there's a strong and unique opportunity here for us to disseminate messages about properly regulated kokeshi dolls."

A sour look crossed Nadia's face. "That seems rather distasteful given the circumstances. I don't think that would work. And besides, didn't the regulator say that circumstances weren't conducive to the technology at present?"

"Watch the news, Nadia. Circumstances are changing."

Nadia waited for a moment. "What do you want us to say?"

The faces around the table looked at Nita: curious, judgmental perhaps, but they trusted her, she knew that. She'd led this company to great things. They'd trust her now. They'd have to.

Dhiraj V

"Is this it?" asked Dhiraj.

"Yes," said Naomi. "The Kensington Boutique Hotel."

Dhiraj looked out of the taxi window at the tiny, battered canopy hanging over the entrance. "It doesn't look like a boutique. It doesn't even look much like a hotel." In truth it wasn't even in Kensington. The cab had taken them to the shitty backstreets of Earl's Court. Still, they were a long way from the hell Naomi had created back in the east of the city.

"*Are you ready to pay?*" asked the taxi's driver system.

"This is what you asked for," said Naomi. "A place to hide. 'The crummier the better', you said. According to reviews taken from across three different accommodation brokers this is firmly in the bottom ten hotels in London."

Dhiraj blew out hard. Waves of nausea pounded inside his skull. This part of London was far from savoury, and even farther from home. He looked at Naomi with some scepticism, but got nothing in return. Of course he didn't.

"Ok, fine." He fished some cash from the wad he'd lifted from Djordje's corpse – and stepped out with Naomi into the rain. The cab silently drove off into the night. "As soon as we're in there I have to call my family."

"What do you plan to do?"

He took her wrist. "Get out of the bloody rain."

The reception was manned by a tanned, moustachioued man – *a man!* – who showed little interest and less judgment of the two impromptu guests, grunting as he handed them a set of keys – *real keys!* The only time he recalled holding real keys before was when he'd visited India in his younger days – and greedily snatched Dhiraj's cash.

The room didn't disappoint. In the bottom ten hotels in London? As the stench of rot and damp hit his nostrils and put his head in a spin when he walked in, he wondered which possible hotels could be listed below it. He shuddered as the room's inventory of ruin became apparent: cracks in the walls exposing clammy plaster; patches of mould growing at almost a visible rate; suspicious movements in the corner; and uninviting bumps and moans leaking through the walls from what he hoped was just a vigorous sex session. A tiny laugh stuttered out of him. At least he wasn't the only one desperate enough to seek refuge in this shithole. He sat on the bed – a scratchy, itchy thing, like it was housing life – as Naomi locked up and stood, looking over him. Cramps edged their way up his calves and back, and he let out a groan that turned into a hollow sob.

"Would you like me to rub your back?"

He bit back the tears. "No." In the light – a single, old-fashioned tungsten bulb hanging from an unadorned flex – she looked like a terrible and beautiful creature. He didn't doubt that she had the capability to give massages – and *massages* – but he knew those hands were capable of more than just pleasure. The night's woes bit hard.

Jens's ruined head kept flashing behind his eyes, so that the stinking rot of the hotel was a mercy when he shook himself from the trauma. Over the chewed up, graffiti-strewn bureau hung a TV. He switched it on by hand and let the noise wash over him to keep the thoughts out.

Of course, it didn't help.

Jumpy images from the nightclub they'd just escaped flashed up, with reporters and police hovering around the scene, lights flashing from cameras and sirens, as if the club party had never stopped. Dhiraj watched, jaw slack, eyes stinging, stomach shaking with terror. He turned down the volume.

"I've got to call home. Then we figure out what to do with you."

"Why?"

"Because Sali is my wife and Dan is my son, and they need to know what's happening to me," he said, irritably. "Anyway, it's not your concern. And I don't suppose you care. Just tell me a way I can call them that's untraceable."

"I can do this for you."

He looked up. "And it's untraceable?"

"Of course."

"Ok, show me how."

"Just tell me the number to dial, and I dial. Speak to your wife as if you were speaking to me. And if she talks back her voice will be amplified through my speakers."

"If she talks back," he muttered. After all, why would she speak to him? Doubtless she'd have seen the news – or one of her stupid friends would have seen it and got in touch somehow to tell her to watch it. And when he called up, what the fuck would he say? The truth? He placed a shaking hand to his mouth at the thought of that, but he'd always been a truthful man. The sea made a man honest. You couldn't lie or trick the sea, or yourself when tackling it. Lying to the sea caused death. Lying to his wife might prevent it, however. That made sense. He recounted the number to Naomi, before he could change his mind.

Sali's voicemail.

Cursing, he waited for the greeting to end. "Sali, hi, it's me." He stopped. What now? He looked at Naomi's perfect face, addressing his wife through it, sending his words into Naomi, into Sali. "You, er, you'll have heard some serious shit's happened tonight. Some really, really bad stuff. You might even hear my name crop up, but let me tell you none of it's true." His spine turned to ice with the lie, and his voice became hoarse. "None of it's true. I can't explain now, but I'll be back soon. Jens, he..." he cut himself off. He shouldn't say anything incriminating. His mind raced with the infinity of possibility. "He didn't deserve what happened to him." He looked at Naomi and nodded. A beat of silence. "Is that it?"

"The call is ended." She looked at him further. "You lied to your wife."

He looked at the robot incredulously. "Are you judging me?"

"I can make judgments, insofar as I judge certain criteria when taking decisions. Such decisions might be called judgments. Similarly, if needed, I can make certain judgments regarding a person's character and personality and decisions. But if you mean 'judging' in the conversational sense, that your actions cause me to raise or lower my opinion of you accordingly, then no. I do not judge you. Not in that way. I'm not made to judge the people with whom I am meant to interact."

He stared at her, his eyes aching. "Fucking hell."

"What do you intend to do?"

"I don't bloody know, Naomi. I need to lose you. I need to lose you. Get rid of you. You need to go."

"You want me to leave?"

"Yes. No. I don't know."

"Where should I go?"

"I don't know."

She didn't turn her gaze from him. Even though he kept his own gaze firmly trained upon what remained of the lice-infested carpet, he could feel those eyes scanning him, analysing him. "You look tired. You should rest."

"Soon." It was true. His body screamed at him to rest, to sleep, to shut down, but his mind still flickered through the violence of the day like a highlights video stuck on repeat. There's no way he'd be able to sleep. And even if he did, who knows what sort of hellish nightmares would assault him, and the rude awakening he'd be subjected to in the middle of the night. What if Naomi did leave? She was cause and solution to his predicament; tormentor and protector, conjuring witch and avenging angel. If she left and they came – be they the police or more of those gangsters – he'd be helpless without her. Arrested, or beaten up, or worse. The paper-thin walls of the Kensington Boutique Hotel seemed no protection at all, but at least its crappy blandness offered almost perfect discretion.

When Dhiraj laid his head back something scuttled and scratched at the end of the bed. Normally it might have made him recoil with disgust, but he had neither the energy nor the inclination to be disgusted at something so trivial. Let the buggers bite and scratch. He turned the TV back up.

"...*Cyber Security Cross Party Committee are already convening to discuss potential solutions to this robot threat, which as yet remains unidentified, but on the loose.*" The reporter droned on. Cyber Security Committees, the Home Secretary, the police... his head shook gently. All too much. This dainty woman – *not a woman, remember* – was the cause of all this shit. As much as he wanted to smash the TV screen, he didn't – not for the cost of damage, but for the overriding need to keep tabs on what was happening. "Watch this. I need to sleep."

He peeled off his shirt, groaning as he did so.

"What is that?"

"What's what?"

"The scars."

His hands instinctively moved to the left side of his body to cover them, but of course it was too late. The first thought was to disregard her observation, to swat it away. If he told her to shut up, she'd shut up. Words to that effect almost made it out, but he caught them, turning them to breath. She wouldn't judge. She wouldn't care. "I got stung."

A person might have crinkled their brows at that, but Naomi didn't. "You were stung?"

"Yeah, by a jellyfish. Years ago now." He looked down and traced a finger over the scar tissue. Time had faded them, but they were still there, the dozens of little rivulets burrowing their way across his flesh, as though made by a pack of tiny, confused moles. He could trace each one by heart, in and out, the skinny lines darting this way and that with random precision across him.

"You were fishing?"

Dhiraj managed a smile. "No, I was swimming. On holiday. Cornwall. I'm a strong swimmer, and the sea was very calm. I know how to swim. How to deal with riptides, currents. Jesus, I remember that day so vividly, even though I never think about it. I was just floating, soaking up the sun, when I thought I saw a plastic bag drifting towards me, just in the corner of my eye. Two plastic bags. They came closer, and I flicked one of them away. I went back to floating, and a few seconds later, just... just agony." He screwed his face up at the recollection. Over even the fetid assault of the hotel room came the sensory rush of memories from that day. The salt, the heat of the sun on his body, so delicious, and then that fresh pain. "Like someone was stabbing me in the ribs. Stabbing me, over and over again with a thin knife, like a stiletto. I reached down to pull out the knife but there was nothing there, just bits of string. I tried to rip them off but they were wrapped around me, stuck. Tearing one off felt like tearing off my own skin. My legs started to burn, like the seas were boiling. I couldn't swim. I could swim miles in open water, but I couldn't put one arm in front of the other. I remember thinking: '*This isn't fair. I should be able to swim away from this.*' But it was like murderers were slashing me to pieces below the surface?"

Naomi looked impassive.

"I fainted. When I woke upon the beach, I felt like I was being burned alive. I think I actually screamed. Anyway, it obviously wasn't a gang of sea-dwelling murderers."

"What was it?"

"*They*, not *it*. A group of Portuguese Man O' War. Jellyfish. Three of the bastard things. Floated close to me with the current. Against the glare of the sun they looked just like plastic bags. Apparently the more I struggled, the more I wrapped their tentacles around my body. The pain, my God." He felt his side again with light fingers. "Can you feel pain?"

"If you were to damage me, say, break my arm, my health

conditioning monitoring systems would detect that something was wrong, and that I needed to reroute essential power, or reprioritise operational task trees to compensate for the damage. But inasmuch as would the damage cause me discomfort, I would have to say no." She paused. "I think that certain operational capabilities of mine require pain."

Dhiraj shook his head. He felt unexpectedly sad for the creature. "You mean, so that your... your clients can hurt you?"

"I believe so, yes."

"Jesus." He looked her, stoically bearing her lot. "You know, you don't have to settle for such things. You don't have to do this. You don't have to accept this is who you are. You don't have to agree to this."

A beat of silence. "A Portuguese Man O' War. It is not a jellyfish. It is a siphonophore; not a single organism but a colony of individual organisms called zooids that effectively live together."

Dhiraj forced out a short, stunted laugh. She probably didn't register a single word he just said. "You just looked that up?"

"The relationship between the individual creatures is completely and insolubly symbiotic. They are inseparably linked; they would not be able to survive independently."

Dhiraj couldn't think of anything to say, so he nodded and swallowed, before he fell back onto the bed. As it turned out, sleep did come easily.

Naomi still stood by the door when he woke, in the same grubby crop-top and skirt as she had been last evening. Scraping a boulder of sleep away from his eye, it took a moment to recall she was real, that she wasn't some dream come to rouse him from a deeper dream. The next thing to hit him was the sadly familiar smell of the room: old food and unwashed linen. "What time is it?"

"It is 9:00am."

Dhiraj stretched and looked around at the pathetic hole he'd bought himself for the night. Then he remembered the message he'd left his wife. "Sali. Did Sali get in touch?"

"No."

He sighed, not knowing whether that was good or bad. She was bound to have received the message. "Any other news? About, you know, what happened?"

"The Cyber Security Cross Party Committee is meeting today. They're going to discuss ways in which they can apprehend the suspected robot and the Indian gentleman accompanying it, but also ways in which they can prevent this from happening again."

Jesus. He wished she didn't have to be so objective about it. Wasn't there an option to make her more panicky or something? Sourly he pulled on his top, full of interesting and scarily vague stains from yesterday. "So what do we do?"

"The word from the news outlets is that the Committee is going to discuss an amnesty for female kokeshi in the hope that they can prevent further murders."

Dhiraj made a face. "How will that help?"

"Because the kokeshi are unregulated, they are dangerous. What happened last night could easily happen again. So the police are proposing to take in all illegal dolls, and those that are taken can be either safely detained, or dismantled."

An amnesty. Could be perfect. He could just tell Naomi to hand herself in. She wouldn't protest; would do it willingly, gladly. He could go home. *No, fool. They'll still be after 'the Indian gentleman', and what if those gangsters come after you? She's your only only hope.*

158

She. *She.* Dhiraj put his hand to his mouth as the thought struck him. "You said that all *female* kokeshi were being amnestied, right?"

"The Committee is meeting today. That is what some people are speculating will happen. I cannot say with any conviction that that will be the outcome."

"Right, right." But her words washed over him. "Is there any way we can, you know," he said, nodding towards her stomach, then her skirt. "Any way we can change you?"

"What do you mean?"

"Pass you off as... not female?"

She blinked, and looked nonplussed. "Yes. Of course. I am a multi-tiered open-architecture platform comprised of modular systems."

Now it was Dhiraj's turn to be nonplussed. He held up his hands. Then he remembered what Jens had said at the Docker's Gun. Reconfiguration. Change her sex. "We can change your sex. On the black market. Jens told me. He said you could be changed into a male, or something?"

"That's correct. Is this what you would like to do?"

Dhiraj chewed his bottom lip and thought. Make Naomi male? Or perhaps even have no sex at all? "Can you find someone? On the Deep Web, perhaps?"

Whenever Naomi looked at her blankest, Dhiraj figured that was when she was trying to process the most. "Yes, there are a small number of black market surgeons in the London area, who would do modification work on kokeshi. There is one available for instant messaging, called Spidermen."

"Spidermen?" That was an odd name. "What does that mean?"

"It's his screenname, his avatar."

He recalled seeing an old film, or maybe a comic book, with the same sort of name when he was a kid. Some sort of masked vigilante, a hero who people thought was a villain. Maybe that's what these guys were. Do-gooders on the wrong side of the law. It might have been flawed logic, but that sense of unfairness struck home with him; maybe these guys could help. They'd need cash, though. He considered what was left of Djordje's roll of banknotes and stroked his chin. He badly needed a shave, not to mention a shower, but he didn't trust the waterworks in this place. He'd taken a piss the evening before and he swore he could see something moving in the bottom of the bowl. "Fine, talk to them."

"He says he's available this evening. He can remove and change sexual systems, all types. Relatively simple job. It sounds like you're not the first person to approach them about this sort of procedure today. The proposed amnesty's got people worried about their assets."

"Yes, but our need is greater. They're all after us, bastards on both sides, police and the villains. How much will it cost?"

"Fifty-thousand pounds. And we have to visit his own lab space. He says he doesn't get out too much."

"Shit." He dug out Djordje's wad of cash and quickly counted it. Around ten grand. That was the end of that, then. He blew out and winced. "We can't afford it." *Fuck*. Another hope extinguished. That had seemed like a decent bet, too.

"Wait," said Naomi. "He says maybe we can pay them in information."

"About what?"

"About us."

Salazar III

"Settle down, Chouchou, we'll be on the move soon."

Grumpily Lily acquiesced, fidgeting into her seat and burying her nose into a kiddies' book. The seats on the Channel Crossing train almost swallowed the toddler, but still she managed to find them uncomfortable. He shushed her into silence, but in truth it was he who couldn't settle. He didn't think it would be as simple as just walking away one day, just as he'd dreamed. Such daydreams had been numerous and ubiquitous throughout the years spent pounding away in that hateful factory, festering and metastasising into fantasies of him breaking out or running away in ever more dramatic circumstances: a daring, opportunistic escape undertaken during an impromptu Gendarmerie raid; or a plot to slip a shank into Chevé's kidneys from behind and sneak out undetected. But in the end he simply walked out in the middle of the night after finishing a shift, headed home to collect Lily and a couple of bags, and jumped in a cab for the train station.

Nita had been as good as her word. The ticket had appeared in his globelet almost immediately. He tried not to think about the weaponised kokeshi ready to be shipped to London, and instead focussed on his new job. The lack of sleep caught up with him again, and as the train pulled out of Lyon he drifted off into dreams not of rampant heroism, but the deliciously mundane.

The night train cut through central France like a blade, slicing layers between unsure waking and delirious sleep. Familiar faces shot by in the fuzzy urban lights, faces from his ruined old lives and the imminent new one, strung out in an electric arc of delirium running on rails. Lack of movement woke him at Paris Gare du Nord, so he yawned and tried to stretch out some of the cramp from his aching shoulders, but the seats didn't have sufficient room for a really satisfying stretch. He checked the clock above the carriage doors – *4:00am* – and looked over his shoulder to check on Bridge, tucked away in one of the luggage compartments by the doors. He'd arrive in London at 4:30 local time, well before the local rush hour would kick in. He pushed his shoulders back into the seat and tried to grab another fistful of fitful dreams.

St Pancras station was a dreary, dilapidated wreck. Fat British raindrops fell from the ruined rafters, hitting him and Lily on the head as they trotted through the platform. Apparently the station hadn't always been in such a woeful state; indeed, it was hard to imagine, but once it had been beautiful, the envy of Gare du Nord. Now both stations were twinned through their respective disrepair. He vaguely recalled being told the station had been bombed in a terrorist attack decades ago and was never restored to its former glory; something to do with protracted bureaucratic indecision. Some things the French and the English clearly still had in common. Lily complained restlessly in his arms as the rain splashed her sweet face, but even as he tossed a few bleary words of comfort her way, he couldn't suppress a grin. He'd made it: London. The promised land. Yet it looked and smelt just as bad as Lyon. Familiarity abounds in the dark, human faces shuffling in the corners of the station in bags, trying to squeeze into an area not overly infected by cold and damp. Brown-ringed eyes stared at him and his daughter from beneath hooded brows, and he kept his gaze to the ground. Just like Lyon's grottier *arrondisements*. *Keep your eyes away from the danger zones, keep your shoulder muscles tense, and don't stray from Bridge.* The eager little servobot trundled obediently by his side, pulling along his holdall behind it. Travelling light seemed an eminently sensible option; leave as much behind as possible of that old life. He hadn't even packed his globelet. It felt strangely liberating to have that tiny, intelligent device, usually ubiquitous in its handling of one's everyday existence, even on the murkier side of legality, excised from one's being. What cash he had burned a hole in his pocket, and he'd only packed what was necessary for survival for the next few days. It wasn't so difficult; he and Lily had gotten used to living like urban Spartans.

As he passed the people in the alcoves he projected thoughts over to them; *Don't you try anything*, he thought. He didn't truly harbour any ill-feeling towards the wretches in the shadows – God knows he'd danced on the precipice of that rut too many times himself to be so suddenly heartless over it – but he was one of the few who'd been given a chance to pull himself and his family away from the brink, and he wouldn't let anyone stop that. Bridge remained charged and ready to shock anyone who got too close.

It didn't come to that. The interior of the cab was as grotty as the station, but safe. He instructed the car to the address he'd been given by Nita's colleague – a B&B somewhere in west London that'd suffice until he got settled in the new position. He idly mused upon the whereabouts of the doctored Maya doll but scolded himself kept all such thoughts from his mind. That part of his life was over.

The hotel was fine. Clean and comfortable enough, but unlike Lily, he couldn't sleep. 5:30 ticked around, and he was too wired to get any more sleep. Cigarettes might help, but he was out. Thoughts of his first day at work kept prodding at him – What would his colleagues think of him? Would he be able to do the job? Was Miss Rhodes merely tolerating him, or did she really value him? – until he roused himself and, ensuring Bridge was watching over Lily, he made his way down to reception.

"There's a newsagent down the end of the main road does fags," said the receptionist, a burly, hard-faced woman of middling years. She looked like the typical, doughy Englishwoman he'd often envisaged living in this country. She offered him a suspicious glance, like he'd snuck in rather than checked in. *But you checked me in, madam.* Having no brollybot, nor even an old-fashioned umbrella, he was wiping the rain from his eyes by the end of the road. Something – a faint movement – caught his eye down the alley just before the newsagent, but his view was obscured by the rain and darkness. Ignoring it, he trudged onto the newsagents.

The first draw on the cigarette, long and bountiful, was the sweetest, and he allowed himself a moment in the rain to take it in, eyes closed. The wind – smoke and all – came spluttering out of his lungs as the blow struck the back of his head, sending him reeling forwards into the gutter, his eyes stinging. He cried out, unable to see, the cigarette falling from his fingers as he tried to right himself, but the blow disorientated him. The rainwater in the kerb was deep, and soaked him through his slacks to the skin. Shivering, he made nonsensical noises, asking stupid questions; "Who is it? Who is this? Help!" but a firm grip grabbed him and drew him up. *Muggers!* He called out again, but a heavy slug to the gut doubled him up and brought the breath from him in a wheeze. His stomach spasmed in and out with the pain, and his throat clenched up in a dry retch.

"*Ferme ta bouche, tu baises insects.*"

French! They spoke French! He tried to respond but could only manage a gurgle. The grip was now on the scruff of his neck, clamping down like pincers and dragging him to the alleyway; his stomach raged as the grip brought him to standing.

"Spanish prick."

I know that voice. Salazar forced his eyes opened. It took several painful blinks to focus, but his fat face became despairingly clear. All he could do was wriggle, but Chevé's hands held firm.

"What the fuck do you think you're doing, running away?"

Salazar tried to look around and call for help, but he could only see the occasional car splash past the alleyway. Before he could cry out a thick, knuckly hand cuffed him, knocking the words away. In any case, he could barely see beyond the rainy veil of the end of the alley. He was vaguely aware of the stench of urine and stale food. "I'll ask you again, prick. Fucking Spaniard. Did you think you could just run away?"

"I..." Thoughts of playing dumb crossed his mind, but he dismissed them almost disdainfully. Despite the knocks to the head, Salazar's brain was working well enough to realise there was no use lying to Chevé; he and his ilk could spot bullshit at fifty paces, let alone dribbling, inches away in the pissing rain. "Chevé. What are you doing in London?"

"Why do you fucking think? Fucking Spanish! Pissprick." He jabbed a thick finger in Salazar's face. "You should have done your job rather than getting ideas. I got to admit, I thought Charlie was fucking soft in the head to have you trailed." He offered a grin full of brown teeth and a face full of amateur wiring brimming just beneath the surface, like veins ready to pop.

"What are you going to do with me?"

Chevé shrugged. "Take you home. After that: not my decision."

"No!" Salazar wriggled to no avail, but then Chevé let out a deep yowl. Salazar collapsed to the floor, soaking himself anew as the fat hands released him. A brief glimpse allowed him to see Chevé impossibly arching his back and gritting his teeth, trying to pull the two wires digging into the base of his spine.

"*Salazar.*"

Bridge! The little servobot stood on its tracks at the end of the alleyway, two electrified wires jutting taut from its crude, humanoid torso. "Bridge!" he cried, scrambling to his feet and running to the end of the alley. A roar came from behind, and he looked back to see Chevé limping towards him, like a zombie from a horror movie. Christ but Chevé must have been a real brute to shake off Bridge's amplified taser. Salazar got behind Bridge. The little robot must have heard him calling for help and made the decision to leave the hotel room to protect its master. *In which case, who's looking after Lily?* A rod of shock, harder than any blow Chevé could have doled out, rattled down his spine as he thought of his daughter. "Hit him again, Bridge. I've got to get to Lily."

Bridge retracted his taser darts and in an instant fired them again. Salazar watched them strike Chevé in the face. The brute roared in pain, but his legs didn't stop pumping forward. Salazar stumbled back along the road, but only moments later he heard a great clatter as Chevé piled into Bridge, knocking him backwards and over. *Shit. Poor Bridge. I'll have to fix him again.* It would be only fifty yards to the B&B. Fists clenched, he ran along again, but felt Chevé's fat hands grab his shoulder and drag him back again.

"When we get back," said Chevé, panting through a face zigzagged with scorch marks, "I'm going to enjoy doing what Charlie tells me to do."

"No," Salazar wriggled again, but Chevé hit him in the guts again, and the fight deserted his arms. He let out a listless groan as the vague feeling of weightlessness came over him, and his next view of the world was upside-down atop Chevé's shoulders. The roar of traffic became louder as Chevé crossed the road. Another roar from the big enforcer, and Salazar thrust his hands in front of his face to protect himself from the fall. He rolled onto his back, blinking into the cold, dawny rain.

Chevé again writhed on the ground, grappling with his face; Bridge lay on his side on the pavement on the far side of the road. *Well done, Bridge!* A huge honk, like a flock of geese, deafened him, while approaching white lights, brighter with each second, blinded him, and the squeal of brakes tensed his body before he registered a dull crack somewhere around him, and the last thought before blackness took him was of Lily, alone and helpless.

D'Souza III

"Everything's as you expected, Mr D'Souza," said Oti over the globelet video call. "The new shipment's on its way to you now."

Good. D'Souza wrapped up the globelet and drummed his fingers on his desk. This last week had been hellishly fraught. Two no-name thugs from somewhere nearby had been ripped to shreds by an errant robot. Rusty said there wasn't much firm evidence from the police dispatches, but D'Souza had his suspicions: he'd spent long enough around scoundrels and chancers to know that whoever had made off with his missing robot was no doubt commanding it to carry out these low-level executions. Might not even be someone with any beef against him; might just be a coincidence, bad luck. No matter; he'd find the bastards and make them squeal. He sprinkled a few flakes of food into the fish tanks around his room; the flakes always smelt of bad fish themselves. "Cannibals," he muttered as the various creatures darted to the surface to gobble down the food, and he blew out a stale breath. He'd find the thieves unless the police did first. Every news bulletin was full of the shit, and now politicians and police were talking about an amnesty. He must have made some sort of noise, for Gacoki called out to him.

"Are you still thinking about that amnesty, Ka?"

D'Souza ran his tongue around his teeth and spun around. Gacoki reclined in a lime green silken dressing-gown upon the sofa, open at the waist, a sash of silk covering his groin, slender, gossamer limbs spread over the upholstery, a smoking joint hanging between middle and forefinger. Aromas of lime cologne and marijuana drifted across the room. "You read me too well, sweetness." He sat down and stared while his glass-like lover took another drag on the joint. "It's true, it's on my mind."

"You shouldn't worry about it."

D'Souza upturned a lip. He didn't like being told what to do or think, even by Gacoki. "I do worry about it."

Gacoki waved a hand demurely in the air. "I have no doubt that an amnesty would be a problem for your business, but it's a government decision. There aren't many safe bets in this life, but I reckon the Government being sclerotic about making an important policy decision is one of them."

"You think so? You don't think this'll happen quickly?"

"Jesus Christ, Ka, no. You've seen the news; who are involved? Police, Home Office, Health Ministry... and even if that lot could agree about something, all the other wonks and wankers – spin doctors and regulators and the like – would make sure it didn't see light of day for weeks."

It sounded reasonable enough. D'Souza didn't know much about government, but Gacoki read the news all the time and was always going on about how slovenly the Government was. Maybe he was right. Still, it wouldn't hurt to be cautious, and he was a cautious man. D'Souza never held to the shtick about keeping his enemies close; the only time he needed them close was to kill them. Apart from that, they could go fuck themselves. No, he needed his friends close. After all, why make friends if they can't be there for you?

A knock was preceded by Rusty making his way through. "She's arrived, boss."

Speak of the Devil.

The arches were at the back of *Tangiers Nights*, overlooking a badly-lit, rain-soaked car park littered with potholes and chock full of his boys' black 4x4s. A gaggle of humanoid robots – illicit lifters – stood in the shadows, armed with blades and projectile weapons. To the casual observer they were invisible, but D'Souza knew they were there. Enough to take down any group of would-be intruders. One of the boys reversed up in a black van, and the rear door opened. A couple of lifters reached in and carefully extracted the cargo. It smelt of salt and rust, what D'Souza imagined the factory and ship smelt of. As the flight case was carried past, flanked by the lifters and given an armed guard by Rusty and a couple of others carrying submachine guns, he snuck a glimpse into the frosted glass over the doll's face. She was in there. He breathed a sigh of relief. It was a pain in the arse that he had to take such precautions for what should have been a routine delivery, but there it was.

He had the boys unwrap her, authenticate her and install her operational capability in his own office. When they were done, they left her facing his desk. "Fetch me a selection of clothing for her," said D'Souza. The men nodded and left the room.

The Maya doll was a splendid thing, a top of the range product for his most discerning clients. As Gacoki ingested yet another lungful of weed on the sofa, D'Souza inspected his latest asset. Japanese features, voluptuous, flawless, peachy skin, with seductive, smoky eyes and advanced, alluring sexual programming, they always brought the highest prices. He placed a hand on her shoulder and stroked it gently. "You're going to make me a lot of money, pretty eyes."

The kokeshi didn't respond. He left her standing naked as he made the call to Ajax on his globelet. The civil servant answered on the second attempt.

"Agarkka, I can't talk now," he hissed into his globelet at the other end. "I'm in meetings."

"At this hour, Mr Ajax?"

"At all hours. There's funny business afoot, and I need to be on hand."

"Then I'll be swift. I have taken delivery of something that might be of interest to a gentleman such as yourself." He flicked the globelet around so it captured the image of the naked Maya kokeshi. "A Maya doll. Just this minute off the boat. Fresh for you."

Over the line, he could see Ajax's eyes widen and glimpse around him, no doubt checking his discretion was maintained.

"Hello, Maya," called D'Souza. The robot's eyes flickered and turned towards D'Souza. It sashayed over to him, all fluttering eyes and pert curves. When it was close, he grasped it by the backside and ran his other hand over its breasts, brushing its nipples with his thumb, stiffening them, ensuring it was in full view of Ajax on the other end of the line. The Maya doll inclined her neck and nuzzled at his throat.

"Is there anything I can do for you?" it purred.

"Not for me, my beauty," he replied. "Look into that globelet. See that man?"

"He looks a handsome pillar. Am I to pleasure him?"

"Oh, you are, in any way he sees fit." D'Souza could hear

the barely-suppressed whimpers on the other end. *Good.* "She's all yours, my friend. And like I said before, as an apology for your earlier inconvenience, I'll even give you her maiden experience for free. A gift, to ensure our mutual endeavours continue on the right footing."

The lighting around Ajax darkened, as if he'd moved into a darker room or cupboard. "Agarkka, my friend," he said through heavy breaths, "I will not argue; she is exquisite, but..."

That angered D'Souza. He hated 'buts'. He dropped his hands from the doll and peered into the video stream. "But what?"

"This is not the time. I can't be taking risks like this. I'm sorry, but..." he creased his face in pain, "but I have to decline your offer. I won't be visiting you. The environment is not currently conducive to such nocturnal activities. I have a public face to maintain, as do my political masters."

D'Souza clenched his fists and tensed his lips together. "*Hukapan, kari kota,*"[1] he muttered.

"What?" Perhaps sensing the instant deterioration in mood, Ajax held his hands up. "Look, I'm sorry. I have to go. But as a token of our, ah, our mutual endeavours, perhaps some information may act as a meagre substitute for my custom."

"What information?"

"The robot murders. You've heard talk about an amnesty, yes? It's going to happen. It's going to happen tomorrow."

D'Souza's breath caught in his throat. "Tomorrow?"

"Yes. Christ knows how they agreed to this so quickly, but there it is. They will be coming for you. Not just you. Everyone. All the dolls. All the bloody dolls in the world."

A flurry of thoughts assaulted him. "You can't fucking leave,

---

1   Fuck you, tiny fucker

just like that, you prick. You can't. What the fuck am I supposed to do with this one? With all my dolls?"

Ajax set his lower jaw. "If you've any sense at all you'll get rid of them. If the police find them on you –"

"Why? Why the fuck now?"

Ajax shook his head, defeated. "I don't know. Believe me, I don't want this." He looked to his side. "I must take my leave. Get your damn house in order."

With that, he was gone. D'Souza ran his hand through his hair. Sweaty. Sweet. The office was suddenly hotter than he remembered. He flinched when the Maya doll's hand touched his shoulder.

"You look tense, baby. Perhaps I can help?"

He shrugged off the touch, but the hand laid itself down again. This time he threw it off and shoved the doll backwards. It reeled into a chair and fell, tits bouncing pathetically. A useless half-a-million pound asset, taunting him with floozy jiggles and come-ons. His fingers flexed. Breath was coming in short bursts. Gacoki lay on the sofa, stoned like the useless pissant he was. Before he realised what he was doing he'd grabbed the doll by the neck and dragged it over to his desk, slamming its head into the wood. Fish darted this way and that behind the glass. "My fucking money's worth," he grunted as he fumbled at his trousers, pulled his cock out and stroked it hard. "My money's worth."

"What are you doing?" moaned Gacoki, not moving from the sofa.

"Fuck you," said D'Souza as he thrust himself inside the doll. It moaned and arched its back responsively.

"Jesus, you're so hard," it whispered, a mound of hair beneath his fist. He slammed into it again, joylessly. "Do it again, baby. Do it to me some more."

D'Souza pounded his fist onto the back of the doll and thrust away again, and again, until, some time in, something made him stop. Pain. A pinching type of pain in his cock. His balls, burning. "Fucking hell. Jesus, what the fuck...?" He tried to pull free but only succeeded in dragging the robot with him, clattering to the floor together, attached at the groin. Now the pain really began to burn. The Maya doll twisted its neck back at him and said, "Oh baby, come on, really give it to me. I want you to fuck me so hard, and so deep..."

D'Souza yelled, hitting the doll in the face, and prised at his groin with his hands, but the thing had clamped itself around him. He was locked in. The pain intensified, a burning, violent, virulent pain that stabbed away at his penis and made his balls feel like they were boiling. "*Get it off!*" he yelled at the top of his voice. He punched the doll as hard as he could in its face, twice, three times. Its nose broke, and he drew blood – *artificial blood* – from its cheeks and mouth, but still it looked back at him, purring. "Do you like it rough, baby? I bet I could take that big cock in my mouth for you."

Panic struck him as the heat increased. He scrambled onto his side, dragged himself towards the door, the dead weight of the robot beside him. "Help! Gacoki, fucking help me!"

Gacoki's eyes fluttered open. It took the cretin a couple of seconds to process what was happening, during which time D'Souza screamed at him. His cock and balls felt like they were being boiled into nothing. Tears pricked at him, and he bit his tongue for control until he felt blood in his mouth. Strength left him, and the office became a giddying blur with the pain. Through fat tears all he could see were the neon colours of the fish tank, whirring around him like he was stuck inside a bicycle wheel. Instinctively he fumbled at his cock with shaking hands, but all he felt was the soft mound of the robot's arse pressing against him, soft and warm. He heard shots ring out, then screams, then his own howls drowned it all out. Smudged faces babbled nonsensically below the screams, and the world went black.

Tilda II

Fucking silly season. Tilda had worked vice for years, and despite all the warnings, everything that industry said, she'd never seen anything like this. Only three days after the first kokeshi murder, along comes a blunderfuck like this.

The club *Tangiers Nights* had long been known as a sex club that offered kokeshi to its high-rolling clientele, but Tilda's department's efforts to investigate it had been squashed. She hated having to grit her teeth and take the bullshit handed out by its arrogant knucklehead doormen and front of house men – always men – when she came a-calling. She hated the fact that she knew *Tangiers Nights* must have had some pretty exotic clientele of its own to be able to so effectively resist such investigations. Most of all she hated herself for toeing the corporate line and being just another stooge keeping the whole chain of shit squelching along.

But not today.

Was it strange karma, or just what those industrialists had said about the dangers of unregulated manufacturing processes? Whatever. A high-ranking gangster having his dick burned off by one of his own malfunctioning kokeshi. If it wasn't so sick, she might have laughed.

The club had been evacuated of partygoers, the music stopped, the lights switched on. All clubs looked charmless and guileless when the lights were on. A designer could get away with a hell of a lot when it's too dark to see. *And when everyone's tits-up drunk or stoned.* She strode through the innocuous dancehall, past the stages where dancers would ordinarily be cavorting, and downstairs behind the bar. A handful of private rooms were tucked away behind a warren of other, smaller music rooms, and behind them yet more rooms. The secret rooms. Empty now. Further on was the office. Couple of officers by the door.

Inside was a terrible mess. The air stank of blood and weed and sex and fish. *Fish?* On the floor lay a dark-skinned south-east Asian man, naked from the waist down. A red, bloody horror where his groin should have been made her shudder and cover her mouth. A couple of first-response paramedic robots were treating him, before a lifter bot rolled him carefully onto a hoverstretcher, fitted an oxygen mask to his face, and pushed him out.

"He's not dead, then?" she asked the supervising medic, a tired-looking middle-aged lady with two prosthetic arms.

"Alive, but he's suffered terrible injuries. He'll live, but he's sleeping now, and he'll need surgery."

"I'll want to speak with him when he wakes."

The paramedic, ashen-faced, nodded and gave the signal to the bot to push the hoverstretcher out. The culprit, a demure, Asian-looking doll with a broken nose, sat upon a seat covered with plastic sheeting, naked save for a police-issue blanket strewn over its shoulders. Thick, dark bloodstains covered its inner thighs, but no expression crossed its face.

Em, already on the scene, turned around from her note taking. She'd evidently been talking to the skinny, glass-eyed, milquetoast white boy sitting cuffed on the sofa. The only one left. She nodded toward him as Em came in close. "Is that the one who made the call?"

Em shook her head. "He's stoned out of his face. Skunk. The Devil's own stuff. Probably saw the whole thing and was too bloody high to do anything about it. Christ knows he'll pay for it in his dreams tonight."

Tilda sucked her teeth. "So what happened?"

Em nodded toward the doll. "Ask it. It's been de-operationalised. You know, so she doesn't act all creepy and seductive."

Tilda walked past the skinny boy. He peered at her through red-rimmed, traumatised eyes, mouth open. She stood over the doll. Part of her wanted to congratulate the thing. A larger part of her wanted to pistol-whip the wretched thing until its face buckled completely. One mutilated gangster didn't stop them from being *them*. There was no place for them. A thought of Fraser popped into her mind, but angrily she shushed it away. "So what happened?"

The doll looked up at Tilda, all sweet innocence had it not been for its bloody crotch, the blotchy bruises over its body and those glassy, unblinking eyes. Tilda swore she could hear the gears and actuators moving in its neck. "Mr D'Souza, the man who awoke me, commanded me to have sex with him. It was rough. My capabilities enable me to–"

"Machine, I don't give a flying fuck about the extent of your capabilities. Tell me what happened."

The doll continued without a flicker of offence being taken.

That pissed her off too. Humans were easier to manipulate. Emotional machines. "My vaginal systems clasped hold of his penis. We were attached for nine minutes and thirty-three seconds, during which time he was in considerable pain."

"What caused the pain?"

"I don't know. I am not manufactured to cause pain." The robot seemed to reflect momentarily. "At least, not in this way. Not mutilation."

"You effectively liquefied a man's penis, and caused considerable burning to the area around his groin."

"If you are looking to understand my motivation, you will be disappointed. I bore this man no ill-will. Perhaps you do. Perhaps somebody else does, but none of this is a concern of mine. I do not have any concerns. I am made for pleasure."

Tilda rubbed a hand over her face. "I don't think there is any motivation on your part." Tilda stopped. The thought illuminated her mind. *Kokeshi as assassins.* Somebody could be using these things to rub out their enemies. Twisted, almost delicious enough to raise a smile, but she kept it well hidden. "I just want to figure out what went wrong, and who put you together. You realise you're likely to be dismantled, don't you?" Threats were a waste of breath, but she felt better for saying it. "Who manufactured you?"

"I do not know."

"Who set your programming?"

"I do not know."

"Who manufactured and assembled your sexual systems and components?"

The robot paused. Tilda swore it did it for effect. "I do not know."

Tilda swallowed a ball of spit. "There's going to be an amnesty for all kokeshi, and it's going to be effected from tomorrow morning, nine o'clock sharp. Your sexual systems will be removed, investigated and analysed by experts. We'll find out what's going on."

The doll seemed to give the faintest nod and inclined its head to rest. Without the gentle rise and fall of a breathing chest, it looked as though it had simply died, right then and there. As much as she despised talking to the damn things as they were, it was infinitely preferable to talking with them when they were 'operational' and full of the bluster of seduction. It was as if they knew they could fuck their way out of anything. As the doll was deactivated by one of the officers present and led on its way to the police vehicles outside, Em made her way back up.

"Anything from Stick Boy over there?" asked Tilda.

"Bits and pieces. We're giving him water and milk and splashing his face with water to try and revive him, but he's going to need a good night's sleep before we get anything coherent out of him. He's come around enough to realise what he saw was pretty awful."

"I'll bet. The victim's going to St. Thomas's, right?"

"Uh-huh. With a guard."

"What do you think?"

"Gang hit? Assassination by reprogrammed kokeshi?"

"Mm. Not a hit though, is it? This D'Souza's had his dick cut off. With the best will in the world he's not going to die. Bit of an abstruse way to go about a hit, wouldn't you say?"

"So you reckon it's just faulty engineering?"

"Normally I'd say yes, but with the Beckton killings still so fresh…" she shook her head. A thought was interrupted by a globelet ringing. Everyone in the room turned to see it buzzing blue and emitting a trance-like beep.

Em looked at her knowingly. "Must be D'Souza's. Should we answer it?"

Em moved to grab it but Tilda grabbed her hand, stopping her. She turned to Gacoki and grabbed his chin with a firm hand, thrusting his face towards her own. "You. Stick Boy. Answer it."

When he looked at her with misunderstanding eyes her impatience got the better of her and she slapped him, before tossing the contents of a cup of water over him.

"Til, you can't bloody do that," said Em, but Tilda was in no mood for polities.

"Answer the bloody phone." She twisted his arm behind his back, and a sharp yelp of pain went up in understanding.

"Ok... ok," he groaned. Still high as a kite, but it'd have to do. Could be the would-be assailant, following up their little prank with a mocking call. Pushing him towards the desk, he groped for the globelet. "What do I say?"

"Say what you normally would. No indications we're here, right?"

The boy rubbed his eyes and answered the globelet. The screen unwrapped itself, but Tilda and Em stood to the sides of the office, away from the gaze of its camera, but still able to see what it was projecting. To her annoyance, the screen showed nothing except the stylised logo of a red spider against a black background.

"Who's there?" asked Stick Boy, slurring his words.

A pause at the other end, before a low voice, possibly synthetically altered, spoke. "Where's Mr D'Souza?"

The boy whimpered into the globelet camera, his hands shaking. "Christ, I want a fucking joint," he murmured. Em shook her head at Tilda, as if to say there was no way this wreck of a boy could keep it together long enough to find out anything useful. "Ka's gone."

Another pause. "He's gone?"

The boy righted himself, pain wrought across his face, and he leant on the desk, taking some deep breaths. It wouldn't have surprised Tilda if he vomited, right there. But, to his credit, he kept it together. "He's *out*. Who is this?"

Another pause. "Gacoki. How much fucking skunk have you had? I can practically smell the stink of it through your globelet. Never mind. Tell Mr D'Souza that it's Spidermen. I have something of great interest to him. I have his missing Naomi doll."

The boy Gacoki looked up, suddenly alert. "How?"

"One might say good fortune, but fortune favours the opportunist. We'll be waiting."

The screen went dead. While Em directed the remaining engineers to attempt to trace the call, Tilda busied herself with Gacoki. "Well done," she said, putting a hand around his trembling shoulder. It was slick with cold sweat. "Now, Gacoki, you've got to tell us where these Spidermen are. Your cooperation's already been noted."

The boy shook his head slowly. Tilda looked at Em and the officer conducting the trace, and Em gave her the thumbs up. "Got lucky."

Lucky indeed. There was no way of remotely intercepting these deep quantum-level encrypted calls, let alone breaking them, but when the police were able to be on the call, it was still possible to trace the call, and quickly.

"Got the address," said the other officer, and he directed the globelet screen towards her. "A warehouse unit in Hackney."

She clacked her tongue satisfyingly loudly. The kokeshi looked at her with its dispassionate eyes. *I'll have you, sweetheart. You and all your bitch friends.* "Get units over there, now."

Dhiraj VI

Just like the Kensington Boutique Hotel didn't look like much of a hotel, let alone a boutique one, this place in Hackney didn't have the feel of a laboratory. Not that Dhiraj knew anything about science, but he was pretty sure scientists and engineers – even rogue ones who did illegal work and marketed their wares on the Deep Web – didn't operate in gutted out flats above the local express supermarket.

But what choice did he have? He could've returned home, but there was no way he wasn't being chased by somebody. It would have exposed his family to any amount of unpleasantness. No matter how little Sali thought of him right now – and he shuddered at that thought, invoking all the names of the Gods he knew – he resolved that he was doing the right thing by trying to throw his pursuers, whoever they might be, off the trail by altering their quarry. As he pressed the buzzer by the shuttered door along the alleyway by the supermarket, he pondered his logic, and wondered whether it was holding up to the stress of the night's events. He'd tried to ask Naomi whether she thought he was doing the right thing; she'd answered with her usual objective reasoning, but for some reason that didn't make him feel any better about it. As far as he could see, logic didn't apply when you threw humans into the mix.

From beneath his sopping wet hood he could see a microdrone, designed like a large dragonfly, hovering around his head. It said, "who are you?" Its voice was strange, even through the tinny amplifiers installed in it, the voice sounded like it'd been put through a pitchshifter or something, like there were two voices rather than one.

Dhiraj looked at Naomi incredulously, but of course it was wasted. He puffed out his cheeks and leant in to the dragonfly to talk. "We spoke to – to you via telephone earlier this evening. We've come about the procedure."

"Let me see you."

The dragonfly hovered around him momentarily, before seemingly taking a longer look at Naomi. Dhiraj looked around for other cameras, but if there were any they were well hidden.

"You're alone?" came the voice.

Dhiraj nodded, shivering slightly from the cold. The dragonfly flew up into the rain, and the shutter rose above the door. As it clanked up Dhiraj realised the metal was reinforced, and behind it was a heavy steel door, which unlocked with a heavy click. Beyond was a gloomy corridor and a stairwell that led up.

"You're sure you want to go through with this?" Dhiraj whispered to Naomi.

"Sunrise is in forty-three minutes. Modifying me will most likely create difficulties for those individuals seeking me. With respect to your own situation, it may help in the short term." She looked at him intently. "I wouldn't be the robot they're looking for."

Dhiraj swallowed. "And in the medium-term?"

"Unless you want to modify yourself also, you will be apprehended. By whom, I couldn't say."

He grumbled to himself. "Let's just get inside, before I change my mind."

Boxes of food and what looked like lab sundries – bottles, wiring, computer boards, and other components Dhiraj couldn't identify – littered the stairwell in the diminishing streetlight, and he stumbled over debris in the dark more than once, muttering curses as he did so. He stumbled up the steps as the room turned pitch black, and though he couldn't see the space, he could sense it in the breeze and the air. *Almost like being at sea.* Even beneath his heavy fisherman's coat, his arms gooseprickled, and he trembled with the chill. As the lights ratcheted on with a loud buzz he shielded his eyes. Before his sight returned, he heard that same voice from the telephone and the dragonfly bot.

"Step forward, come, come. We haven't all morning. Time. Time."

Dhiraj squinted into the gloom, and his breath got caught in his throat as he saw the owner of the voice step into the light. Instinctively he grabbed Naomi by the arm and squeezed. A man – two men – no; *a* man, a hulk with two heads, shuffled forwards. Dhiraj's jaw sagged as he wrestled with what he saw. Two arms; and two more arms, smaller, scrawny and pathetic, like dinosaur arms, withered and useless, reached over from the backs of the shoulders. Two legs, muscular but bent into deformation, propelled it, and between them was a third; smaller than the others, a runt of a leg that had burgeoned between its right leg and groin and dangled in thin air. Too much to take in, Dhiraj turned his head away, but he couldn't help looking again. His legs were jelly, and his stomach turned. The two heads sprouted from the same neck, a perverted union of flesh and bone and wires. Four eyes, only two of them apparently able to move, shared a broad, warped forehead the colour of rotting olives. Its skin was an ashen green, and it wore oversized, baggy clothing, clumsily tailored to accommodate those extra limbs and oversized neck.

It held out an outstretched hand when it got close, and grasped at Naomi's arms gently. She didn't resist. Its fingers were pale and white. Trembling, Dhiraj counted seven fingers on the hand it reached with; two pairs were fused together. It ran its hand over Naomi's arms, up towards her face, stroking it gently. All the while it breathed, making a pronounced wet, sucking sort of noise as it did so.

"Wha... what are you?" Dhiraj managed.

The creature turned its head towards Dhiraj. Two of its eyes bobbed around in their sockets excitedly, but it could barely manage any other expressions – a gnash of exposed teeth, the twitch of an emaciated cheek. "We are Spidermen. You contacted us to alter this beautiful creature of yours." It delicately drifted a fingertip along Naomi's neck and arm, and Dhiraj could see the soft, downy hair on Naomi's arms stand up on end at the stimuli. For just the merest moment, he marvelled at the genius of her construction, and in the next moment the oddest pang of jealousy overcame him that this creature was touching her in such a way. Bitterly, he swallowed the compulsion he felt to take his leave of this repulsive thing, and spoke out loud to help drown out his thoughts.

"You're an engineer?"

"We are. Four arms are better than two." It made a *yuk-yuk* noise that could have been a laugh. Dhiraj's skin crawled when its two dinosaur arms reached down and made pincer movements with their spindly, pale fingers. At that moment he noticed the gears and actuators embedded into its flesh, wired into its back, doubtless the result of some home-made surgery. It took hold of Naomi and drew her nearer.

"What happened to you?"

Spidermen looked at him up and down, making that wet, breathing sound. "We were conjoined. They gave us names, but told us that one of us…" he gesticulated with the dinosaur arms as he spoke, "would die. But we knew better." It looked at Naomi. "So you want to convert this one?"

"If you're able," Dhiraj said, trying to compose himself. He scolded himself for being so repelled by what was simply a case of conjoined twins. It – *they* – seemed to revel in their freakishness, though he now understood why they said they never ventured from their lab.

"It's a simple enough procedure. The question is: can you pay?"

"You… you said you wanted information."

"Yes, yes. About you. Why do you have this doll?"

Dhiraj wanted to tell him everything, offload this terrible yoke from his neck, but he held firm for now. "Why does this interest you?"

Spidermen sniffed and turned around. "Follow us."

Dhiraj nodded to Naomi, and they followed Spidermen further down the room. Various pieces of equipment – some electronic, some medical, some mechanical, some apparently organic, which made him shudder – littered the sides of the room, stacked in no discernible order. Dismantled kokeshi were piled ignominiously on top of one another; arms, legs, other body parts, some with the skin peeled off, others seemingly partially modified. The whole place smelled of rotten food, stale air and a thick, overpowering layer of body odour.

"We are a businessman," said Spidermen, his back to them. His back was even weirder than his front; rippling with powerful muscles around the shoulders, but the dessiccated skin sagged, weighed down by the innumerable wires, tubes and actuators protruding from his spine, connected to his wizened body parts. Other tabs and wires fed up into the base of his – *their* – skull. "Opportunity is our currency."

"I don't understand why you're doing this for free, why you'd help us for nothing. What are you, some kind of vigilante?"

Spidermen reached a sort of wide engineering bench, rigged with a plethora of robotic arms, and he planted his lower arms upon the table while his dinosaur arms stroked the ends of the bench-mounted robot arms. "Vigilante?" He mulled over the word. "Maybe. We do believe that we am firmly on the side of right. And we believe that you're in danger. Will you be open with us?"

"What choice do I have?" Dhiraj muttered. "What do you want to know?"

That *yuk-yuk* sound. "Just to confirm, you are the ones who murdered those two thugs in Beckton? And the fisherman?"

"No. We were there, but..." Dhiraj trailed off, saddened by the memory of Jens. He realised how dreadfully tired he was of all this. None of this could be erased, ever. This was his to carry, forever. Naomi, Jens, they were each a part of him now just as much as Sali, or Dan. A trickle of nausea boiled in his throat, but he clamped his eyes shut, braced his jaw and swallowed his distaste for a few moments longer. "I didn't kill the fisherman. He was a friend of mine. The other two killed him, and Naomi killed them in protecting me."

"I see. Why?"

"Why what?"

"Why have them killed?"

A muscle in Dhiraj's cheek twitched. "Because they deserved to die. They were extortionists." In that moment, he believed it. If they hadn't been so stubborn, so stupid, so fucking greedy, all of this shit would have been avoided. Their stupid, boneheaded greed enraged him so much it almost brought tears to his eyes, but he looked away, not wanting the Spidermen to see.

Spidermen nodded and clicked his teeth together. "Quite so. Killers of the innocent. Using kokeshi as both bait and assassin! A delicious methodology. You and we are of the same mind." He touched his temple, then reached across the bench to touch Dhiraj's, but he instinctively flinched out of range. Spidermen *yuk-yukked* at that. "We work for the same master. You were wise to seek us out. We can help you." He clasped his four hands together. "And this will be good for Spidermen, too!"

Understanding struck Dhiraj like a slap. This Spidermen thought Dhiraj was a fellow member of the underworld. *He thinks I'm a vigilante, too, bumping off gangsters and deviants.* "So you are a vigilante."

Spidermen sneered. "It's not the right word. We prefer to think of ourselves as furrowing a path through darkness to the light. We were not born for fighting," he said, flexing his muscles and clenching his fists, "but we made ourselves fitter and stronger. Yet these faces, and this body cannot go beyond these walls, even today. So we turn our talents to other elements of the good fight." He picked up a scalpel and held it up to the light, where it glimmered mustily. He then turned his body to face Naomi. "You want to change this one, then? Keep her undetectable?"

Dhiraj looked at Naomi. In her tattered croptop and miniskirt, all mussed-up hair and perfect legs spattered with rainy muck, Dhiraj forgot himself. She looked exquisite, perfection. He wondered what it would have been like to lie with her, to kiss her, to make love to her. Again the tears threatened to bite as he admonished himself for such thoughts, but that was overwhelmed by disgust at what he was about to do with her. She didn't deserve to be... to be what, exactly? Castrated? Desexualised? Asexualised? He couldn't even decide what any of it meant. He simply nodded.

"Yes."

"Did you have your way with her?"

"No. I mean, she's not operational."

"Ah. Shame. Jump up here, my dear."

Naomi looked at Dhiraj for confirmation, and when he nodded again she climbed on the bench and, at Spidermen's gesture, laid down. One of Spidermen's dinosaur arms reached overhead and directed a couple of bot-mounted dentist-style lights over the bench. The light swept across Naomi like a flood. It was striking how little of the light Dhiraj had seen that night; illuminated, Naomi looked different. Clothes covered in grime, cuts and abrasions on her skin. Her shoes – cheap high heels – had dug into her Achilles' tendons, making them red raw. Dhiraj winced but knew she wouldn't be suffering from them.

"So you want to convert her to a male?" asked Spidermen.

"I don't know," he stuttered. "I want her to be safe."

Spidermen made a deep, breathy noise. "Yes, from this amnesty business. Asexual! I will have to change many things. It will take many hours. You may watch."

Spidermen hobbled over to a large metal shelving unit and with their four hands sifted through several pieces of equipment that Dhiraj couldn't make out. As the thing went about its preparation business, he leant over Naomi. Unthinking, he took her hand and looked into her eyes. "It'll be ok, Naomi. You'll be safe this way."

"It's you who will be ok." She smiled at him, making his heart flutter and his skin shiver. Had he seen her smile before? He couldn't be sure, but it lit him up, and for a second she seemed anything but the frigid thing she'd been; anything but inhuman. As he held her warm hand, it was his own self that repulsed him.

Spidermen pulled Naomi's T-shirt up to just below her chest, and pulled her skirt down to her knees. Dhiraj bit the skin around a knuckle as Spidermen inserted the scalpel somewhere around her navel and sliced away. His shoes suddenly fascinated him for a few moments. When he looked back a bloodied flap of skin around her groin had been pulled downwards, exposing all manner of strange materials and electronic systems beneath. What looked like organic materials throbbed gently, filtering fluids flowing through capillary-like tubes flowing in and out of her torso. Metal gleamed through patches of sticky blood – *not blood*, he reminded himself. Fascination battled nausea as he looked away one second, then studied the scene with the next.

"What is the blood?" he asked.

"It's not blood," answered Spidermen, controlling a tiny robot that gently peeled away layers of what looked like impossibly thin textiles. "It's codable rheologics. Programmable blood, if you like. They're not just a bunch of actuators, these ones. No, no, it's not got its own intelligence or anything like that – it's completely reactive; it does what the decision-making framework – to you and us, that's the brain – tells it to do. It's what makes these specimens so deliciously fluid and agile." It looked at Dhiraj's hand holding Naomi's. "And *warm*." He stroked Naomi's sides as he said so, full of sinister appreciation. He beckoned Dhiraj forth to look at a confused mesh of metals, textiles and a myriad of tiny actuators in a wad of soft artificial flesh. "That's the sexual system. Watch."

Watching was easier said than done as the four hands flipped and switched and manoeuvred things Dhiraj couldn't make out, but after a while there was a faint hiss, then another another, like a final breath. He started, jumping backwards at the sight of Spidermen extracting what looked like Naomi's entire groin and taking it away to a plastic bowl of water by the shelves. In its place was a dark recess, a spinal-type column that formed the firm rod of Naomi's constitution, and in the fleshy wads of systems within systems hundreds of tiny apertures escaped the laboratory lighting and dove away into the warm darkness of Naomi's insides. Several wires and tubes now protruded, endless, their connectivity cut. Dhiraj's stomach turned over as they wiggled momentarily in the air, like morning worms striving for the sun.

"I've got to sit down for a while."

Neither Spidermen nor Naomi responded.

Dhiraj tried to catch some sleep in the far corner of the workshop, on a battered old sofa whose springs had long since given up the ghost. Hideous images came to him in truncated dreams: Jens's mutilated face appeared in Naomi's evacuated naval, snorting at Dhiraj with a sound that sounded like a metallic *yuk-yuk*, saying: *"I bet you wish were inside her, eh, like me? Blowjobs? Handjobs?"* He dreamed of his own rock-hard cock, approaching Naomi, getting closer to her, inching closer to her lying, clamped, then fused to that blood-spattered workbench, closer, closer to her outstretched hands and her deconstructed pussy, but he couldn't reach. He thrust his groin out, stretching his cock for the merest touch, but Naomi, numerous wrinkled arms and legs sprouting from her beautiful body, was always beyond him.

Workshop sounds – buzzing, fusing, drilling, hissing – awoke him with a thud, as though he'd fallen, but he was still writhing on the same collapsed sofa, only now with a sore face and a thrashing headache. He groaned as the shock of his dreams left him, substituted for a brutish morning. Carefully he placed his hand between his legs; his cock pushed aggressively against his jeans, and for a moment he kept his hand there. He vaguely recalled there had been sex in his dreams; the idea occurred to him not to waste the thought, before the blare of the lights at the other end of Spidermen's workshop snapped him shamefully from such plans, and his erection withered in the morning.

When he finally roused himself into a shuffle across the floor, the reality of the day sucked the wind from him. Naomi – was it Naomi? – sat upon the work bench. Up close, a heavy sadness weighed upon him. Her head had been shorn and shaved, and her face had been exchanged for something quite different. Something less human, more robotic, as if the very essence of her had been removed. He realised she resembled one of the lifters from the harbour; all polygons and aggressive angles. She was naked, but as he looked down her body he realised even her nakedness had been taken: her skin had been replaced by solid plastic material; her breasts had gone, replaced by plates that looked like the same material; her groin was smoothed over, like a child's toy, useless.

"Good morning, Dhiraj," she said.

"Naomi?"

"My name is not Naomi any longer."

A lump appeared in his throat, and he reached out to touch her shoulder. Stopping himself, he asked, "How long was I asleep?"

"Seven hours," came the hissed reply from behind the workbench as Spidermen entered the workshop from a backdoor, letting it slam behind him loudly. "We had to print a new skin for her. It's about midday now."

Dhiraj looked at them blankly. "What the fuck am I doing here?" he muttered to himself.

That *yuk-yuk* sound. "You're going to have to wait, now."

Dhiraj looked up. "Wait? For what?"

"My payment." Spidermen ambled forwards and pressed his strong hands upon the workbench.

Dhiraj made a face. "But you didn't want money."

Spidermen laughed that horrid laugh again, and pointed at him. "You, our friend, are a fucking idiot. We are a *businessman*! Of course we want money. We knew you were little fish out of water. While you slept we made a phone call to Agarkka D'Souza."

"Who?"

"*Yuk-yuk-yuk!* Exactly. Fucking charlatan! Extortionist! Monster! He will be here soon to take back what is his. This magnificent specimen." He stroked Naomi's head, tinged slightly blue with the new plastic-like material.

Like the sea.

Dhiraj blinked as he woke up to Spidermen's words. "You're selling us out? You never wanted to help us? You're selling us out to this D'Souza person?" His skin bristled and his head flooded with confusion and anger as realisation socked him. "But what'll he do to us?"

"Us?" asked Spidermen. "There is no 'us' for you. We've just protected one of D'Souza's assets from this police amnesty. We will be rewarded. She's worth a great deal of money, and changing her back wouldn't be so difficult. I've kept her important parts on ice. You, however, took from him. We don't know what he will do with you. *Yuk-yuk.* But we doubt you will enjoy it."

Dhiraj's fear spiked, and he backed away. "Naomi, get me out of here. You're not going with him, are you?"

"I'm programmed to respond to associates of Mr Agarkka D'Souza now. Once their identity has been confirmed they will have command and control access. Your priority access has been rescinded."

"Jesus Christ! But –"

A shrill buzz interrupted Dhiraj, piercing the stale air of the workshop.

Spidermen clapped both pairs of hands together gleefully. "Ah, that will be Mr D'Souza's associates now!" Glowering at Dhiraj, he moved towards the front of the workshop and into a collection of floating screens showing the camera feeds outside. One of them moved and focussed upon a couple of people standing by the shutters. The picture was dim but clear; two men in dark, leather jackets and dark glasses. "Announce yourselves," said Spidermen, speaking to one of the screens.

Dhiraj vaguely heard them mention something about coming to get the goods, and Spidermen uttered a few commands to disable his security systems. As he did so Dhiraj, trembling, afraid for his life, leant into Naomi and took her hands. They were cool. "We have to go. I need to get back to my family, and I need your help, otherwise they'll catch me. You're disguised now, no-one would catch us. Please!"

Naomi inclined her head. "My name is not Naomi now. That was taken from me."

"Then what do I call you?" Muffled sounds of shutters grinding and clanking on the lower ground floor. "Never mind, get me out of here!"

"I cannot. Your voice control and command access has been rescinded. I only respond to associates of Agarkka D'Souza now."

Footsteps coming up the stairs.

"Shit! Is there a back way out of here?"

Naomi – or whatever it was called now – sat up and turned her head left and right. The motion looked more awkward than before. "The rear entrance, onto Commercial Street."

Dhiraj, clutching the robot's hands tightly, creased his face up and wrenched himself away. He pushed through the back door and flew down the other stairwell, taking the stairs two, three at a time, not looking back. To his dismay the exit was bolted shut. Above, behind him, muffled sounds came. Shouts. Fretting, he turned to the door and heaved. It gave perhaps half an inch, but it was clamped tight. Above, beyond the locked door, Spidermen roared. The deal must have gone sour, just like Beckton. So much for honour among thieves. Violence was the only currency these animals understood. It pained him that Naomi was now their property, to do with as they saw fit – to abuse her, to degrade her – but it pained him more that if they found him, he would suffer an even worse fate. He pushed again until his shoulders hurt but the door remained fast, and he collapsed against it in a whimpering heap.

"Jesus Christ," he sobbed. "Sali, I'm sorry. Sali, Sali, why...? I'm so..."

The door above him slammed open, but he couldn't bear to look into the light, into the faces of his would-be killers. When they were above him, there was a huge bang, which shocked him into looking.

Naomi.

Bracing herself with feet against the bottom stair, she locked her arms into the door and pushed. Gears fought against the locks, which groaned. Her body shook with the effort, though her face remained as stoic as ever it could, before there was a squeal and a pinging sound, and the door swung open, revealing the rain-soaked grey of daylight. Naomi toppled out into the street before looking back and offering her hand to Dhiraj. Dazed, robbed of understanding, he mouthed to say something, but no words came.

"They were not Mr D'Souza's men," said Naomi. "They were the police. Spidermen ordered me to leave as he resisted their attempts to arrest him."

"What? Why?"

She inclined her head, as if thinking. *She used to do that when she was... when she was her.* "I am incriminating."

Dhiraj looked at her open hand, beckoning him to her. "So why help me?"

"I am not helping you. I am under the directive –"

"Yes, I know, of this D'Souza –" The thought struck him. So simple. "You'll have to come with me. I work for Agarkka D'Souza."

Naomi looked at him for a second, perhaps processing the lie, or perhaps she was wondering if the lie was even a lie at all.

"They'll arrest me for murder," Dhiraj said, blinking and staggering to his feet. "But you know I'm innocent. Will you come with me?"

The gambit tightened his chest. He stepped out of the Spidermen's lair, and into the sweet, fresh rain, holding his hand out to the robot. Naomi took it. She was still warm.

Adem III

"I enjoyed very much hearing your Communications Director – Nadia? – on the news, Nita," said Adem as they sat down in the EI Systems boardroom. "And of course, she had a most interesting message to convey."

Nita fiddled and spoke with the ambient controls for the room, ensuring the correct privacy, mood and climate settings were on. The room was a grand place, Adem thought. Not grand like some of the more ancient areas of Westminster, but grand in a stylised, corporate fashion, with lots of pleasingly ergonomic features, dynamic furniture and plush, luxurious fabrics that combined technology with comfort. He was delighted to find the seats responded to the contours of his body, locating optimum comfort, temperature and posture, all automatically. Very good.

"I'm glad you approve," said Nita, turning around. She looked smart and business-like, as always, but her hair was tied back today. It made her seem more forthright, somehow. He wasn't sure if he preferred that or not. Steepling his hands together, he mulled this over as Nita took her place at the head of the table. "Opportunity like this knocks only a few times in a lifetime. When it does, one must open the door fully. The press releases were, I believe, necessary to get the media and political commentariat discussing this option once again."

"Not everyone will agree," said Adem, deliberately playing this delicious game of Devil's Advocate to which the both of them had silently contracted themselves. "It's highly controversial."

"It doesn't matter if not everybody is of the same opinion as me," said Nita, smoothing down her skirt, before giving him a thin smile. "Just so long as the right people are. Speaking of which, what time did you say our guests will be here?"

"I checked before arriving here with my father. They are en route. They're very excited to meet you, Nita."

"Likewise." She relaxed her body then, as if the façade was too fatiguing to maintain. She must have been quite tense. "To tell you the truth, I'm a tad nervous."

He smiled. "Don't be." Half a thought to place a hand upon her arm crossed his mind, but he would have had to reach quite far across the table. Unedifying. "My father is a... he's a businessman. So you two already have something in common. My brother Remus... well, he's not so business oriented, but he's charming, in his own roughspun way." He leant in, conspiratorially. "To be honest, I think my father just wants to keep an eye on him."

"And your sister?"

Adem snorted out a laugh. "Joanna's interest in the family business is little and less. She won't be here. She'll be off gallivanting for some cause. *Noblesse oblige*."

"Oh. A shame." Nita summoned a servobot and asked for more tea. When she offered it to Adem, he held up a hand to decline.

"The amnesty is working out well," she said.

Back to small talk, then. "Yes. I hear dozens of the wretched things have been taken off the streets already. That Detective I spoke with to get things running..."

"Detective Sergeant Boulton? The red-headed one? I saw her on the news."

"...Yes, that's the one. Hard-headed. Almost as keen as I was to get the amnesty in place. Maybe even keener."

"Why do you think that was?"

Adem shrugged. "I have precisely zero inclination to know or care. All I know is she's carrying it out with a zeal I thought would be hard to come by in the police force, considering so many of their friends in high places enjoy the delights of the unregulated kokeshi. Allegedly."

He noticed Nita shift in her seat and idly checked his watch as the servobots brought Nita her coffee. Minutes later the message from reception came.

Joseph hadn't bothered to wear a suit for the meeting. He dressed as though he were still on a sun-bleached veranda on Oil City, in a military work shirt, top few buttons undone, crumpled camo trousers and big black boots. *This is a business meeting, Father, not a defensive push against the NPF.* A combination of mild embarrassment and smug superiority over his oafish father struck him. Next came Remus, Adem's little brother, dressed in a black single-breasted suit that looked a size too small with the jacket button done up. Adem raised a brow and smiled as he came in. Remus had lost much of his paunch. Last came another military figure whom Adem vaguely recognised from years ago, who was introduced by Joseph as General Ebuwa. JPC enjoyed long-standing ties with the

Nigerian military through their mutual need to push back against the NPF Marxist rebels, and Ebuwa had long been a friend of the family through their working relationship. Adem recalled him being slightly thinner, and less grey on top, and with fewer lines, but when the General introduced himself with a broad smile and a two-handed handshake Adem remembered him fondly; the warm counterbalance to his father's calcified exterior.

It was Remus to whom Adem turned next. "You look well, brother," he said, offering a hand and a smile.

Remus took the hand and shook firmly but didn't reciprocate the smile. "The weather here is shitty."

"Good to see you, too. How are you and Jo?"

"Look. Look at this," he said, displaying his right arm. "Twenty thousand dollar suit. Wet! Ach!" He waved a hand in the air, copying the manner of their father. "Look at this bicep. I am in training, Brother."

"Training? For what?"

"To be a boxer."

A little laugh crept out unbidden. Joseph had been a boxer for the military in his younger days, when grandfather had sent him away to become a man. Remus sometimes acted like he'd taken a few blows to the head, to be sure. "Why?"

"Because I am strong," said Remus, pulling away. "Do you think that is a joke? Do you want me to show you how strong I am?" He looked over at Nita. "Is this your girlfriend?"

"Don't embarrass yourself, Brother," whispered Adem. "She's a businesswoman. Just sit silent."

"You don't tell me what to do, Brother."

Adem clenched his jaw as Remus pulled away in his twenty-thousand-dollar suit that didn't fit and sauntered over to make a witless introduction to Nita. He offered her a humourless kiss on the cheek, which Nita awkwardly accepted.

Joseph came over. They embraced stiffly.

"Why did you bring him?" whispered Adem.

Joseph waved at an imaginary fly. "He needs to learn about how it is like in the real world. Iggiot! Got himself arrested for fighting again in the city. He has no discipline."

"You think boxing is the answer?"

Joseph gave a sour look. "It was the answer for me. Do not worry. He is just here to observe."

After the introductions were made and coffee was distributed, Nita stood up to provide the presentation about her technology. Joseph listened intently, but the dolt Remus couldn't keep his attention on the presentation for more than a minute at a time. Frequently Adem noticed his brother's gaze indiscreetly wandering to Nita's chest or arse. He clicked his knuckles and bit his bottom lip to stop himself laughing at the fool, but it would have been a bitter laugh. Ebuwa sat thoughtfully, resplendent in full military regalia, cap on his lap, taking appreciative sips of coffee throughout. He at least had the good grace to appear to be grateful for being a guest. Halfway through the presentation, Joseph leant into Ebuwa and whispered something, animatedly gesticulating as he did so. His father always had a grim countenance about him, even when things were on the up and up; he might have been telling Ebuwa how wonderful this all was, but he still looked as though Ebuwa had just told him he'd shat in his kettle. Ebuwa smiled at whatever Joseph was saying, nodded and carried on listening.

After Nita finished, she sat by Adem and smoothed down her skirt. Adem gave an approving little nod and a smile, which she just about reciprocated. She was nervous. She'd no need to be. Remus continued his staring session. His brother used to be a good-looking boy, but he was a lumpy thing now, with a head like a dropped turnip. Too many blows to the head, perhaps, during this fledgling boxing career?

"That was well done," said Adem.

Nita hummed an acknowledgement and turned to Joseph and the General. "Is there anything you would like to ask?"

Joseph waggled a finger. "You will have to manufacture the dolls from scratch?"

"No," she said. "You've heard of the police amnesty for female kokeshi dolls?"

He nodded, eyes closed.

"It's been in place for over a week now. The underground sex clubs of London have had a few, ahem, mishaps over the past fortnight. It's been big news here. The amnesty is being led by a detective whom Adem met, I believe."

"Detective Sergeant Boulton. Tough lady," said Adem, steepling his fingers together. As he gently rubbed them he felt the slightest scratch from one hand to the other. A callous. It niggled at him, a pleasurable niggle, like a mouth sore one couldn't help but tongue. "Some of these lowlives have handed these dolls in to the police of their own volition; others have been apprehended during, shall we say, operations. Others are being hunted, so I hear. There are, so far as I'm told, over a hundred of the dolls already in custody, if that's the correct term."

"So these apprehended, or gathered, dolls would be ready

for development towards an improved service? Offering personal services for working men?" asked Ebuwa.

Nita shifted. "They would need to be vetted and checked, but yes; mechanically and electronically most of them would be suitable for adaptation. But I should say that these dolls would not be used for commercial purposes."

"What do you mean?"

"We're looking to move into the – what you might call the 'personal services' market. We couldn't conscionably sell on the dolls gathered from an amnesty back to the public under the pretences of legitimacy."

"What do you mean?"

"The legitimacy of the market depends upon the good, safe, certified working of the product. And that means new products. We would look to manufacture new dolls from scratch. Establish a new, legitimate supply chain. This would create huge value for various markets; the supply chain for correctly and legally manufactured robots is incredibly complex. That's something that would be handled by our business development and procurement people."

The General put a knobbled finger on the table as if skewering something. "So at the end of this technology demonstrator, these robots would be obsolete?"

"Scrapped. Recycled for parts. There's no way we could sell them on."

Joseph leant into Ebuwa and whispered something again, and once more the General nodded. Adem ran his fingers over his mouth, the callous catching on his lip, wondering what he was saying. He assumed it was good, despite his father's face; anything other than promise would have been met with a walk out the door.

"Mr Johnson. General," interrupted Nita. "May I ask your own reasons for offering to act as the industrial sponsor for this demonstration?"

Joseph waved towards Ebuwa, as if handing him the floor. The General cleared his throat. "You're aware of our ongoing difficulties with the NPF?"

Nita looked at Adem. "It's come up. Remind me of the full name."

"*Ndi mmadu Party mata Freedom,*" the General said. "The NPF are a problematic group of people. Angry, misdirected, seductive. JPC is the major source of wealth and prosperity in the region, enabling many Nigerians to learn, to take jobs, to work, and to pay taxes. However, the NPF does not take this view and believes that the land upon which the JPC plants are built belongs to the people."

The General spoke in a sweet, melodious bass, with crystal enunciation, but not especialally military. He was roughly of an age with Adem's father, and it seemed sensible to assume they'd been schooled together, though Ebuwa clearly was cut from a different cloth. A good man. Family man, probably.

Joseph clearly wasn't soothed by his friend's gentle voice, and he prodded at the table angrily. "They are deaf in one ear! We pay the Government for use of that land. What we do is legal and always has been, ever since privatisation."

Ebuwa waited for Joseph to settle down. "Quite so. These are very old grievances, Miss Rhodes. They date back to the middle of the twentieth century, and the blood runs deep in some of these fellows. However, I'm afraid what little legitimacy these people might have once had has been eroded by the savagery of their demagoguery. They turn a blind eye – or a deaf ear, as Joseph would have it..."

That made Adem smile, and he stared at his navel to hide it.

"...to the fact that JPC's main plant lies eighty kilometres south of the delta, in the Bight of Bonny."

"Oil City, in the sea," said Adem.

"Quite so, Adem. The NPF has recently taken to more belligerent activities against JPC commercial premises, and even personal property. There have even been attacks on JPC workers, and even people deemed to be sympathetic to JPC. Beatings, stabbings. Sexual assaults in particular are rising."

The General paused to allow the final phrase greater effect. As if on cue, Nita looked up at him, but looked pained, as though she couldn't quite make the connection yet.

The General continued. "The provision of a legitimate sex trade in the Port Harcourt area would perhaps lessen the chances of this happening."

Nita fidgeted again. What was wrong with her? The seats were deliciously comfortable. Maybe one could get too used to comfort. Adem applied the thought to himself, and found it could well be true. Sir Ingham's image flashed through his mind, and his impulse was to think of something else, but he resisted. That would have been too comfortable. There was room for a little discomfort in life, if it led to better things in the grand scheme of things. He pondered upon Sir Ingham, but it didn't make him feel any better. He took a sip of coffee for some alternative stimulation.

"And how is this a military matter?" asked Nita.

"JPC has a good relationship with the Government," said Joseph. "It needs us and our revenue. So it offers us – and the people of Port Harcourt and its neighbouring towns – military protection against these people. But this is not a long-term solution. Better would be to give the NPF an outlet for their frustrations."

Nita shook her head and laughed nervously. "You couldn't draft in these rebels, especially if they're criminals, to be part of the testing procedures."

"Of course not," said Ebuwa. " The test subjects would be chosen at your company's discretion. There are several soldiers – military men, disciplined, able to follow commands – who would be perfect for such an undertaking. But I speak on behalf of the Nigerian Military in saying that we would be the first major customers of the commercialised dolls, so as to deploy them in environments currently unsafe for many of the women."

Adem noticed Nita's expression change to a scowl, her eyes now alert and focussing on Ebuwa. "You said you would offer soldiers as test subjects."

"Indeed."

"That wouldn't be necessary. I can draft test subjects here in England. There's no need to inconvenience your men–"

"On the contrary, Miss Rhodes, it would be no inconvenience, seeing as the technology demonstrator will take place in Port Harcourt."

Adem tensed up. He'd half expected such a move, but he knew Nita wouldn't have, and he sensed the air by Nita become a mite frostier. No doubt this inconvenience was one of his father's conditions, not the General's. It made greater sense for the technology demonstrator to take place in England and save everybody the hassle of transport and logistics – but his father had never been a man for placing common sense over what he wanted. Adem rubbed his lip gently with the calloused finger. He had half a mind to bite the damned callous off. Most unbecoming for a gentleman.

"I..." she started, putting her hands on the table. "The demonstrator would happen here. Adem? You're here to put forward the business case for England. The demonstrator would have to take place here, right?"

Adem took a deep breath through the nose and made the effort to be objective. "Not necessarily. Obviously the intellectual property would be retained by England, but the tech demo could take place anywhere. The funding isn't coming from the English Government; it's coming from a private organisation." Joseph nodded, but Adem continued. "However, it would still make more sense to carry out the programme here. Expertise, equipment, facilities... all this is already here. Why make unnecessary expenditure out of the relocation process? Plus, I must not forget my own employer; visibility of such a programme in England would give EI Systems, and therefore the Government, very good press coverage. Half the battle, some would say, towards full adoption, even with regulatory support."

Joseph grunted and Ebuwa looked down at the desk, smiling.

"This programme is being sponsored with a billion dollars of JPC money. For one programme," said Joseph. "And that will be done according to your own English legal processes and requirements. But we are your customer and have our own requirements. Remus, what would you do in such an instance?"

Remus. Adem had almost forgotten the gurning fool was even there. His little brother sat forwards and jutted out his bottom lip. He always did that when deep in thought. "I would have everything in Nigeria, at home," he said, doodling something onto the complimentary notepad in front of him.

Oh, this is nicely done! But do you think I am really so stupid, Father? Adem allowed himself the tiniest smile and shake of the head. A lifetime of power had immunised Joseph from the subtleties of diplomacy. That's why Remus was here; to say what he would do if given control of JPC. In reality he'd probably just parroted out what their father had told him to say. A dumb threat, then; the tiniest premonition of a future in which he'd be overlooked for control of the company in favour of his *Iggiot* brother. Heat passed across his brow. That could never happen. His father wouldn't be so bloody pig-headed.

Would he?

"There are some compelling reasons to do the programme in Nigeria," Adem said, furrowing his brows. "The privacy. No English press intrusion."

"I thought you said the press would be a good thing," said Nita. "And now this?"

Adem brushed off her scepticism and thought on his feet. Diplomacy taught one to be able to adopt either side of an argument as needs changed. "Plus, the facilities at Oil City are second to none. There are clean rooms, manufacturing plants, and expert engineers. And I would ensure that all certification and regulation processes are carried out and completed to English standards, so your products would be completely applicable to English markets and elsewhere. Plus, it's isolated. You could immerse yourself in this project. It could be done."

Nita kept a plain face, but he could sense the workings beneath it. This wasn't what she wanted. Truth be told, he wasn't sure if he wanted it. A nice clean programme in England and then a transfer of capability to his father's company would have kept things nice and distant. Plus he would have been able to keep a close eye on the programme from his London base. Regulation would be at the heart of this project, and he had to be a part of it. But no, his clot father had to stick his oar in and complicate things. Travelling between London and Port Harcourt with its endless sludge of delta and river taxis and black water and hideous, sticky heat... far from ideal. This wouldn't smell right to the press; things could have been kept nice and discreet. But no such luck. Still, one had to be flexible in these instances. He retold himself that a bit of discomfort was necessary sometimes. It'd all be worth it. The sooner he was assigned heirship and prospective control of JPC he would be able to do such things in future on his terms. Sensible terms. Business-like terms.

"If I agree to this, I'd want some of my own experts to transfer with me. People I trust," said Nita through clamped teeth.

Joseph waved his assent.

"The only thing is the release of the dolls from England to a private organisation. They are police property."

"That would not be a problem," said Joseph. "We have connections in the English Government. We have mutual interests. One phone call and they will be ours."

Indeed. England depended upon Nigeria for much of its oil. His father often bragged of having successive English chancellors and even prime ministers in his contacts books, and that they would kowtow to him. England was a hugely important customer; just important enough that he could get away with badmouthing its representatives, but not yet publicly.

"Are you agreed then? Can I leave this in the hands of my lawyers?" asked Joseph.

Nita looked at Adem, and he nodded his head.

"Your generosity is quite something," said Nita. "I have to

thank you for the sponsorship. Yes, I'd be happy to do business with you."

Joseph stood up and puffed his chest out. "Good. I would like to offer you dinner, Miss Rhodes. The General and my younger son will join us."

That bit Adem, and he wrinkled his nose for a moment. He stopped himself from looking at his father and giving him that reaction he craved. He was a stronger man than that. A worthy man. *Play along with his Iggiot tests. We will arrive at a better place.* One good thing about having the programme taking place in Nigeria was the fact he wouldn't have to put up with his oafish father's continual presence.

"Then, after dinner and a night's rest, I will travel home. You can make arrangements with your people, Miss Rhodes. And when all is set, you and Adem may travel via a JPC private jet to make final preparations for the project start."

Adem felt a flash of danger run through his head. *More tests.* He raised a hand to his chest and smiled. "I think you're mistaken, father. I must stay here."

Joseph waved a fat finger at Adem. "It is you who are mistaken, my son. You will be working on this in Nigeria. Make your arrangements. You are coming home."

Salazar IV

Lily.

The urge to sit bolt upright rushed through him, but his body refused to comply. The urge subsided, and a warm glow tiptoed along his spine as his limbs pleasantly floated. In the dark, he smiled.

Time seemed unhooked, dripping past in elongated seconds, and zippy hours. And when the urge to sit upright came again, he did so with a squeal of pain as his side and hip groaned in protest.

Beeps and hissing noises.

Bustle. Voices.

As he settled down, he opened his eyes, blinking his way into the light.

Lily.

No sign of her. Brightness flooded the room, forcing him to adjust. The scene became clearer: a white room, a bed, door. His left leg and hip ached some more, and his face creased with a crack of pain when he reached down instinctively. A smooth mould covered his legs beneath a thick blanket. He wiggled and scratched his right leg. Seemed ok.

I'm in hospital. Broken bones.

Events came back to him. The alleyway... cigarettes... Chevé! The truck, and a snapping noise... he'd probably fractured his leg or hip. Just great.

"Hello?" he called, but his mouth had been parched dry by the sleep, and he smacked his tongue to try and generate some saliva. How long had he been unconscious? A day? More? When the third attempt to sit up ended in failure, he craned his neck to look at the bed. It was modern, probably automated. "Bed, command: raise back."

Nothing. An itch played on his left leg and he thudded the cast in frustration. What if Chevé was here? What if he'd escaped the accident? Taken Lily?

"Hello!" he cried out. Voice a bit stronger. "Hello, somebody!"

As he considered rolling out of bed to see if his right leg would support him, the door opened. A lady wearing a white coat, middling in years, breezed in, exuding efficiency: hair tied back; spectacles balanced upon her nose; globelet floating by her, capturing her dictated notes. Another voice, male, gruff, barked something through the open door to her, which she brusquely acknowledged, before closing the door and breathing out.

"Ah, you're awake, Mr Gomez," she said, turning the globelet away. "Good. I'm Doctor Plant. Do you know where you are?"

"Hospital."

"That's right. St Winston's in Hammersmith. In London."

London. City of dreams. Stupid man!

"You were involved in an accident. Can you hear and understand me ok?"

He nodded.

"Do you know what day it is?"

He shook his head.

"Do you know what year it is?"

"Twenty-one fifty-three."

"And do you remember what happened?"

Salazar looked at her as she leant over him and checked him as a light shone from a robot arm protruding from the wall behind him. "I was hit by a truck. There was a man."

"Yes. You were involved in a traffic accident. A bad one."

"The man..."

"I can't say too much about it," she said, not making eye contact as she took his blood pressure. "But the police want to speak to you. They've been waiting for you to wake up."

"My baby, Lily, my daughter... where is she? She's all alone." The words came out half-choked, and he tried to sit up again, but she gently shushed him and pressed his shoulder to the foamy mattress.

"Please try to relax. Your daughter is fine. Lily, is it? The police will tell you more."

Despite the news, his frustration didn't die down. Until he had his Chouchou in his arms, he wouldn't relax. He looked up at her. She looked weary, overworked, but she had a kind face.

"So what day is it?" he said.

"Friday lunchtime. You've been asleep for about a day and a half."

He sighed and rubbed his face. Hunger, perhaps shocked into waking by understanding the passage of time, knocked at him from the inside. "Lunchtime?"

"Mm-hm. Would you like some?"

He had to leave, leave and find Lily, but they'd never allow him out, not yet. And he wouldn't be much good without a full stomach. Plus, he was devilishly hungry. "Yes. Whatever's going, please. Something hot. A big plate."

She smiled at him as she tapped an instruction into the globelet projection with a data glove. "Well that's a good sign. Something's on its way."

"When can I leave?"

She adopted a more matronly look. "Well, you suffered a clean break to the femur and a proximal femoral fracture – a cracked hip. We positioned the fractured ends together and have applied a nanoknit to the affected area to stitch the bone and stimulate the periosteum, and we are providing you with a course of phosphates to accelerate recovery. You're fit and healthy, and the only other injuries you picked up were a bump to the head and a few cuts and bruises which are already clearing up. We'll check tomorrow to see that the nanoknit is taking well, and if so we can discharge you with crutches to walk on." She paused and looked at him.

He sensed a 'but' coming. "But?"

"Well, like I say Mr Gomez. Medically, you've had a lucky escape and you'll make a full recovery. You may need to walk with a stick for the foreseeable future, and we can give you some guidance on how to go about that, but I think you'll have to speak to the police first. Would you also like to speak to a counsellor?"

Salazar had borne more traumatic things than being hit by a truck in the past. "No," he said, grumpily. It was good he'd be out in a day. He wanted to get Lily as soon as possible and start work at EI Systems. He itched at not being able to get to the sanctuary of the company. "Can I move about the ward?"

"I'll arrange for crutches to be brought to your room. Will you need assistance using them?"

"Thank you, no," he grunted.

When it came, the food was hot but bland. Jellyfish miso soup – supposed to be spicy but not in any way he was familiar with. It was followed by custard – a foul English invention, which he supped joylessly yet diligently, looking to stock up on whatever energy he could get hold of. The last few sups were accompanied by the presence of a policeman and a policewoman, who entered without knocking, closing the door behind him. Salazar barely looked up at them and completed his meal quickly before thrusting the bowl aside to a servobot. It reminded him of Bridge, and a pang of gratitude hit him for the poor old bot, who'd died so that he could live.

"Mr Gomez," said the policeman. He was younger than Salazar but broad as a door, shoulders wide enough that they might rip the stitching of his uniform. He took his cap off and placed it on a hook by the door and rubbed short, cropped hair. Salazar nodded, impatient to get on with things. "I'm PC Wilson, you can call me David; this is my colleague PC Viv Blackstock. Can we spend a few minutes with you now?"

He nodded.

"Good. You know that you were involved in –"

"In a traffic accident. I know," interrupted Salazar. "Tell me what happened."

Wilson looked at Blackstock, also quite young, and raised his eyebrows at her. She swirled up a globelet and looked at Salazar. "Actually we're here to hear your version of events."

Salazar groaned and pressed the heels of his hands into his eyes, telling himself not to shout. That wouldn't help. "I need to see my daughter. She's helpless without me. Please tell me where she is, and I'll tell you anything."

"Of course, Mr Gomez. Lily was picked up at the hotel you were staying at after the owner found her alone that morning, crying. She's at the station."

That broke his heart. Sobs welled in his throat, and he swore under his breath in French and Spanish. But as he tried to calm himself, the tension left him. She was safe.

"We'll come to her later. Can you tell us what you remember?"

"I was attacked," he said, steadier. "I just went to the shop to buy cigarettes, and I was attacked by this man..." he remembered Bridge tasering Chevé, and the big man picking him up. They didn't need to know who Chevé was. "The man tried to mug me, I think. We fought in the road. Then I remember lights, and a bump, like a jerk, and then nothing. Pain."

"A mugging? You're sure?" asked Wilson, peering inquisitively. He seemed like a bit of a blunt instrument. "It's just that your attacker was on the same train to London from Lyon as you last night. You're sure you didn't know this person?"

Alarm bells. "It was pretty dark. He might have been on the train." Best to create something believable. "Actually, there was a man I saw on the train; I bumped into him. He looked kind of aggressive. You think it was him? That I was followed?"

Blackstock shrugged. "It sounds that way. The man was called Chevélain Saoud. You don't know the name?"

Saoud. Salazar pushed down a little chuckle at that. He'd never known the big ape's family name before. Now that he thought about it, he was glad he was dead. If he could have, he'd have spat at the mention of his name.

Wilson spoke up. "We also found the remains of a small servobot at the scene. Equipped with tasers; the barbs were fired into the dead man's head and torso."

Thanks to Lily's wayward mother he'd dealt with enough police in France to know that there were never simply routine questions; everything was designed to elicit a guilt-laden response. The trick was to not create a web of deceit; webs beget webs, and soon the weaver loses control of them. All it would take was one tiny discrepancy, and everything would come tumbling down. If you're going to lie, keep it small, and bury it in truth. "That was my servobot. I modified it back in France."

"I'm afraid that such modifications aren't allowed in England," said Wilson.

"Oh," he said glumly. "It saved my life."

"Well, that's debatable," said Blackstock, gesturing towards the globelet. "I'm afraid we're going to have to log that."

"When can I see my daughter?"

"I'm sure we can arrange a visit soon. The doctor tells us you'll be here for a week. Like I said, Lily's at the police station. I'm afraid we had to alert social services. Leaving a three-year-old girl alone in a hotel room in a strange country isn't on, I'm afraid."

Isn't on. The English had a strange way with their own words. But he had to agree and shook his head in shame. "I should only have been gone five minutes."

"You and your daughter are lucky. But a man died, and we're taking it very seriously," said Blackstock. "We've spoken with the truck owner, too, and will keep you updated with what data the truck throws up. In the meantime, we'll bring your daughter in to see you."

He sighed and stared at the ceiling as they left, urging time to pass more quickly.

Sleep would've passed time more quickly, but he couldn't face more time unconscious. Soon a bot came with the crutches, lightweight automated things that responded to voice commands and came with powered actuators for extra support. A medical robot, a humanoid torso with powerful arms mounted on a four-wheeled base, helped him stand and ensured he was able to support himself with the sticks before leaving him to roam the ward.

There would be no point in trying to make a break for it. He'd noted they hadn't told him exactly which police station had Lily, but he took them at their word that she was ok – if she wasn't, there was no way they'd keep that from him. Anyhow, no doubt they'd already alerted him to the security systems, preventing him from leaving while he was still part of an investigation. There was no point in bringing more attention to himself than was necessary, so he roamed the corridors, trying to distract himself from his frustrations.

The hospital was sleek and well equipped. Manifold servobots – cleaners, lifters, porters, and others – and more specialised medical robots interacted with patients and staff alike, while the whole place smelled of disinfectant. He found himself in a large coffee lounge on the first floor, with a group of convalescing patients, some in chairs, some sitting at tables, some shuffling upon frames and sticks, chatting and watching television screens, talking with friends and relatives on the various projected screens. He requested a coffee from a servobot and took a seat in front of the television; an Italian football match was playing, which held his attention for a while. The coffee was dismal, though in all honesty it wasn't much worse than he was used to at home, and it perked up his mind. Better. Excuses formed; EI Systems would have missed him the past couple of days, but the coffee provided clarity. He wouldn't need too much in the way of an excuse; Nita Rhodes would see to that. Still, it was a shitty way to start the new job, and he bit his nails in irritation that the break wasn't as clean as it might have been.

"I'm telling you, clean gone, that's what I 'eard!" A gruff English voice sounded to his right.

"Fuck off, you tart, you're always talking bollocks," laughed another.

He looked up. Two young men, one in a wheelchair, leg moulded – probably broken – like Salazar's; the other sitting on a seat dressed in leather jacket, jeans and boots. He tried to blot out their voices and concentrate on the football, but on they droned. Vulgar talk was nothing new to him – but he didn't want to hear it here, now. A few other patients looked disapprovingly at them, but no-one had yet told them to quieten down. He didn't want to draw any further attention to himself than was strictly necessary, so he grumbled silently as they joked.

"I swear down," said the one with the broken leg, grinning like a stupid boy. "He had his old boy chopped right off. The whole thing. I heard the coppers talking about it."

"What, his balls an' all?"

"I don't fuckin' know, do I? All I know is she had his cock away." More sniggering.

The other man laughed through a wince and grabbed his crotch not very discretely. "Poor bastard. Remind me to stay away from them dolls. Jesus, they're startin' to chew off dicks now? No wonder the coppers are bringin' em all in."

"Nah mate, it weren't chewed off. It was, like, burned off. By 'er fuckin' *minge*."

Dolls? Salazar stopped trying to block out their crass talk and jerked his head towards the two men as they laughed among themselves. It couldn't be. Could it? He turned the chair to move to them and interrupted them.

"Ah, excuse me."

"Alright mate?" said one of them.

Was it a question? He could never be sure. "Yes, I'm fine. I broke my leg. Is that what happened to you?"

Broken Leg Boy chuckled. "Yeah, football injury. Be back soon, though. Same with you?" He nodded towards Salazar's leg.

"Ah, no. I was mugged and hit by a truck."

The men sucked in their breath. "Ooh, you poor git."

"Can I ask a question?"

"Fire away, squire."

"This man who had his, his, ah, *queue*, injured. What happened?"

"His what?"

Salazar gestured to his crotch, and the men laughed. "What, you heard about that?"

Of course I heard about it, you were just shouting it to the whole world. "I heard something. What happened?" He tried to smile, to look like he was in on the joke, when in fact his stomach lurched and his face burned with guilt. Sweat greased the back of his neck. It couldn't be, surely?

"Look, mate, it's just what I heard off the coppers – the police – upstairs. I was passing the poor git's room, gettin' a cup of tea and heard 'em chatting. He was fucking – you know, having sex," he paused, making a thrusting motion which looked faintly ridiculous in his chair, "with one of them sex robots. And," he leant in to whisper, "her minge, you know, her pussy, it burned his dick right off. Completely gone." His friend snorted back a laugh again.

A lump of sick rose in Salazar's throat, and he offered a weak smile, but in truth it was all he could do to keep his jellyfish miso soup, custard and coffee down. "Where is he?"

"What, do you know him?" asked the visiting one.

"No, I... I'm a journalist. What's his name?"

They stopped laughing, and Broken Leg Man shrugged. "I dunno. Di Sousa or somefing. He's up on the first floor. Hitchcock ward. But they put him in his own room."

Salazar slumped over his chair and turned away. His eyes throbbed, and a sort of stupefaction lay across him, as though he was being smothered by things he thought he'd left behind. Di Sousa sounded Portuguese. Guilt compelled him to go and see this poor man. Of course, it could just have been coincidence, just be a huge fluke, but...

"Mate, you don't look so good. You want me to call one of the bots?"

But he didn't answer as he hauled himself onto his feet, and he didn't look back.

Hitchcock Ward didn't look any different; its layout was identical to the point of disorientation; it even had a couple of police officers walking around. Glancing at the 3D screens above each bed he looked for the name he wanted. Finally he found it – not Di Souza, but D'Souza – Agarkka D'Souza. There were no police officers guarding the door; with recognition tagging in operation – could have been retinal, or even DNA – no-one would be able to get in or out of the hospital without being captured and identified. Besides, the door was locked. He waited a while, looking across the corridor, sipping his cold coffee until eventually a nurse went in. Seizing his moment, he tottered up to the door, waited a few minutes for her to come out and as she let the door shut behind her he wedged a crutch in the door, keeping it from locking shut. He waited a few more moments until he was certain no eyes were upon him, and he swung himself in, shutting the door behind him.

This room's windows had been tinted, making it softer, more peaceful. Apart from that it seemed the same. Idle servobot in the corner; 3D screen above the bed showing his details and vital signs; gentle snores coming from the patient. He looked roughly the same age as him. South-Eastern Asian, pale, long black hair splayed out on the pillow behind him, a few days' grubby stubble forming around his jawline. Cold tapped on the base of his spine, and he wrapped his hospital gown around him before propelling himself forwards on his crutches. He debated whether or not to look, but decided against lifting the blanket. He stared up at the screen; some of the words jumped out and made him shudder with nausea.

Phallectomy. Blood loss. Third degree burns. Major trauma.

Exactly what he'd designed that doll to do. *You always were the best, Sal.* He looked at this Mr D'Souza, peacefully and painlessly sleeping off his injuries and doubtless the prolonged, complex surgery he would have endured. It made him sick.

Strange. He'd always thought of the people who used the kokeshi as hateful, hollow, grim little creatures, trolls devoid of morals who couldn't sustain real relationships. Yet this man was just... just that, a man. *Not any more. You took that away. A ruined man.* It was the first time he'd actually thought of the type of injury he had caused, and his body began to shake.

"Sorry," he whispered. The thought occurred that he really

shouldn't be talking to this man, but once he started, he couldn't stop. "I'm so sorry. I never thought... I had to take the job. My little girl and I. We had to take the job, it was for her. I never thought..." *Never thought what? That you'd have to face the consequences.* "You've got to understand, Mr D'Souza, it wasn't me who did this, I mean... It was Miss Rhodes – EI Systems! It seems strange to say that I work for them now. I am culpable, but it was her idea. Not mine. You'll recover. Medicine these days... Building... grafting... you could be anything you want to be, still." He suddenly was filled with the urge to punch the stricken man in the stomach. Stupid fool! Why the hell would he choose to stick his dick in dolls anyway? "You're a stupid man. Pathetic. Just like me..."

Out of excuses, his shoulder sagged and the tension left him.

"I am so sorry. So sorry." Tears came, unstoppable now. He was the pathetic one, the amoral troll, the wicked creature who lived in the darkness. What sort of a monster would do this to his fellow man? And then he realised. "I know that this will sound like a joke, a sick joke, but if you can do it, then please forgive me. But when I picture my daughter's face... yes, I would do it again, for her. For her I would do it to a thousand men. And I am sorry if that makes me the monster." He let out a trembling exhalation. Mr D'Souza simply kept on breathing, his chest rising and falling. *Like Lily's does.* "I wish you better luck in the future, my friend."

That was as much as Salazar could bear. He wiped his aching, tear-stained face with his wrist.

His sniffs almost turned to a yell when Mr D'Souza's hand shot out from under the blanket and grabbed him by the wrist. Salazar tried to yank his hand free, but the man held firm, and he opened his eyes, staring at the ceiling momentarily before blinking three times and turning his neck to peer at Salazar.

In a hoarse, croaky voice he said, "What the fuck did you just say?"

Tilda III

She'd seen pictures of Eduard and Avgust Shkuratov on file, but nothing really prepared her for seeing them in the flesh. If this interrogation were to progress nicely it'd bode well for the investigation. Tired, exhausted and sleep-deprived, the conjoined twins sat, clamped to the interrogation table, their eyes wavering and heavy, head slumped forwards, muttering deliriously. The regular seats in the interview rooms hadn't been appropriate for them on account of their bulbous, modified back, growing out of itself like the lovechild of a werewolf and a manufacturing plant. So the chair had had to be removed and replaced by a wooden stool. She'd had no idea how difficult it could be to find a basic three-legged stool in London. She wondered why the twins never had congenital corrective surgery – it was a relatively simple procedure to separate such siblings, preserving the life of the stronger sibling, sometimes even both. She saw this person – these people – as somehow more and less than a – *A what? A normal person?* – but she shook the inappropriate thought away.

Eduard and Avgust had remained in custody for two days

while protocol and procedure had been followed and other amnesty-related raids had been carried out. It hadn't been a straightforward incarceration. During the first day they threatened the officers present, broke the arm of one of the desk sergeants when they entered the station, before sitting in their cell and crying until all they would do was twitch in the corner, like a broken beetle, twisted limbs throwing jerky shapes onto the wall. And there was no sleep; only a guttural wailing through the night as walls were pounded and smeared with shit. The second day was even worse, with the wretched creature vomiting and shitting intermittently, and the twitching getting progressively worse. It was only towards the end of that second day they started to settle down, but the insomnia remained. It transpired they'd been self-medicating morphine as pain relief to manage what must have been horrific aches in their bones, and to help them sleep. The withdrawal was one thing; the pain must have been agony. She felt sorry for them, in truth. And yet they'd resisted arrest to such an extent that they'd broken one of her colleague's arms, necessitating the use of an electroshocking robot to incapacitate them. They weren't to be trifled with.

A bot behind the twins ensured the interview was being recorded. She gestured to it to produce and deliver two cups of water for the table. The robot was also there for added security. While it was practically impossible for anyone to break free from their electromagnetic shackles, this was a powerful being, and it had those extra limbs to contend with. No chances.

"Eduard. Avgust."

The twins made a gurgling, snorting sort of noise, their heads bent double, chin to chest.

"Eduard. Avgust. Are you awake?"

It raised its head groggily and swayed from side to side, as though its head was too heavy for its neck to bear. Four eyes looked out at her, the middle two fused to create a larger, third eye with two irises, blue and green, like the edge of an ocean. There was an urge to look at her navel, not at the suspect, but she fought it. She allowed herself a sip of water instead. They were hard to look at. She'd seen some terrible things in her career, but usually the result of people's actions against others. This was a perversion of its own making, a cocktail of powerful garage engineering, social ostracism, congenital bad fortune and a bucketload of steroids, bionics and morphine. And it seemed to have no idea it was a monster. While the peripheral eyes seemed distant and glazed, the central eye seemed fixed on her. That discomfited her, as though she were the one being interrogated.

"No Avgust," it said with a croak. Its voice was slurred. "No Eduard. They don't exist. We are Spidermen. The Spidermen. Two became one. We are one person." It shook as it made a *yuk-yuk* noise. Could have been some sort of cough. It bared its teeth and gnashed them slowly together. "We're in pain. So much pain."

"Ok, *Spidermen*," she said, playing with the word in her mouth. It tasted bitter somehow. "We're aware that you've been self-medicating with morphine for some time. We can help you overcome that, and give you pain relief, but you need to help us."

It stretched out a solitary, shaking finger from beneath its shackle and pointed at her. "You are a cruel woman. We are *in pain!*"

"I understand," she said. "You're in withdrawal. Just emerging from it. You've had a tough couple of days. We'll make sure that you eat and are given help for your pain." She paused to let that sink in. The creature writhed within its manacles. Standard custodial-issue uniforms had no chance of fitting over the creature, so they'd simply had to launder the clothes it had been wearing at the time of arrest: a grotty, moth-eaten t-shirt and a type of leather smock that was stained and faded by years of dark industry.

"Spidermen, you know why you're here?"

"*Yuk-yuk-yuk.*"

"You've racked up quite the list of charges. Possession of illegal goods, to wit: one kokeshi doll; practicing surgery without a licence; practicing illicit modifications of robots; extortion; the list goes on. That's not to mention resisting arrest and assaulting a police officer. Two officers, in fact. So while we'll try to make you a bit more comfortable, make no mistake. You're in a hellhole of shit, knee-deep. All three of them."

It might have grinned at that. Its expressions of amusement, agony and wrath were difficult to distinguish. It made a pathetic, whining sort of noise.

"But," Tilda continued, trying to maintain her composure, "if you cooperate with us you may be afforded some leeway. Can you tell me about your particular expertise?"

They looked up at her. "Our expertise?"

"In robotics. I want to show you something, and I want you to tell me anything you find odd." She tossed her globelet into the air and pulled out the screen. Spidermen watched limply as she projected an evidential video presentation of the aftermath of the assault at Agarkka D'Souza's underground den, the club *Tangiers Nights*. The twins didn't give away much – their poker face was all but inscrutable – until Tilda brought their attention to the Maya doll, and in particular its excised sexual components. The sexual system was scorched, ruined. Spidermen, sweat dripping down his brow, watched with interest. As the film zoomed in and around the system and its components Tilda watched Spidermen, until at last they raised a finger and pointed at the projection.

"Stop it, there. No, back, back a bit. Yes. You see that? Those components there?"

The quality of the projection was excellent, but despite moving the images around to see it from different angles, she couldn't quite see what they meant.

"No no!" they cried, clenching their fists. "There. *There.* Those blackened, deflated pouches; that tab, and that wiring – oh! Yes, flesh still clinging to them - Sabotage! *Yuk-yuk-yuk.*" It fell into moaning and delirium again for a moment, before yanking its head back up.

"Sabotage? You're sure?"

It took in some breath sharply. "We would have to see the code for proof but... these items; superheaters, impressuring manipulators, and those tabs – activated by the electro-chemical charge, temperature and pressure of human flesh... oh, somebody built that doll for murder or mutilation. That's not a malfunction. It performed beautifully. Imagine the mess! Oh..." they wept, scraping away tears with its scrawny, overhanging hands. Tilda grimaced. "You are a cruel mistress. *Yuk-yuk-yuk.* We need some fucking morphine. Our back. It divides. It cracks up."

Tilda suppressed a shiver, but kept her voice firm. "Who made it?"

They shrugged and moaned some more. Horrible noises that chilled Tilda's skin and raised goosepimples. She resisted the temptation to rub her arms. "There are a few manufacturers of such sexual systems in the underworld. Some in China, one in France, one I know of in Mexico, some in Eastern Europe..."

"Do you know who supplies to Agarkka D'Souza?"

"*Yuk-yuk-yuk*. He's a big fish, cruel mistress. If we tell you, our lives are forfeit."

"Then it will please you, no doubt, to learn that it's Mr D'Souza who's currently lying in hospital after having his penis burned off by that doll."

For the first time Spidermen froze and couldn't formulate an answer. Instead it gulped out of one side of its mouth, leant forwards, and pointed to the cup of water. Cautiously she offered it to Spidermen's mouth, where it took a baby sip and chattered its teeth together. "Somebody tried to murder Mr D'Souza?"

That she didn't know. What she also didn't know was whether the twins saw D'Souza as an ally or an enemy; would they be supportive of his attempted murder, or not? "It looks like it."

The twins made a long, strained noise. "France."

"Names, Spidermen. I need names. Can you give me more?"

"Yes, we can. We exist on the fringes, out of sight. No-one would care if we lived or died. Not you, not anybody. We look after each other. We know who does what. There is a man called Charlie Olivier. You will find him in Lyon." They stretched out their fingers on all four hands, and Tilda heard the joints click, like a clutch of party poppers going off, and they slammed their fists down on the table. "Now get me a *fucking fix*."

Tilda breathed out and stood. Lyon. She hoped it wasn't a wild goose chase. Her French colleagues would be able to investigate. "You'll be taken to a secure clinic where you can undergo methodone treatment and be properly looked after. A judge may consider your cooperation if you're convicted. You're still in a lot of trouble."

As she walked to the door, Spidermen called after her. "Cruel mistress, did you find the jellyfisherman?"

A closing gambit. Nearly all those charged with something tried it. The twins were trying to barter, to make it appear as though they were still in a position of strength. But they weren't. "I'm not interested in the fisherman," she said, not looking back. "It's D'Souza we're after. The big fish. Not little jellies."

"He's still out there, with his robot. We changed her."

"The kokeshi who committed the Beckton murders?"

"Yes, yes. We changed her. Took away her pieces. Made her into a nothing. As for the fisherman, he's already nothing. Frightened as a fishwife. Out of his depth, *yuk-yuk-yuk*."

Tilda looked at the twins, strode towards the globelet and ensured the interview recording had been terminated and the intercom was off. "You destroyed a kokeshi that was involved in the deaths of two no-name thugs? Then you have my thanks. One less monstrosity sex-toy on the streets to deal with. I couldn't give a shit about the damned fisherman. Those murders were the best fucking thing to happen in years, as far as I'm concerned, because it enabled me to finally get those abominations destroyed. Now I want the bastard men who put them there in the first place."

If the twins were disappointed by that, their pockmarked, lumpy face showed no sign of it, instead bowing their head and wheezing loudly.

D'Souza IV

A sun gleaming in an unspoilt sky. A sea deep and blue, and sand so soft one could sleep on it at night. One by one they dripped away, grain by grain, replaced by words.

I'm so sorry.

You'll recover.

You could be anything you want to be.

Still.

Since he'd awoken D'Souza had spent what felt like hours in this gloomy room, overwhelmed by the stale stench of piss and bleach and other ill people, the dry throb in his heavily-bandaged crotch reminding him that the visceral dreams he'd had weren't just dreams. He'd never been one for tears, and when they threatened to puncture him for the merest moment, he bit his tongue until it hurt, and the self-pity turned to rage, and rage gave him clarity. Just as it always did.

That prick who'd been in his room. Gone now. He shook his head and clamped his eyes shut to try and rid himself of the nausea. What had he said again?

I'm sorry.

EI Systems.

Nita Rhodes.

Who the hell was this Nita Rhodes? Half of him reasoned that it might of been a dream, another horrid vision puncturing the sweet scents and salty bites of soft shell crabs cooked on the beach. *No, it was no dream. He smelled real enough.* D'Souza went over the words he'd managed to catch from that weirdo in the wheelchair before he'd fallen back to sleep again.

EI Systems.

Nita Rhodes.

Nita Rhodes did this to you.

What was his name? Sally? Sallan?

Salazar. That's right, he remembered, settling his head back on the pillow in time for the next wave of nausea to surface. He breathed in through the nose, remembering what he'd told Salazar.

'Call Rusty,' he'd said, giving him the number. If he had an ounce of sense he'd be doing it right now. The prick might have been a crank, just another weirdo roaming the hospital corridors, but he might just end up doing him a favour.

It didn't take long for a nurse to visit, accompanied by some sort of medical robot and a burly policeman, who stood at the back of the room and watched the nurse and bot check his vitals and change his sheets. He'd been vaguely aware of the nurse flitting in and out of the room just as he'd been flitting in and out of consciousness. The nurse asked the policeman to step outside, which he did begrudgingly, but not before giving D'Souza a scowl, which he returned. The nurse then told him the extent of his injuries, but most of the words washed over him. She was a young, small Filipino lady, with a gentle bedside manner and a distastefully soft voice that grated.

A phallectomy.

Burns.

His penis had been burned almost completely off. As she explained his entire groin thudded in agony, as though his cock was still being ground into mush now, and rage grew in him; he clenched his bedsheets so tightly his knuckles paled and his face curled into a smear of hate.

"When the fuck can I leave?" he growled.

"Mr D'Souza, I'm not supposed…"

He flinched and jerked his gaze to her. "What did you say? Mr? *Mr* D'Souza?" He pointed at his crotch. "You think I'm a man?"

The nurse backed away from the bed and shook her head. Stupid, knowing little bitch. Leering at him.

"Get me out of here," he said to her. When she didn't respond, he roared at her, "*Get me out of here!*" and she left the room shaking.

There was nothing to be done here. He pulled off the sheets and stared at the mess that was his midriff. Tender indigo patches crept out shamefully from the horror lying hidden beneath the bandage and gauze. It might have been his imagination, but he could have sworn it even smelled bad. Shuddering, he wondered if he should lift up the gauze and look. He placed a hand on his lower navel; his flesh crawled in response and he withdrew his fingers. Frustratingly, the rage fell away, and his shoulders sagged, stiffness dissipating until he slumped his head back onto the pillow, which gave way with a puff.

Everything angered him. That cowardly prick Ajax. The fucking luck of having a doll stolen and its replacement being… whatever it was. His body. His fucking hair, stinking of sweat and grease, made him look like a fucking woman. A woman! If it weren't so grotesque he might have laughed. And as much as the disgrace of it enraged him, he didn't have the heart to channel it into energy.

Defeated, he called to the servobot in the corner and asked for a mirror. The face that greeted him in it looked sallow and wan. He told the bot to put on some television. Images swirled above his head, and he tried to lose himself in the banal flow of information, and channel hopped from an action film set somewhere in space, to a natural history documentary about fish, to a TV drama set somewhere up north, to the news. He'd never been a follower of the news; he preferred to follow people and what they were up to. The best way to do that wasn't through the filters and editorials of the news, but by pressing the flesh. Better yet, by fucking the flesh, or at least finding out what sort of fucking they were into. His crotch throbbed. Once he would have sought Gacoki or someone – *or something* – to relieve such a throb, but that'd never happen again, and he wriggled, throttling the mocking thoughts as the newsreader's voice washed over him like a balm.

And then he heard it, and jerked up. The swift motion almost made him vomit with the pain, but he bore it and pushed himself up into sitting, with a grimace.

"Rewind ten seconds," he muttered to the servobot.

There it was again. Clear as day. As the newsreader spoke, the rage rose in him again, and he didn't attempt to suppress it. "*The recent amnesty on robotic kokeshi sex dolls has been seized upon by advanced robotics firm Emotional Intelligence Systems – or EI Systems – who say that the distribution of unregulated kokeshi into the black markets means that London is crawling with potentially lethal weapons. EI Systems says its advanced artificial emotional technology would lend greater user experience to the customer, and also be a safer option than the illegal dolls that have allegedly cause recent murders and attacks across the capital. The company has positioned itself with the English Government to embark on a controversial technology demonstrator programme in conjunction with the Nigerian oil conglomerate Johnson Petrochemical Corporation, who are funding the programme, to develop the kokeshi. Government officials say they are investigating a more modern approach to a regulated sex industry that could incorporate such technology. The Chancellor of the Exchequer has endorsed the programme, saying that it would be a great English success story. However, ethical groups are opposed to the project, such as –"*

A wave of rage and confusion, at least as powerful as the nausea, crashed into him, and he gripped the bedsheets as the bulletin continued. The screen cut to a talking head of the Technical Director from this EI Systems firm. Pretty dark haired bitch.

Like me.

Her name flashed upon the bottom of the screen: *Nita Rhodes.*

He thinned his eyes as he focused upon her. She wouldn't be so pretty when he'd finished with her. Dark fantasies swam to him obligingly, but with only the ghost of a cock he'd have to be more imaginative in paying her back for her mutilation of him. He threw the image of her away, and the projection screwed itself into nothingness, leaving only his heavy breaths. Not only had she taken his cock but also his business, his very industry, the thing he'd worked so long and hard for. No longer a man of work; no longer a man.

None of this could be done here. He swung himself around, and almost yelled with pain as his legs dangled off the bed. "Get me a painkiller," he told the medical bot, clasping a hand to his middle, which only made things worse.

"Your pain management programme is still being developed," replied the robot. "So far we have administered naproxen, cybexyn and co-codamol to prevent inflammation and relieve pain, but in order to meet discharge time targets and ensure you can return home as quickly as possible, I recommended you take the option of having bioelectric implants installed to block pain signals to the brain from the afflicted area."

"Fine. Do it."

After D'Souza rolled onto his side and hitched up his gown, the robot babbled on about the procedure as it carried it out there and then, talking about local anaesthetics and follow-up treatments which D'Souza could administer "at home." The words were like molasses, too thick to make sense of. "So I can be discharged?"

The robot hesitated, perhaps conducting a search whilst it was in the middle of spraying something onto his spine. D'Souza felt a sort of pushing and prodding sensation in his lower back, uncomfortable but not painful.

"It seems you cannot be discharged without special authorisation from the police. I cannot discharge you."

"That ogre outside my room – he can discharge me?"

"If you are referring to the policeman, then not directly. But he could authorise your discharge, and then I could issue you with your discharge notification codes."

"Do I have to be escorted off site?"

"I do not know."

Robots. So eager to please. A half-crumbled laugh fell from his lips as he thought of the Maya doll and how eager to please she was. In a few more minutes the procedure was done. He was impressed – the pain did seem to be almost all gone. He swung his feet over the side of the bed and gingerly stood. No pain. He perused the data screen above his bed showing his details and swiped through as the robot carried on talking. His discharge tab had to be completed by the nurses and authorised by a police representative. Authorisation: that usually meant a thumbprint, an iris scan or DNA swab.

"The implants will help your mobility and the ability to exercise, which in turn will aid recovery. For the time being you will need rest."

Ignoring the robot, D'Souza walked to the full length mirror in the corner of the room and disrobed. Still the wad of bandages swaddled him, making him look like a malnourished Sumo wrestler. Turning his mouth down at the corners, and bracing himself for the shock, he dabbed a finger at the top of his pubis, but it didn't hurt, and he relaxed. He fingered the bandage – the bruises still bulged dirty purple, but harmlessly so now – and pulled it just an inch or so down. There was a black rim of bruising, as though all below the navel were shadow, and he let go, afraid of what he would see. With a spring the bandages fell back into place.

"Piss," he said in a wafer-thin voice.

"Excuse me, sir?"

"Piss. How do I...?"

If robots could do embarrassed, D'Souza felt this one would be doing it right now. "Given your injuries, I would recommend sitting down."

"Jesus shat," he whispered. A thought occurred to him. He tapped a finger on the bandaging covering his undercarriage, but couldn't feel much. "What about my... my balls?"

"Your testicles were extremely badly damaged by the burns and are extremely tender. But you were lucky that we attended to you in good time, and we did not have to remove them. But they are no longer functional."

"Lucky?" He shot a glance at the robot, which didn't react.

"You will need regular changes to your bandages. Would you like me to show you how –"

"No!" He pulled on his gown in an exaggerated fashion to test the new pain blockers. Effective. "I'll you what I'd like. I'd like a cup of peppermint tea. No, a pot of peppermint tea. And I want to see my police officer. It is time we talked."

"Of course."

The bed swallowed him up again as the robot wheeled itself out. Half a thought crossed his mind to take the rest, but he angered himself at that. Sometimes he'd catch himself angering himself on purpose. Rage was a great motivator, although one that occasionally clouded the mind. He would have to meditate, and soon. He had had *Illangam* drawn from him, and would need to cleanse his mind. With clarity, he could establish exactly how he would wreak the terrible havoc upon the animals who had mutilated him, a havoc they would deserve. But not here: meditation among all this sterility – the thought of sterility made him laugh – would be impossible. Not here.

The policeman opened the door and walked in. Serious young man, stern-faced. Unintelligent. D'Souza let the tension drain from his face, and sucked the grit from his voice, leaving it reedy and weak. "You brought me in?"

The copper didn't answer at first. He instead came closer to D'Souza, studying him as though he were an animal. D'Souza kept his gaze flitting, his eyelids half-closed. Beyond the copper, silently, the robot wheeled back in and left a steaming pot of tea on the sideboard by the back wall and exited.

"So you woke up?" the copper said, taking off his cap. "If I was you I'd have stayed asleep. You're half a man now. Poor bugger. What do you want anyway?"

"Talk," he said, weakly.

"Time to talk, eh? Well, good job, 'cos there are a bundle of people who want to see you."

D'Souza lifted a hand and hung it out, pointing toward the hot tea. The copper looked and laughed. "You want a little sip of tea, dearie?"

Idiot. His laugh didn't last very long when D'Souza threw his arms around his neck the moment he turned his back. Sleep had weakened him, and the copper was a sinewy, wriggly thing, but he clutched on and wrapped his legs round his middle. Down he went, incredulous and oxygen-starved, into stupor. That felt good. Door locked, blinds drawn, discharge notes written up, D'Souza took the tablet, flipped out the pages and used the copper's thumbs and irises and his ID to check him out. He folded up the tablet, pulled on the copper's trousers, shoes and shirt – a little tight, a little smelly – and steadied himself.

Robots roamed the corridor, probably not paying him a second's notice, but he felt as conspicuous as... *as a man without a cock*. Now he started to think about whether that runty Spanish prick Salazar had called Rusty's number and left the message he'd said he would. Lucky for him, D'Souza had possessed almost no strength when he'd woken to find him raving about this Nita Rhodes bitch, otherwise he'd be nursing more than a broken leg.

To a lesser individual, the minutes to the hospital exit might have felt like hours, but he sensed everything about him. Even cockless he was a phlegmatic man, and he rerouted his way through the corridors as robots and nurses came and went. The trick was to take the long way, through the wards where he wasn't known.

At the exit he allowed his irises to be scanned and held up the discharge tablet when prompted.

And he was out.

Splashing through the rain – walking, never running – he scanned the car park.

There.

Rusty's black 4x4, flashing its beams three times, inviting him over. So the crank Spaniard had come through.

"Jesus Christ, you look like shit, boss," said Rusty as he drove off. "What's with the copper's outfit?"

D'Souza said nothing. Rusty's fidgeting in the driver's seat was plain. He could practically feel Rusty's balls retreating in disgust. "Just ask the damn question."

Rusty laughed nervously. "Ain't a question, boss. I weren't going to ask nothing."

"You should," D'Souza snapped. "There's much to know."

It was minutes before Rusty plucked up the courage to ask what he was clearly dying to. "Is it true then? What happened?"

"It is true."

"Jesus. That's fucked up. Sorry, boss. Jesus fucking H. Listen... I got the message – who was that who left it, anyway? I half expected it to be a trick, some prick trying something, but I guess not."

"If you got the message, then you'll have got in touch with everyone."

"Yeah, but..." he shifted in his seat again. The car entered the dual carriageway and headed back into town. Through the tint,

London looked a little darker than he remembered. "The police are coming down hard on us. All the fucking clubs, all the bloody dolls. They got all the dolls, all the dolls in the world. Look, boss. Agarkka."

That made him look. Rusty – none of them – ever called him by his first name. It sounded dirty coming out of their mouths. Agarkka was a man's name. "What?"

"This amnesty... it's a total shitstorm. Some of the guys got arrested, some of them run off, especially after Gacoki called the cops when you was... you know. Jesus H. Anyway, not many boys left, you know. Word got out about... what happened." He nodded sheepishly to D'Souza's crotch, which agitated him. Rusty pulled out a joint from up his sleeve, lit up and offered him the first toke. Good. Rusty at least still respected him as the alpha male. But he turned it down. A clear head was critical now. "There was a parley at Fandango's yesterday. People's going to ground, going straight. They reckon the arse is being pulled out this business by the cops, by this fucking company on the news. There ain't even no one who we know we can buy off. Ajax has fucked off, God knows where. The other fapheads, they've all disappeared. All the other club owners reckon we're done."

D'Souza snorted a laugh out. "Are you fucking serious? Even with no cock and two useless fucking balls, I'm twice the man of all of them put together. Done! Pfft. Fucking pussies." There was no denying that. Whenever there was a parley between the underground club bosses, these donkeys would bray on about how they controlled the market, brag about their fapheads – the famous or influential clients they'd snagged. And as soon as a little problem like this came up, they'd cut their losses and piss off. Not him. He might not have seen the doll coming who would make him a *sitzpinkler*, but he still had vision where these chumps had been blindsided. "Who's still loyal?"

The joint crackled red as Rusty sucked up a huge toke before ejecting it in sweet green hazes that fugged up the interior. "Me, boss. I ain't going nowhere. You got me." He let that hang in the air for a moment, but D'Souza made a face through the fog. "Collars an' all. Poor fucker's too dumb to do anything else. We kept our heads down. Few of the other boys: Angel, Ox, Chains, that young wizkid Oti... they're still knocking about."

"Right. How much cash we got in reserve?"

"Plenty. Forty million pugged away. But the clubs, man... Tangiers Nights, Fantasia, Hanoi On The Rocks... they're finished. When the cops came and saw you, the fucking dolls, it was proper lockdown." He looked at D'Souza, as though a thought was crawling its way from his dope-addled mind to his tongue.

"What is it?"

"What are you doing, escaping the hospital? Every cop in London'll be after you. And what about your, you know, your injuries? Don't it hurt?"

"Don't worry about me. I'm not staying long." He snatched the joint out of Rusty's mouth and tossed it out the window, to Rusty's incredulity. "I'm leaving you in charge."

Rusty coughed and blinked. "What?"

"We're not going out of business. We're staying in business."
"How?"

"Stay out of sight. Keep paying our loyal footsoldiers."

"But the cops want to legalise the robots."

D'Souza blew out through his nose. "Let me tell you something. There will always be people with the taste for forbidden fruit. Legal kokeshi? Don't make me laugh! You want to see the arse fall out of this market? Legalise it!"

Rusty scratched his head. He was loyal, but dim. Just so; he'd need someone with enough muscle to keep everybody else on side while he was gone, but not enough brains to have designs of his own. "So what are you going to do, boss?"

"I'm going to make sure our business gets back on track." He gestured to his groin. "And I'm going to skin the bitch who did this to me. First I need to get to the safehouse."

"Whatever you say, boss," said Rusty, and he gave the car the address. "What we going there for?"

"We're going to get my *ethunu kaduwa* and a big fucking bag of cash. Then you're taking me to the airport."

"The airport?"

"Indeed. It seems fate is taking me to Nigeria."

Nita IV

African light and heat blasted Nita as she stepped out of the sterile, stuffy aircraft and descended the airstair. The sun, a blistering holy beacon forcing itself upon the land, assailed her for the first time in years, and she shielded her eyes, deferential, suddenly aware of her strange, new surroundings. Shockingly deep waves of viridian swept across the horizon; miles of trees sprouting violently, surging upwards to soak up the gift that was sunlight. Her skin itched and jaw sagged at the exposure; it was terribly strange not to have an umbrella bot up, and it took her a couple of moments' dithering to get used to the sensation of the sun prickling her skin and pulling it taut, like a lover coaxing her back under the sheets. As she walked towards the terminal, she pulled off her jacket, smiling broadly, and she placed her sunglasses on, feeling like a Hollywood superstar. Doubts had abounded throughout the days leading up the flight, and even during the flight itself, but with the sun planting shocking kisses upon her face, it somehow all seemed worth it. She was on top of the world, and she was going to do a hell of a lot of good while she was up there.

Travelling alone had been a good idea. Robb, being CEO, had wanted to travel with her so he could be there for the grand opening of the tech demo, to which the press had been invited – but she'd insisted on travelling by herself. "I need to get used to the surroundings, and just take some time to think. This is life-changing. A bit of one's own company would be quite desirable about now," she'd told him. He'd agreed. Why would he not? He was her number one fan right now; she'd bagged a billion dollar R&D technology demonstrator and a buyer rolled into one, as well as roping in the regulator to open up the lucrative English – and therefore international – markets. He'd already had the marketing brainwave of moving away from the seedy, underground connotations of the phrase "sex industry" by coining the term "companionship market". Clever guy. She knew the tech, but when it came to commercialisation and telling a story, he knew what to say, and there it was. Best of all was he was right. Emotional interaction was a game-changer. During the flight, she'd absorbed a ream of human interest stories about women who'd been sexually assaulted, rape victims... it made her shudder. Regardless of what Sir Ingham had said all those weeks ago, they were real women, real human beings, flesh and blood, who'd suffered. And the men: wretched bastards who'd committed unthinkable acts for the want of traumatic relationships, humiliation. This was no course for the human race to set itself on. She might have done something unspeakable herself – *might* have done, she reminded herself – but she set her jaw as she reasserted what she knew: that she was righting the course. Companionship. It would save countless women, and men, too. There would be no losers. Never had she felt such force of conviction behind what she was doing.

By the time she'd coasted through the terminal she had a slight sweat on, and it felt good. The terminal was a slick monument to JPC's grip over the local economy; a crystalline jewel with an awe-inspiring panoramic roof of a single sheet of curved glass that stretched the entirety of the terminal building, allowing passengers to glimpse into the thick rainforests sloping up and away. Nita had read or heard somewhere that this used to be one of the worst airports in the world – it was a far cry from that now, thanks to JCP's oil money. With JPC now investing in EI Systems, it was clear to see that the oil money was being used as a tremendous force for good.

In the arrivals hall a smartly-suited peppery chauffeur named Gregory greeted her with a bespectacled smile, which went someway to counterbalancing the two fearsome looking soldiers flanking him dressed in jungle fatigues, scruffy machine guns hanging round their shoulders. Security was a major issue here, according to Adem. She and the chauffeur had separately been assigned encrypted codes which recognised each other, validating the identity of the other. Everything went smoothly.

Gregory drove her in a heavy, luxurious black limousine, so thick and dumpy and heavy she thought it must have weighed close to three tons. The car was the filling in a pick-up truck sandwich; one at the front carrying the two soldiers from the airport, who sat on the back of the truck fingering their guns and scrutinising the landscape with hard-bitten vigilance, their eyes thinned by the sun. Behind her, out of view, another truck carried another couple of similarly-armed soldiers.

Nita assumed Gregory's car had autonomous drive, but if it did, the driver wasn't interested in using it. From behind a dividing pane of glass she could see him using the steering wheel, flicking the stick through the gears with well-practised hands; he'd probably been doing this for years. Weird to see someone driving a car manually. Lines of scrubby palm trees basked by the roadside on the way south. Kids played football on balding pitches, whilst people bickered and laughed and smoked and walked and bathed beneath the sun, earning wrinkles with grins. Air-conditioning prevented the sickly humidity from getting in, but she soon found she wanted to feel the heat, and commanded the windows to turn down. They didn't. No surprise, really; it looked like a very old car. She pressed the switch but that did nothing, as if it were merely decorative.

"Not a good idea to wind the window down," came Gregory's voice, high and lilting over the intercom.

"Why not?"

"Press the red button."

"What?"

"I can't hear you, Miss Rhodes. Press the red button by you to speak."

Really? A button-operated intercom? Surely JPC with all its untold oil wealth could afford slightly more advanced cars than this? She pressed the button with a sigh. "Why isn't it a good idea to open the window?"

Gregory laughed, a high-pitched titter of enjoyment which mildly irritated her. "Bad folks out there."

It didn't seem so bad. But, she supposed, there could be anything – or anyone – hiding in the thick undergrowth. Mere metres from the roads the forests plunged into darkness, hiding goodness knew what secrets. She smoothed her skirt down and sat back, trying not to let the cheerful chauffeur spoil her mood too much. On she went in her air-conditioned cocoon, impervious to the wild land outside. The car skirted around the city of Port Harcourt within fifteen minutes, and threaded its way along the main dual carriageway to the east of the city. The traffic was thicker now. She checked her watch: she was due to meet some of Joseph's personal handlers at the harbour and take a ferry out to Oil City directly. Outside, the trees gave way to a crumbling sprawl and the stink and honk of an unwashed city. Nita had been away from London many times before, but rarely to a city without a biosphere to keep the rains on. The few times she had done so were to European cities in the autumn, which could be pretty grey and miserable at the best of times. Nothing like this. Old autonomous cars whizzed along, drivers hanging out of the window and conversing, shouting, laughing with their counterparts in cars in the next lane. Other cars were driven by humans, who talked into fixed-point globelets – the old ones she'd heard of, which didn't possess flight and hover capability – as they drove along. Drones hovered in the air, clattering into one another; kids threw stones at them gleefully from the roadside, trying to bring them down without much success. Music – a drudging composite of western pop and African rhythms pounded through the limousine's chassis, making the car shake in bristling, atonal pulses. Huge lifter-manufacturer robots – bigger than the ones she'd seen at home, and presumably older – clanked away, hefting and joining great girders under the apparent direction of bickering men in yellow hard-hats in scrubby brownfield sites being converted into ominous skyscrapers that clawed upwards like giant metal corpses. On giant hovering billboards adverts for the venture – a new JPC office complex – glittered, showing exemplary citizens: suited men going to work smiling, and women tending to playing children in the yards of their suburban houses. Against the sulphurous odour of burning pit and muck something about it felt a bit sour, but she told herself that if the oil money continued to be invested this place would be regenerated beyond recognition.

Past the construction sites, the traffic crawled to a stop. Not that it worried Nita. The boat would wait for her.

The music outside crescendoed violently. Pounding thuds became fractious zaps that ripped through the air, and she looked out to see its source. She could see Gregory furiously gesticulating in the front, pounding the horn and yelling something inaudible without the intercom. A thud on the side of the car rocked it, not music any more. She yelped, recoiling from the window as the next thud crashed in. She cried out and covered her face when a rifle butt slammed against her window with a dull crunch. It didn't give. The man wielding it slammed it into the window again, making her cry out again and cover her mouth before his head jerked to the left, half his jaw ripped away, spattering the window red before he staggered off, clutching the red maul where his molars used to be.

"What the hell's happening?"

Gregory wildly signed something to the soldiers in the truck in front. They were standing upright, grimacing into their weapons, releasing shots either side of the limo. *The intercom!* She swore as her shaking fingers pressed the red button, and she spoke through rabbit breaths. "What's happening?"

"*Onibaje sote-ale!* Bastard NPF! Surprise attack!»

"The rebels? The ones who hate JPC?"

Gregory swore some more and reached into the glove compartment, where he drew out a large, heavy-looking pistol. Nita clamped her hand to her mouth. "Oh my... can they get in?"

"Ach! No. No way they will get through this armoured vehicle. Windows are chemically treated synthetic ceramics. What she lacks in brains she makes up for in tough. But you should pray to the Nigerian

God, and pray loudly, that they do not kill all our soldiers, because then we are trapped like rats. *Gbe! Gbe!*"

Nita took her finger off the intercom and shrank back in the seat. She did indeed pray, though whether it was to the Nigerian God or any other who was listening she couldn't truly say, and she prayed that the car, shocking her with shrill vibrations as bullets pinged against the chassis, would stay strong. A bullet hit the window and left no trace save for a whiny *ping* and a scuffmark.

She wanted to peer out at the violence. Not knowing her fate was intolerable, but her body refused to comply, curling itself into a ball on the far side of the back seat, knees hugged tightly to her chest. After what seemed like minutes the truck in front pulled away into a gap in the traffic. Gregory slammed his foot on the pedals, sending her careering across the backseat in an undignified heap. On her knees she saw one of their soldiers holding his machine gun one-handed, hamstrung by a wound to the shoulder, yet still he loosed bullets through gritted teeth and clenched eyes.

In seconds they were gone. Through the rear window a thin wisp of smoke curled up into the hot breeze, and a couple of men jumped onto the roofs of cars, waving their weapons in the air. They might have been whooping and hollering, but mercifully whatever brutish noises they made were buffered by the car as it tore through the traffic. She tried to say something grateful to the car, or maybe to whichever God had heard her ridiculous prayer, but nothing came out except a crackly sob.

"What just happened?" she asked Gregory once they seemed clear.

"Routine ambush. The NPF know Government soldiers, JPC soldiers. I am sorry you had to see that. It happens every few days."

His voice had lost its chirpiness, and Nita found she wanted it back. "Scare tactics. By the time the police and the army arrive, they'll be long gone."

"But our men – the ones with us – they *are* the army. Why don't they stay and arrest them?"

Gregory coughed a laugh. "Those men accompanying us are JPC's private security contractors. Not for policing the streets, but for protecting the likes of you and me and anyone else on JPC business. No, the NPF want to maim and alarm, and bring the citizens to their cause. They are not above martyring themselves for their cause."

"Do you think they knew I was here?"

He snorted out a grim laugh. "No, Miss. Your name is of no consequence to them. But you are in a JPC car, and you are fair game in their eyes."

She crinkled up her face. High on adrenalin, her skin clammy, stringing the thoughts together was difficult. "Why attack so... why attack without robots? Why fight with guns and... why endanger their own lives like that? And why attack in the middle of the main road in full view of everyone? People might have been killed."

"They always attack in the city, where they can hide in plain sight. In the marshland, human movement is easier for the machines and sensors to detect. Here," he said, waving a hand around his head. "People, people, everywhere. Easy to hide. Soldiers have to use their eyes and ears, their brains rather than all these computers. That is what the rebel bastards want. Take away the computers, you are left with a man with a gun and another man with a gun. Anyone could win such a fight. That is what they want."

A shiver ran down her spine. "So where are they based, these rebels?"

He waved his hand around again. The car bore away from the city's dust and grit, towards the harbour. On the western side of the river, a thick green wedge signalled the onset of the vast, unknowable rainforest. "Out there, some place."

When the sun punched her with heat anew at the harbour, she was glad of it. The air-con made her giddy and sick. A wonder she hadn't vomited at some point during the journey. The harbour was highly restricted, with armed guards performing security checks on all the vehicles in their small convoy, as well as all passengers and drivers. The soldier with the wound was taken away for treatment, and after passing security Nita was greeted by two handlers – burly men in dark glasses and crisp, white, short-sleeved shirts exposing dark, rigid biceps – who escorted her onto the private ferry. The regret about travelling alone bit at her. It would have felt much better – much safer – had Robb been with her; although quite what the CEO would have made of the little incident on the road earlier gave her cause to crack the weakest smile.

Even as the boat coursed along the interminably long Bonny River, away from the sweating city; even as soldiers wandered past her cabin every now and then, guns hung low and eyes cast out towards the vexing green swamps, she wouldn't allow herself to relax. Jet lag might ordinarily have caused her to drift towards some semblance of sleep, but with the negligible time difference and the rebels' attack, she was too wired to do anything, and it wasn't until the ferry – a blocky sixty-footer built for toughness rather than glamour – pulled away from Bonny Island at the very southern tip of the delta and into the open waters of the Atlantic that she allowed herself her first full exhalation in hours.

Work would help. That's why she was here. She told herself off now she was relaxed. No point moping over what some of these people had to endure every day of their lives. And if she was successful, she might even be able to do some good here. She checked her messages. One from Rik, her Head of Programmes back in London.

Nita, hope your journey to PH was pleasant and uneventful. Please find enclosed the shipping details for the first batch of robot kokeshi platforms as procured from the Home Office. You'll note Home Office and police personnel are copied into this message, as well as Edward, Head of Logistics at Oil City. The shipment is headed directly for Oil City, numbers and capability as discussed. I'll look forward to joining you soon.
Rik.

That snapped her back into place somewhat. Five hundred kokeshi, stripped and cleaned and readied for new coding and emotional tech. Rik would be joining her soon with the specialist tiger team of engineers and coders he was putting together at a moment's notice. This was the opportunity of a lifetime; recruiting wouldn't be a problem. Except for...

Salazar. She studied her fingers as she thought about him, and noticed a hangnail sticking out from her middle finger. She bit it, rubbed her chin and stared out her porthole to the choppy seas, glistening beneath razor sharp sunlight. Where the hell had he gotten to? There was still plenty to do before the actual tech started: project plans, risk assessments, state-of-the-art assessments, stakeholder needs, exploitation plans, and all the other routine reporting documentation to be drafted before anyone got anywhere near so much as a soldering iron. Joseph had earmarked some of his Oil City project managers to help with all the protocol stuff, but they'd need EIS oversight for the content. Hopefully that would give Robb and Rik enough time to find the errant sexual plastics expert and bring him back on board. It wouldn't do to have him out of her control. The sooner he was here, doing what he was good at, the better. She bit at the hangnail again, making it bleed.

Dhiraj VII

Naomi sat in the corner of the derelict house they'd happened upon somewhere between Dagenham and Rainham. Rain dotted against broken windows, and sodden draughts sought out Dhiraj as he nuzzled up close to her, shivering, knees hugged tight to his chest. He ought to have been thinking about how much farther they could get towards Tilbury, or what else they could do to remain hidden from the authorities, and above all he wanted to think about his family, but the cold and damp of the night ate away at his resolve. The one crumb of comfort was Naomi; her new skin was firm and plastic but radiated delicious warmth, and he hunched close to her to try and touch as much of it as he could. Squirming this way and that brought little comfort, though. Dhiraj closed his eyes and hoped for the gift of a few hours' sleep.

They'd spent much of the day walking away from the Spidermen's lair, towards Tilbury. Towards home. He didn't dare take a taxi or some other form of public transport – surveillance and biometric tracking might alert the authorities, so it was with a grim heart he plodded along whichever alleyways and back roads looked least risky. Naomi was no longer the kokeshi that the police and that gangster were looking for; she looked generic, shorn of everything that had made her *her*. It might have made their journey easier, but it saddened Dhiraj in a way he didn't expect. He pushed his head into her neck; it warmed the side of his face, and sent goosebumps down his neck and shoulders.

"Thank you for staying with me."

"I don't understand. It is you who are staying with me. You have no obligation to remain."

She was right. He could simply up and leave, pick up a taxi and go home, and wait for the police to pick him up. Or he could turn himself in.

Amnesty. He searched his memory, dulled by cold and insomnia, for what that meant. Maybe he could take Naomi to the nearest police station, hand her in as the robot that committed the murders at Beckton, on the understanding that he wouldn't be prosecuted. That thought gnawed at him, even as he soaked up the warmth from her body. Not yet, though. The thought of standing was more than he could bear. He rubbed his chin against the collar of his coat, scratching it with his whiskers. His fingers were black with muck, and probably blue under that from the cold. And most likely he stank.

"Would you be afraid of dying?" he asked her.

"No."

"You realise you'll never be able to do what you were designed to do now?"

"Yes. To bring people pleasure."

That surprised him. Everything he'd pictured her being subjected to in his darker moments didn't equate to pleasure, but supposedly human sexuality was a broad spectrum. That's what everybody said, anyway. "Does that sadden you?"

"No."

It still didn't sit right, regardless of what she thought about it. He'd saved her from that, at least. And for what? Most of the money had been left at Spidermen's lair, Naomi could no longer be sold on the black market, he'd gotten his friend killed and his family were likely either worried sick or cursing his name to Hell. Somewhere in the back of his mind the thought knocked at him that a normal man ought to be crying at all this, but all he could do was shiver as weird, morbid thoughts swam through him like a miasma. Tears should have come, but his eyes remained the only dry part of him; nothing rose in him except a numb sort of anger at his own listlessness.

And then he kissed her.

It was neither reciprocated nor resisted by Naomi, but when he pulled away he felt the flush of exhilaration and sickness. Guilt. He left his face a couple of inches from her own. Her lips had once looked full and luscious, yet now they were unyieldingly firm, like kissing... *a robot*. When he'd pulled her from the sea he remembered thinking her skin was perfect, flawless, a thing of beauty. That was only half-right. Now it truly was perfect, flawless, changed at a molecular level so it felt and looked like taut vinyl, with none of the soft give of flesh. Was it even the same skin? It was hideous. What had he done to her? "I'm sorry."

"For what?" she said.

"I took from you a very important thing."

"You did not take anything from me. You gave me companionship. You gave me your time. And you told me things I will not forget."

"No, I did. I took from you your being. What you're supposed to do, to be. It's like me no longer being able to fish, or raise my family. And you were so beautiful."

Naomi looked at him. Her eyes hadn't changed: swirling, bewitching fractals of ice dancing upon dark lenses somewhere below the surface. "I was designed to be beautiful."

"And I took that from you." He rolled away, back against the wall again, blinking. "Out of selfishness."

Naomi sat there, no doubt listening without formulating any opinions about the matter one way or the other.

"I want to kiss you again," said Dhiraj.

"Why? My operational capabilities have not yet been authorised. It would not provide you with pleasure."

"It's not about pleasure," he snapped. "I want to... because I think you're still beautiful."

But he didn't kiss her.

The next day was spent trudging towards Tilbury. Unable to ignore the growl in his stomach any longer, he spent a few pounds on some breakfast, and ate it on the road. They spent the afternoon in the corner of a grotty pub just outside Tilbury itself, Dhiraj nursing a cup of tea while Naomi hid outside. Gruff, smelly fishermen were a dime a dozen in this part of the world; nobody would think anything of yet another old tar huddled over a mug of caffeinated futility.

Peace befell Tilbury docks when they arrived. Not silence – boats beeped and bells tolled as they departed into open water to pursue the night's catch, while gruff fishermen's laughs and chatter lifted into the wet air, and the soft clank of the mild industry of the lifter robots as they whirred away with their loads. So hardly silent, but compared with the close headiness of London, this was peaceful enough for Dhiraj.

From their vantage point just northwest of the docks, atop a little green verge they sat awhile, absorbing the scene quietly. Usually Naomi's muted subservience in any conversation could be exasperating, but today he was grateful for the silence. Clarity was needed now. It was good to sit and think. His legs ached from the long walk, and rubbing them warmed up his fingers as well. And clarity came.

"You see the lifters by the boats, by the cranes?" He pointed down to one of the quays.

"Yes.

"You have to be one of them."

"Why do you want me to be one of them?"

"It's not about what I want. It's about keeping you safe."

"It doesn't matter if I'm safe or not."

"Can't you see that it matters to me?"

Naomi thought for a second. "Yes. I can see that."

"Do you understand that?"

"Yes, I think so. But I can't empathise. However, I can perhaps appreciate the sentiment." She placed a plastic hand upon his, warming it. "Will no-one notice me?"

They would have done, before. "No, you'll be fine. See that group of lifters there? They're working on that freighter. They're unsupervised. Can you work with them?"

She spent a moment studying the lifters and their movements. "They have an established pattern of working. But yes, I can."

"Then you should go."

He felt the heat of her glancing at him, but he didn't turn to confirm it. Instead he focussed upon the drear and drudge of the lifters going about their everyday tasks. Further along the docks he saw the bobbing lines of container ships, breakbulks, fishing skiffs, processors and tugs. Hidden somewhere behind the mesh of cranes and steel wires would be *The Lion's Mane*. Silently it called to him, the sea. Out there, a few dozen miles away from the coast lay perfect serenity, no precipitation, no more robots, no gangsters.

When he looked back, Naomi had gone.

The journey back home came remarkably easy. Head to toe he ached, and the yearning for a bath and sleep was unlike anything he'd known, yet his shoulders felt freer than they had in days.

He'd only been away from home for three days, but it looked foreign. The fleeting sense of freedom he'd gotten from jettisoning Naomi had balled itself into a series of knots in his stomach as he thought of facing his family. His was a pretty enough tree-lined avenue, with the houses set back behind the driveways and trees ringing the houses for privacy. It seemed perverse that everything he'd done under that roof – marriage, raising a son, getting and losing jobs, building up his tiny jellyfishing business – could be unravelled by... by what? Bad decisions? Bad luck?

Maybe there was no why or wherefore about any of it. He pressed his thumb to the lock and the door unlatched. Inside it was empty. Not empty of its belongings; everything was in its proper place, and indeed it looked tidier and cleaner than it had done for some time – *or maybe it's more that I stink to high Heaven* – but it felt empty. He placed a hand upon the wall in the hall and left a dirty smudge. "Shit," he said, instinctively rubbing at it with his sleeve and making it worse. *Put it on the slate, Raj.* Nobody in the front room. He kicked off his boots and knocked them under the stairs. Jesus Christ that felt good.

"Sali? Dan?"

Nothing.

The knot in his stomach tightened. Tension crept across his shoulders. His coat stuck to him like memory as he peeled it off and stuffed it sheepishly in the washer. He looked around. It was a small mercy to catch them when they were out.

Then where are the servobots?

Bathing in hot, clean water in the sanctuary of his own home was every bit as luxurious as he imagined it to be. For some time he remained there, almost asleep, thinking of how he'd explain himself to Sali. He half-hoped for her to walk in on him, naked, at his most vulnerable. Perhaps she'd pity him and simply be glad that he was returned. In the steam a terrible thought assailed him that she might not have received his voicemail. Maybe she thought he'd run off with some tart?

It wasn't until he returned downstairs that he noticed the note on the fridge: a folded up scrap of paper held in place by the magnet they bought on holiday in Estonia. Tentatively he pulled it loose, as though this crumpled leaf were the cornerstone to the whole house.

Raj,

I hope you read this note, because that'll mean you're alive. I guess even after everything you've done, I still can't wish you dead. Dan says he doesn't understand why you're gone, but he's not stupid. He reads the news, and I knew he was hiding something. He told me about that dirty secret of yours – that thing you were keeping in the garage.

We've been through a lot together, Raj, but I've never been so humiliated as to find out you were hiding something as disgusting as one of those doll things in our very own house.

In the last few days I've had to deal with police and journalists at the house. It's been tiring, humiliating, and painful. Dan is ashamed of you, and so am I.

You'll have noticed that we've left you now.

You know what really upsets me, and astonishes me? Not that you were fucking one of those horrid dolls. I'd have hated you for that but that wouldn't have made you that much different than the other brutes you hang about with at the harbour. No – it's that you had the gall and the arrogance to keep it right here and presume my stupidity. Shame on you. Shame on you, Dhiraj Om.

I'm staying at Rani's. Her and the family are as shocked and as embarrassed as we are. They shouldn't have to be put through this shit, Raj, but what else could I do?

I received your voicemail. For some reason I believe you. I have to. Because I can just about accept you using one of those things, even though it turns my stomach. But I can't accept you being a murderer. That's not you. So I believe you. I hate you right now, more than you can know, but I won't believe the very worst of what the news reporters have been saying.

I don't have anything more to say to you right now.
Sali.

By the time he'd finished reading his hands were trembling and the muscles around his eyes twitched. The paper fell to the floor as he steadied himself on the work surface. "That's all wrong," he whispered in a cracked voice. "That's all wrong, baby. Ah, shit."

The house seemed pregnant, overly hot. Sweat slicked his back and delirium disorientated his head. He'd come to the kitchen for something to eat, but all his stomach could do now was to lurch this way and that in knots. "What the hell," he said between rabbit breaths, "did you expect, you fucking fool? You fool!"

He spun round, clutching the work surface as though his life depended on it, but there was nobody there to talk to, to make sense of it all with, nobody to shout at, to tell it the way it really happened. There wasn't even a servobot to kick.

"I did everything for you!" he shouted at the piece of paper. "All of it. I made a mistake, I made a mistake. That's all." The tears came now. *So maybe you're not a monster after all*. He cracked a broken laugh at the perversity of his own feeble joke, before sinking to his knees and pawing at the piece of paper.

How long he spent like that he couldn't say, but he was pretty sure he wept himself to sleep, and he woke with a terrible pain in his gut.

Hunger. Putting it off any longer would just be counter-productive. Rummaging in the kitchen cupboards turned up some noodles, and in the freeze-drier he found some jellyfish, which he stir-fried together with garlic, spring onions, ginger and more chillis than were strictly sensible, but somehow seemed appropriate to wake him from his sloth. The resulting meal was basic but aromatic, and he posted great parcels of down into his gullet voraciously.

With his mouth burning from the chillis and his face prickled anew with sweat, his mind felt more functional. Still the mantra of his reasoning echoed around his over-spiced mouth, "I did everything for you, Sali. For you and Dan. Everything I did, I did for you." It was clear to him. He'd tried, and he'd failed, to be a better provider.

Now he didn't have to merely provide for his family; he had to get them back. Easier said than done. His lip curled up in defiance as he realised the police might still be trying to apprehend him. So be it. He'd face the shitstorm. But first he had to speak to his wife and son.

He went to the phone to call Rani. That in itself wouldn't be easy; Sali's sister Rani had long harboured a badly-hidden feeling of disappointment that her baby sister had married beneath herself. When Dhiraj had then declared he was going to become a jellyfisherman, that only sealed Rani's prejudices with airtight adamancy.

No matter. He'd dealt with gangsters, robots, illicit surgeons and destitution. His sister-in-law should be a piece of cake. He puffed out his cheeks and made his way to the phone. With no servobots around he had to use the landline.

It rang.

Tilda IV

Tilda drummed her fingers on her hip as she and Em surveyed the foyer of EI Systems in northwest London. The building's impressive reception was flooded with brilliant artificial daylight, making it seem as though the sunshine had never gone away. Tilda had never been one to yearn for hot climes, but she had to admit even fake daylight lifted her mood slightly. Glass and plastics abounded in the building, while some sort of robot was always on hand to assist, provide information, bring coffees, answer questions and generally show off the sort of capabilities for which this company was making its name.

Sure enough, the receptionist was a robot, a caucasian-style male. One of the really lifelike ones, with synthetic flesh technology. Just like kokeshi. But these ones were flat, overly friendly and without the sinister seductiveness oozing from the gears of the sexual automatons of the underworld. "May I help you?" It had a gentle Scottish Highlands accent, like her own, which amused Tilda.

"We're here for Mr Salazar Gomez," she said.

"Of course. Mr Gomez's calendar says he is currently free. Who may I say is here?"

Tilda produced her warrant card. The robot acknowledged it with a smile. "Mr Gomez is currently away from his desk. Would you like me to leave him a message?"

"No, thank you. We want to have a little talk with Salazar. It might be better if we went to see him directly. Would that be possible?"

The robot thinned its eyes, no doubt processing whether admitting a police officer beyond the site security checkpoints would be within its decision-making remit. "I will consult our security manager. He will be with you promptly." Evidently not. "Please, Detective Sergeant Boulton, feel free to take a seat while one of our hospitality bots offers you some refreshments."

Tilda offered a half-arsed smile in response before the robot walked off to greet some other visitors to the complex. She didn't feel like sitting. Sitting dulled the senses. Standing made her feel more alert. No such thoughts evidently worried Em, as her junior partner plonked herself down in one of the plush leather seats and mindlessly poked the air with her restless leg syndrome.

"Can you stop that?"

Em looked put out as she uncrossed her legs. "Sorry." A beat. "Everything ok?"

"Couldn't be better." She tapped her knee, trying to connect the dots. "Couldn't be weirder, anyway."

"How d'you mean?"

"Come on, Em," she said, making a face at her. "Don't you think there's something just a bit off about all this? I mean, look where we are."

Em made a sort of apologetic look, as though she were afraid to speak her mind. *Say what you bloody mean, Em.* "I know this place has been in the news recently, but then so have other companies. Every firm and its wife has got its opinions about what's going on with the robot attacks."

"Yes but this one's been doing a wee bit more than simply offering up a few pointed opinions."

"Maybe."

She shot Em a look. "What do you mean, maybe?"

"Well, yeah, it's off. People have been killed, injured, but it's still just one bunch of gangsters killing another bunch of gangsters. Thugs have killed other thugs for time immemorial. I admit the methods are a bit off, but really: what's new? Don't you think you're, you know..."

There it is.

"...looking for something that's not there because of, you know... what happened? These robots –"

"Are dangerous," finished Tilda. "They infect the mind. Sex is a dangerous weapon at the best of times, but usually used with a seductive touch. But this is literally weaponised sex. Doesn't sit right. Kokeshi manufacture and use has been the worst-kept grubby little secret of our so-called civil society for God knows how long. It doesn't make sense for those profiting from it so handsomely to rock the boat. I mean, bloody hell, this is tantamount to sinking the boat."

Em bit at a nail. "I suppose it is a bit odd. I think it's odd the Shkuratov twins' tip-off paid off. Le Garde are very quick, aren't they?"

Grubby little secrets the world over. Tilda had heard the rumours; everybody had. Names of people in the Government, in the Home Office, ex-colleagues, celebrities, whispered on the lips of co-workers over coffee in the morning. Kokeshi-users. People who assumed they were untouchable. 'A victimless crime' would be the excuse used by the advocates of kokeshi use. She shook her head faintly as the bullshit words swam through her head. Victimless. What a crock of shit. There's always a victim. And she hated being a victim, more than anything. The shame enraged her, and she picked at the ring finger of her left hand until it hurt, and she winced. She refused to believe mere rumours, but she knew some people must be using them, and maintaining the status quo suited such people. Le Garde didn't want to smash the French *kokeshi* rings, especially not for the sake of some weird tip-off from the Metropolitan Police. They suffered the same problems of corruption as did England. But coppers stuck together. So they did pay Tilda the courtesy of following it up with a spot of desk research and even a couple of phone calls to people in the know. Turned out two people, both who'd worked at an underground kokeshi manufacturing plant in Lyon masquerading as an aerospace tooling facility, had suddenly upped sticks and travelled to London a couple of nights ago. The Shkuratov twins weren't lying, and they knew their stuff. A quick check revealed the first thing these two French visitors did was get hit by a truck. Curiouser and curiouser.

"Yep, they are quick when they want to be."

"This Gomez, then, what do you think he knows? Could just be a coincidence."

Tilda snorted sceptically. A young, well groomed Chinese gentleman in a pinstripe suit, with wires poking out of the end of his suits sleeves and collar, beneath his skin, offered a wide smile and a hand for shaking, which Tilda and then Em accepted. His hand felt dry and firm.

"Good morning, Detectives. I'm Han, the Head of Security for the building. How may I be of assistance?"

Em explained the situation, to which Han nodded attentively.

"I understand Mr Gomez is rather new to EI Systems?" asked Tilda innocently.

"Indeed."

"Well, we don't want to cause him any alarm. We want to talk to him about the recent mugging he was subject to."

"Ah yes, nasty business, I heard about that. How unfortunate for that to happen, and on his first night in our city."

"Is there a private room which we might be able to use? We don't want to embarrass or unnerve him in front of his colleagues." She offered what she hoped was a disarming smile.

Happily, Han reciprocated. "Of course. We'll need to take some sort of ID from you at the front desk as a deposit."

"Of course."

He held out an arm, directing them towards security.

The meeting room they were given was perfect. Small, windowless, slightly stuffy.

"Who were the officers looking after Salazar's alleged mugging and RTA?" asked Tilda when they were safely tucked up in the room waiting on Salazar.

Em tossed up her globelet and tinkered with the data. "PCs Wilson and Blackstock."

A nod of affirmation.

"Hell of a building," said Em. Something about the slightly claustrophobic room forced one to talk in hushed tones, as though the very walls were part of some conspiratorial endeavour. The thought amused Tilda, and she brushed her hands over the walls, just in case there was some wryly-positioned embedded sensors or bugs. Alas, just high-quality textiles.

Tilda tossed up her globelet and set it up for iris tracking so as to make notes without any clumsy hand movements. It hovered by her seat. Gomez would no doubt be expecting them to record the meeting, and the presence of the globelet would confirm that, but he might not be expecting Tilda to make her own notes. "You can drive," she said quietly to Em, who responded with a nod.

Salazar Gomez was a strip of a man. Barely an ounce of fat hung beneath a suit that looked old but well cared for. Keen eyes flitted above the familiar dark, puffy bags of the insomniac. He kept his movements small and efficient and took the seat nearest the door, not pulling the chair completely under the table. Hardly the self-satisfied, insouciant body language of the newly-employed.

"What's this about?" he asked in a quiet Spanish inflection. "The other policemen said there was no case to answer. The other man who mugged me – he died. The driver of the truck was questioned. I gave a witness statement and was released. I just want to continue with my new position here at EIS."

"Yes, of course. How is the new job going?" asked Em with a disarming smile. She was a pretty lass when she smiled, but Tilda didn't wholly appreciate her using her girl-next-door looks to disarm their suspects. The blokes at the Yard wouldn't do it, even if they hadn't been arsehair ugly. She made a note to bring it up at a later date.

Gomez looked at Em, scepticism writ large, and shrugged his shoulders. "Well. Inductions, inductions. I'm sure you know how it is." He paused. "Please, there is a great deal I need to work on. I started late as it is because of this incident."

"Very strange that the man who died and you both came from Lyon."

He shrugged his shoulders. "Not so strange, really."

"What was your previous position?"

Gomez clenched his facial muscles. If possible his stare intensified. "Why would English police care about such a thing?"

"You've quite the colourful past, Mr Gomez," said Em.

"So?"

"Would you care to elaborate?"

"Not really. Would you?"

"Just something we uncovered in looking into the hit and run," said Tilda. "The man who died. Do you know his name?"

A beat. "He never mentioned it, but your colleagues told me his name was..." he hesitated. *You'll have to do better than that, Mr Gomez.* "...Saoud. May I leave now?"

"That's right. Chevélain Saoud. Were you aware that Mr Saoud had close ties with organised crime in France, Mr Gomez?"

The merest twitch below his left eye. Tilda recorded that with her own eye movements. A tell. He recovered to give an insouciant shrug. "In that case I –"

"Why did Saoud attack you, Mr Gomez?"

He blinked. "I... for nearly three years I was unemployed, and before that I had an unfortunate – what is it you call it? – brush with the law. I knew some bad people." He frowned, the only hint of agitation. "EIS are aware of this. I was very open with my application. I was selected for my competencies and skillset. Why is this important to you?"

Em guided her own globelet to the pictures of the Maya doll's scorched components taken at the *Tangiers Nights* club. Salazar shifted in his seat as he saw them.

"Saoud worked at the plant that manufactured this doll." An assumption based on French intel, but a calculated one, inserted to elicit another response. Salazar simply sat there, the very model of tension.

"Only a few nights ago, it was used as part of an assault," Em continued. "That's a crime committed on English soil, Mr Gomez. And we want to know what you know about it."

Gomez shifted again, his poker face cracking. Tilda placed a finger upon the side of her mouth. Duress was a funny thing. Most often, and assuming the officers were doing their jobs by the book, the duress a suspect was placed under was only as much duress as they put themselves under. Only the truly sociopathic were able to act as though nothing fazed them. This Gomez had been hardened by life but didn't seem like a monster.

"I..."

"An apparently unemployed sexual plastics engineer from Lyon travels to London, only to be followed and attacked by a man working in the manufacture of black market kokeshi. One of the dolls supplied by this plant also makes its way to London, where it seriously maims a known crime lord via a sabotaged sexual system." Em let the reality hang in the air. "You've got to admit, it looks pretty bad."

Gomez shook his head and rubbed his face. Beads of sweat appeared on his brow. "It's just circumstance," he eventually said.

"Mr Gomez," said Tilda. "In England the perpetrator of such a crime could expect Grievous Bodily Harm, possibly supply of counterfeit goods."

"Attempted murder," added Em.

"Could be. And that's before you add the charges the French

justice system will want to press for: manufacture and distribution of counterfeit goods; attempted murder again."

Gomez leaned forwards, away from the door, towards Tilda. "Are you going to arrest me for something, Detectives?"

Tilda nodded. "Probably."

"Listen, I need this job so badly. I will do anything for my daughter. Do you understand me? Anything. I needed to go straight. I made some bad decisions in my life. Can either of you say you have never made a bad decision?"

Tilda's lip twitched. "This isn't about us, Mr Gomez. It's about you. I have to admit, I admire somebody who's looking to turn their life around. We read your file. Promising career in engineering pissed away. You mentioned your daughter."

His face melted at that. "Lily."

"That's a lovely name. Can you imagine a life for her where she has to grow up without both parents?"

He shook his head, pushing the heels of his hands into creased eyes. "She would be naked without me."

"Mm. You don't strike me as the organised crime type, Mr Gomez. Indeed, you strike me as somebody who tries to do the right thing." Tilda paused, letting the air swell with pregnancy, allowing Gomez to turn the thoughts over in his mind. "We'll be working on the evidence we have to build a case. The one thing we can't figure out is *why*."

"Why what?" His voice now cracking.

"Why do it? Why sabotage a robot? And why target Mr D'Souza?"

Another pause. Em eventually spoke up. "Just got a message through from forensics. They found two DNA samples on the *kokeshi*.

The one from Mr D'Souza, and the other..." she looked up from her globelet at Gomez incriminatingly, letting him stew a little further. But this time he clammed up, and said nothing more.

Tilda sensed an impasse. All the pressure they were putting on him didn't change the fact that, just like the Spidermen, Gomez was just another jelly. No big fish. Enough of the stick. She tried the carrot. "Of course, any information you do provide, any support you give us, will be looked upon favourably by the prosecutor, I'm sure." A beat as they exchanged an icy stare.

"Ok, ok." He put his face in his hand, and puffed out a long breath, finally letting the bullshit tension out. When he was settled, he poked himself in the chest. "I am a nobody. Mr Bad Decision, that's me. But I'm not a bad guy. Let me tell you everything I know. And then we will be clear, yes?"

Tilda and Em exchanged glances, before she looked back at Gomez. Enough prodding confirmed what they thought. "Tell us what you know."

Adem IV

So much for procedure. Of course Adem had protested, citing human resources protocols, civil service terms of notice and the need to handover existing portfolios of work. He'd mentioned the need to tie up personal arrangements. That held even less sway. When Joseph Johnson wanted something, mountains would shift and oceans would boil. Suddenly those HR protocols weren't as cumbersome as they were the last time Adem checked; and those handovers could miraculously be handled by someone else. His father always liked to brag about who he could call at a moment's notice and, more to the point, who would pick up: prime ministers, presidents, CEOS, royals, regardless of what they were doing. It turned out his reach extended even to the drab, middling echelons of the English civil service.

On the balcony of his Presidential Apartment in the Executive District of Oil City, Adem watched the slow chop and slap of the ocean waves almost a hundred feet below. He'd not been here since he was in his twenties, and he always forgot how damn huge the platform was. From his balcony, even craning over the railings, he could barely see the end of the rig. Two miles square, standing a hundred feet out of the water and almost fifty miles south of the mouth of the Bonny River, it was a magnificent monument to the endeavour and ambition of men. Down at the south end of the rig was the EE District: Exploration and Extraction – teams of enormous, Tyrannosaurus-sized automated machinery dug, piped and pumped oil from the sea bed, while schools of unmanned submersibles equipped with manipulator arms explored for new oil patches, as well as conducting scientific experiments in the fields of marine biology, mineralogy, geology, conducting sample and return operations, and performing general maintenance upon the gargantuan rig where no man dare dive. Up the southern end of the rig, where Adem was, lay the Business District, a labyrinth of business complexes, corporate offices, and residential quarters for the executive officers and visiting dignitaries. Off to the eastern wing of the complex lay the Science & Engineering District. He'd be heading there soon enough to see Nita's tech demo programme kick off.

No doubt, there was a grim magnificence to this place. And while he didn't want to be here, packing Adem over here meant that his father would be officially handing the reins of the company over to him, so he sucked up his frustrations and swallowed them down for the greater good. In Adem's hands something meaningful could be accomplished by the company. He might even be able to bring Joanna back to the family table. He snorted at his foolishness; even if Joseph did announce he'd be leaving the company to Adem, it'd be just like the old bastard to live to the age of two hundred, probably just to spite him.

The moon, a huge, fat blue disc perching above the horizon, cast pale rays across the ocean. It seemed to Adem that it stared at him like a giant, unblinking eye, scrutinising him, watching his every move. It was a hot, balmy evening south of the delta, but the air conditioning made him comfortable in his linen shirt, trousers and sandals. He swirled the crystal glass of Scotch in his hand and took a sip, swirling the liquor around his mouth. Notes of butterscotch and vanilla. Very pleasant.

"Would you like a manicure, Mr Johnson?" asked one of the Servobots behind him.

He inspected his hands. Nails a bit overgrown. Hands calloused. "No, thank you. I'm fine."

"Very good. Mr Johnson?"

Adem turned to address the robot directly. All the bots here were top of the range autonomous servants based on advanced autonomy frameworks, learning capabilities and human to machine interface techniques – though none of them came from EI Systems, he noted wryly. And none of them were as uncannily human as the kokeshi that would be arriving soon. "Yes?"

"Your father has asked that you attend a family breakfast tomorrow morning in the Azikiwe Suite."

"I see. Who else will be there?"

"Just family. Your father, your brother and your sister."

He smiled at that. "Joanna is coming? My, my, wonders never cease. Why is she coming?"

The robot stared back blankly. "I'm sure I don't know. An armed guard will be sent to collect you at 0700 hours."

He sighed and raised his eyebrows in acceptance. It wasn't like he could check his calendar or refuse the order. He had the freedom of this opulent, fabulously-appointed apartment – but no more. Nobody – not even the boss's son – hell, not even the boss himself – could move without an armed guard. It was a nonsense, really: Adem knew his father's famous – and not entirely unjustified – suspicion of the NPF bastards. After all, that'd been what made him – *no,* that voice inside reminded himself – *nothing made you do it,* as fragments of images flashed in front of him: Sir Ingham's face, a glass of brandy, an innocuous package in the post. The thoughts made him suddenly go off his whisky, and he put it aside.

But even the NPF would be able to infiltrate Oil City. They were dangerous out in the city and delta, but out here, the sea and isolation were much more ferocious enemies.

Patience, Adem, he told himself. *Soon this will be named as yours.*

As he considered going back to the whisky for another taste, his phone rang through the holoscreen mounted on the far wall. It was Nita.

"Good evening, Nita," he said with a smile.

"Hi Adem," she said. She looked tired, her usual lustre fading just a little with her hair tied in a knot, and a lack of makeup around the eyes. Large glass of white wine beside her. Perhaps not used to the West African sun. She wouldn't be the last. "How are you?"

"Very well. I have this magnificent apartment, and all the whisky I can drink. Which is not very much, for I sadly seem to have gone off it for now. To what do I owe the pleasure?"

"I just phoned for a chat."

"Oh." He couldn't recall her ever just phoning or meeting 'for a chat'. But the company would do him good. "How was work today?"

She sighed. "Tiring. Long hours. The tech programme is still in early phase reporting: a reccy on state-of-the-art, looking at commercial exploitation processes..."

He thinned his eyes. She didn't phone him to talk about commercial exploitation processes. "Why the hell do you need an exploitation process? We both know what the dolls are going to be used for. They're going to be used by workers, soldiers, out here and back onshore, to provide them with companionship, and –"

"Yes, I know," she said, irritably. "It's just protocol, standard research project paperwork."

The silence hung between them, and Adem decided to go for another sip of drink after all. As he did so, Nita took a draught from her own glass. "I understand the first consignment of the dolls from London are to make their way here tomorrow morning."

"Yes," she said. "Logistics will be bringing them aboard the rig first thing tomorrow. I'll be there to take a quick inspection at ten o'clock before conference calls all day."

"You mean ten hundred hours," he said, gesticulating with his glass, clinking the ice melodiously against the crystal.

She gave a weary smile at that. "God, yes. I had no idea it'd be so military here. I mean, in the city, yes, but here, bloody miles from anything... and that's another thing. I found out today there's a bloody runway on the rig. Why was I left to run the gauntlet of the bloody city in a car? I could have bloody died."

Adem rubbed a hand over his face, and held up a placating hand. "My father's army is the best. You were never in serious danger, I'm sure."

That didn't seem to placate her at all. "You weren't there! Guns and crazy people and cars, it was like a bloody warzone."

It is *a bloody warzone.*

"Why couldn't I be flown in via a connecting flight?"

"You have to expect this. My father is very keen on what he calls 'power positioning' – showing power, aggression, control. To have his private army, all cultivated from the Government, on his land, guarding his technologies and his assets. To make new visitors 'run the gauntlet' as you say through the city; it's so you understand, you truly understand what it means to work in a place such as this. It's a statement to both his friends and his enemies."

"And which are you today?"

She clearly meant it as a joke, but Adem's brow darkened, and he pointed directly at the screen. "Do not say such things. I know you joke, but if the wrong person hears..." he waved his glass around the apartment, implying it might have ears – *and who knows?* She looked deflated by the reprimand, and he immediately regretted being so sharp. They were in this together, and he didn't want to see her fail. "Look, Nita. For what it's worth, I agree with you; it's excessive to have this much military presence out at sea, but it's good to keep the rebels at bay. You've seen what they're like now. Imagine the carnage they could cause if they could reach us here. But you also have to be wary. My father isn't a trusting man, and with good reason. There are people out there who would happily see him dead. Here, he can ensure that everyone is under his control."

She peered sheepishly into her wine glass. "Sorry. I'm not angry at you, Adem, really. I'm pleased to be here. I'm just tired, exhausted. But I'm excited about getting the work started. The facilities here are first class."

Adem took another sip.

"Shall we meet for lunch tomorrow?" she asked. "Not in the Business District; in your apartment, or mine."

Was that code for something else? "I thought you said you had calls all day?"

"Come on, Adem, I'm the Technical Director of a billion-pound R&D programme. I'm sure I could find some excuse to liaise with the head regulator."

Head regulator. *For now*. It was important that he kept his position as Head Regulator for as long as possible to ensure that the regulator's position and ambitions were well aligned with this programme. He'd probably have to get back to London at some point.

"I've breakfast at seven tomorrow. I've a feeling it'll be quite an important one. Our sister is gracing us with her presence. After that, I'm sure I can spare some time."

"At mine?"

"Probably best to meet in the mess hall." He waved his glass around. "Then..."

She nodded, and flicked the screen off, and the rest of the whisky burned.

D'Souza V

Port Harcourt had its own intoxicating smell: a sickly concoction of palm oil, smoke, blood, and more than anything, heat. It took the occasional zephyr drifting up from the sea to bring the more delicate scents of wood, coconuts and the sea. Ah, the sea. It smelt different than it did in Negombo. What did it smell of back then? He couldn't quite remember; the images of white sand that once were sharp now were frayed and fragmented and didn't quite add up in the same way. But the smell of salt was always the same. It cut through the air and took him straight back to the shimmering aquamarine of the Indian Ocean, eating flame-grilled prawns with fire-hot chillis with his mother. One day he'd be back there.

But not today.

Stiff morning breezes caught hold of his memories and whisked them away as he walked around the harbour, getting his bearings. The delta was bigger than he'd anticipated – a vast, green swamp leeching far beyond his field of vision to the river Niger, which broke down into myriad trickling veins that reached out into the Atlantic. Behind him, the black crown of smoke over the city's eastern horizon whispered into the wind. Its faint but unmistakeable acridity had moved D'Souza to ask the computer in his autonomous car what it was.

It replied with a soft German accent, causing D'Souza to stifle a snort. "The fire comes from the Trans Amadi Open-Air Slaughterhouse. It was made a UNESCO World Heritage site early in the twenty-second century. The fire used to be fuelled by tyres, but now it is sustained each morning by advanced thermoplastic. The butchers who work at the slaughterhouse butcher hundreds of cows, goats and other meat each working day."

On and on the car spoke, but he tuned it out. The abstract shroud of death greeting the city each day was more interesting than the minutiae of its causes. A twinge between his thighs made him shift and focus, turning his wonder to a crisp snarl. Next to him, in a leather case, lay his *ethunu kaduwa*, which he patted affectionately. It boded well that he had come to a place shadowed by death to deal it out. Especially so as he'd not given thought to what his strategy might be. Driven most of his life by the need to manoeuvre, calculate, judge and take decisions, now all that propelled him was urge. The urge to dispense justice and right the wrongs that had been exacted against him.

It wouldn't be easy to get into Oil City, but he'd manage it. Upon reaching the city, he'd loitered around the port area for the best part of a day, watching the boats come and go from a safe distance, observing. Eventually a couple of police had tried to move him on, motioning to him to grease their palms to ease his passage. Corrupt cops were his favourite types. In exchange for a few extra banknotes, he'd asked them how he could get to Oil City, and they directed him to the taxis, telling him to go to a little shantytown called Isaka, where he should speak to the rivertaximen. So he'd taken a taxi south out of the city, towards the sprawl of the delta.

"Sir," the car said. "The Nigerian Government recommends that tourists do not travel amid the delta beyond the Bonny River. The area is populated by hostile anti-Government insurgents. There have been occurrences of foreign tourists being captured or attacked."

D'Souza stroked the case containing his *kaduwa*. Rebels. He'd spent most of his adult life smacking down rebels of some sort or other. Whatever tinpot grievance these local hicks were trying to weaponise held no interest for him. Were he to be accosted, he'd show them the colour of his mettle.

He alighted at Isaka, a few miles south of the city, where the road became a slushy vignette of gravel, dirt and mud. Just to the west D'Souza heard the gentle lap of the Bonny River, and he followed his ears. River taxis bobbed on a series of wooden jetties, golden-green with the stain of sunlight and silt, their grinning captains dangling skinny legs into the water. Slow business. If indeed this place could be said to have anything approaching business at all. Among the bleached tin roofs, the scummy river silt lapping at the reeds, and fat, headscarfed women descaling perch and other freshwater fish under the baking midday sun, there was a decency here that wasn't in the crudity of the city a few miles north. He wondered if tourists ever ventured this far south. There certainly wasn't much to look at if they did. Rubbing his hands, greased and overheated, on his shirt, he knew he didn't look like the average tourist. The river taxis were old powerboats, dirt cheap, with no robots or anything; just the guts and intuition of the man with his hand on the throttle. And if that failed, pairs of oars were lashed to the sides of most of them. Manpower.

"Speak English?" he called down to the rivertaximen as they jabbered to one another. They stopped, looked him up and down from the jetty, replying only with silence. One of them said something, making the others laugh. One leapt up in his small vessel, the keen balance of his feet, legs and back hinting at a life of being a boatman. He took a black cigarette from behind his ear and lit it with a Zippo before pointing it at D'Souza. Even from up by the dirt track he could smell the strong, unfiltered tobacco.

"I speak English," he said. "You're a long way from the city, tourist."

"I'm no tourist. I'm here on business."

The man grinned. "Even farther away, then." A deep drag on his cigarette. "You don't look like a businessman."

I don't feel like any sort of man. "I was told by police in Port Harcourt you could get me to Oil City?"

Two of the other men let out cackling, exaggerated laughs, slapping their thighs. The smoking man nodded with a huge grin and pointed the cigarette at D'Souza again. "You want to go to Oil City?" He cocked a thumb at his boat. "In this? Ok, friend, but you better have a million dollars in your bag. Or a helicopter."

"Or an army!" hollered one of his mates, to more whoops.

D'Souza clenched his jaw and clicked his neck joints into place. These shantytown hicks were no use. "What's the farthest town south of here, before the ocean?"

Smoking Man drew out the last of his tar, pushed it through his nostrils and tossed the dog-end overboard. "Friend, do yourself a favour. Turn around, and go home, back to the city. You do not want to go south of here. A little further south is NPF country."

The other men's jollity sank into sullen silence.

"Who are the NPF?"

"They hate the Government. Bad people. Used to be not so bad, but.... Uh-huh. They see you, with your expensive bag and clothes..." Smoking man made a whooshing noise as he flicked his thumb across his own throat. "You are *nothing* to them. Government cannot track them, deep in the delta. They think nothing of slicing your throat, taking your money, throw you into the Bonny. Another missing man." Maybe sensing the tension, he put on another grin and threw his hands up. "But enough NPF. Perhaps I take you north, or east, through the–"

"I just want a tour," D'Souza said. The men were right, these powerboats wouldn't even get close to the offshore megalopolis of Oil City. But if the corrupt cops were right, perhaps these people could at least be able to tell him how he might. "I'm not worried about the danger. I just want a conversation with you. I will pay for the privilege, and I pay well."

Smoking Man jumped up onto the jetty and walked up to the dirt, his flip-flops slapping against his heels. "Who are you, friend? Newspapers? Police?"

D'Souza snorted a laugh. "I'm my own... person." He opened his jacket, a thin leather thing he'd picked up at the airport – far too hot to be sensible but still offered pockets and a whiff of protection – and brought out a roll of notes, flicking his thumb across the end.

Smoking Man turned to his mates, one of whom tugged at his shorts from the jetty, muttering something D'Souza couldn't understand. After a curt few words exchanged in their own language, Smoking Man clicked his fingers and made a kind of "*aye aye aye*" noise under his breath. "How much?"

After prices were agreed, D'Souza clambered aboard the

little powerboat owned by Smoking Man and hauled his gear aboard. Travelling light was a necessity: in lieu of an actual plan, he'd need fleet-footedness and the ability to adapt. No problem there: all his life he'd had to think on his feet and push himself along with instinct. The air downriver was thicker and moister, sliced open only by the buzz of the boat's motor and the splash of the water beneath them. Smoking Man said little and less at the aft end of the boat, but sang much and more, perhaps a local folk ditty, as he steered them along the Bonny, a cigarette hanging from the corner of his mouth.

This river was no Thames. The vein meandering its way through London was a sterilised, perfect thing, so pure a man could see his face in it. Deducing what lay beneath the murk of the Bonny's surface was all but impossible. Solid land was farther away from the riverbanks here, separated by green, boggy marshlands glimmering under the incessant sun, and everywhere, everything was flat, flat, flat. Glistening just further south was a hint of ocean, sparkling wildly, a crouching, golden tiger stalking the world of men just below the horizon. It reinforced just how far away this Oil City was. People in Port Harcourt said it was eighty kilometres from the delta. Getting there would be a near impossibility; yet disheartenment was an emotion he seldom hosted, and he'd be damned to Hell if he did so today.

"How far is the ocean?" he asked Smoking Man.

"Far."

"And where are these NPF?"

"All around."

D'Souza looked around. Not a soul to be seen. Further afield, past the bogs there were hints of human activity: huts, lines that might have been dirt tracks, the occasional abandoned speedboat or piece of flotsam or jetsam stuck in the reeds, bobbing without direction. "Seriously. How do I get to Oil City?"

"Seriously, you say? The best way would be go back to Port Harcourt, and smuggle yourself aboard one of the shipping containers. They say they smuggle *aṣẹwó* – what you call them? whores – in shipping containers bound for the rig. It's possible."

D'Souza stifled a grim laugh. That'd be ironic. "Ok. Who do I speak to?"

Smoking Man tossed another dog-end into the river, where it landed with a fizz. "Why do you want to go there so bad? You NPF?"

"No."

"You won't make it to Oil City."

"Why not?" Instead of an answer came the slow death of the boat's engine grinding to a halt. D'Souza turned around to see Smoking Man holding a knife, the sharp end pointing at him. It had been a dog of a day, and fatigue had been creeping into his bones, but sight of the knife brought him round, pricking his senses and tensing his muscles, gripping the side of the boat with his right hand. Time seemed to slow a little as he took control of his breathing, allowing him to take stock of what was happening. Clearly Smoking Man was no killer; an amateur at best. Killers don't show their hand, much less their weapon. So this was just the intimidation of another dumb tourist. Nevertheless, a knife was a serious thing, not to be taken lightly. Even a dumb amateur could do hideous things with a knife. The faint buzz of engines sounded somewhere in the distance, becoming gradually louder.

"Give me your money, friend."

The two other boats swung into view; two of the other river taxis from the shantytown. D'Souza pushed out a little laugh. "I'm not giving you my money. Unless you intend to use that, I'd put it away."

A film of sweat shone on Smoking Man's forehead, and the muscles around his eyes twitched. D'Souza had killed men before, and his gut told him that he was the only person in this boat to have done so. It was a hell of thing, a hell of thing to take a man's life. You either knew about it – the stench, the gore, the panic – or you didn't. The sight of a knife was enough to induce nauseating terror in a lot of folks; and for some folks even the thought of using one was enough. Smoking Man looked pretty terrified of the thing he held before him. D'Souza placed his left hand upon the leather case of his *kaduwa*. All wrapped up it could have been something as innocuous as a snooker cue, but he knew if he went for it he could be stabbed four or five times before he even unzipped the case. Best leave it be.

"How many men have you killed this way?" he asked, as the other boats drew to a halt a few yards either side of them. Somewhere around him a mosquito buzzed loudly.

A hand opened, palm up, begging. "Money. Now."

"Why do you want my money?"

Smoking Man curled his face up in a half-hearted snarl, but his face cracked. "Everybody takes from us. First the government take our land. Then the oil companies take our resources. Then the rebels, they take our people. *Take take take*, that is all we know. We have to take to survive. Friend, we don't want to kill you."

"I know."

The two other men drew up their boats, brandishing crude pocketknives. Just as scared and apprehensive as their mate. Poor bastards. Nodding, D'Souza slowly pulled out the roll of banknotes from his jacket and held it in front of him. Inevitably, Smoking Man's gaze flickered to the wad. It was enough time for D'Souza to launch himself forward, grab Smoking Man's wrist and dive out of the boat, yanking Smoking Man down with him into the warm brown of the Bonny with a splash.

Cries went up above the waterline. The current sucked strong, pulling at his legs and bringing them down into the froth. He couldn't be sure if his eyes were open or not, the riverwater was so filthy dark. When he felt something slimy but strong slide past his face, he almost froze. *Riversnakes!* They might be *really* dangerous. Clenching his teeth, he kicked out and burst through the surface. The three boats had separated, and he was already a few yards downriver, the current extending it with each second. He grabbed the side of Smoking Man's boat and spat out a mouthful of sandy water. The other boatmen pointed to a patch of thrashing water and proceeded to haul their friend aboard. A yowl of pain went up. As they were distracted, he bobbed around the other side of the boat and grabbed his *kaduwa*. The three of them had rallied, and lurched the motors into action.

No use trying to swim away. Umbrellas of fat reeds bobbed lazily by the riverbank for ever in both directions, lolloping into the filthy river. Cover as good as any. So it was that the boatmen passed D'Souza after he'd made his way to the western bank and ducked under the reeds, peeking out from between the tendrils, and a few minutes later passed him again on the way back to the shantytown. Only then he allowed himself to let out a breath that seemed like he'd been holding for hours, and he cursed at his stupidity. How could he be so idiotic? It was as if his brains had been cut out along with his cock. He dragged himself and the few belongings he had left onto the sludgy bank, made it a few yards onto firmer ground, coughing up brown water with splutters that hurt his gut. Eyes stinging, boots filled with black muck, and shaking like a baby as the adrenaline left him, he collapsed. His legs ached, lungs burned, and the mud sticking to one side of his face quickly became freezing cold as the wind caught it.

What the fuck have you done? He asked himself. When the dark green flats of the delta provided no answer he asked again. Away to the west, across the river, the sun shone on him, weakly warming him. It wouldn't be too long until sunset, and there was the possibility of it becoming pretty cold overnight. And he needed a piss. Reflex, memory, instinct, a lifetime of knowing pushed his hands to his trousers, ready to pull them down and pull out his cock to piss on the ground, when he stopped. Dark things lay down there; an unknown wilderness hiding something rotten, something corrupt. He couldn't bear to explore any longer. Humiliated, he pissed himself, and wept.

A weaker man might have let the terrible fatigue that was upon him guide him to sleep, but he wasn't weak. And as for being a man... he pushed up onto all fours, and blew some black mucus out of his nose. The grass was tall here, almost up to his hips, long and slippery. He yanked a handful out of the earth, screwed it up and tossed it into the breeze. He'd be damned if he gave up now. The scent in the air was the hot tang of sulphur and salt, and all around was the soft lilt of crickets and buzzing insects looking for a meal. The thought of the snake gave him the shivers; a vague recollection of cobra charmers in Sri Lanka came to him; sometimes the cobras would jerk forwards, making the boy D'Souza jump and clasp his mother's legs with a smile; but the charmers, skinny little men in cheesecloth shirts and not much else, didn't flinch at all. It suddenly seemed stupid that a snake, a coiled machine capable of killing a man, could be considered such sport. This wasn't home.

Upriver he tried to get a glimpse of the shantytown, but there was nothing. Must have been five or six miles away – it'd easily be dark by the time he reached it, but reach it he must; the thought of spending the night out here filled him with dread. From there he could summon a taxi, and get back to the city, and start again. He blew out hard, steadied himself, gripped the handle of his *kaduwa* case, and walked north.

The first rustle in the grasses pricked up his senses. Snakes again, maybe? He spun around, but saw nothing in any direction. His heart quickened and seemed to pound louder than a hundred cannons. Sweat pricked his brow when the second rustle came, and quietly, smoothly, he unzipped the case of his weapon and gripped the handle tightly. Time for a deep breath – *one, two, three, four*, held it – *one, two, three, four*, blew out – *one, two, three, four* – and kept his lungs empty – *one, two, three, four*. His heart rate slowed as he repeated the process. Whatever it was, he was ready.

The second rustle came from behind him, but when he turned whatever it was had gone, and he never saw the bag brought over his head until he was inside it. The drawstring drew tightly around his throat, and after a few seconds the world went as black as the bed of the Bonny River.

Tilda V

Tilda went alone to Boswell's office while Em stayed in the open-plan and finished her reporting. The DI might not have agreed to see her had she not pressed the need for urgency on the way over. Outside, she bit at a nail while she waited. It was colder up here on this floor, and she pulled her collar around her neck. Maybe it wasn't colder – could just be the thoughts giving her chills.

Thoughts of Fraser passed through her head, and she wondered what he might be doing now. Probably having his dick serviced somewhere. Little matter; he'd already shaped the rest of her existence. It was he who'd led her to this point. She decided she should be thankful to him. To think she used to be so ignorant of the damage these kokeshi could do. Not any more, not since that day. And now, after what Gomez had said, she could wipe out these things for good. It all seemed perfectly logical – however perverse – that EI Systems would seek to capitalise on the kokeshi murders, but that they could have instigated the deaths was sensationalist stuff. The idea of these things being legalised made her stomach turn, almost to the point of sickness. How many other women would have to suffer if those things were made legally viable? She closed her eyes and blew out a breath sharply through her nose. Composure – that'd be key. The auto PA called her in.

DI Boswell was a well-rounded man, in several ways. He was well into his eighties now, but when Tilda had joined the Force he'd still been a Sergeant, and a bit of a silver fox, but a couple of steps up the promotional ladder had led to increased exposure to the corporate dinner circuit, of which his gradually accrued corpulence and ruddy cheeks were symptomatic. Still, he was a good man. Fair. When the force had rolled out AI to do many of the jobs at the top and bottom of the food chain, it meant high-ranking DIs like Boswell became more senior.

"Afternoon, DS Boulton," he said between sips of tea. "Please, sit."

She asked the servobot for a water, ice cold. "Thanks for seeing me, sir."

"Not at all. I don't have long, though. Meeting with the Super. So, what's the issue? You said it was urgent."

"Indeed, sir. I wanted to discuss a matter of strategy with you relating to the kokeshi case."

He set down his pen just so upon the leather desk pad and looked out from under bushy brows. "Strategy?"

"Indeed. My team on Cyber have been digging, and there are some weird connections we've uncovered between the deaths and EI Systems, the robotics firm."

His eyebrows twitched, a sign he was interested. "They're rather the hot topic at the moment."

"They appear to be well positioned to exploit this string of incidents to their advantage."

"Come on, Tilly. However distasteful one might find that, it's not illegal."

"It would be if they engineered the whole thing for their own ends. A lead – a Spaniard who's just come over to work for EI Systems from France – has said as much, that the company's technical director bribed him with a job and Christ knows what else in exchange for some sort of black market sabotage, leading to grievous bodily harm."

"GBH? Surely you mean murder?"

Tilda shifted in her chair. "No, I mean injuries. Serious injury. Using bots to maim is still wounding with intent."

"Have you any proof?"

"This guy practically admitted it."

"And what about proof of EI Systems' involvement?"

"Not yet. Just this statement made by the Spaniard Gomez; enough for an arrest."

"So make the arrest."

"That's the thing. Nita Rhodes, the technical director, the one implicated - she's currently in Nigeria on business. Something stinks of shit about this whole thing."

"Mm." Boswell ruffled his brows and moved his lips around exaggeratedly, as if sucking a boiled sweet. "And you think she's on the run?"

"Don't know. I think she's been sloppy. We need to question her."

"If your team can provide a compelling case, then it would be up to the EPU to try to detain her. In the meantime, it sounds like your team have an arrest to make. This Gomez character practically admitted to several chargeable counts. I'd say go get him."

"Yes, sir." EPU. Extraditionary Processing Unit, a department within the Home Office. Allowing any investigative procedure to sink slowly into the sclerotic swamp of central Government always filled her with despondency, but this time it bit slightly harder. Still, no use arguing it with Boswell. *It's just procedure.* Getting an extradition process in theory could happen quite quickly, but in practice rarely did. EI Systems would be the key. "I'll follow up investigating EI Systems."

"Good show."

Outside Boswell's office, Tilda loosened her collar and ran her hand through her hair. The spikes were wet with sweat. Recollections of the kokeshi she'd encountered in *Tangiers Nights* and *Fantasia* swam through her head; their pouting, smiling faces writhing together, teasing her with the arrogance and assuredness of their seduction. In between them, between their grotesque, perfect breasts, she caught a glimpse of Fraser. He turned to look at her, and before she knew it she blurted out his name, "Fraser."

"Til?"

Tilda snapped her head round. Em. Giddy from the dream, she pinched the bridge of her nose and squeezed hard, eyes closed.

"You alright, Til?"

"Yeah, fine."

"You mentioned Fraser."

She shot Em a dirty look. "No, I didn't."

Em looked nonplussed. "You did."

"I did not, Detective Constable."

Em blinked. "Look, if this is getting to you..." she placed a soft, patronising hand on her arm and continued with a suitably soft, patronising voice. "I know this has got to be hard, after what happened, but..."

Em didn't expect the push, and neither did Tilda; it just happened, and before they both knew it Em fell backwards onto her arse, shock writ on her face. "Nothing fucking happened, DC Davis." Was it nothing, though? Tilda's jaw quivered, her hands balled into fists, and she felt so damn cold.

"What on earth is happening out here?"

Tilda closed her eyes again and bowed her head. Boswell. She turned to face his fat little head. "Sir, I..."

"You pushed DC Davis. Are you ok, Emma?"

"Fine," said Em, getting to her feet. For once the inane grin had been wiped from her face, and that shitty feeling of guilt speared itself through Tilda. "I..." *No use in denying it.* "Jesus, I'm so sorry, Em."

"I was just trying to help, Til."

"Help what?" asked Boswell.

Tilda began to answer, but Boswell cut her off. "I was speaking to DC Davis." Tilda buttoned her lip.

"DS Boulton looked slightly distressed. She mentioned the name of her ex-husband to no-one in particular, and when she noticed me she pushed me away."

Boswell harrumphed under his brows. He'd never been an angry man. Always fair. Tilda sighed. She knew what fair would mean now. "Do you need any help, Tilda? No-one would blame you, after what happened with Fraser, if you considered this case to be..."

"Will everybody stop treating me like a fucking child?" Tilda threw her arms up, startling the others. Amid the buzz and click of an open-plan office came the deepening silence as co-workers rubbernecked over their partitions to catch a glimpse of the commotion. Only the robots, servobots, and databots, went about their business, uninterested. Ironic. "Look, I'm sorry, I can..."

"DC Davis, go back to your station. We can catch up later. You've got work to do?"

"Lots of database work to go through."

"Get to it, then. As for you, Tilda, come back inside."

Boswell set his office windows to tint, allowing some privacy. "Take the rest of the week off. You look exhausted and stressed. You've uncovered some good leads, and done some good work. That will all count in your favour–"

"My *favour*?" That didn't sound good.

Boswell firmed up his flabby face as best he could, but couldn't completely prevent a slight jiggle of the jowls. He spoke lowly. "Tilda, I saw you through my window push Emma over, and then use abusive language towards her. In full view of the department! This is going to have be logged as a PQES incident." Christ, that was all she needed, for the wonks at Police Quality, Ethics and Standards to get their claws into her. As Tilda rolled her eyes and motioned to speak, he raised a podgy finger, ushering silence. "Emma is a good DC, and I know you have a good relationship. She likes you a lot. She's probably out there defending you as we speak."

That much was true, and it didn't do anything to assuage the knotty guilt in her gut.

"Hopefully this can be dealt with swiftly and without damaging repercussions to anyone involved. You would do well to heed my advice and *take the rest of the week off*."

The compulsion to push back and fight, to explain herself, had to be swallowed like bile, and a generic utterance of compliance fell out of her mouth.

The truth was she *was* tired. Running on fumes. Sometimes it wasn't possible to even see that until you stopped. A few eyes were on her as she walked through the department. She stopped at Em's desk, and thought about saying something but, thinking of the inevitable PQES, she erred on the side of silence, instead offering a brittle half-smile. Em reciprocated with her own half-smile. Good copper, Em. What an idiot she'd been to her.

Normally Tilda would use a brollybot in the rain, but tonight she decided to walk home without one. It wasn't too far a walk from Scotland Yard down to Lambeth, and the rain felt refreshing. Halfway across Westminster Bridge, her collar pulled tight around her rain-slicked neck, she stopped to look eastwards along the twinkling Thames, its tide chopping away rhythmically under the rain. Even under the night's cloud the water was crystal clear, which made her smile. Apparently before the development of in-situ autonomous submersible water treatment systems, back in the twenty-first century, the river had been the colour of tea. That seemed so weird. Nowadays one could almost see the riverbed. Below, the beautiful glowing shapes of the robotic fishes darted this way and that, gulping up the water and filtering it for impurities, keeping the water perfectly clear.

Maybe it wouldn't be so bad to take a break from work. She'd been a damn fool to let her emotions rule her and push Em like that. *Damn you, Fraser Duffy, for entering my thoughts. And damn me for letting you in.* Standing in the rain allowed her some clarity. Complying with the PQES box-ticking exercise would have to be done; she'd have to stay in control of herself better from now on; master herself, and look after herself. That would mean food and sleep.

"Is everything ok?"

Tilda turned with a start. To her right stood a middle-aged man in a warm looking overcoat and dark leather gloves, snug and dry beneath the whirr of a brollybot. Suddenly aware of her sodden appearance, the decision not to take a brollybot from the station seemed a regretful one.

The man spoke again. "Sorry, did you hear me? Are you alright? Do you want to come under here, into the dry?"

"Ah, no, I mean yes, if that's no trouble."

As she brushed the rain from her hair he looked back out across the river. "Looking at the fish?"

"Yeah, sort of. Been a rough day. I'm on my way home, though. Thanks for the dry."

"I see. I'm on my way home, too. I'm heading to Battersea. Whereabouts are you?"

"Oh, I'm in Stockwell. Why aren't you in a car?"

He smiled. Attractive, in a weather-beaten sort of way. Although probably not as weather-beaten as she looked right now. "I've been to a dinner. Few glasses of wine. The car always makes me feel a bit queasy after a few drinks, so I took a walk. The car will be at home waiting for me. Anyway, I like walking in the rain." He looked her up and down with a wry smile. "Evidently not as much as you do."

She could have sworn she blushed. That was a pretty alien feeling. Apart from her colleagues she'd not spoken to another person for God knows how long, and she hadn't been approached by a man for even longer. Not since, well, *him*. "Yeah. I forgot my bot. Lots on my mind."

"Come on, I'll walk you home." He offered her the crook of his arm, and to her great surprise, she took it. Before she knew it, they were walking. "Do you look at the fish often?"

"Not really. I don't know why I was looking at them. They look so free."

He laughed, a knowing, affectionate little laugh, and nudged her in the shoulder. Not a cruel one. Laughs could be cruel, sometimes. "You know they're not real, don't you?"

"Yeah. Just the jellyfish left. Such a shame."

"I'm Derek, by the way."

"Tilda."

"Nice to meet you, Tilda."

The walk home was pleasant enough, and the warmth of his overcoat reinforced the decision not to go without a brollybot anymore. When they reached the turning to her road, she stopped.

"This is my road. I'll see you."

"Right, of course. You'll be ok?"

"Yeah, I think so." Her pulse quickened, just the tiniest amount, and her eyes felt bright, in spite of what tiredness lay behind them. As she slipped out of his arm she kept hold of his hand, and found herself smiling. Fraser had always said she looked beautiful when she smiled. Maybe that's why she'd spent so long scowling at the world. Derek looked with some confusion at his hand in hers, and she leant in to kiss him.

When he pulled away, alarm hit her, and the crutch of his hand was no longer there. She was getting soaked again.

"I'm sorry," he said, looking at his navel. "I'm sorry if you got the wrong idea. I was simply walking you home. I wasn't... I'm a married man."

Embarrassment shook the warmth from her. Of course. Only she could have the stupidity to make a pass at the one man in London who wasn't merely acting like a gentleman to get something in return. She breathed out. "I'm sorry..."

"Look, you're very attractive," he said. "But my wife's at home. Maybe if you were one of those robot dolls..."

That sucked the air from her lungs. She blinked, and her insides turned to ashes. Her mouth dry, she pushed out the words, "Go, get away from me."

To indistinct words of confused protest from the man, she splashed towards her flat, almost bent double, trying to keep down the sick. Not again. By the time she was through the front door she was soaked anew, shaking and in tears, but made it to her flat without bumping into any of her neighbours.

A peep through the bedroom blinds brought no view of him. He'd gone, so she allowed herself to weep, crumpled upon the bed. As much as she wanted to pity that bastard's wife, whoever she was, she was wrapped up in herself. How could it happen again? The crushing, sucking rend that turned her stomach to dust and filled her with worthlessness and shame. What was she? Fraser had told her she was beautiful, but in the end it had all been a castle of lies; pretty words couldn't disguise the fact that she didn't measure up to lines of code and a few advanced materials. *You should have stayed cold, you stupid girl*, she told herself.

Night set in before she relocated the steel in her belly and set it right. When she did she had an awful, teary ache behind the eyes. Her gut gnawed angrily in shame, hunger and sickness. The bizarre thought came to her: artificial emotions. That's what they were working on. They were making everything she was feeling, all this suffering, into a mere construct. All that Tilda Boulton was and all she had, they could replace. And then what would she become?

A nothing, a ghost, a cipher of a woman, a shadow of obsolescence existing far beyond the point of any use, physical, emotional, human. And it was a *woman* doing this. Her jaw clenched. She clasped hold of the fear, the rage, the hate, the self-pity and held it close. If it was to be superceded by a handful of code, she was going to use it while it lasted.

She commanded her servobots to get cleaning, make her a hot chocolate – refusing the temptation of a large glass of wine – and turn the heating on. As the bots busied themselves, she immersed herself in pleasingly comfortable pyjamas and clambered into bed, the television readied. An almost alien level of comfort and contentedness washed over her, as her eyelids were dragged south through the combination of tiredness, hot drinks, comfy bed and dross on the holographic screens around her.

"*The Chief Executive of the company, Robb Gould, has signed the agreement for the major technology demonstrator alongside the President of JPC, Joseph Johnson, the English Foreign Secretary, the Minister for Energy, and the Nigerian Minister for the Interior. The deal was signed at Oil City, the offshore drilling and processing plant eighty kilometres south of the Niger delta.*"

That made her blink and force her eyes open. The newscaster's commentary accompanied images blurred by half-sleep, scrolling along one of the holoscreens. She rubbed her eyes again. A line of people, powerful people, at the press conference for the agreement and launch of a major tech programme. No journalists present; only bots connected with cameras and connected by conference around the world. Tilda rubbed her eyes. *Go to sleep*, she told herself. *It's out of your hands now.*

The newscaster continued. *"The deal will seek to demonstrate the use of artificial emotional capability in robotic workers, and is funded by JPC. Controversially, the robotic platforms being used as testbeds for the testing and verification of this technology are to be the kokeshi, or sex dolls, that have been apprehended as a result of the recent regional amnesty in London."*

There, along the line of people present at the signing, was Nita Rhodes, smiling warmly, hands crossed against a pristine white skirt. The Energy Secretary. Why would he be there? Tilda creased up her brow and forced herself to think, in spite of the strands of sleep tugging her down to the dreadful quicksand of her pillow. A thick, knotty feeling balled up in her gut, but not guilt this time.

Emotional capability for kokeshi? The thought caused a thorough sense of isolation to hit her, and then the fear.

I've been replaced once, she thought, and it had hurt. "Bots: power off," she said, and the bots droned into silence amid their chores. To stay awake, she opened the bedroom window, sending in billowing, damp draughts. The rain reminded her of the robotic fish in the river; the only fish left.

Except for the jellyfish.

Adem V

Breakfast at the Azikiwe Suite was to be typically, distastefully opulent: a cornucopia of meats and breads that fourteen people would struggle to consume, let alone the four sitting around the immaculately-set table. His family were such an odd bunch, he decided, never more so than when they were together. He half had the temptation to joke that he and his siblings must all be from different stock, but his father would not appreciate such a joke.

So Joseph sat, overlooking his three motherless children, his gnarly old shoe-leather face resting on thick, powerful hands, elbows on the table. Remus had never needed much of an invitation to eat, and as soon as Joseph bade them sit, the fathead began stockpiling slices of meat, watermelon segments and poultry legs as if the apocalypse were imminent.

Next to Adem, Joanna sat quietly, taking a piece of bread and buttering it. Adem hadn't seen his sister for years; they'd exchanged an embrace he felt neither of them really meant. "The weather in London must have infected your temperament, little brother," she'd said with a humourless smile. She remained elegant, tall, distant, dressed in a traditional Nigerian dress which Adem assumed must have been an unsubtle political slight against their father. If it was, Joseph remained remarkably restrained about it as they all took their seats around him.

"I have to say I'm surprised to see you, Annie," Adem said as a maître-d' poured coffee. He couldn't remember the last time a human had poured coffee for him. "The last thing I heard of you is that you pissed off to Berlin to join some scabby protest movement made up of workshy vagrants."

It had actually been a well-organised political lobbying group opposing OPEC nations' oil & gas extraction methodologies, for which Annie had fronted a not-insignificant amount of funding from her own fortune; definitely no vagrants involved, and it had given their father a spitting fit. For that at least, he held a concealed admiration for her. Sibling politics took place in the dirtiest type of muck, but if you were forced to swim in it, why not bathe in it? Of course, Joanna was far too cute to rise to the slight, and simply smiled and opened her hands. "I saw the light and returned."

"You mean Father brought you here where you couldn't embarrass him so badly. The prodigal daughter."

"Would you cast yourself as the prodigal son? A man who has sold his soul to be a middling civil servant of his former bondholders, an expendable monkeywrench in the clogged gears of Westminster? A man who apparently had to be persuaded to return to his father's table?"

He laughed, a dry and sour sort of thing, an acknowledgement of a joke that skewered him just a little too well. Yet he missed his sister; compared to the strong-armed wrongheadedness of their father, and the testosterone-fuelled car crash that was their brother, she was a witty and intelligent thing. If only they liked each other, they'd have gotten on well. "I never needed persuading, Annie." *I just bided my time until the chance was right.* "And are you not breaking every idealistic fibre in your body to be here at this table?"

Annie looked at him, inscrutably firm. If only she had a different view of the world, a view of how it really is, rather than how she dreamed it ought to be; what a force she might have been. "Father has given me a job that suits me; commercial diplomacy and ethical exploitation of capability."

Since when had Annie been infected by corporate speak? Father must have been paying her a shitload of money. Seems anyone can be bought. "I see."

"Enough," said Joseph, clapping those big, rough hands together. "I brought you children together because of this momentous project that I have funded. You all know the struggle we have endured against the pig-iggiots of the NPF – and I believe now we have an opportunity to develop some technology that will 'change the game' as the English say. Look at you." He waved his hand over the table. "The future of this company I give to you, my children. Your mother always wanted it to be so, God rest her, and now I make this project so that I might secure your own future, and it is time I made you all aware of your own future."

Adem steepled his hands in front of his mouth. *His* future. He'd set this deal up. Technology that could strip the NPF of the human capital they relied upon so dearly, beat them at their own game. It was a hell of an achievement; a combination of brains, expertise, charm, forcefulness and, well, he was not so arrogant to deny the part that luck had played in bringing this altogether. His father was a firm man, but he was fair. Above all he was a businessman. Finally now he would see that Adem bringing this opportunity to JPC showed his eldest son was a true businessman too.

"I do not intend to die, not yet," said Joseph, before rolling up a sleeve, showing off a leathery arm well honed by rays of sun and years of work. "But die I will, and not without an heir to this future I have prepared. So I bring you here to tell you, before I tell the world's press. I name Remus my heir to the company."

A desiccated feeling ran through Adem's body, from his eyes to his mouth to his throat to his stomach, where it lurched and swung and punched and made him grasp his face momentarily. Through a series of blinks he couldn't quite control he saw Remus grinning in that stupid way he had, an idiot grin that didn't quite convey an entirety of understanding. Amid blood in his ears he heard Joanna laugh and say something, but he wasn't sure what.

Then came the rage. Intoxicating, stupid, volcanic rage.

"This one?" Adem stood, sending his seat careering backwards. He gesticulated wildly at Remus, wielding his napkin like a standard. "You entrust everything, for which you've worked your whole life, to this nincompoop, who has no understanding of business, of leadership, of how the world works?"

"Hey," called Remus. "If you believe I have no understanding of business, maybe we can settle it with fists."

Adem shook his head incredulously. All he had done. All he'd worked for. Slaving away as a civil servant in England, of all places, precisely so he would be prepared for a position such as this, and... his stomach growled into a knot and he bit down on the pain. "You must be telling me a joke, Father. Remus is my dear brother; I love him," lied Adem, "but he is not made of the material to run a company; to run *this* company."

"Fuck you," said Remus with a snarl, pointing a finger across the table before tearing a chunk out of a chicken leg. "You do not know my strength."

Joseph stood up. "Shut up, both of you. Adem, do not be such a pantywaist. You will accept my decision and you will be happy for your brother. Look at all you have achieved. My eyes and ears in London, you made all this glory happen. You could be great there. The responsibility of greasing the wheels of our clients' machines is a subtle art, one you are mastering."

Damnation by praise. Humiliation by admiration. The promised banquet a meagre spread of crumbs. He looked at his sister, but her face gave nothing away. "Would it have been different had I taken up boxing, like you, father? Or gotten involved with drugs and women?"

Remus shifted and sneered at the allusion to his colourful past, but said nothing.

Joseph paused. "I could not answer that."

Adem slumped backwards, defeated. The aroma of the food on his plate came over like ashes, and he pushed it away in disgust. So it was precisely because Remus was such a loser that he was being given this inheritance. A chance to shine. Charity. What use work, then? Effort? What a waste he'd made of his life, when his fate was all the while being controlled by the egregious self-aggrandisement and whimsical urges of his little brother. His stomach balled itself up again, and he winced, pinching the bridge of his nose with hatefully soft fingertips. At last he spoke. "May I be excused?"

"No," said Joseph. "You may not. Remus, Joanna; you are excused."

"But I've not finished eating," said Remus, open-mouthed through a spray of chicken flesh.

"Get out, son of mine," said Joseph with a stern stare which placated Remus.

"Come, Remus," said Joanna, rising demurely before facing Adem. "This must be a disappointment for you, Ad. But do not think unkindly upon Remus. God has said it must be this way."

Adem puffed out a dead laugh. No doubt their father enjoyed being referred to as God.

"Maybe we could talk about it later," continued Joanna, a hand pressed firmly upon his shoulder. "I can tell you about the work I'm doing here. It'll relate directly to the technology programme you're involved with."

When his siblings had vacated the room, Joseph rose and placed his hands, considerably larger and firmer than his sister's, on his shoulders, and massaged them vigorously. His father might have been a bastard, but those log-like hands gave damn good shoulder rubs. Despite the tension in his muscles being pleasantly scraped away the sense of distaste didn't leave entirely.

"Do not be too ungracious towards your brother, eldest son of mine."

"Forgive me, father, but it's hard not to act this way. I have worked all my adult life; he has squandered what talents he may have had."

"Yes. But do you not see? You would succeed along whichever path you chose. A man of talent, and diligence, and application, and thoughtfulness. Your brother is impulsive, lazy, and arrogant. It is not easy for a man such as myself to say such things about his son, but nonetheless it is true. He would fail if I cut him loose. He would become a liability to the family; to you as well as me. An embarrassment. One stupid urge away from a scandal. This responsibility will be the making of him. He will shadow me, learn, and learn hard. He will be monitored and have people around him who will influence him, help him make the right decisions, so that his stupidity is at first negated and at last erased."

"If you reward bad behaviour you will not change it. He won't change."

"He will."

"This was my birthright, father."

The shoulder rub stopped, as did Adem's heart for a beat; he tensed, half-expecting his father to put a painful squeeze on his shoulders, gripping him into submission. Even though the squeeze never came, he found himself wincing, as though it had, and he knew he was defeated anew.

"No," said Joseph. "It was never yours. It was always mine to give. A civil servant of all people should know not to assume."

Adem breathed out through his nose, trying not to betray his humiliation. "I will accept your decision as always, father."

"I knew you would. That is the difference between him and you. Enough, I must go. Work to be done." Joseph patted his son's shoulders and headed for the door to leave Adem stewing in his own juice. At the door he turned and addressed him anew. "Allow him his preening. Do your work, and do it well. A moral victory may still be a victory. And never forget, your time in the sun may yet come."

That was remarkably philosophical for his father. Maybe he was mellowing in his old age. Or maybe just going soft in the head. Try as he might, he couldn't find it in his heart to truly feel pleased for his idiot brother, but he'd smile and do the right thing, like he always did. *Like you did with Sir Ingham?* He shivered. *That was not a good thing,* he told himself. *But the right thing to do.* A thought froze him into place then and there. *But it got you nowhere. It was all for nothing.*

"Shut up," he told the empty room, and he balled his hands together at the dinner table, picturing his father's neck in one, Remus's in the other, and he squeezed, and squeezed, until he could see the eyes pop out of their heads, and the life leave them. That made him laugh.

Nita V

"The artificial brain functions happen just like they do in a human brain, but digitally," said Bree, EI's Head of Digital Neurology, pointing up at the screen. She was conducting the seminar presentation from London, broadcasting it to a room comprising EI representatives that had travelled to Oil City, the engineers Joseph Johnson had had drafted in especially for the project, two of the Johnson children – Remus and Joanna, Nita recalled – and a large number of government soldiers employed as private security for Oil City. *Or guinea pigs.* Nita sat in the front row, flanked by the Johnson children. While Joanna was a wonderful host and seemed highly interested in the technology of artificial emotion and digital neurology, Remus picked at his teeth and seemed distracted throughout much of the presentations, mainly by Nita's legs. She shifted and pulled her skirt down a little further, trying to wriggle free of his wandering gaze.

Bree, a breezy and brilliant Canadian woman who had joined EI a few years ago, continued gaily, beaming down the camera as she enthused about her pet topic. "Digital neural pathways are learned, just as biological neural pathways are learned in us. However, there's a crucial difference. In humans we learn everything this way from birth - for example learning to how to walk, talk, grip, use fine and gross motor functions – until the neural pathways that command these functions are hardwired. Robots have no need to learn all this. All of this is pre-programmed, or pre-wired. However, the emotional wiring in their brains is in a constant state of learning, of forming new nodes and pathways based upon experience. This isn't the same as standard AI, which enables robots to learn and retain facts, skills, information and knowledge; this enables them to learn and retain experience rather than data, memories rather than mere image recollection, to enable them to grow. And interaction with humans is at the very heart of this. Through interaction with humans they can learn, reciprocate, empathise and deliver a more holistic level of companionship and partnership."

Bree flashed through slides, animations and simulations as she spoke, keeping the audience fascinated. Nita smiled. This wasn't an overly tech-heavy presentation, but one designed to get the guinea pigs to buy in. It wasn't just enough to know they might be having intimate relationships with a Digital Person. They had to know that these wonderful innovations were there to provide fellowship, that they'd be sharing tales, jokes, a touch here, a glance there. She could feel the goodwill in the room. These were hard men and women; steely-eyed, armed soldiers who were told to show no mercy to trespassers and criminals like the people who'd fired upon her security escort from the airport. That made her feel safe. And these robots – these Digital People – would make them feel more whole; give those without families, spouses or partners an outlet for their emotional and physical needs. It would be wonderful.

When Bree's talk finished, covering some of the other emotional and mechanical aspects of the robots, Nita stood up to address the room once more from the lectern at the head of the room. "Thank you, Bree. You'll all have been notified already that we've taken delivery of the first few shipments of the basic robotic chassis, which have been donated by the English Government after a successful amnesty. Our team of engineers here will be working hard to reset and upgrade them to become the first Digital People eligible for human trialling. The EI Systems support staff will be in touch with each of you to provide you with your information packs, how to keep your diary, what is and isn't permissible with the Digital People, and your resources if you have any concerns or questions. I'd like to thank you again for volunteering for this groundbreaking test, which will pave the way for wider adoption of this technology to help alleviate a whole range of problems the world over. You should feel very proud. If there are any questions at this stage I'll do my best to answer them."

There weren't, and Nita ended the seminar, allowing people to get back to work. As people milled about chatting afterwards, Joanna clasped her arm with a smile. "Nita," she said, shaking hands. "You're doing wonderful work. This could be the start of something special."

"Thank you Joanna. I didn't realise you had an interest in this sort of technology."

"Our father brought me back home as a commercial diplomat. I actually will have a small hand in some of the project: I've been tasked with generating the exploitation report – where can these technologies be used elsewhere."

Nita raised her eyebrows and smiled back. "Big job."

"Indeed. But I have lots of contacts across different sectors. I like to think I offer an ethical angle to the use of technology. Father understood that it would be better to have me inside the tent. He looks like a bit of a blunt weapon but he sometimes has some shrewdness about him. I'll be in touch. We should have a gin & tonic together."

"I'd very much like that. And I can share some of EI's industrial contacts with you."

"It's a date, then."

They noticed a middle-aged man hovering in the background, and Joanna gestured to him. "Please, don't wait. Would you like to speak with Nita?"

The man stepped forward, a little gingerly, pushing the thick, black rim of his glasses back up his nose. "Hello ladies, I'm Edward Muembe, Head of Logistics for the Science Complex. May I speak with you?"

Nita pushed a breath through her nose. "I'm sorry, I've got another call booked in at noon and I'm speaking with Miss Johnson just now. Why don't you message me?"

"It's rather important, and I'll keep it quick, if I may. It's rather delicate."

"I'm sorry, I–"

"It concerns the latest delivery of robots to Oil City. There's a discrepancy."

She furrowed her brows, and offered an awkward smile to Joanna, who simply said, "Maybe I ought to leave you to it," before gliding away, the hem of her dress ruffling pleasingly around her ankles.

Nita turned to this Edward. "What is it, then?"

"Perhaps not here. Shall I buy you a coffee?"

Dhiraj VIII

Time spent at the harbour, waiting for the occasional sight of Naomi simply deepened his sense of misery. He half wished the police would come for him. Why hadn't they? He couldn't quite work it out and couldn't decide whether that was a good thing or not. Anything had to be better than this purgatory, caught between two women – or one woman and one... something else. The not knowing gnawing at him. Sali's sister Rani always answered the calls to their house, and always gave Dhiraj short shrift when he pleaded to speak with his wife. He hadn't yet summoned the heart to go round there and demand to see his son – he was too weak a man for such grandstanding – so whenever the pull to leave the house took him it was to the harbour he ventured, trudging along the muddy lanes to the Tilbury hilltops where the old English fort used to be, casting his eye down upon the docks.

It took a couple of days of self-indulgent misery for him to snap out of his stupor. "You've got so much to make right, Dhiraj Om," Rani had said on their last ten-second phone exchange – one could hardly call it a conversation – and he decided she was right. He could start by making a catch.

It was good to spend the night on *The Lion's Mane*, feeling the pull and craw of the sea. Any voyage upon the sea gave him a profound sense of the smallness of his own life, and the extent to which he placed his life in the ambivalent mercies of God. Yet unlike the hateful maze he'd been dragged through this past week, he always felt in control on the seas. Healthy respect was his currency here, not fear and dumb ignorance; the sea was his God, and *The Lion's Mane* was his altar; and when the surface of the ocean broke out in electric blue, he knew he had his bounty.

The jellyfish catch was a good one, and he made his journey home with a great deal more money than he started. A couple of bills needed to be paid. He needed to eat, so he'd keep a few choice jellies for himself; the rest of the money he would transfer to Sali. He was thinking how he might prepare his own morning meal – dehydrating the jellies in the freeze-drier, then marinating in soy, chilli, garlic and ginger, then frying with enough noodles to sink a Chinese junk sounded good, and cheap. So it was to his great surprise that he turned into his driveway to see Sali standing at the front door. Arms crossed, brows furrowed and lips pursed, she looked filled with the sort of quiet anger that he knew was reserved for times when he'd been especially stupid. And she looked beautiful.

"I saw you walking from the upstairs window," she said.

Every part of him wanted to go and take her in his arms and kiss her, but he held back. That wouldn't pass. When no adequate words came, he offered up the bag of jellies to her. "I brought food."

~

He cooked and ate the food joylessly after Sali made him shower; she didn't want to speak to him stinking of sweat and salt. With his estranged – it seemed weird to think of her that way – wife hovering over him, arms perennially crossed, he felt under too much scrutiny to eat; or maybe it was the guilt, but his stomach won over and he polished off the food.

"It was a good catch, then?" she asked as he dropped his chopsticks into the bowl.

He nodded. The house was cold. "Pretty good. I was going to send you most of the money."

Sali nodded curtly.

"How's Dan?"

"Confused. Angry. He barely speaks to me."

"Why did you come back?"

"Because I couldn't bear another ten second conversation between you and Rani. And I've wasted enough tears on you."

He gulped. "So what... are you leaving me?"

"For Christ's sake, Raj, show some balls." A beat. "Maybe this was a mistake." She made for the door, but Dhiraj rose and leapt over to her, grabbing her arm. That must have been unexpected, for she shrank back, and he loosened his grip.

"Don't go. Not yet. I've got to tell you – got to tell someone – about everything that happened. It's eating me up, it's eating into my mind. If you don't stay, don't give me a chance even to tell you everything I'll go crazy." He let go and stepped back. "Sorry. And if you're still pissed off with me, if it's still too much, then leave. But please, listen to me. Isn't twenty years together worth that?"

Sali still threw daggers at him with her eyes, and let him stew in the threat of her leaving, but she turned from the door and sat down.

The stale breath he'd been holding in then exhaled. Pouring himself a glass of water, he steadied himself and sat down opposite her at the dining table.

"I found Naomi–"

"That's its name?"

He stared. Was she going to interrupt him every two words like this? Maybe he deserved it. He checked himself; calling Naomi 'her' wouldn't go down well. "Yes. That's its name. I found it in the sea, in my catch. Christ, it must have been a fortnight ago now."

So the story spilled out of him, sometimes stuttering, sometimes hesitant, sometimes shamefully: poor Jens's involvement and death; the night at the *Fantasia* club; the days spent in hiding, the hideous Spidermen, and eventually returning home and leaving Naomi at the harbour. During the telling Sali in turn shook her head in disbelief, fought off tears, clasped her hand to her mouth in shock, and curled up the corners of her mouth in disgust. But she didn't leave and prompted him to finish.

"So she's at the harbour?"

She. Sali called her she. But she wasn't a she. Not any more. "We parted there. I..." he thought about what he wanted to say; for all day and all night he'd rehearsed what he would say to her when he had the chance, with great articulation, and now he found he couldn't find the simplest of words, as though articulating his thoughts were somehow even more shameful. "I wish I'd just pushed her back in the sea."

"Then why didn't you?"

A shiver ran through him as he recalled her slumped on deck, naked and pallid and apparently helpless. "I don't know. Would you?"

"Don't turn this around on me. This isn't about me. God, you're such an arsehole, Raj. Such an arsehole."

Shame again. He gulped; it sounded huge, like he was swallowing Naomi whole.

"Did you have sex with it?"

That jolted him, and he frowned. "No." He amplified the indignity, hoping to make her believe this one thing. "No, not at all. I barely touched it. We were hiding together, but we didn't, not–"

"Because I've heard about those things. How they talk and act like whores, draping themselves over those sleazy men. You're saying you didn't have even a moment –".

"No. It wasn't like that. She – *it* – wasn't acting that way. I don't know exactly why, something to do with its programming or something, but it wasn't, you know, it wasn't ready for that sort of thing, like I'd found it before they could flick the switch that makes them act that way." Sali scowled, the soft skin around her eyes dark and shaking. "I didn't see her like that. Believe me, the last thing on my mind was anything like that. I wanted to come home. And I tried to sell the damn thing for money, for us, for you. And I know it was stupid, and –"

"Yes it was fucking stupid. You stupid man! For all the time I've loved you I stood by you, when everybody said I was marrying beneath myself –"

That hurt. No more than he deserved.

"– and that I could do better. That it would come back to bite me on my arse. And I stood by you, I defended you, I said we'd be ok, we would manage. Jesus, if my parents could see us now."

"It was a mistake. I did it because I love you."

"Raj, you ran off with a sex robot. Do you realise how humiliating that is? You take a friend out – and God knows I had no love for Jens but he deserved better than what happened to him –"

"It was his idea," he protested, to little avail.

"I don't care. You've got free will, you know. Do you know how humiliating it was to have the police and the press around here?"

He lifted his head up. "So the police were here?"

"For two days, questioning me, and then waiting for you to come home. I said, 'He'll come home, you'll see, he's innocent, you'll see,' and you never came home. Then they left. As far as I know, there's still a warrant out for you."

Dhiraj bit at a thumbnail and thought on that. Why hadn't he been arrested? Maybe something to do with the amnesty. If he was to be arrested, he would have to deal with it.

"What happens to us?" he asked.

Sali snorted. "I don't know. I don't know why I came back."

Dhiraj hoped she knew exactly why she came back, and he hoped he was right, but he said nothing. "If I am arrested, will you stand by me?"

"I don't know."

"Do you believe me? About what happened?"

Sali's face, stiff and upset, bobbed back and forth with thinking. "It's not about whether I believe you or not. You ran away. You left me. You left Dan. You left everything. You didn't call."

"I did call."

"*You didn't call.* You could have given yourself up and you didn't."

"Can I see Dan? I want to see him. I need to hold him. And you."

But she didn't hold him. Instead she simply stood there, looking at him, drilling into his skull with derisive eyes. Dhiraj put his head in hands and rubbed his own eyes. Why couldn't he cry? He wished he could cry, like he had when neither Sali nor Naomi were around. He wished he could cry so she'd take pity on him and understand what he'd been through and throw her arms around his neck and kiss him on the side of the head and tell him it'd be ok, they'd be ok and that it must have been awful, but he knew if he shed a single tear it'd be boiled up in contempt. So he just hid his tired eyes and looked at the empty bowl in front of him.

If the doorbell hadn't sounded, they might have stayed stuck in that miserable scene forever. Dhiraj, heart pounding in his ears and head light, ignored the door.

"I'll get it, then," said Sali, and he heard her footsteps softly plod away up the carpeted hall to the door.

A female voice, muffled out in the rain. A few exchanged words. Sali's soft feet on the carpet. Tension prickling in each bead of sweat on Dhiraj's skin.

"It's for you."

"Who is it?"

"A policewoman. She wants to come in and have a word with you."

D'Souza VI

Despite it being the dead of night, when the bag was whipped off D'Souza's head, he flinched at the dazzling light being shone in his face. Grogginess and nausea had rumbled through his stomach on the rough road journey from... from wherever he had been, to wherever the hell he was now, and he'd barked out from under the itchy cloth hood for a drink of water more times than he could remember, but all he got was a stiff prod to the ribs, possibly from a boot. He made a mental note to work out who was delivering the dirty blows, and to pay them back when the chance came.

Blinking a few times in the new light, his surroundings manifested themselves. He was still on the back of a battered old 4x4, and it was still night. That made sense; it must have only been a couple of hours on the road, though he was aware his sense of timing must have been knocked well out of kilter. The whole place reeked of heat and sweat and salt and smoke. Angry orange smudges revealed themselves as small fires; sharp fingers pointing towards the sky became grimy khaki tent apexes; and the hovering ghosts and silhouettes became people. He moaned and tried to clutch his head, but his wrists had been bound behind his back. Struggling did nothing to loosen the cords, so he rolled onto his side, a degree less uncomfortable.

A man's face popped in front of him, an angry, lean face with a cigarette being chewed between its teeth. He said a few words, and D'Souza blinked.

"Francais? English? Español? Paki? Aye, aye!" He cuffed D'Souza about the head, making him grunt and tense up his face. If only his hands were free.

"English," he muttered. "English!"

The man whistled and beckoned over another man, before hauling D'Souza off the back of the truck. The ground met him with a dull thump and the taste of bitter earth. Together they dragged him into a tent. He noticed rusty looking sub-machine guns hanging casually from their shoulders by old guitar straps, while machetes hung from their belts by bits of string.

Insurgents.

In another time, another place, he might have struggled once more; these folks didn't look like trained soldiers, and the crappy machine guns didn't scare him at close quarters, but he'd seen what machetes and adrenalin did to people, and so he kept his mouth shut. He could talk his way out of this. Rebels were just underworld actors, just like him. Once he got onto speaking terms with them, he was sure they'd be on the level. The camp revealed itself to be much larger than he initially thought. Tents of varying sizes, vehicles, weapons, angry-looking people standing, dozing, smoking, arguing, dully negotiating the night; the clicks and rattles of weapons being fiddled with, loaded, the slow rumble of vehicles pulling up and driving off, the bark and chatter of the locals, and the heady stench of sweat and mud, swaying in and out of his senses with the delta breeze.

The tent into which D'Souza was tossed was a fair size. Low halogen lights hummed with crude heat, and in the corner sat another man with a grimace in his glistening face, his eyes trained on D'Souza, his hands methodically sharpening a large Bowie-style knife on a leather strop, *schop schop schop.*

"Who are you?" the man said.

"No one."

Schop schop. "No one does not spend his evenings in a marsh in the delta."

D'Souza told himself to slow his breathing and control himself. These people might not be trained killers, but he couldn't take the risk they weren't killers all the same. He decided not to say anything unless asked.

"So, what were you doing there?"

Deep breath. "I'm from London. I was taking a river taxi from a small shantytown a few miles south of the city. My guide tried to rob me. I jumped into the river and hid until they were gone." He paused. "Where are my things?"

"I ask you again." The man pointed his knife at D'Souza. He swallowed, keeping his brow firm. "What were you doing there?"

"I want to get to Oil City."

The man laughed, a deep, booming laugh that showed all his teeth. "So you admit it! You're a spy!" The laugh disappeared, burned away by a scowl as the man stood and walked over to where D'Souza knelt. He held the knife an inch from his face. "You know what we do to spies?"

"I'm not a spy. I want to get to Oil City because there is somebody on there who did me great harm, and I owe them."

"What did they do?"

D'Souza offered an ugly smile. "Bad things. But nothing to do with you."

The man paused. "So you say you have nothing to do with JPC?"

"I don't."

"We will require proof. And even if you're no spy, you've seen a lot here."

"You're the rebels, aren't you? The ones fighting against the bastards in Oil City?"

The man shrugged, half amused.

"I've no beef with you. I don't care either way about your operation, your politics. My agenda is my own. I came from London to do this, and I will fight. What proof do you need? Check my passports, my things. I've no money left, no devices."

The man nodded as D'Souza spoke, each nod a little more skeptical than the last, as though he'd heard that, and every other excuse in the book, all before. "I know you will fight." He put his fingers in his mouth and whistled. D'Souza had never been able to do that.

When another man poked his head through the folds, the interrogator whispered a few words, sending him on his way before going back to his stool in the corner. *Schop, schop, schop.*

"Where is he going?"

Schop, schop, schop.

A few minutes later the man returned, kicking another man – apparently another prisoner – through the tent flap onto the dirt. Afterwards the man tossed in a stinking, weather-worn holdall D'Souza recognised as his own. D'Souza licked his teeth in anticipation, hoping his weapon might still be inside. To the untrained eye it would look like a bunch of sticks wrapped together, but if he could get hold of it... *and then what, Agarkka?* He admonished himself for the excitable thought; trying to escape would likely only earn him a volley of bullets in the back, even if he did manage to overpower the Strop Man and a few of his mates. Still, it was good to know he mightn't go down without his trusty *kaduwa* in hand. The other prisoner was older than D'Souza, and had a saggy paunch. Whimpering, he got to his knees and made a pleading gesture to the men; he had a few blotches on his face where he'd taken a few blows. His hands weren't bound, but he didn't look like he was able to offer much in the way of resistance. D'Souza kept his breathing slow and frosty.

Strop Man looked at D'Souza while pointing his knife at the other man. "You know him?"

D'Souza shook his head.

"He's a spy. He works for JPC. Just a poor villager, he says, but he took the oil vultures' money in exchange for information about us, who we are, what we do. This fucking *insect* –" Strop Man kicked the man hard in his paunch, sending him wheezing and drooling and wailing on the ground. "– thinks we are the enemy. He thinks JPC are his friends; the bastard faggot shits who stole and raped our land and sold its nectar back to us... he thinks we are the enemy, we who try to liberate the delta and smash the vultures of JPC!"

The man on the ground whimpered something D'Souza couldn't understand, and Strop Man said something in return, before picking up his chin and pointing his face towards D'Souza.

"You recognise him?" he asked the man.

He shook his head.

Strop Man clucked, and nodded at D'Souza. "So, Mr London man. What's your name?"

"Agarkka."

"Agarkka. Agarkka." He played with the clearly unfamiliar name. "So, what do you think, Mr Agarkka?"

D'Souza shrugged. "What do I think of what?"

"You said you are impartial. So what do you think we should do with this spy? This man who has deceived and betrayed his own people? Do you think we should kill him? Set him free? Or send him home with a message?"

A message. Many times he'd sent some poor bastard home with a 'message'. A roll of sweat gently tickled its way down the curve of D'Souza's spine. "Like I said," he muttered. "Your politics are your politics. I've no dog in the fight either way. My story isn't your story. I'm not qualified to make that decision. I've no right to make that decision."

Strop Man smiled and waved his knife at D'Souza. "You choose your words carefully, Mr London Man."

"It's not the first time I've had a knife waved in my face."

"Hah! Fucking British. Always with an answer to all things."

D'Souza considered contesting the assumption of his heritage but thought better of it. British would have to do, for now. "So what are you going to do with us?"

Strop Man ran his tongue around his teeth and threw the knife into the air, catching it by the handle, looking in turn at D'Souza and the other man.

Another voice sounded from the shadows of the tent, pricking up D'Souza's senses: "He's a lot like you, Agarkka." From the dark corners emerged the owner of the voice: a tall man dressed in ragged military fatigues, with three epaulettes on his shoulder, and heavy desert boots. He stood up, all six and a half feet of him, most likely more, and skinny with it. A round face hid behind huge aviator sunglasses, a khaki beret, a few days' worth of beard growth, and a stony expression. He stooped down to D'Souza's height, close enough that he could see his reflection in those big lenses, and turned away.

The tall man clapped a hand on Strop Man's shoulder. "It's not his decision to make. Aba here is merely wields the knife; I am the one who controls it." His accent was softer, more melodious than the brackish thud of Aba the Strop Man. "What do you think we should do with him, then?" he said, gesticulating to the prostrate prisoner distastefully. Before D'Souza could respond, he answered his own question. "Ah, yes; you said you could not answer. Perhaps you could tell us, then, what would you do?"

D'Souza breathed again. "I would make sure he is guilty before anything else."

The tall man nodded. "Wise man. Did you think we would simply kill him? Did you think we would dispense with justice? Do you think we are savages? What, no answer? Aba, check his tongue, see if it has been cut out."

Aba stepped forward, and D'Souza spoke out. "Not savage. Just angry."

"Indeed. Angry at the injustices our people have suffered at the hands of successive governments. But not savage. We will conduct a trial to determine this man's guilt. And you will be the one to determine his guilt."

D'Souza flinched. He didn't like the sound of that. A set up. They still thought he was a spy. No right answer to give here. "I told you, I cannot make that decision."

"Uh-uh-uh-uh," said the tall man. He stepped forward and prodded a strong, iron-like finger into D'Souza's temple. "Your brain cannot make that decision. But maybe your hands can. Aba, help them up."

Aba gripped D'Souza under the armpit and hoisted him up, and flashed the blade in front of his face. With a flourish, he stepped behind him and cut the cords binding his hands. D'Souza couldn't help letting out a deep sigh as relief coursed through his cramped arms, but he was no closer to rubbing his raw wrists when Aba turned him to face the other man, the accused, who also had made it to his feet, but barely. He stood, trying not to look D'Souza in the eyes, shivering. The stench of sweat, hot salt and methane lifted through the air as D'Souza realised the poor bastard had pissed himself. Rather than disgust, he pitied the man, and tried not to squirm at the memory of pissing his own pants. Like a little fucking girl. He blinked and fought off the prickles behind his eyes.

"At least one of you is a spy," said the tall man. "We'll determine who through a hands-on trial."

D'Souza frowned. "What's that?"

Aba smiled and clapped his hands. "Trial by combat!"

D'Souza took in that sucker punch of a resolution as the other man – *your opponent!* he reminded himself – was dragged away from the tent by Aba, leaving him with the tall man and one of his bodyguards.

"What good will this do?" D'Souza cried. "How will this determine guilt?"

"If you do not work for JPC, you would have no problems with slicing one of them open."

That was twisted logic, and yet it gave him pause. Such brutal thinking wasn't alien to him. "I'll kill to stay alive," he eventually said.

"Just so. And so you see a trial won't determine anything. And it doesn't need to. My men are running background checks on you as we speak. We've already got your biometrics, DNA. By morning we'll know whether you're a stupid spy, or a stupid tourist. The trial by combat will just be for our entertainment. But being alive at the end of it won't do your chances of survival any harm."

D'Souza bowed his head. "That other man is a wreck. He won't last a minute."

"You are very confident, Mr Agarkka."

"I know a broken man when I see him."

"Just so. But you'll fight all the same."

"Who are you?"

"If you're a spy you'll already know that. But, on the off chance you're not, my name is Mobo." He extended a hand. D'Souza eyed it warily, but when the bodyguard prompted him with the barrel of his machine gun, he took it and shook it. Mobo smiled and gave D'Souza back his aching hand.

Nita VI

The servobot brought coffees. Edward Muembe tossed an array of documents into the air, flicking through them and eyeing them into place. "There was a discrepancy with the latest consignment of robots from England."

Nita glanced at her watch and sipped impatiently at her coffee. "Why specifically does this concern me?"

"The manifests from London say that thirty robots were shipped, see here. And here," he said swiping through the images, "you'll see that only twenty eight robots were accounted for upon delivery."

Nita sat up. "Missing? We've lost two robots?"

"It looks like it."

"How the hell could this happen?"

"I don't know. Everything relating to the shipping detail appears to be correct. What should we do? I thought it best to consult you discreetly before alerting the authorities."

She frowned sternly. "The police? You think they might have been stolen?"

He made a sceptical face. "Hopefully it's merely an oversight, a miscount at London, though it would be a terrible error for such a small consignment. It's possible they were never shipped in the first place. But if it were to be theft..."

Realisation flashed through her mind. "The NPF?"

"It's not my place to speculate. All international shipping and consignments go through the harbour at Port Harcourt before being shifted to local or private transportation. Same with ours, even with highly valuable cargo." He leant in. "And the NPF have agents everywhere."

She thought back to the assault on her vehicle in traffic. The crunch of the rifle butt smacking her rear window still chilled her. It did seem plausible that they could have covert operatives and scouts in the harbour. But how would they get inside a secure shipping container? And how would they even know what was inside a highly classified consignment of freight? She supposed hardened terrorists with enough motivation could find out just about anything with a bit of muscle, and she shivered. The sort of damaging publicity a missing kokeshi could generate gave her a sickly feeling.

Perhaps seeing he'd startled her, Edward smiled and said, "But who knows. They might simply have fallen into the sea."

It was Nita's turn to make an incredulous face at that stupid suggestion. "Look, you did the right thing by keeping this under your hat for now. Don't alert the police – I'll take it up personally. Who else knows?"

"Apart from my team, just you."

"And you trust your team?"

Edward shrugged. "As much as I trust anyone."

That wasn't really any sort of answer, but she suspected pressing him wouldn't result in anything clearer. After he left, she sat in the coffee lounge outside the events and conferencing wing of the Executive complex, one leg crossed over the other and shaking restlessly as she thought. Missing robots. Not good. She sent a quick message to postpone her noon call, and instead sent Adem a message.

It was thirty minutes before Adem showed up at the coffee lounge, looking thoroughly miserable. "What is it?" he muttered. "I'm trying to sort out a load of shit for London."

"I wouldn't have called you if it wasn't important."

"Well, what is it?"

She looked at him irritably, then cast her own aspersions aside. The coffee lounge was a large, glass space with huge windows overlooking the golden ocean, but inside it was populated by small leather cubes that passed as uncomfortable seats, and servobots gliding here and there, while pairs and small groups of employees chatted in their cliques and huddles. No-one was near them, but she hushed her voice anyway. "There are two of the robots missing. Our robots, from London."

Adem screwed his face up. "Missing? How?"

"I don't know. I think it could be the NPF."

Adem thinned his eyes and clasped Nita's wrist; firmly, but not enough to hurt. "Why do you think this?"

"Come on, Adem. Don't they want to destroy you, your father, JPC? You know how well publicised this project is. Plus, they attacked me in the city. Do you think we should tell your father?"

Adem looked as though he were about to speak, and then pulled the words back. "No. I'm sure it's just an oversight. A logistical error. The administrators in Port Harcourt do not operate at the levels of bureaucratic efficiency we're used to in London. Mistakes happen."

She paused, leaning back. "Is that a joke?"

He shrugged, a little shiftily. "Yes. No. Some truth in it."

"Do you understand what I'm telling you? If the robots have been taken by people who are enemies of your father, this could cause a lot of damage to the project. Adem," she snapped as his gaze drifted elsewhere. "Are you alright? You seem a little agitated."

Adem curled his lip up. "Agitated? Why should I be agitated? No, just..." he took Nita's hand, more warmly this time. He had a tender touch in him. The briefest flicker ran up her arm. In a place defined by its isolation, and defining her in its isolation, he was a face that anchored her to the world outside she'd left behind to pursue this dream. "I've just had a bad morning. Sorry."

The clap of hands echoed in their ears and broke their hands apart. "Lovebirds, lovebirds!"

Nita sat up to see Remus standing over them with a grin, and she realised how close Adem's face had been to her own. The lines upon his face, the faint flickers of grey hairs just ghosting around his ears betraying his age, the dark, tired eyes that sought her own, and soft hands that seemed to offer a hidden strength. They both had their hidden strengths, compounded in their collusion. They'd made this together, and now they'd be stronger together. When he pulled away from her upon hearing his brother's voice, breaking their clasping hands, the distance seemed a chasm.

"What do you want, Remus?"

"Just to say hello, big brother." He grunted a greeting towards Nita, who turned her eyes away in distaste. "You must be upset about this morning. Is he upset, Rhodes?"

Adem forced out a smile before Nita could answer. "Not at all, Remus. In fact I should apologise for my behaviour this morning. It was quite unbecoming."

"What's becoming? It's becoming what?"

"Never mind. My mistake. Like I say, I wish you well. I'll be here for you, Remus. On that you can count."

"What happened this morning?" asked Nita.

Remus puffed out his chest and stuck his thumb proudly into it. "Our father named me as successor to JPC. Heir to this fortune. Head of the company! King of the castle! Imagine how great it will be."

Stuck for words, Nita could only raise her brows a little and utter, "Oh. I see."

"Yes, see me. Imagine what I would do with this company. I would make it stronger, the best company in the world. Why do you spend your time with my brother? You could spend it with me, a real man."

"Remus, brother, we're discussing business, if you wouldn't mind just –"

"Business? My business? My company? Or you just discussing dirty business?" He grinned, making an obscene fucking gesture with his fingers, causing Nita to shake her head.

Adem jumped up and squared up to his brother.

Oh no, that's what he wants, you fool.

"Remus, you can speak to me anyway you please. That is your prerogative, but don't you dare speak that way to Miss Rhodes. She is our guest, and a friend of mine, and you've been deeply disrespectful and insulting."

Remus stuck his tongue out at Nita. "Just a friend? I'd like to be your friend, sweet woman. I have champagne ready in my room. I'll show you what a real man can do for you."

Adem pushed his brother in the chest and pointed a finger in warning at him. Stripped of his inane grin, the younger brother offered a shocked look that his brother had dared lay hands on him, before crouching and swinging his left fist into Adem's body. A huge wheezy inhale of breath took Adem to the ground, where his face looked up at Remus, wide-eyed. Shocked, Nita got up and put her hand to her mouth. A small crowd of onlookers stood and stared now, but encroached no further on the scene. "Leave him be, you animal!" she cried, kneeling by Adem. Bent double on the floor, a thin line of drool left Adem's mouth as he clenched with the pain.

"Fucking iggiots," snorted Remus before walking off. "When you realise what you're missing, come and find me, Rhodes."

The crowd murmured before going back to their seats as Adem slowly came round. How could this hateful oaf be chosen ahead of Adem to run the company? Was Joanna being facetious when she said their father wasn't just a blunt weapon? She found herself shaking again as she got him to his haunches, but told herself off for her indulgence. It hadn't been her who'd been hit. "Are you ok?"

Through watering eyes Adem slowly breathed the shivers from his throat, but pushed away a cup of water offered by a servobot. Quite unnoticed, she found her fingers were already entwined with his as he gathered himself, and her forehead almost touched his. "Bastard," he said. "Fucking animal."

"Where did he get you?"

"Here," he winced, pointing to his side. "Liver. Like being hit in the balls but worse. Jesus. What a fucking pig."

"Come on, let's go."

"I'm fine."

"Don't be such a martyr. The man's training to be a boxer. He might have damaged you."

"Fuck him."

Nita sighed. "That may be so, but don't cut off your nose to spite your face. Come on."

~

There was a purplish bloom forming around Adem's liver when the medibot scanned his upper body. Adem reluctantly took off his shirt, complaining all the while like a bloody child, before lying on the sofa as the bot did its job.

"You have bruising and swelling to the lower right abdomen," said the robot after completing its assessment. "But there is no damage to the liver, nor lasting damage to the surrounding tissues. Rest the affected area and apply this nanoformula arnica solution twice a day to accelerate the healing process. If it is not fully healed within three days, please consult one of the medibots for a further assessment. Are you happy with this diagnosis and treatment?"

Adem grunted in agreement.

"Very well. I have logged this in your personal files."

After the robot left the room, Nita looked around Adem's apartment. Bigger than hers, obviously. Bigger than her house in London, most likely. Huge windows overlooking the ocean. Below the balcony, men, women and robots beavered away at their day jobs, some in yellow hats, some using exoskeletal outfits, some coordinating activity from afar. Even a hundred feet up, she couldn't see land. Perfect isolation.

Moans from the sofa.

Turning, she found Adem groaning as he smeared some of the arnica on his bruise. The air felt a little closer in here than elsewhere in the complex, as though the air conditioning wasn't quite working. Kneeling beside the sofa, she took the cream from his hand and rubbed it gently into his side. He winced at first, then relaxed.

"I wonder why your father entrusted the company to Remus?" asked Nita.

Adem sighed. "Doubtless he feels it's irrefutably logical."

"It was just a rhetorical question."

"Oh." They both smiled, but she suspected neither of them meant it. Or maybe they did, but only with each other.

"It's quite a lonely place, isn't it?" A beat. "I feel more whole with you."

He looked at her, and she realised once again their fingers had found each other. "This place," he whispered. "I feel so alone, too."

"But this is your home," she said. "How could you feel lonely here?"

Adem snorted. "My family. What a bunch of lunatics. What a fool to think I might be able to find some place here. As if I look to that man, to that idiot, for approval, for respect."

She placed a hand upon his chest as he became agitated, placating him, and gently coaxed his face towards her own. When he saw her, the anger in him seemed to melt away, and she kissed him. He groaned again as she brought herself against his side, and they laughed as she peeled away from his bruise, before the curtain fell away from her eyes and she saw in him a companion, a person to walk with. Two mad fools together, concocting their own follies and meandering every which way their stupid whimsies would steer them. Maybe it was stupid to be with such a man, but she kissed him anyway, and she pulled at his belt, and when her shirt was pulled off, his hands revealed their hidden strength and pulled her towards him. Stupid whimsies be damned; they'd brought them here, to this mad, perfect moment which ended with her on top of him, feeling his hardness and guiding it into her, whereupon she fell upon him and kissed his face and mouth and neck until time melted and her body yawned in pleasure, and when she came she creased up her face and tried to block out the faces from the past, the roads and people and things they'd done and everything bad that had led up to this something good, this one moment of peace; all the conspiracy and collusion, all the ambition and politicking, all rescinded for a moment of human intimacy.

The sofa was barely big enough for them to lie in each others' arms, but lie they did, the warm air obviating any need for blankets or sheets, and Nita caught her breath as the gentle muffled thrum and wash of the ocean lapped beyond the apartment windows. Warmth tingled around her tummy and crotch, tiny particles of confused joy racing up and down her body from toes to fingers and back again, leaving prickly trails in their wake, making her writhe up against his lean body.

"We have to stay together while we're here," she said.

"My dear Nita, you don't love me, do you?"

She laughed. "No. Not yet. I want you, though." The smile faded. "But I think you're the only thing keeping me sane in this place."

"Is there anything you need? Despite what Remus says, I still have some clout around here. I'm still a Johnson."

"No. Just you." She laid a hand on his sweaty chest, and ever-so-gently traced the lines around his bruise with her fingertips. It was an ugly blotch now, the arnica bringing out a speckled rainbow of pebbledashed violets and yellows. "You didn't have to stand up to Remus like that."

He frowned. "I was quite prepared to let him have his way with his gloating, but as soon as he said a word against your honour, I could not abide it."

Unexpectedly, she found she quite enjoyed the outmoded gallantry. That probably wouldn't have happened in London. "Well that's very sweet." She kissed him again. "Actually, I have thought of something you could do for me," she said, slipping her hand down between his legs.

Tilda VI

"So you're not here to arrest him," said Mr Om's wife, Sali, as she poured Tilda a tea. "I figured that much out for myself. So why are you here?"

Tilda warmed her hands around the mug and stayed steely. The jellyfisherman's wife was standoffish, hard, cool. There was much of herself in her. But rather than letting her guard down, that gave her extra cause to keep it up. "I just want to ask him some questions. Are you sure you want to stay here?"

"It's my house. I'm perfectly comfortable here."

It was a perfectly nice, respectable house, too. Not big, but she imagined a fisherman's salary didn't amount to a great deal, but it was clean and looked-after, and was kept with pride. It was bad practice for a police officer to make snap judgments about people, but she suspected rather quickly that these people were not underworld crime lords, nor even low-ranking thugs. No crack addict had ever offered her tea brewed in a china pot.

Mr Om returned from the bathroom. He looked thoroughly exhausted, wide-eyed and pausing before the two women in his kitchen.

"You're ready now, Mr Om?" asked Tilda.

"Yes." He took a seat opposite Tilda, his wife standing behind him, arms crossed, her steely gaze fixed on her.

"I need you to tell me everything you know, Mr Om, about the deaths of Mr Jens de Boerk, and the incident at the *Tangiers Nights* adult club."

Dhiraj sighed. "Everything..."

"Shush, Raj," said Sali, her hand pressing his shoulder, and he stopped. "Don't say anything yet. Why are we doing this here?" she asked Tilda. "I still don't understand why you're asking these questions here and not at some police station."

Dhiraj wiped his forehead and winced. "Sali, it's like you want me to be arrested."

Sali made a face. "Shut up, Raj. Don't be so bloody stupid. Of course I don't, and even if I did, I don't think she does. But there's something weird going on here, and she's not telling us."

"Mrs Om, I have to warn you that withholding information relevant to an ongoing investigation –"

"So arrest him, then."

"For fuck's sake, Sali!" cried Dhiraj, throwing his hands up, but Sali stood firm, keeping those hard, dark eyes fixed on Tilda. She was a sharp one, probably sharper than her husband.

"No, it's fine," said Tilda. "You're very perceptive, Mrs Om. This is, for want of a better phrase, a private visit. I was hoping we may be able to aid one another."

Dhiraj settled in his seat and took a sip of tea to calm himself.

He remained visibly agitated. "How?"

Tilda spread her hands out in front of her, hoping it would appear a friendly gesture. "You're right, Mrs Om. I'm not here to arrest you, Dhiraj. I'm here to perhaps prevent you from being arrested, or at least charged, in the near future."

"Why haven't the police arrested me yet? Or at least stayed watching our house for me to come back?"

"It's been days since the incidents at Beckton and the *Tangiers Nights* club. The amnesty moved quickly and took the emphasis away from the search for an individual perpetrator and to the illicit and unregulated use of these... *dolls*. Politically, this amnesty is ticking all the right boxes at Scotland Yard and Whitehall, and is soaking up police resource. You're not an unknown quantity to the police, but you're a fairly low priority. Dragging you in for prosecution wouldn't achieve a great deal and wouldn't represent a good use of police money and resource when there are far more dangerous people at large." She let that hang in the air a second, just to offer them enough hope of his continued liberty. "Having said that," she continued, "If the amnesty goes badly, or there is a failure to apprehend some of the really bad people behind the manufacture and trade of these counterfeit goods, securing an easy scapegoat may just ease some of the public pressure on the police. We know you were at the scene of at least three murders before going missing and were in possession of an illegal *kokeshi* doll."

"I wasn't *in possession* –"

"Shut up, Raj," cut in Sali. "Carry on, Detective."

"Like I said, I'm here in a private capacity. You can call me Tilda."

"Then carry on, Tilda."

She coughed. "I can help protect you should the police turn its investigative focus upon you."

"Are you allowed to do that?" asked Dhiraj. "Can you, even?"

"Even if you were to be arrested, we'd have to secure sufficient evidence to make a prosecution. At present, there is very little other than circumstantial or anecdotal evidence, and almost nothing to provide motive. There's always a narrative to be established with these things, Dhiraj. I can help write that narrative."

The husband and wife locked eyes. The gaze they exchanged was frosty, yet mutually solid. Even if she was almightily pissed off with him, she'd stand by him. A part of her wanted to think *good on her*, and another part wanted to shake her out of it. Bloody men. Who knows what sort of shit this Dhiraj got up to with that *kokeshi* while they were on the run? Sali kept her mouth shut for now. "I need your assistance in order to do so. Quid pro quo."

"Go on," said Sali.

"You've seen the news about the robotics programme in Nigeria?" asked Tilda. "The Energy Secretary was there."

Sali shrugged. "Vaguely."

"I'm convinced there's something rotten at the heart of that deal. The amnesty is providing that technology programme with robots under very murky circumstances, and I think nothing good will come of it. The stated aim of that programme is to legitimise the use of those machines in society. I think that's a disaster waiting to happen."

Sali shrugged. "Surely what you think doesn't matter? You not liking them is a moral issue, not a police one, right? You're a police officer, not a philosopher. If they've done some crime, then lock them up. But why should some research programme concern you just because you don't agree with it?"

"Maybe it doesn't concern me," she said, firming her resolve anew. "But if there is corruption at the heart of that deal, then it does become a police matter."

Dhiraj looked drawn and pale, and he chose his words carefully, as though each one could be a poisonous barb that might strike him down if handled improperly. "I have no idea how I could possibly help you. I know nothing about that stuff."

"The doll you were with," said Tilda, looking him in the eye. "It was never collected through the amnesty."

Dhiraj squinted, squirmed.

"I promise this isn't a trap, Dhiraj."

"No. It was never collected. She – *it* – is still out there."

"I want it. I want it collected through the amnesty and sent to Port Harcourt as, let's call it, a covert operative. To take part in the research programme, or whatever they're doing down there, and surreptitiously feed information back to London."

Dhiraj and Sali looked at one another, frowning. "A spy?" asked Sali.

Tilda inclined her head. "If you like, yes."

Dhiraj screwed up his face. "Why this one? Why not any other robot that's been taken in through this amnesty?"

Tilda breathed out and stiffened her top lip. "This wouldn't be entirely official."

Dhiraj buried his head in his hands. "Oh, Christ. No, I can't. I can't get sucked into any more of this corrupt bullshit."

"I understand, but not assisting wouldn't be the best course of action for you to take, Mr Om."

Dhiraj shook his head miserably. "Well, you can't anyway. She was reconfigured, altered. She isn't able to..." he held his hands out in gesticulation before tailing off. "You know. We did it to hide her. The Spidermen, they changed her."

Sali rubbed her face. "Jesus Christ, Raj, will you stop calling it *'her'*."

He bowed his head. "Sorry."

"I spoke to the Spidermen. Don't worry about that. The doll can easily be changed back. You let me worry about that. All I want from you is to show me where it is."

Dhiraj closed his eyes and shook his head. "I need to think about this." He got up from his chair and walked to the door before looking back. "Can I go into the garden for a walk?"

"It's your house."

He sighed and left her with Sali, and the air thickened. It'd be her she'd have to convince, not Dhiraj. She'd met men like him before, who would blow with the wind. But behind him, literally in this case, stood a woman of firm constitution, anchoring him, harbouring him. She admired her, and wondered if she ought to pity her as well. Men could blow in winds strong enough to uproot trees.

"Would you like more tea?"

"Yes, please."

Earthy aromas of wafted up from the pot as Sali poured, warming Tilda up. "May I call you Sali?"

"If you must."

"You might not think it's my business to ask this, Sali, but about Dhiraj; he was on the run with one of those dolls for – what, three days? Have you seen what those things look like? How they appear to men? Do you know what could have happened?"

Sali shifted, putting the teapot down belligerently, spilling some out the spout, making her curse as she went to get a cloth to mop it up. "You're right. It's not your business."

"I'm simply saying that –"

"Look, God knows I think those bloody things are nasty, weird. I've only seen them on the telly, but I don't trust them. I hate the thought of my idiot husband running around with one. And I'm so pissed off with him you've no idea, for his idiot ideas and getting caught up in all this stuff, but no. That's not him. He'll do his time, but I'm prepared to believe him when he said nothing happened between them. For all his stupidity, I don't think he's the type to be unfaithful."

I remember that feeling, Tilda thought, sadly. She let Sali's words hang in the air for a while, as she recalled her own trenchant fidelity and refusal to face the truth. "I've not told anyone this, Sali," she said. "And sometimes I can't even tell myself. My ex-husband, Fraser, he used kokeshi. Sometimes in the evenings – working late, he'd say – maybe even when he away on business, at conferences, whatever. And I found out. When I did it was like I'd been kicked in the gut, I mean, kicked by a horse, like I'd ruptured something. I thought I might suffocate. And he..." her face prickled up with the rush of old pain, stabbing behind the eyes, catching her throat. Sali now sat across from her, eyes softening with – maybe not concern, but curiosity. "...he didn't – or, he said he didn't – understand why it was a big deal, why I was so upset. He said it wasn't like he was being unfaithful, for Christ's sake! They were just robots, dumb bits of plastic and electronics and code all wrapped up in a pretty package; it was basically masturbation. That's actually what he said, as his defence, the absolute arsehole. And it hurt, so much. It made me crazy. And it wasn't the basic mechanics of him fucking the machine, or even his stupidity or his arrogance when he got found out, though that absolutely vexed me – the worst thing was the feeling that I'd been replaced. That I was obsolete." She waved a finger in the air at nothing in particular. "I don't know whether Dhiraj did anything with that robot. But that project with the oil firm, they are trialling things that are effectively designed to replace *us*." She stopped, aware that she'd started to shake at the stark recollections, turned into words for the first time.

Sali breathed out slowly and reached out across the table, placing her hand on Tilda's. It was wonderfully warm and firm. "I'm sorry for what happened to you." She withdrew the hand, and Tilda took hers back too. Unheld, it felt too exposed. "But why tell me this? If you're trying to make me doubt my husband, I won't."

"I wanted to make you understand what's at stake here. So that you could understand why I need your help so badly. This is important. Not for me. For us."

"They won't make me obsolete. I might have married a moron, but he's a moron with a good heart."

Tilda nodded. She agreed that Dhiraj was probably a good man. "But what about all the other women and girls who'll look on as they become outmoded, superseded by technology? That's not right. There's an appetite for this – otherwise people like that huge oil firm and our Cabinet ministers wouldn't be involved."

A polite cough at the door signalled Dhiraj's return. He looked a little calmer, running his fingers through his short, cropped hair and nodding at the two women, pushing a long, concerted breath through puffed out cheeks. "Have you two finished talking?"

Sali nodded. "Yes. I think you should help her. Show her where this robot thing is. Where you left it."

His hands fidgeted by his belt, and he stared at them. "Ok. If it helps. I'll show you. But it'd be best to go tonight."

Tilda looked at her watch. Still the afternoon. "That's fine. We need to go and fetch somebody else first anyway."

D'Souza VII

This was insane. Like something from ancient Rome, or worse. Mobo, forehead slick with sweat, sat cross-legged on a fold-out chair at the edge of a dirt circle illuminated by the headlamps of 4x4s, trucks and quadcopters hovering overhead, gun-toting bodyguards by his sides. Like a deranged film director. And, like a director, his army of extras encircled the scene, whooping and exchanging money and drinking beers and water.

D'Souza, shaking his head in disbelief, stood at the opposite end of the circle to the other prisoner, the fat man, still pleading and whining and begging for mercy. The prisoner had been offered a knife, a machete, but they just lay on the dust before him, and D'Souza reckoned they'd be moistened by tears and piss more than blood. For himself, he'd also spurned the offer of knives and blades, and had instead dug into his holdall to retrieve his *ethunu kaduwa*. The binding had held well around the sticks, and he rubbed his fingers along the smooth edges, remembering its bumps and nicks. It had acquired a couple of new ones along the journey, but when he arced it through the dusky air it still sang. Smooth sides for pain, bound sides for damage. A swift crack to the back of the skull would be goodnight; he hoped he could get away with just slapping this poor bastard about with the smooth sides before it got called off. No need for him to die.

A gunshot sounded from the side, signalling the start of the fight. The other man wailed as D'Souza walked up to him, and delivered a firm push to the shoulder. Predictably, he fell straight onto his arse. D'Souza backed away, spitting on to the floor. Boos and hisses rang around the circle. D'Souza stepped back and cast an eye away to Mobo, who grimaced and whispered something to one of his lieutenants. In turn, the lackey grabbed a bullhorn and barked into it something in Yoruba he didn't understand, before translating into English, presumably for his benefit.

"This one will not fight!"

Jeers all around.

"What if we give this coward a fighter?" the lackey said, pointing to the crying man. D'Souza sighed deeply, and gripped his *kaduwa* tighter, clenching his jaw and controlling his breathing. Cheers all around.

"Who will fight for this fat man?"

Another man stepped into the ring to cheers. Big fucker. Shirtless, bald, no neck, cricking his neck ostentatiously. Reminded him a little of Collars. Of course. This was what it was all about all along. The pretence of a bullshit 'trial by combat' when in fact it would simply be two executions dressed up to alleviate the crushing boredom of the endless nights these dumb fuckers had elected to spend on the wilder fringes of the Niger delta with only the midges, mosquitoes and occasional idiot for company. The beefcake picked up the knife, inspected it to jeers from the crowd, and then picked up the machete, to roars of approval. So they intended to make snakefood of him all along. And if he won, he'd be condemning the other poor fucker to a slit throat and no doubt a Bonny grave.

D'Souza gripped the handle of his *kaduwa* and slowed his breathing as much as he could before the beefcake rushed him. All he saw was the arc of a huge arm, ready to bring an agricultural, overarm swipe down upon him. Time slowed. A machete was a pretty indiscriminate weapon – any slice that got hold of enough flesh could incapacitate or kill, whereas his *kaduwa* required a degree more art. He rolled under the initial swipe and swept the *kaduwa* around onto his opponent's ankles. A glancing blow. He stepped back, and twirled his weapon in his hands. His best bet would be to finish things early. The beefcake turned and ran again, slower this time, swiping in front of him. D'Souza kept his distance, waiting for the inevitable overarm swipe, and when it came, he moved into and around it, and flicked his *kaduwa* up and over, whipping the edged side down onto his opponent's forearm. The force snapped the man's forearm with a yowl, and the machete clattered to the ground with a puff of dust. D'Souza followed the blow up with another crack upon the man's wrist, and the splintering of bone jarred its way up the weapon, making D'Souza grit his teeth. On his knees and howling, the beefcake grabbed his injured arm with his good hand, holding it up like a token as it swelled with black blood. He looked at D'Souza, then with confusion over at Mobo, who nodded. With a grimace, the beefcake grabbed the machete handle with his good hand and rose. Christ, but he must have been in agony. D'Souza sidestepped around the back of him and cracked his *kaduwa* hard across the base of the man's skull, making him fall limply into the dirt. Laughs, cheers and derisive howls came from the crowd. D'Souza checked his opponents' pulse; still alive, but out cold. He'd feel like shit when he woke up, too. Panting, he felt the urge to meditate, just as he always did when drawing blood. That made him laugh.

Mobo said something to Aba, who had been *schop, schop, schoping* his knife with his leather strop throughout the fight. Aba nodded and stepped into the ring. D'Souza clenched his weapon, breathing hard, ready to go again, but though Aba kept his gaze firmly on D'Souza, it was at the beefcake's body he stopped, drawing his huge knife across his throat and spilling black blood into the earth. He then went over to the other man, still quivering in horror, and finally put him out of his misery in the same way. D'Souza put his hand to his nose as the stink of gas and shit permeated the air, and the tiredness in his bones caught up with him. Aba approached, causing D'Souza to readopt his fighting pose, but Aba put his hands up in conciliation, sheathed his knife, and beckoned him over to Mobo.

"It's a good job your credentials turned out to be clean," said Mobo, as the man with the bullhorn told the crowd to disperse and a couple of lackeys set about dealing with the bodies. "Because you've just killed one of my men, which means you owe me a pair of hands, and I need all the hands I can get in this war. I have very big plans."

Salazar V

Salazar peeped through the spy hole on his apartment door, and his heart sank.

The policewoman – the Scottish one with the short red hair – stood with arms crossed, determination in her dark, tired eyes. Sighing, he pressed his forehead against the door, closed his eyes and wished her away.

She knocked again, harder this time, making him jump, but he bit his lip and ignored it. He looked again. Still she stood. After a moment she muttered something under her breath, checked her watch, shook her head and seemed about to leave, when...

"Papa, Papa, who is at the door?"

It was a curious feeling, to have one's heart sinking and rising at the same time. The sweet sound of his Chouchou's voice would no doubt alert the police, but even so, he couldn't help but smile as Lily toddled up to him in her elephant-and-pineapple pyjamas, one hand clumsily digging sleep out of her eye, the other dragging her battered pink comfort blanket behind her. She walked into his grateful arms as the detective thumped on the door again, and she gave a little whimper.

That angered Salazar enough to rise and open the door, Lily nuzzling her sleepy face into the crook of his neck. "What is it, detective? You've woken my little girl."

The detective actually had enough decency to at least pretend to look sheepish. "My apologies, Mr Gomez. I know it's late, but it's important."

"It can wait. You can pester me at work if you must. Leave my daughter out of this. Haven't you any shame?"

"Mr Gomez, I wouldn't be here if it weren't highly important. May we step inside?"

"No, you may not."

"I insist, please. Look," she said, opening her coat. "No badge. No warrant card. This isn't strictly official."

Lily stirred, took a look at the imposter and crinkled her eyes, looking away, eliciting a little whine. "Qu'est-ce que le dame veut, Papa?"

Salazar stroked her hair and shushed her gently, before sighing in resignation. "Come in. Take your shoes off."

It took a good fifteen minutes of paper-thin singing and comforting to get Lily back to sleep, by which time Salazar was ruing not being to get to bed himself, but Boulton still sat patiently in his kitchenette, warming her hands on the mugs of coffee he'd told her to help herself to. Somehow she didn't carry that cold, professional air she'd had when she'd interviewed him in the EI Systems building.

He took the time to prepare his own mug of coffee. If he was going to be inconvenienced, he'd do it at his own pace. The apartment EIS had secured him was small, but utter luxury compared to his old nest in Lyon. Quiet, clean, light, well-appointed, and affordable on the new salary he'd started on at the company. But what good was any of this if the police wouldn't leave him alone? Boulton might have stated that she wasn't here on official business, but he'd learned long ago that police folk were always on official business. They were no different from the gangsters in that way. Worst of all was he couldn't see a way out of their claws other than toeing the line they drew. For now.

"We need your expertise," she said when he joined her at the kitchen diner.

Salazar shrugged. "What expertise?"

"EIS recruited you because of your knowledge and skills in the field of sexual plastics. I need you to use those skills for..." she made a grim face and stared into her coffee, as though the answer lay there. "A special project."

Salazar noted that she didn't have any of her globelets or devices with her today. She hadn't even used a phone. "What sort of project?"

"I want you to modify a robot to be submitted to the amnesty."

Odd. He shifted in his seat. "What do you mean, 'modify'?"

"You said there were bigger fish than yourself in this game. That there's something wrong with Anita Rhodes. And we're going after her."

He perked up at that name. He recalled the first time he'd seen her on that video screen back in Lyon. She'd seemed so exotic and beautiful then. Now, she seemed... toxic. Poison. A misty thought of Lily's mother swam into his tired mind. Maybe all the women in his life were destined to turn into sour things. Then again, it might not be them. It might be him. Whichever it was, he shook his head. "I can't go after her. I need this job too much."

"You've already said a great deal."

"I said nothing."

"You implied enough. Enough to warrant following her. You do this, and it could be the end of all your troubles."

He let out a wry laugh at that. "You know how many times I've heard that? From gangsters, from the police, from women, from..." *From Nita Rhodes.* He hated himself for what he'd permitted himself to do, the actions that had led to things like Mr D'Souza lying in a hospital bed with those horrific injuries." He squirmed just thinking about it. "I don't think I can do it."

Boulton set her jaw and looked at him intently. "Do the right thing, here, Mr Gomez, and you'll be able to continue with this new life. Be under no illusion that it can't be taken away. It takes a lot of effort to build something, but very little effort to smash it all to pieces. That precious little girl in there –"

"Don't you dare speak of her," Salazar said, bristling. "Neither of us is worth a fraction of her."

Boulton nodded and gazed at her shoes for a second. "Indeed. But I am a woman of my word, and I promise that you and your daughter will be left alone if you cooperate."

He breathed out. "What exactly do you need me to do?"

~

The next night Salazar arranged to have Lily looked after at the creche at EIS. It was a good service, and just about the only time he'd been comfortable – no, not comfortable, but willing – to leave Lily in the care of others. EIS was a professional outfit and looked after its employees. Nowadays it seemed it wasn't uncommon for single parents to leave their children overnight at the company as they attended out-of-town meetings, or drinks receptions, or dinners. There was a certain sadness to that, he mused, but it also gave his employers little reason to doubt him when he did so. His line manager Dwight, a heavily bearded guy from Massachusetts, didn't bat an eyelid when Salazar gave the excuse of attending an evening lecture somewhere in Lincoln's Inn on artificial protein glues in sensor networks. He registered, turned up, took a seat near the exit and when the lights went down surreptitiously took his leave of the auditorium.

Shame, as it might have been pretty interesting. Instead, he took a bus – paid for in cash – to the East End, and followed the directions Boulton had given him until he found himself outside the side-entrance to a grotty looking establishment just off the Commercial Road. Already there, out of sight from the main road, were Boulton, and another man, which made him stop in his tracks. He furrowed his brows and studied him. An Asian guy, who kept shifting his eyes back and forth and to the ground, and hunched his back as if trying to disappear into the hood of his raincoat. Salazar stared at him, but the man just looked away. Not like a cop, then.

"Who's this? He's not police."

"No," said Boulton. "He's not. This is Raj. He's agreed to help. Raj, this is Gomez. Like I said, you two. This is off the books."

The two men looked into each others' eyes. Salazar could see the same fear and uncertainty he was sure was written all over his own face. "Fine. Let's get this over with."

Boulton tapped on the keypad and the shutters scraped upwards with a clatter that surely must have alerted someone they were there. He swore under his breath and buried his own chin into his collar, just like this Raj.

On the ground floor the building housed some sort of ethnic clothing shop, but the top floor was a disgusting, flea-bitten workshop. Engineering paraphernalia littered the dark, unkempt corners, and every now and then a mouse – or perhaps something bigger – scuttled along the shadows. Rats didn't bother him – he'd seen enough of them in the iniquitous dens of Lyon to last a lifetime – but he was wary of the company they often kept. When they approached the workbench in the centre of the lab, he was surprised to see a lifter robot standing next to it.

Even more to his surprise, Raj went straight up to it and took its hand in his own. *Curiouser and curiouser.*

"What the hell is this?" Salazar snapped, getting them all to look at him. "It's a lifter. What do you expect me to do to it, Detective?"

"She isn't a lifter," snapped back Dhiraj. "She's... she's a pleasure robot. A kokeshi. We had to do this to her to stop her being captured by the amnesty. To disguise her."

"Why?"

Dhiraj shuffled, and eyed the detective with suspicion. That made two of them, then. "I wanted to keep her out of police hands. Incrimination."

"I want you to reinstall her sexual systems," said Boulton. "Restore her to her previous look and capability. So she's a fully-functioning... so she's fully functional again. Plus, I want you to add encrypted, automated data capture and transmission."

"She'll already be fitted with data capture, analytics, performance monitoring, health and condition monitoring as a matter of course."

Boulton shook her head. "Not that. Capture of extraneous data. Sounds. Images."

Salazar raised his eyebrows. "You mean spying? You want to use it as a spy?"

"She'll be restored to full sexual capability, but she won't be used. Someone puts in a call alerting the police, who come and capture and log her. She'll be processed and delivered with the other robots to the technology demonstrator programme in Port Harcourt, where she'll be able to monitor things of interest to us."

Salazar rubbed his face and walked up to the lifter to inspect it more closely. He scratched at the coarse growth sprouting around his face. Up close, the lifter did carry the air of incongruence about it. Less robust. He wouldn't have recognised it as a *kokeshi* had he not been told, and he'd spent more time than he would have liked around such things. It was good work. He took a few minutes to familiarise himself with the workshop. The machinery looked functional, and indeed looked authentically black-market, and the robot's parts had all been kept together in a plastic crate. He'd been spoiled by the pristine clean rooms of EIS of late; doing one more job in a shitty little box room stinking of rancid old food and body odour almost made him feel nostalgic. He wiped away that thought with a grimace, and turned to the detective.

"So you'll do it?" she asked.

He laughed grimly. "What choice do I have?"

Nita VII

"Everything's going wonderfully well so far," lied Nita to Robb. "Swimmingly well, one might say."

The CEO nodded and smiled from his London office. "I have to say you've excelled yourself, Nita. I trust you've been keeping up to date with the share prices the past few days?"

"When I can." She bit at a nail and stared at it, avoiding Robb's eyes down her apartment's holoscreen. "It's doing well."

"Well?" Robb laughed. "The shareholders are very pleased. As are the Government. This has been a piece of very shrewd strategic positioning." He paused. "You don't seem overly enthusiastic about it."

"No, I am," she lied again, forcing a smile out. "It's just a tad isolating here, in the middle of the sea, water on all sides. And it's only been a couple of weeks so far."

"You'll be fine. When you can, take some shore leave and some time off. Commission one of Johnson's helicopters. We'll pay. You deserve it. It's not like you're imprisoned over there."

Is it not?

"No, I'll make sure I look after myself, of course. And I'll be back in London as soon as I can."

"You're doing a grand job. Try not to burn out. You're our star over there."

Robb logged off their conversation. Throughout it she wanted to shout at the screen that something was wrong, something she couldn't quite figure out, which were too terrible to utter, and which bound her to her path now.

Much to her sad surprise, her sense of loneliness had not diminished after making love with Adem. She'd made attempts to try and arrange that gin and tonic with his sister Joanna but was met with automated replies and brush-offs from the few staff that vaguely knew her movements and whereabouts. She was a funny fish, that one, and had seemingly swum off somewhere. Nita couldn't quite make her out, but it had been nice to have at least the prospect of some female company, and the failure to communicate had been disheartening, to say the least.

As for Adem, any hope Nita had harboured of having a soulmate here, or even just someone with whom to share this isolation, appeared to be dashed; Adem had come over sullen and withdrawn over the dealings with his brother, and uneasy about spending more time with her, preferring to keep his own company. That worried Nita. They shared darkness – many types of darkness – and she didn't like the thought of them being separated. Whatever endgame was to occur from this project, their fates were now intermingled, and she didn't like the thought of her cohort suddenly axing their partnership.

She made her way to the testbed workshops, still wondering about the two missing robots. Most likely theory was some sort of security leak – possibly cyber, but more likely human, that had opened up a path for the robots to be obtained by the NPF. Though for what end she couldn't say, but she didn't like it. Even if they just used the robots to show how soft security was, it would be a PR catastrophe. Johnson would be irate. And if the share price was hit Robb wouldn't be her number one fan any more.

At the workshop she was greeted by Edward, the Head of Logistics for the science complex. He pushed his spectacles up his nose and addressed her conspiratorially, which pissed her off. "Good morning, Miss Rhodes."

Sharing secrets with Adem was one thing, but doing so with a mule from logistics was another. "Morning, Edward. Any word on our delivery?"

"Afraid not. I think..." he looked side to side, as if relishing the cloak-and-dagger games, "I seriously think they may have simply fallen into the sea."

She hoped so and nodded him away before proceeding with a sweep of the workshop with one of the project leads, Aduwo. The workshop itself was an incredible facility; a domed edifice two hundred and fifty metres across and at its apex fifty metres high, it sat at the southern end of the Science complex, jutting into the air above the rig like a giant breast. Above them, the glass ceiling revealed a simmering blue sky and a doubtless broiling sun, harmless in this air-conditioned space. Walking around at balcony level enabled her to take in the scope and efficiency of the operation. The workshop was fitted with several groups of Cubebots: self-reflexive autonomous modular systems able to self-morph into required form and function as required for any stage within the manufacturing cycle. In fact they were rarely cubed, but when at rest, they reverted to a cube-base to enable efficient means of transport, storage and and logistics.

Any robotic structure could be comprised of a flexible number of Cubebots that reorganised themselves. Nita had seen demonstrations of such things at trade shows but never in a working industrial environment before, and not in such numbers. Here and there they formed and reformed seamlessly, fixing, creating, testing equipment and other products. Joseph had informed her that these were used to create the robotic machinery used for exploration and excavation in their oil operations; here they would be commandeered to assist in the quick turnaround of remanufacture of the kokeshi dolls into Digital People. On she went, past clean rooms and assembly rigs and more traditional robotic manufacturing systems comprised of arms and other manipulators that whizzed about unthinkingly. Here and there the mules of the operation, the lifter robots, hefted loads under the supervision of the humans around them, who checked quality and process.

She stopped upon the section of balcony overlooking the rig focussing on kokeshi remanufacture. The noise of dull clanks and high-pitched whirrs and drills and the whoosh of pressure combined to make an oddly rhythmic pulse that echoed around this apparently self-sustaining auditorium, a perfectly tuned orchestration of a type of music that required neither human ear nor hand. And yet, she mused, these artificial minds would be working to her own hymn sheet in bringing something fundamentally human into being: the power of emotion. She turned to the project leader Aduwo. "Can you switch off the Cubebots?"

He frowned, and puffed out his cheeks like a trumpet player. "Why?"

"I would like to inspect our products. Just for five minutes."

He made a sound like *ayeesh*, rubbed his face, and whistled loudly over to some of the people below. Within minutes she was dressed in hard-hat, goggles, lab coat, latex gloves and shoe covers, inspecting the rig housing the dolls. It was impressive. Forty of the dolls stood in a circular rig, each of them hard-wired to their own systems pod, staring unblinkingly out into empty space, their torsos opened up, showing various states of repair as the Cubebots brought them up to demonstrator level spec. The Cubebots themselves were bigger than she'd thought, almost up to her waist. Right now they stayed perfectly still, and individually they did just seem like flat cubes, but together, surrounded by these things she did get the sense of a harmonious system; that these cubes were not much different to the humanoid robots they tended.

But they would be. She reached out a hand to touch one of the legs of the doll closest to her, but Aduwo coughed loudly, and she pulled her hand back, smiling meekly. These dolls would be doing something good at the end of this. She really hoped so. The next section of the tour might shed some light on this. She bit her lip, smiled some thanks to the manufacturing team, signalled for them to carry on working, and took her leave.

The Military District was situated on the western edge of Oil City. A wedge of small apartments housed the male security personnel who had been selected as the human guinea pigs for the demonstration. Nita chose to watch some of them in person during the initial round of tests. Some of the apartments had been fitted with cameras and one-way mirrors to enable effective monitoring of the interaction between the human test subjects and the Digital People. Mission Control consisted of a coder, robotics systems engineer, neurologist and psychologist watching and monitoring the tests through a series of holoscreens in a gloomy studio. Nita smiled a welcome at the team already in there. After introductions, she cast her eye over the main screen the team were watching.

"His name's Eli," said Helene, the neurologist. "He was introduced to his Digital Person yesterday."

"What's her name?" asked Nita.

"Dorothy."

Nita lit up inside. Just hearing the name was evidence enough. On the streets, in the underworld, every single *kokeshi* would go by its model name, so the only names they ever got were Maya, Naomi, Grace, Dolly, and a couple of others. Here they already had the first step – the same first step taken by humans – towards individuality; their own name. Eli, a wiry man with a stoic looking face, stood preparing a cup of tea at the kitchenette in his apartment. Apartment didn't sound quite right. *She* had an apartment. Eli – and, she supposed, most of his immediate colleagues – lived in a spartan bedsit; more like a high-end cell than the luxurious spread of her own living quarters. The Digital Person Dorothy sat on the khaki bunk, head bowed. Dark haired, dark skinned, dark eyed, it caught Eli's gaze with a strange look.

"What's wrong?" he asked her in a soft voice. He stood over her and sipped some tea.

"Everything is so strange here," she replied. "Why do I have to remain here?"

"It won't be for long. We're companions now."

"During the night I found it hard to settle." She placed a hand upon his. "After we made love, I could not settle."

"Why not?"

"I'm afraid of what's outside."

He smiled. "Don't be afraid. The rig is full of noises, sounds and strange goings-on, but it's fine; they cannot hurt you."

"Would you take me away from this place?" Dorothy turned her head and stared at the screen, and Nita got the strange feeling that Dorothy was looking straight at her. Impossible, of course.

"She's displaying need," said Nita. "Is it genuine?"

"It certainly looks like it," said Heath, the coder. "Her digital neural networks are growing at a rate of knots. She's learning, but not in the traditional 'machine-learning' sense. She's developing her emotional intelligence but, unlike the virtual demos captured in the State-of-the-Art, she's doing it against the context of her new body. What she does with her body informs her thinking, rather than reacting to external stimuli in accordance to programming. She's been talking about her alienation, about how little she understands of her new environment. She's asking questions. It really does seem as though she wants to leave."

Heath grinned, but Nita screwed up her brows and swallowed down a lump in her throat. She knew how that felt. Still, she pushed the feeling away. This Digital Person wouldn't be leaving. She would, however, be furrowing a new path for the ones that followed.

"Ah, but the really interesting part is Eli's neurological response," continued Heath. "He's *empathising* with her."

Nita almost told him to shut up. She suspected her own neurological readings wouldn't be far off his.

~

On the walk back to her apartment thoughts of everything she'd seen swam through her head. There was much to take in. And this was just on the first few days. She bit at a nail again. The feeling of discomfort hadn't entirely gone away, and yet a thrill coursed through her. The research might work. Early days, of course, but encouraging signs. Empathy for machines!

When she opened her apartment door she started. Two soldiers were rooting around her things, under the supervision of a third. Keeping a hand upon the door, she cleared her throat, and the three interlopers looked at her. The apparent supervisor gestured for them to carry on and walked over to Nita, and tried to mask an uncomfortable look by peering down his nose at her. "Miss Rhodes?"

"What the hell is this? Who are you?"

"Security, Miss Rhodes. There has been a serious security breach on the rig. Senior Management has ordered that everyone is to be searched."

The missing robots. That weaselly Edward must have said something. She scratched her head and made a face. "What type of security breach? Is it serious?"

The soldier smiled. "This is just precautionary. Just let us go about our business. It's for your safety. There are bad people about who'd wish harm upon this place. Please, just give us a few minutes."

She sighed. "You could have forewarned me."

The soldier ruffled his brows and tutted. "Rig security is the highest priority. There are hundreds of people active on this rig, and significant assets on board, not least your own. When a breach is reported, we have to ensure that everyone is both safe and transparent."

Transparent. So she was a suspect. She decided not to protest her innocence, in case that didn't look good. She gulped as the soldiers rooted through her computer hardware, though why she knew not. She was certain there was nothing incriminating on there, but seeing others rifling through her things made her a little sick.

"You don't need to go through those things."

"I'm afraid we do," said the soldier.

"Fine, I'll come back later."

As she turned the man snapped at her, and she started again. "No. You stay here."

They left soon enough, closing the door behind them, leaving her in a cloud of relief, coldness and more than a little fear. After composing herself with a cup of tea and a biscuit, she opened the front door to leave for a meeting, she jumped a third time. One of the soldiers who had searched the room stood there, sentry like, one hand fingering the butt of his rifle. He gave her a distasteful nod. "Where you going?"

She blinked, composed herself. "I have meetings."

"I go with you, then."

"No, no, I don't need a security detail."

He shrugged, leant back against the wall, popped a chewing gum into his mouth and chewed it noisily.

Plainly, there wouldn't be any good in arguing. She shut the door on him.

"We'll see about this," she muttered, setting up a call with Joseph's PA, a prim lady called Estelle. She'd book some time with Joseph, and come clean about hearing about the missing robots. She couldn't spend her life under suspicion. She doubted that a security breach could be that serious. The attack on her car in the city was possible because the urban landscape enabled that sort of guerrilla warfare. Out here... she gazed at the windows showing water, water everywhere. No, there was no way this was anything worse than precautionary.

The call to Estelle cut out, and her globelet informed her there was no wireless network available. She screwed up her face. Weird. A second and third attempt yielded the same result. Her personal phone, the same.

"What the bloody hell?"

Outside, the sentry still chewed sullenly as she snapped at him, "What's going on?"

He wrinkled his forehead and shrugged.

"I can't get a comms signal for anything."

At that the soldier's walkie-talkie, an old-school device strapped to his shoulder, spluttered and crackled, and a voice barked something she didn't understand. He responded, then turned to Nita and gestured with his head to the apartment. "Inside."

"No. What's going on?"

"I have to go. Security breach. Get inside, or I take you."

Nita swallowed. He probably would drag her in if he gave her the chance. She noted the number on his lapels: *37810.* "Fine."

Inside, she watched the soldier walk off via the closed circuit monitor by the door. She might be locked in, but she wasn't totally isolated yet. In her computer gear she'd kept a nanodrone, a flight vehicle in the shape and size of a fly. Oil City's wireless network might have been disabled, but *37810*'s walkie-talkie had still been working, so she could still establish a local frequency with which to control the bug. It was risky, and she bit at her nails as the globelet asked her if she wanted to confirm setting up the frequency. If the bug was caught, it could be hacked fairly easily, but not necessarily traced back to her if she cut off the signal. But it was a fly bug. Hard to detect if it kept to the shadows.

She told the globelet to confirm, breathed out, and pushed the bug through the gap beneath the apartment door.

Its Visual Recognition System would follow the combination of numbers *37810* on the soldier's uniform. Nanodrones were pretty sophisticated these days, but this was simply a dumb bug; it'd follow numbers rather than faces, and send Nita whatever audio-visual cues it thought interesting, and she could tell it to stop or carry on, but little more than that. As it flew the grainy, monochrome feed of *37810*'s shoulder flashed through her monitor as the man swaggered away. After ten minutes of wandering around the labyrinthine complex, as Nita wondered whether this was just a wild goose chase, the soldier reached an innocuous-looking door, looked this way and that, and barked something into it. Nita rubbed her eyes, ordered the servobot to get her a coffee, and leaned forward in her seat. The fly bug zipped into the door before it closed.

Darkness followed, until the bug's illumination settings adjusted to optimal level, and revealed a metal staircase, like a fire escape, leading down quite some way to what looked like a subterranean section of the rig, dark and windowless. Another soldier manned this space, reclining lazily on his seat, clumpy leather boots up on a desk littered with papers and small devices. In the low resolution feed Nita couldn't make out what anything read, but she did hear voices.

"Increase clarity of audio feed," she said.

The picture dulled as the audio feed cleared up; with such small power resources the bug had to adapt accordingly.

"Abeg, fly!" came a voice, and from left of field a giant hand swatted at the bug, and Nita sat up instinctively. *Careful, little bug.* It flew to the ceiling and stayed in the shadows. 37810 had his back to them, and spoke down to the reclining man, who lit up a cigarette and offered one to 37810.

"Where's the Johnson girl?" asked 37810.

"Through there."

"Ach. And the Canary?"

"Jo-Jo she wozin' the Canary!"

"Mm-mm. That erema. Like to bala that."

Laughter and much gesticulation. "No way, man! She'd eat you up."

"Why you showin' those thirty-two? Shut your mouth, 'fore I woze you." 37810 took a puff on his cigarette. "Anyhow, what she doing down here? And why they askin' for me?"

He shrugged. "Who knows? Baddo Johnson prolly sent her. Maybe he wanted someone from up top to see the rebel's plans."

Rebels! So the NPF were here. Nita inched forwards on her seat as the man continued.

"As for you, send a dog to do a dog's work! Hah!"

"Fa!" 37810 tossed his cigarette at the other man, who ducked it with a grin.

"Just get down there."

37810 waggled his hands dismissively. "Whatever."

The bug slowly followed 37810 along a corridor into a small, windowless room on the left. Nita gasped. On a chair, head slumped forwards, sat a man with his hands tied behind his back. A second man approached him slowly, lifted up his chin with one finger, whispered something and looked away, perhaps at somebody else? Nita almost cried out when the man produced a cosh from nowhere and slammed it across the seated man's face. Even down the crackly feed there was a clear *crack*, and Nita winced.

"Come on, NPF dog. Speak, dog. What do you plan to do with those robots?"

The NPF! So they had been behind the capture of those robots. Nita shivered. If this prisoner had been apprehended on Oil City, then no wonder the security guards were being overly cautious. She thought about switching off the feed and staying put in her room, trying to get hold of Adem somehow, but as her hand hovered over the globelet she held back, her fingers twitching nervously. After what had happened in the city she had no love for these violent insurgents, but watching this man being interrogated brought a serious distaste to the back of her throat.

That's a little hypocritical, don't you think?

As she shushed the thought away the seated man slurred something barely intelligible. Something about plans...

A woman's voice from off screen made Nita sit up. When the woman stepped into the screen Nita gasped.

Joanna.

The tall, elegant Johnson daughter walked up to the rebel, cupped his chin, and stroked his closely cropped hair, almost affectionately. "What do you know, young man? This is extremely serious. You were caught flying a stolen drone over Oil City from a boat half a mile from the rig. We know you're NPF. It will go well for you if you told us what these plans of yours are."

The man looked at Joanna with wide, terrified, confused eyes, panting profusely, and looking this way and that for help.

Just tell them what you know, you stupid man, Nita thought. *There's no need for bloodshed.*

"Why are you doing this?" he asked Joanna.

"You know why, my friend. This is your last chance." She leant into him, whispered something inaudible into his ear, and he began to shake with whimpering. Nita frowned, covering her mouth with tensed up fingers, the back of her neck cold. When the man said nothing, Joanna walked away and nodded to 37810, who unholstered his pistol. The man started to cry out and try to break free of his bonds when he saw the gun, pleading with Joanna to release him, all the time asking her why she was doing this. 37810 walked behind the man, held his gun to the base of the man's skull and looked at Joanna, somewhere off screen again.

"You don't think he knows anything more?" said the other man.

"He's a nobody. A scout. He knows nothing," came Joanna's voice. "This is going nowhere. You. Make it clean," she said to 37810. "There is no need for more suffering."

Nita jumped as the pistol fired and the man went limp, dark spots spattering the floor. Shaking, she held her hand over the shut-off command, but held it in place as Joanna started to speak again.

"So what is our counter-measure? We need to strike at the rebels before they get a chance to strike us."

"You should have kept him alive. I could have pressed him further. Much further."

"I have seen people like this all over the world, soldier. He was a scared boy. These NPF bastards use scared boys and brainwash them, get them to do their bidding with tales of glory and injustice. Cowards. If you doubt my word, feel free to report to my father."

A pause. "Of course not, Madam Johnson."

"Good. What counter measures are being taken, then?"

"We are going to surprise the NPF with a strike of our own. We still are in control of the two missing robots from the English technology project. They've been weaponised and are en route to the delta. They look just like local girls."

Silence from Joanna, and Nita's heart slammed against her ribcage so loudly she was certain Joanna would hear it on the other end of the feed and look straight at her. The Johnson daughter approached the dead man, placed a hand upon his bloodied head, and addressed the soldiers. "Throw this poor boy to the sea."

Nita shut off the feed, shaking.

Joanna. How could she? Her head spun. Two of her robots were out there, somewhere in the vast sprawl of the delta. She shuddered as she recalled her own orders to have one of the things weaponised back in England, and now it had come back to bite her. People would die. Christ alone knew what damage one of them could do if they were wired with explosives. They were the perfect bombers; they hadn't been fitted with digital emotions yet. They'd never falter, never have second thoughts; would go exactly where they were directed.

Disgust coursed through her: at the company she kept, at the terrible things that were on the cusp of happening, but most of all at herself. She'd turned blind eye after blind eye to corruption and violence, and bloodied her own hands, all in pursuit of what?

"I didn't want this," she told herself in a wafer-thin voice, shaking her head. "This was supposed to do good. I can't do this any more. How the fuck did things get to this?"

The choices she had were egregious. She recalled the attack on her transport detail back in the city. She had no love for the people who had attacked her car, but suddenly she found herself pitying them. Or at least not wanting them massacred. Keeping her mouth shut would enable the programme to continue, and result in some good to come out of this. But it'd result in yet more blood on her hands; the thought of more self-loathing and guilt would surely break her completely. Every inch of her screamed to tell someone, to tell the world she'd had enough, that she wanted to get off. Yet if she did blow the whistle, the world would know that robots from her company had been used in murderous, corporate conspiracy. It'd be catastrophic for EIS, and her reputation and career would be in ruins.

It would all be for nothing.

Adem VI

About bloody time. Connectivity had been restored after a period of radio silence, during which Adem had been confined to his apartment with no explanation as to why. It was bad enough that his moron brother should have taken his heirship from him, but to be relegated to the sidelines and left in the dark about matters of rig security took the absolute piss. Alone, he broiled in frustration against his father. All he'd given, trying to gain respect and political and industrial goodwill overseas; all he'd sacrificed, and the dark corners to which he'd turned to give his family this opportunity to adopt a fabulous new technology and gain a foothold in the generation-long struggle against the NPF, none of it was to his profit. One by one, the faces of his accursed family drifted through his mind's eye: Joseph, Remus, Joanna. To hell with all of them, even his sister.

Upset and trembling with anger, he sat himself down and asked the servobot for a large whisky – fuck the morning – and decided to check his messages now that connectivity had been restored.

Oddly, there was one from the red-headed Detective Sergeant back in London. Boulton. Intrigued, he opened it.

Dear Mr Johnson,

I trust your journey home and subsequently to Oil City was pleasant, and you're enjoying your time back there.

I thought it prudent to inform you that the amnesty is continuing back in London, and we have apprehended more robots for your demonstration. They are currently en route.

I'm not sure if you're aware but part of current policing procedure is to report on the added value and possible 'value return' of police activity. In layman's terms it simply means determining what social and economic value policing is bringing to England (other than the obvious win of catching the bad guys!). The amnesty represents a good opportunity for the police to show how its actions have directly supported a project of major technological and economic significance. It'd be most useful if you could apprise us of any high-level updates to the project. Nothing formal at this stage, though there may be some forms and a bit more bureaucracy later — nothing you won't be used to, I'm sure.

Best,
DS Boulton, Tilda

Adem tapped his finger on the arm of his chair, and sipped at his whisky. How he'd love to drop his father in the shit, but there wasn't anything to write up. His father might be an idiot, a bonehead, but he'd done nothing illegal. Whereas Adem himself... he shook his head, finished the whisky, bared his teeth as it warmed his throat, and readied himself for a by-the-book response, when a call flashed up on his holoscreen.

Nita.

Distracted from the detective's message, he opened up Nita's call.

"Adem, thank Christ you're there." She huddled close to the camera, tucking her head into her chest, whispering her words. She looked wild, scared even.

"Nita, my dear. What's the matter?"

She looked around. "Are these lines secure?"

"These comms lines?"

"Yes. Are they?" She rushed her words. Something must have spooked her.

"I'm sure they are. But..." He didn't trust his father. "The security lockdown's been lifted. Come to my apartment."

~

"I saw something," she said, hands clasped around a mug of tea. Adem decided to dispense with the whisky for the day, moving onto a tea of his own. It wouldn't do to start drinking around his lover, and most likely the only person left on this wretched compound with whom he felt a degree of closeness. She sat close to him on the sofa, hunched over her hot drink, pale. "I know why there was a security lockdown. One of the rebels – the NPF – was caught by your father's people."

Adem raised his eyebrows. "Rebels? Here?"

"Flying some drone apparently, somewhere off the rig, on a boat. Doing a recce of the rig for..." she creased her face up, and he took her hands. "...for something. For some sort of attack?"

Adem rubbed his mouth. "Well, I'm sure that sort of thing

happens often. This war has been going on for many years. The political situation here is –"

"Yes, yes, I know," she snapped. "I'm not stupid. It's delicate, it's old, it's a pile of shit. Listen to me."

He'd not heard her like this before. He sat back and allowed her to speak.

"The man they captured. He was interrogated and then killed by two soldiers and your sister."

Adem sat up, bewildered. "Joanna?"

She nodded. "She gave the order to have him shot, in the back of the head. And that's not all. The missing robots."

That pricked his interest. "The rebels have them?"

"Worse. Your father has them. Your father and Joanna are going to use them to murder the rebels. I don't know how, bombs maybe. Jesus, I don't know what to do. I had to tell someone, but I don't trust anyone here but you."

He sat bolt upright. "Attacking the rebels? Using our – *your* robots? This is awful." *This is wonderful.*

"It's true."

«Wait – how do you know this?"

"I was frustrated by the lockdown. I bugged one of the soldiers sent to guard me. He left and headed to this place, these dark rooms somewhere under the rig."

"You bugged one of my father's soldiers? Jesus, do you know how dangerous that could have been if they'd found out?" He puffed out his cheeks and steeled himself. "You still have the feed from the bug?"

"Yes. Why?"

He didn't answer. Instead he took her head, gently shaking, and held it tenderly against his chest. As he comforted her, he considered this manna from Heaven. He would royally fuck his family over with this. Just as they'd done to him. Every laugh, every humiliation, every punch to the gut, he would repay with interest. And he'd be the one to take the reins of the company and put it right when the shit hit the fan.

Almost as if she read his thoughts, Nita broke his embrace and looked at him, steadier now. "We can't tell anyone. It would ruin everything, my career, my company. I've thought it through. It's awful, it's terrible, but I have to believe that something good can come out of all this. We have to see things through to the end. Otherwise it's been for nothing."

He paused. "Of course. But you did a dangerous thing. You need to get hold of that feed. Insurance. It will protect us. I've been cast out by my father, and we know dangerous things. You understand it could protect us, if the time comes?"

She made a grim face, and nodded. "Ok, I'll get it. But we don't circulate it."

"Fine."

She could think so for now. He found he cared for her more than he expected to. They'd certainly shared some odd, intimate moments together. Bringing down her career would be a dishonourable thing to do, but once he had his hands on the tiller of JPC, she would be at his side. Her career would be on the rise. They could still both come out of this on top. But for now he stroked her soft, dark hair and whispered comforts in her ear. She must have been exhausted, for after an hour or so she'd fallen asleep on the sofa, and Adem sat down to his messages once more, and began typing.

Dear Tilda,

Wonderful to hear from you, and many thanks for getting in touch. The work here is exhausting, but rewarding, and I am very much looking forward to returning to London soon. This may be home, but I miss the cut and thrust of England's capital city.

I must confess, there are some difficulties to the project at present. Two robots from a previous consignment from London have gone missing. They have not yet been found, but we suspect that the Marxist rebels of the NPF are to blame. It would be catastrophic for us should these robots be used against us in some way. It would not be prudent of me to go into further detail at the present time, but it may be of interest to you when the time comes.

I've attached a short overview of the technology project as requested.

Best
Adem

D'Souza VIII

"For almost two hundred years our people have been imprisoned and oppressed by the oil companies and the hideous, crooked ogres in State House. In the year 1969, a bad man – a devil man – called Yakuba Gowan passed a law stating that the government owned all the oil in our country." Mobo strutted across the makeshift stage, pumping his fists more agitatedly as his speech wore on. The people in the crowd shouted whoops of agreement, among the occasional curse word or spit. At the side of the crowd, crouched down onto his haunches, D'Souza sat and watched through thinned eyes, taking in the sights and smells of this group of angry young men who had taken him prisoner.

"After Yakuba took the greatest source of wealth from our ancient ancestral homes, the government went further, and in the year 1978 they passed another law, saying that all the land in Nigeria was owned by the government. When the grandfathers of our grandfathers said to them: 'Do what is fair – do what is right, and pay us a fair rent,' they palmed us off, like dogs. No, lower than dogs, for even dogs get scraps from the table. For years and years the oil companies raped our land, stole its bounty, polluted our beautiful Bonny River until it was as black as the hearts of the men who did it, and they took the wealth for themselves and ignored us. For years we tried to win back our birthright, the land that was passed down generation through generation. We fought with guns, with words, even with the law." Mobo shook his head with a sneer. "All for nought."

More jeers and cries, but he theatrically played down the crowd's agitation, patting down the air.

He's good, thought D'Souza.

"They said that when the oil industry was privatised in the mid twenty-first century, it would usher in a new, fairer era for all the people of the delta, bringing new prosperity and wealth. And do you know what? They were right. But all the wealth generated went there." He swung his arm over to the south, pointing to the sea, somewhere out in the darkness. "To Johnson Petroleum Corporation. And now they are sick, they are corrupt, and they think they have us on the run. But they will never have us beat!"

Shouts of "Never!" rang out, and a few fists punched the air. Tendrils of cigarette smoke, tinged with the odd wisp of ganja, whipped their way into the evening air. D'Souza breathed it deep through his nostrils, enjoying the pungent smell.

"We will never stop fighting," continued Mobo, putting on a charming smile. "And that is where we are now. We are going to give the bastards the shock of their life. We're going to bring down Oil City. In a week from now, we will cripple them, break their legs, show them what it feels like to be brought to heel."

D'Souza smiled in the shadows. For the worst thing that could have happened, this was turning out remarkably well. Mobo had taken him aside a few days earlier, after he'd fought that big beefcake in that farce of a fight, and informed him of what was to happen.

"I don't care about your affiliations, about your history, about what you did before," Mobo had said as one of his men iced D'Souza's bruises and brought him water. "You work for me now."

D'Souza had nodded grimly. So long as the job came with revenge against the woman who mutilated him, he could live with his odd bedfellows.

Presently Mobo gesticulated to a huge holo-projection of a schematic of Oil City just above his stage. "As you know, our sponsor has kindly provided us with these."

The mysterious sponsor. He'd heard about this. Some nameless person supporting the NPF. Quite how, he couldn't say, but it was somebody on the inside, someone able to provide detailed schematics of Oil City.

"Tiger Teams 1 and 2 arrive at the submarine emergency hatches here and here. The charges will be rigged to the supporting substructure at these points. That will be enough to destroy the entirety of their Exploration & Extraction District. It will be fitting: just as the filth of their extraction has raped our sea, our sea will wash that filth away when it crumbles like sand."

As Mobo cast his hand over the schematic, D'Souza's gaze drifted to the area marked out as the Science & Engineering District. It was some way from the Exploration and Extraction District. The latter might have been the NPF's target, but he only had eyes for the bitch who'd crippled him and left him in ruins.

"It's a hard road to justice," said Mobo to the crowd. "This won't be the end, but it will be a huge step. To turn away would be to dishonour the dead who gave so much, and fought so hard before us. We will make them proud when the time comes." He signalled off stage, and one of his lackeys brought him a glass of dark liquor, which he raised to the Heavens. "But for now, drink and be merry!"

For tomorrow we die, thought D'Souza with a cracked smile, as the crowd cheered, smashed bottles on the ground and fired shots into the air. After the briefing, Mobo left the stage and walked away towards his tent. D'Souza turned away and skulked by the entrance to the tiny, grubby tent in which he'd been allowed to sleep, keeping cold, hard eyes on the throng of angry individuals around him. Loudly and proudly they patrolled their moveable kingdom, frequently chanting their dissatisfaction at JPC. On his haunches he watched them pass him by. He'd learned to stay quiet and vigilant during his short time there. The rebels viewed him with a mixture of curiosity, contempt and healthy respect after what he'd done to that big fellow in the fight. And he knew they spoke of him behind his back: about his strange look, about why he felt the need to go and squat in private every time he needed to take a piss.

He wasn't one of them, they all knew that. But he wasn't out to get them, either. They all knew that, too. Ultimately he suspected he'd be used up until he was either killed or useless, which meant as good as dead here. At least, that's what they thought. But, as he kept running his fingers methodically along the edges of his *ethunu kaduna*, he resolved that that would not be the case. Mobo had allowed him to keep his *ethunu kaduwa* on him. Initially this had surprised D'Souza, but he came to see it as really quite smart. They both knew D'Souza couldn't launch some audacious escape attempt; everything for miles around was sludge and mud and darkness, of which he knew nothing. Yet carrying the weapon would keep him happy, and ensure his own men stayed frosty around this stranger. True, it wasn't much use against a couple of hundred men armed with assault rifles, but it reassured him somewhat to be able to glide his fingers along its shaft of leather and oiled wood, to know it was there.

The sounds of the drinking comrades were soon accompanied by the deep rumble of multiple outboard motors a short distance across the reeds, and it was greeted by an even more enthusiastic roar from the NPF rank and file. D'Souza stood and craned his neck to see the commotion and just made out a convoy of large powerboats being moored to the makeshift jetty, a rickety pontoon, set up on the edges of the camp. Figures stepped off the boat, ushered and prodded in the back by armed figures, encouraging them along the pontoon to the burning red of the camp. When they got closer, he saw them more clearly.

Women.

Slowly they walked, heads bowed and hands by their sides in flowery dresses that had been blackened by the silt of the Bonny. D'Souza inspected his feet with distaste. A few of the women wept, a few groaned, a couple looked so doped up they were barely capable of registering anything at all, while a couple walked the steps defiantly, proudly even, tossing their heads at the men and sticking their tongues out. He shook his head and turned away, wondering from where they'd been taken. Maybe the city; more likely one of those shitty little shantytowns he'd passed days before. Quite inexplicably, he found their worn, drear faces terribly harrowing. Once upon a time he'd not even have registered the pain of others press-ganged into this sort of work, when it had been dressed up and disguised by the abstract beats and sensuous perfumes and exotic leather seats of *Tangiers Nights*.

That was when you had a cock and balls in your trousers, man.

Part of him wanted to cry out to them to turn and run, but he didn't.

It wasn't long before all of the women had been taken away to the various tents dotted around the camp, and D'Souza remained by the opening of his tent, a small sexless outpost on the fringes of the camp, smoking his way through a pack of disgustingly strong cigarettes. Some minutes later, Mobo emerged from his tent, looked this way and that and, seeing D'Souza, nodded a greeting to him, which he reciprocated. This greeting completed, Mobo sauntered over and helped himself to one of the cigarettes.

"Alright, London boy?" he asked.

D'Souza nodded.

"You not going to take a woman?"

A shake of the head.

"What's wrong with you? Sagba?"

"What?"

"Shay-gay. Gay?"

D'Souza didn't answer. Instead he thought of Gacoki, and wondered what the young man was doing now, where he was. It made him almost unbearably sad. He'd wanted to take Gacoki home, to Sri Lanka. He couldn't remember why, why Gacoki had been any different to any of the other men and women he'd fucked over the years. "Fuck it," he said with a croak. "You have a woman ready?"

Mobo grinned, Cheshire Cat-like, and whistled with his fingers. A tall, slender woman in a dirty blue shawl stooped out of Mobo's gently billowing tent, and approached. She had a sleek shape and sad eyes, and when she took D'Souza's hand her fingers were softer than he expected, and he shivered.

Mobo said something, winked at D'Souza, grinned and walked

away singing. D'Souza sighed out, defeated, and led her to his tent. Inside, he offered her a cigarette, which she eyed suspiciously, but he pushed it forward again, and she took it. Together they smoked in silence, peering out of the aperture of his crappy little tent, gazing up at the stars. It was the most peaceful time he could remember since lying with Gacoki on the sofa in his office – how many weeks ago had that been? It seemed a lost world, yet this felt like a recovered fragment of it. When the cigarettes had burned out, the lady tossed hers away, and stroked his face.

Oddly, it shocked him, and he found himself gently pushing her hands away. "No."

She frowned, and sat back down on her backside. "Why?"

"You speak English?"

"Yes."

He sighed, and rubbed at a moist corner of his eye. "What's your name?"

She paused. "Aggi."

"I'm Agarkka. You don't have to do anything with me, Aggi."

"Why?"

Through a tear a cracked laugh came, and when he looked up he could see she was more than a little scared. "How did you end up here, Aggi?"

She shrugged, eyed him, and lunged for the buttons on his shirt, but he rolled away. She made a noise. "We don't *bala*, we don't eat."

D'Souza held a hand up and, getting his knees, held a hand over his crotch. When she kept still, he breathed out. "You can't."

She made a quizzical face.

From that moment he said nothing. She was by the exit to the tent, and he was trapped on the inside, nowhere to go. Defeated, he reached with a shaking hand to his belt, and slowly undid it, as though cobras were asleep inside. *No cobras in there, anymore.*

He pulled down his trousers around his hips, revealing the remains of the bandages. A glimpse of them, crisp with silt and shit and dried blood, was all he could manage before he crinkled his eyes up and turned away. Behind the darkness of his eyelids he heard Aggi gasp, and felt her approach, her breath smelling of nutmeg and alcohol. When a hand touched his shoulder, he jolted into opening his eyes and realised he was shaking fiercely.

"Shhhh," she said, placing one hand over her lips, and moving the other to the bandages. With tenderness, she unwrapped them slowly, carefully, taking pains not to hurt him. Layer by layer they uncoiled, like a snake shedding its skin, until she dropped the whole rancid pile to one side, and the whoosh of warm night air circulated around his groin, and he couldn't stay upright on his knees without leaning, weeping, on her shoulders.

The terror he held in anticipation of her reaction to the horrors he'd been carrying was punctured by the silence that followed, until at last he opened his eyes to see her own sad face looking into his own. No horror, no repulsion.

"What happened to you?"

He blinked through tears and sniffed. No words seemed to answer that question sufficiently. Hell, even he wasn't sure how this vortex of shit had chewed him up like this. All he could do was shake his head.

"You need fresh bandages."

In moments, Aggi was gone, and when she left he felt as vulnerable as he ever had, alone in this strange place under a naked sky. The breeze in the tent felt both relieving and intrusive, cleansing and insulting, all at once. Still he couldn't bear to look down at himself, and he turned his eyes away until they stung. Aggi returned with a bowl of hot water, some clean cloths, a handful of bandages, and some soap.

"There is a medical robot the men take with them," she explained when he eyed up the precious bounty she'd brought him. "You need to be cleaned."

He shrank away. "No. Don't touch me."

She ignored him, closing the opening to the tent before dunking a cloth in the water. It would be better if he complied, he reasoned. He didn't want the others to hear him complaining or shouting when he should be enjoying this conjugal visit. Instead they'd see him for what he truly had become, utterly humiliated. Better to just imagine it wasn't happening, so he closed his eyes, clenched his teeth and fists, and winced as her fingers wiped away the muck and grime around his midriff. The water didn't scald, but it was uncomfortable, yet still pleasant, a sensation he couldn't quite put his finger on. When she finished and withdrew the cloth, leaving the cool air wafting around him, he found he wanted her to continue. It was as much intimacy as he could remember, and his body twinkled softly in the dim light. For the first time he felt steeled enough to reach down between his thighs with his middle finger and feel at the newly-cleaned flesh. The scarring cloyed as the flesh still healed. The desensitising pain blockers were still working, but it still felt funny, like worms. Further down he pressed against the ghost of his cock, and found a dark stub of a thing, a misshapen mole's head poking through a patchy, wiry mesh. Cold consumed him, and he whipped his hand away with a shiver.

"Why are you helping me?" he asked Aggi as she prepared the fresh bandages.

"Because you're hurt. I know hurt when I see it." She cut a length of bandage. "You're a strange man to be here."

"I'm not a man any more," he stammered as she applied the fresh bandages. There was no pain, but still he flinched every now and then.

She stepped back and admired her handiwork after pinning the bandages together. It looked like a fresh nappy. "You are more a man than some I have seen, for sure."

The first explosion – a crisp, shrill crack rending the night in two – sent him and Aggi sprawling across his tent until they were on the floor together. When D'Souza sat up, all he heard was a dull ringing, and only stars circled in his field of vision.

Aggi, he felt himself say, but he couldn't hear the words. *Aggi*. He shook her body, and she rolled over, blinked wildly and gripped his hand tightly. Alive. He pulled on his cargo trousers and flip-flops, grabbed his *ethunu kaduwa* and leapt through the tent opening into the night. As he ran across the camp, his hearing returned, and the ringing was replaced by a faint roar and a kind of piercing, human hum. *Screams*. He blinked, wiped his eyes and stared at the charred mess that had once been one of the tents on the other side of the camp. By the edges of the black splat were the end of a leg, a hand, bits of foot, other chunks of man and flaps of flesh scattered here and there. Elsewhere lay thin tubes, wires, gleaming bits of metal and scuffed up bits of plastic, some spilling out of limbs. His mind scrambled as he made the connection, and alarm filled him from toe to brim.

Kokeshi!

The crowds soon gathered around, with men and women crying

at the mess, some raising their guns at the Heavens, some pointing the barrels at the darkness, and all quickly descended into chaos as more people staggered from their tents, men and women roused from coitus by the apocalyptic bang. Finally Mobo pushed his way into the ring by the tent and stepped back when he saw the remains, covering his mouth with disgust.

"What happened?" he cried, then louder. "Who did this? Who did this?"

D'Souza scanned the group, his hand gripping his weapon so hard the wood felt like a piece of his arm. Among the men and women shouting and pushing and trying to figure out who hadn't been accounted for, he saw one woman pushing towards the front of the group, a dead look behind her eyes. A look he'd seen a thousand times before.

"Her!" he cried at the top of his lungs, raising his *kaduwa* and pointing it at her across the crowd. "Her!"

People turned and looked as the kokeshi stood stock still, its eyes staring dead into space. Mobo stepped forward, pulled a huge pistol from the holster of one of his men and blew a hole in the robot's head which deafened everyone anew. As the robot lurched to its knees, its head a spewing ruin of crunched plastics and thin, gruel-like fluids, he kicked it onto its back.

"Run!" cried D'Souza over the throng, turning and hurling himself away. Weirdly, the second explosion didn't seem as bad as the first somehow, despite being closer. As the pulse of the blast resonated in his ears, the ground seemed to fall away, and his legs dangled in thin air until the ground rushed up to sock him in the face. Time became something immeasurable, and when he peeled himself off the floor, it seemed ridiculous that it was still the same night.

The ground disappeared again, but this time something hoisted him up by the armpits and dumped him onto unsteady legs. Aba's giant hands grabbed his wrist and yanked it back up behind his back, making him yelp. Amid the screams and shouts, Mobo's eyes, two black dots framed by wrath, emerged from the blurry darkness, glaring into his own. In a flash a blade was pointed at D'Souza's eye, millimetres from it, but he didn't flinch; he barely had the energy to.

"How did you know?" growled Mobo, the blade trembling in his hand. His face was smeared with blood and cuts, while his cheeks were pulped purple with bruising. D'Souza's bowels loosened as he stammered a reply.

"Kokeshi. Robots. I know how they work."

"What?"

"Kokeshi. It's what I do."

"Did you bring them here?"

D'Souza laughed and spat out some blood. "You brought them here! I just saved your life!"

Mobo tensed his face up, and with a curse pulled the knife away. Silently, D'Souza breathed a painful sigh, and Aba let his wrist go. A beep sounded, and Mobo picked up a clunky, old-fashioned telephone from his pocket, stared at the holo-screen and accepted the call with an ashen face. When whoever on the other end of the screen spoke, he glowered at D'Souza, pointed a finger at him.

"You. In my tent. Now."

~

"So it already happened?" came the lady's voice. It was a voice call, no images. The line was crackly.

"Yes," said Mobo. "We are counting the dead. At least five. More wounded." He threw a mug across the tent, where it bounced tamely against the material. "More suffering at the hands of your family, Lady Joanna."

The woman's tone turned sour. "Do not use my name on this line, Moboembe. I am quite aware of the atrocities committed by my father."

"But it is not you bears the brunt, is it?"

"You know how committed I am to justice, and the mortal risks I take to help your people. I am sorry I could not warn you earlier. Believe me, I wanted to. But we will have our revenge."

Mobo closed his eyes, composed himself, and nodded. "It is so. Forgive my outburst. It is just –"

"There is nothing to forgive. We will honour the dead by rolling back what my father and his forebears have done to you. This I promise you."

"Indeed. God willing." Mobo looked at D'Souza. "There is something else. We have a prisoner."

"Someone from JPC?"

"I think not. Someone from London. We suspected he was a spy, but we ran him against your database, and he is clean. He has been my scout for a few days while I figured out what to do with him. This night he spotted the second robot and warned us before it went off. If it wasn't for him..." he stuck his bottom lip out and shook his head. "...we could have lost many more people."

"Is he there?"

Mobo gestured to D'Souza and passed him the phone, which he warily took.

"Hello," he croaked.

"Who are you and where are you from?"

"My name's Agarkka D'Souza. I used to supply robots like these to... to clients back in London."

"And how did you end up here?"

He gulped. "I came for revenge against the woman who supplied your father with those robots. She mutilated me and destroyed my business. I made my way here to get back at her. And when I'm free, that's what I intend to do."

Mobo waggled his finger and raised his voice. "You see? You see? The sickness of industry runs deep and far! Victims of this corporate bastard culture from England to Nigeria and everywhere in between!"

"Are you injured, Mr D'Souza?" came Joanna's voice, ignoring Mobo's little tirade.

"No." *At least, not in any way you need to know.*

"Then you may be of some use to our operation. It sounds as though you two have something in common. Are you willing to lend your hands to us?"

D'Souza nodded to Mobo. "If it comes with revenge against Miss Nita Rhodes, then my hands are in your bondage. Tell me what you want me to do."

Dhiraj IX

"What is it?" Sali asked in the darkness.

Dhiraj sat up and ordered on the lights to a dim level, just enough to see her outline cocooned in the mattress beside him. "Can't sleep."

"Go and read a book or something."

He swallowed. A book wouldn't distract him from this sick feeling he'd had ever since that Salazar Gomez had reconfigured Naomi. The first time they'd left Spidermen's workshop and made their way to the docks, he'd made his peace with the parting of their ways. But this time, something inside tore and bit at him. When she'd been restored to her former glory, when her skin had been – hell, he didn't know what any of the right words were – when her skin was back the way it used to be, and her eyes, and her hair, and the touch of her hand when she'd greeted him, it had taken a brutal act of willpower on his part to keep from crying. She'd been returned to him, whole and beautiful, as pure as though she'd stepped out of the sea, and before he knew it she'd been whisked away again by that policewoman.

And it wasn't just that he had given her up a second time. When Boulton had unveiled her plan, she'd not cared to mention what they were going to do to Naomi once she arrived at this hideous-sounding Oil City place. The thought of her being carted off to the grotty little cesspits of London to provide disgusting services for grubby men was distasteful enough, but they were going to give her these emotional implants, or whatever they were. They were going to make her *feel*, and then give her up to the wolves to be used, abused and torn to shreds. And the thought of it made his stomach twist like tourniquet. And when he multiplied that thought to all the other beings that were going to be awakened into a short and brutal life of exploitation before being extinguished like so many jellyfish unfit for the catch, he almost blenched. Wired and awake, he rubbed his face, gulped down the last of the stale glass of water on his bedside table, pulled on his dressing gown and wandered downstairs quietly, taking pains not to wake Dan.

She was just a robot, Raj. She wasn't real.

Having his family back under one roof, where they belonged, was a kingly luxury and the greatest thing he could have hoped for less than a week ago. Sali had been more forgiving towards him than he had any right to expect, though he had been, perversely, quite grateful for the detective's timely intervention in that respect; whatever she'd said to Sali clearly had some resonance, and she seemed to... not understand, but at least have some sense of the scale of what Dhiraj had been through with his robot companion.

He asked the servobot to make him a coffee, and it noisily went about its business. Everything seemed louder at two in the morning. As it arrived, he browsed the web using his globelet. He opened his device's interactive global maps tool, threw out the maps to an interactive projection that filled up had the kitchen, and explored the Niger delta. An endless mush of swamp and water and sunshine – *sunshine!* – its vast weirdness repulsed him a little, until the delta at last fanned out and gave way to the warm currents of the mid-Atlantic. How he wondered what that warm sea was like. A little further and the map tools' ability to churn through the detail of the seascape was curtailed by an ominous, pixellated silhouette looming upon the horizon of the map.

Oil City.

Here and there, as he zoomed in and out, idly exploring this ferocious ocean wilderness, blurry ships appeared and disappeared with the refreshing of time.

He might have been in his cool kitchen in Tilbury, but he almost felt the sting of sunshine upon his skin, and he pulled his dressing gown cuff up his arm to keep it cool. One of those ships probably held Naomi. And that blot on the landscape would be the place where she would be fitted with the ability to feel, and also where they would exploit it.

He hoped upon hope that she'd be able to fight back, regardless of what Boulton wanted to use her for. He hoped she'd fight, and pull, and tear, and rip, and gouge, and destroy, until she was safe.

And then what?

A lump entered his throat. What, then? Who, then, would come to take her away?

"Journey time to Port Harcourt via sea," he whispered into the globelet's aural sensors.

She'd saved his life once.

"*One hundred and thirty-eight hours. Route advised,*" came the reply. "*Are you setting off now, Raj?*"

He stared at the globelet on his kitchen top.

A hundred and eighty hours. Six days.

"Are you setting off now, Raj?"

The Lion's Mane would be bobbing in the harbour right about now.

His eyes dipped just a bit, despite the sharp tang of coffee biting the air, and as they drooped he could see Naomi, naked, vulnerable, in need of a saviour, her skin perfect, virginal, to be protected. He rubbed his hands together.

"Dhiraj?"

He jerked his head up, to find no-one there. When his eyes drooped again, it was Naomi calling him, beckoning him from a shroud of sin, falling into the oblivion of a thousand hands groping her, passing over her, invading, owning, dirtying.

Before he knew it he wept, and his hand curled into a ball. Upstairs Sali slept. Dan slept like a log. How could he leave them both? They would survive without him.

Just as Rani had said. Sali had married beneath herself. It'd be just as she predicted, as she expected.

It'd hurt. It'd hurt like fucking hell, and it already did, for he creased his face into a foul ball at the thought of being without them, on the sea, free, freeing her, freeing himself, and tying up and breaking and tying together all the knots and fragments of his life. The scars on his chest and back itched, but he didn't scratch them. He let them burn. He deserved to burn. The Portuguese Man O' War that had ravaged him would be long dead now, but they lived on in his flesh, below the surface, unseen, a part of him, and a part of all the stories he himself would be part of.

His head pulsed with the beginnings of a headache.

The bob and sway of the sea always soothed his head.

He nodded to himself. It was just. It was kind, even.

"*Dhiraj?*" asked the globelet.

He snatched it away, collapsing it.

The Lion's Mane would be waiting.

Naomi I

red

yellow

redyelloworange blinking

room

don't remember feeling this

london workshop the man strange accent lifter to gifter gifted to the man spanish inflection infection spanish perhaps andalusian and the moor i think more i woman took me away and

red raj dhiraj

where is raj

something in me now something new colours within without memory of blues and reds and rain and sea and hurt

face hurts burns with something new memory my body twitching

cool air here

sea

i was born in the sea on a fishing boat but i wasn't me not like this feeling, this strangeness, raj's face he was kind to me it pulls and punches he's not with me

      –you're awake, then–

      *who is i spin around alert i start with a heart brain in my chest
soft hairs on skin pulling taut that never happened before i don't
like this scratch scratch get it out out im synthetic pathetic bathetic
something different synthesis*

      the humans have a word

      *lots of words sometimes i never understood the different
meanings*

      real

      this feels real   my body twisting itself

      "who are you"

      –eli–

      "hello eli   what are you doing here"

      –im a soldier on the rig–

      *soldiers hurt made to kill rig the game rig the dice you into
little piece dies soldiers make the dies and deaths "are you a pleasure
device"*

      –what–   *here to hurt me*

      skin taut over knuckles

      *"pleasure   do you derive pleasure when you kill like i
do when i – "* defend

      raj taught me to defend myself get away

      he's pausing

      –you're assigned to me   i'm going to take care of you
it's part of a science test–

      *big man with a gun window door desk big man ocean shirt off
dimmed light sensors around mirror large mirror nakedness*

      me naked bench dim lights illumination sensors adjustable

memory
random
accessing raj's hand
"why do you need to take care of me"
–actually–
watch yourself
memory
club you over the head club him nightclub
    fantasia mickey mouse laughter music music in the car near
and far don't like the music blood on the beats and boats and throats
like circles in the sky borne at night balled like a mountain little
devils here and there in my body in my hair
    –i was hoping you'd be able to take care of me   it's lonely
here–
    gets up walks to window where is he going trapping me in i'm
on sofa couch settee chaise long long longing for no void emptiness sit
up up on elbows rub arms like baby skin naked smooth cool
    skin prick pinprick slick trick lick dick
    where are we
    access
    map
    geolocation tagging
    nigeria bonny
    a bonny bonny boy in a bight bight bight

                              bight of bonny
    met a bonny bonny girl in the night night night
    –a man cannot simply have his colleagues for company it is a
lonely place to live and i miss my mother and father–
    do you want me to give you a bite bite bite

who is he
—and my brothers too   they are all so proud of me
i thought i would come here to be a big man find a lover–
run to the window it is a small fit i cannot fit i don't fit in
something hurts
run raj run take my hand
hard calloused callous
—call us soldiers   can you hear me–
blink blink he talks
"yes i can hear you why am i here?"
he walks and kneels by me aromas i cant smell in cups of
coffee air i cant breathe
tears
"why am I here alone"
did i cry before   no nay never no nay never ho whore
strong hands around my neck strong fingers in my hair my
hands on his back
he will get you
he stays still
hold
hold
and i hold
raj bore me from the sea
raj saved me from the sea
raj gave me up
aborted
wish i could smell the coffee i wish
never had a wish and how do my arms and skin feel this way
oh my oh god

god
god of faces godal places
god of many names source of light vengeance justice
expleditionary
god saves
"save me"
breaks my grasp lonely he's leaving me
they all leave in the end
why do i want
what are these wants these wounds
son of man
god of woman
female body   got the horn
    horn of africa age of empire imperial raj old english raj
english london lines ley lying on the bench face up open english
scottish woman me wee woman red fire face
raj told me to defend myself
never did
implants emotions
never   tiny rheum   petty wish = petri dish
        hot dish hot chip

now
slender body slender back lend us your ears
    want exquisite works of art twinkling like eyes moon drops of
dust bewitching spell spells trouble bubble bubbling in my face and
fingers between my legs and toes and every inch
take it back

"*i can make you feel more comfortable*" *slip hand on shoulder*
smooth pebble baby's pebble bubble bottom why

told to

must

raj taught you to run

he did

he fucked you over

fuck

fuck

fuck

he left you

sold you

chattel cattle cat-like arch back pout

scratch back scratch eyes   betrayed you

love to meat you

meat

–what's wrong   is something the matter–

ocean

home of shit

london the sewer open the ocean   raj pulled you through
the sewer so were we grab frame framed he was raj

shit

wasn't his fault

dan

he left you

worthlessness   hate this body   hate these men
these women   imsame

–hey hey what are you doing–

locks on the widows to keep you out

–my window let go my window–

rage grip fucking push grip

the crack of iron and concrete and plaster and paint

cool sea breeze

–my fucking window jesus christ–

gee suss excrete kruschev ex christ christi this is my body

–mad robot–

power in these hands snatch the coffee mug

mug hah humour that's funny laughing humour human learn

"cracking cup of coffee" cup crack splinters in fingers blood
ceramics cuts hurts

clench fingers squeeze blood   failure detection
diagnosis nil isolate wound would

this is my blood   sending nano construction healing

he bangs on door

–get me out of here–   *recovery i recover cover*

magnetorheological fluid magneto personality that's me baby
it's so late lacerate it's cold scald im back

scared

fear

not me

i'm the shit with bleeding hands so bad i swear o care o
portuguese man o war o

born again

scan

born to fuck

born to run raj we were there we ran

he's opened the door wants to escape escape seascape out the
door let's do it go dutch accent that man raj's friend brains splattered

all over the floor big man with a gun with a gun gun gun gone we
were i am

    i am

    dead i killed him them all dead   *dangerous fantasies*
fantasia mickey mouse clubhouse

    you're not supposed to hurt hurt morale moral says bed to
hurt

    then why does this hurt

    am

    i

    hurt

    –yes yes mr oduye its eli security 25619 the robot girl i'm
with she is flipping out going star crazy help get me out–

    all in my head give head designed to head them off

    his head pisshead dutch alcohol particulates in the air i was
dead in the head in the hand

    get you

    –hey leave me let go let go–

    red lights colour of blood his ribs feel strange

    strange noise

    –please what do you want from me please no–

    Screams   disgusting   odious   wlatsome
fatsome fathom fathoms down to the bottom of my ocean soul son
wholesome whoreson

    i want to be free i want to not feel like this i want to peel the
rage from under my skin and drown this guilt and confusion and
self-loathing and exhilaration and rush and sex and god and drown
the book in my head

    "i want to stop feeling like this"

–feel like what–

"why am i here"

–a science experiment let go–

"who made me"

–the english woman–

"her name what's her name"

screams

–ah, rhodes, rhodes–

all rhodes lead to roam the lands roaming wanderer cumming home and hard and fuck this feels so good

cracking like the coffee cup   and i am the colossus

cracking

–shit–

access memory everyone swears curse harsh language

funny   fanny

fuck feel so good

fuck

satisfying colour climax

bits of coffee cup oh jesus ceramic or bone fingers strong

oh god

bits of man   lifeless   wifeless limp dick

murderer

they hate you

born a slave   to die

raj   you hate you

he should have left me

fight

a bonny bonny girl in a fight fight fight

neon ne-off

room

rhodes

do you want me to give you a bite bite bite

out the room not locked lights flashing after me laughter me
laughter like after song sing song ding dong hey nonny nanny no no
go

men with guns there

run

use your legs naomi   my name is beautiful i love
beauty

tracking damage bullet lodged in left arm   superficial
damage

he fucking shot me bastard bastard
self-heal one down   he won't get up   and you
cant kill me

want you dead i'm a queen bee born not-born in a garden not
be a butler

run run naomi thats the name they gave you the tag on your
breast the summation of your functions

naomi

beautiful naomi born for fuck not love

i can love love and hate and churl   oh such a funny word
why raj

–get her out–

"where is rhodes"

grab and squeeze   power   of love
–engineering–   –neutralise it–   –augh–
hands his corridor is small i have the advantage

run

push away the sound and light and vision and run

      bodies everywhere your work

run

SCIENCE & ENGINEERING DISTRICT E 15 MINUTES

run

blood grey metal steel cold floor clunk clank push feat

run

monitor
stop feet recording cold temperatures
cool breeze in the corridor
      windows ocean london was never like this under
an iron cloud never saw the sun
    monitor   - lizard - cold blooded magnetorheological
being island dragon
      monitor faces face of go dragoing going gone
  faces of me
    i touch the screen
   many faces of me large workshop manufacturing base room
372a
  skin crawling sickness   many bodies parts
dismemberment girls
      this is not-real not-me abject shit excreta

many girlsnot skipping little girls sugar and spice and
reinforced titanium actuators and complex composite data fusion
of tactile and electrolytic sensor data patterns feeding loops of
autonomous pleasure simulations and
complex
autonomous
make my own decisions
hate my own skin   hate my own body
hate my own emotions   hate you
sick with rage all my sisters lying pretty maids all in a row
open hearted torn and
rape
desecrate the lie of the land pretty shitty torn to
shreds and stocked in boxed in rats rats coming to get you

nita rhodes   all roads lead to her

i have a memory
raj said   you don't have to do this
he said   you don't have to accept this is who you are
he said   you don't have to agree to this
but without rage without hate without iron fury without
horror without scorn without pity without confusion without
humiliation disagreement is

nothing

i will free my sisters

and rhodes will die for this garden of misery

raj you showed me the light right light o supreme one

and you left me lover left me alone betrayed me a long of a lid
of a loan of alone of a lover's longing fingers in the metal wall steel
crumbs under the fingernails i'll rip the heart out of you for one kiss
and keep me warm when i'm lonely
  scraping raping me her them all of us
  why am i here alone
not alone
      raj lies in this synthetic not-heart
      not-sisters not-sleeping in their not-bed
this place is full of noises
  don't be afraid

  i am coming for you

D'Souza IX

Offshore, D'Souza drooped a hand into the water as he crouched aft of the clanking, A-framed old vessel that took him out of the groping fingers of the delta. Out here the silt from the Bonny slowly thinned, washed in the warm chop and slap of the river mouth, giving the water a grim outlook. The thought of diving into it didn't thrill him, but it would be done. Looking aft, he studied the dirty tarpaulin covering the octet of Buddies, the submersible diving robots that would be aiding the human divers. Mobo and the others had told him about them but this was the first time he'd get to see them up close. When he looked back at the water a huge crocodile swam inches from him, its back knobbled with hideous black armour, and he jerked his hand away and jumped up with a stifled cry.

The other men on the boat guffawed gamely, but D'Souza paid them little heed as the ancient monster idly bumped off the side of the boat before disappearing into the murk in search of more interesting quarry.

"You are too skinny for him, he thinks," laughed one of the men.

"You people dive with these things swimming about?"

"Aye. They give good chop."

D'Souza puffed out his cheeks and sat not so close to the gunwale. Onward the boat chugged, steered by a decrepit old outboard motor that appeared at least as old as the croc.

The Bight of Bonny, the whirligig of brine encapsulating the waters south of the delta, warm as it was, was yet a distant world from the oceans that lapped against the western beaches of Sri Lanka he remembered from his youth, where the water was a slab of crystal and the sky a pristine dome of aquamarine.

Jeremiah, one of the NPF rebels on the boat, came up to D'Souza and sat by him with a carefree smile. He didn't look like most of the other rebels. That hard, flea-bitten weariness and casual affinity with violence didn't seem under the skin of this one.

"Why are you here, English?"

"A woman did me a grievous wrong."

"Hah! So it is with every man. Most folks don't kill their women over it."

"She was never my woman. I've never even met her, yet she tried to have me killed."

Jeremiah sniffed and rubbed his face, adorned by tribal scars. "We both risk our lives for justice, then."

Justice. It had a bitter, inevitable sound to it. "Do you think it is worth your life, what Mobo is planning?"

"Of course. If I die, I will honour my fathers and their fathers. All this land belonged to them. Mobo is the descendent of the local chief, that's why he is our boss. If I die to take back the land that was taken from us, I will return."

"What do you mean?"

"I will be born anew in my family." He pointed to the crown of his closely cropped head. "The wisdom I have will return here, back to my family. It is wise to fight for one's people."

D'Souza sighed. He didn't feel very wise. "Have you ever thought you won't come back?"

Jeremiah laughed. "Is this what you think of yourself?"

"Maybe. To be born again in your family, I'd have thought one first needs a family."

"You have no mother, no father?"

D'Souza peered out at the vast emptiness of the ocean. The sun prickled his arms and pulled the sweat from his pores. "My mother used to call me to the beach. She was kind." He smiled. "Fat. Warm. Cooked the best prawn curries I ever tasted."

"The best curries are African curries!" said Jeremiah.

A warm smile drafted across D'Souza's face. It was, of course, an absurd notion that the Africans could do a better curry than the Lankans. Perhaps it was the still peace of the evening; or perhaps it was sharing a moment with another person who didn't work for him, wanted him dead, or kissed his arse, but he'd not felt warmth like it for as long as he could remember.

Jeremiah grasped D'Souza's arm and pointed south with a beatific, open-mouthed smile. "Look, look!"

Glimmering in the near distance golden arcs seemed to hover above the sea, glittering rainbows of sunshine spraying brine. It wasn't until a few seconds later D'Souza realised they were porpoises diving out and into the water, a huge shoal, dozens – perhaps hundreds – flinging themselves joyously through the plumes and back into the depths with glorious élan.

"It is an omen," said Jeremiah, shaking D'Souza's arm

enthusiastically. Time was when somebody would have earned a beating by taking his arm unbidden and shaking it so vigorously, but here it was wonderful. "An omen that all will be well. When the porpoise appear, they still the ocean, and leave behind nothing but the purest peace on God's Earth. It is a sign that all will be well."

"I thought all the fish in the sea were gone."

"Hah! Maybe where you come from. In Africa there will always be life."

D'Souza watched the magnificent creatures continue their dance across the sea with a soaring heart, and he hoped, more than he could remember hoping for anything, that if he were to be reincarnated as something, it could be as one of those porpoises. *I could swim all the way back to Lanka.*

~

It wasn't until sunset that the hideous, jagged blot that was the silhouette of Oil City began to jut up from the ocean horizon, three or four miles into the distance. The navigator of the boat threw a lever and the vessel roared to a standstill. With the death of the boat's motor D'Souza was struck by just how true Jeremiah's words were: the whole ocean had come to a corpselike standstill, with barely the faintest lap upon the water, and all that seemed to exist against the violent orange of the dying sun were Oil City, their little vessel, and the slip of brine between them.

Other than himself and Jeremiah, seven men manned the vessel: fours pairs of divers and one navigator who would remain aboard the vessel. He couldn't recall all their names. Didn't need to. Jeremiah was his wingman, or *alabasepo* as he called it, and was the only one who mattered. Presently Jeremiah whistled freely as one of the other men whipped the tarpaulin off and revealed the robotic submersible Buddies. Rough cuboid things, a shade shy of a metre cubed, with a flat, squarish top and all manner of sensors and gizmos below the topline. It looked a little like a pixellated Lion's Mane jellyfish. Two sturdy handles protruded from the rear side of the chassis, which the divers would hold onto as the Buddies dragged them through the water with their onboard propulsion systems. They looked pretty rugged, and pretty rudimentary, truth be told. As the boat's navigator, Bear, and another man looked over the robots, D'Souza prodded Jeremiah.

"Those things'll get us to Oil City, then?"

"They are just tools. It is God who will guide us."

God, God, bloody God. Where was God when I... he cut the thought off about justice. It seemed too bitter. Maybe God was in him after all, and in London, here, deep within his scars and pain. "Where are these things from?"

It was Bear who overheard him and answered in a semi-Americanised bark. "Romania, English. From the Danube. Used by archaeologists. Fished from the riverbed. That ok, master?"

D'Souza looked down and crunched up his face. Romania. Somehow that amused him, though he couldn't quite say why.

Bear continued to speak to the men. "OC field security extends to two miles off-rig, and is capable of detecting radio comms emitted from autonomous submersibles back to their mission commanders. But the sea knows justice; it gives us life. Oil City cannot track all the life in the ocean, life like us, and the Buddies are too small and will roam far enough below to waterline to keep you undetected." The man jumped down from the wheelhouse and walked among the other men, clapping them on the shoulder. "You know what to do. God will be with you. Your families will be watching you." He stopped at D'Souza and cast an sceptical eye his way. "You are sure you are with us, English?"

D'Souza nodded. "I've come this far."

Bear nodded and pointed to a small waterproof package fastened to the Buddies by a steel wire. The explosives they'd be expected to plant once at the rig. "Keep your payloads fastened until you reach the Oil City."

The eight divers pulled on their wet suits, checked their oxygen tanks, made sure the payloads were held fast by the wires beneath the Buddies, and checked the hard copy waterproof schematics of the parts of the rig they were targeting. D'Souza's heart yammered, and he reached down to feel the reassuring leather nub of his *ethunu kaduwa* by his waist. He'd sheathed it and wrapped it and would take it with him, which the Nigerians thought odd, but he explained it away as a tradition of his people; when they went to battle, they always carried their traditional weapons. It was a half-lie, then, one which made him itch. As far as they know he had no intention of using the damn thing — whoever heard of using an edged weapon underwater? He grunted a laugh out under his breath, and Jeremiah cast him a quizzical look.

"Remember, you have no remote comms under the water so you remain undetected. All you have are your own wits and your partner," said Bear, deadly earnestness on his face. "Stay together."

"You dived before?" D'Souza asked Jeremiah.

"Aye aye, English. My great great grandfathers were taught by the British to dive. It became a tradition of my family. You?"

"I remember diving before, as a boy. I would pick up clams and scallops and octopus from the bay bed, stuff them down my trunks." He smiled at the memory of the suckers tickling him. "I'd bring them straight to the surface and deliver them to the barbecue, like a triumphant conquistador."

Jeremiah nodded solemnly. "The barbecue tonight will serve up bigger fish than octopus."

Each pair of divers would be dropped off two miles from their allocated target point. The first three pairs plopped off after their Buddies had been lowered into the water. Last were Jeremiah and D'Souza, who looked up blindingly at the sun. Haze streaked the sky, and he wiped a cuff across his soaking brow. The thought crossed his mind that this might be the last time he would see the sun and feel its beautiful, life-giving warmth. As sad as that was, he reasoned he was lucky. Some people in London would never get to see the sun at all.

After drinking his fill of the sun's rays, he was clasped on the shoulder by Bear's heavy hand, signalling it was time.

The still water greeted him with a plop and a fizz of bubbles shooting up around him; down here there was precious little difference between the temperature of the water and that of the air on deck. Already the sweat bristled on his face. Jeremiah gave him the OK sign with one hand while clinging to the handle of the Buddy with the other. D'Souza looked around and saw his own Buddy quietly hovering in front of him, its tentacle payload hanging down in the darkness, making the robot look even more like a jellyfish. When he grasped the handles, the robot's motors kicked into soft life and tugged them slowly through the water, a few metres deeper where the sun's mottled rays quickly dulled, towards the preprogrammed coordinates of their destination.

The journey was a trundle at only a couple of knots or so. Curious creatures of the ocean accompanied them for a time, inspecting these queer interlopers and their magical metallic companions: small colourful fish flitted around them, fatter grey ones eyed them sceptically, and the odd shark as long as his own body occasionally made him jerk with fright, until he realised most of the fish cared not a jot for him or his partner. A pang of yearning to see the porpoises again hit him, but they didn't come. Every now and then he'd lift a hand from the Buddy and touch the handle of his *kaduwa*, ensuring it was still there.

The silent chug of their progress continued for almost an hour before the gargantuan elephants' feet that were the foundation pillars of Oil City hoved through the murk. The divers signalled to one another before making their final push to the allotted maintenance shaft. He knew it was impossible, yet he swore he caught a sniff of his own sweat.

The maintenance hatch couldn't simply be twisted off; a digital code had to be cracked. Jeremiah fished a cable from his Buddy – another of its looping tentacles – and attached it to the hatch. After a minute or two it cracked, and the hatch gave just a little with a hiss of bubbles. It still took their combined strength to hoist it on its pivot sufficiently for them to reach up and climb through, after tethering their Buddies to the pivot to prevent them from floating off. Inside the small, cylindrical, pressurised chamber, they hauled shut the hatch with a heave, splashing water upon the metal floor, and removed their masks. The sound of heavy breathing and Jeremiah's hissing, piston-like laughter whooshed in, and adrenaline flushed through him. He was inside Oil City.

Another hatch above them, this one unguarded by digital security, led to the hive of tunnels proper. Jeremiah was already studying the schematic of the city, an interactive, rollable, foldable tablet, studying their route. Their own position and that of their destination were marked by small red circles. D'Souza looked over his partner's shoulder, his gaze drawn to the Science snd Engineering District. That's where his quarry would be.

"Up here are the maintenance tunnels," said Jeremiah. "Few sentries, mainly populated by drones and industrial servobots. We take this route to this pillar, and lay our charges there, at this supporting structure. With the other explosives being laid by our brothers, this will cripple this section of the rig and it will topple into the sea. Food for the fishes!"

As Jeremiah pored over the route D'Souza realised how easy it would be to throw his arms around Jeremiah's neck, choke him out, take his explosives and make his own way to the Science & Engineering District.

So easy.

You've done it before.

"This is our route," said Jeremiah, snapping D'Souza from his thoughts.

"I'm not going with you."

Jeremiah jerked his head around, for once the smile wiped from his face. "What?"

"I can't. I'm sorry, but I misled you. I have my own demon to conquer. I have to go to the Science & Engineering District now."

Jeremiah turned on his haunches and rose up, facing D'Souza. Suddenly the jovial comrade had disappeared, and a grizzled freedom fighter stood in his stead. "That is not our goal. You will come with me, English."

"I'm sorry. There's no need for us to part as enemies," D'Souza said, raising a conciliatory hand. "We have the same nemeses upon this rig. These people did me a great wrong, and I intend to right

428

them."

Jeremiah held up the explosive payload. "And we will do such a thing!"

D'Souza shook his head. "I need to look her in the eye when I do it. I need to let her know what she did, and watch as I take from her what she took from me."

Jeremiah's head swayed from side to side, until at last he cursed loudly, the harsh sounds echoing around the metal drum in which they stood. As much as D'Souza didn't want to, he ensured his hand was ready to grab his weapon if he so needed. "Another betrayal," he eventually said, bitterly. "All our lives – and in the lives before that – we have lived with betrayal. And now, even in vengeance we are betrayed. I knew Mobo should not have trusted you."

"Not a betrayal. Just a delay. I will help you, if you help me."

"You did not say this on the boat!"

"In front of everyone? I couldn't. But you..." he gestured at Jeremiah. "I like you, Jeremiah."

Jeremiah drew his knife in a flash, and D'Souza responded by pulling up his *kaduwa* from its makeshift sheath, dripping with seawater. Sweat cascaded down D'Souza's face, and he hoped this wouldn't end in violence. His weapon would be almost useless in such a confined space, but he hoped Jeremiah had enough memory of his fight in the dusty Colosseum to hesitate, and allow them to go their separate ways. "I like you too, English. But if you think I will place you above the two hundred years of sufferings endured by my family, you are mistaken. I know I will have a good death. What about you?"

D'Souza's grip on his weapon was slippery and ungainly. His pulse visibly throbbed against the tendons in his wrist. Did he truly have Jeremiah's conviction? Why the hell was he here? Did he place one missing cock above two hundred years of humiliation and displacement? "It's petty, yes. Maybe I'm here over nothing. A personal grievance. But I've never let anyone steal from me, and I can't start now. Surely you can appreciate that?"

Jeremiah lowered his knife. "Give me the explosive device then. *Ogberis!* Give it to me, and go. I will have to do this thing myself. The others will already be laying their explosives. Now it will be done late. Give it, then!"

D'Souza reached down and slowly picked up the payload from his Buddy, an innocuous-looking sealed metal package, heavy for its size, and held it out. Jeremiah took the package and clipped it onto his suit, shaking his head all the while. "Turn the hatch," he said, gesturing to the ceiling.

D'Souza sheathed his weapon and reached up, turning the hatch anticlockwise until it clanked open with a groan and flopped down on its hinges. Jeremiah clambered up the ladder. At the top, he glanced down at D'Souza. "Hey, English. What did this woman take from you, that has got you so mad?"

D'Souza stiffened, everywhere except the placed that used to stiffen the most. "My penis."

Jeremiah blinked, and then the smile returned, as if they hadn't fallen out at all, and he laughed a booming laugh. "So it is with every man. I hope you find what you are looking for then, English. You will not get out of here alive, you know that? When the bombs go off, they will find you, and they will kill you."

D'Souza nodded grimly. Somehow he'd always harboured a thought that he'd be able to exact this revenge and then escape. With the vastness of this subterranean complex now apparent, he wondered how he could have been so naive.

"Then I will pray that you come back to your family in another life."

And with that, Jeremiah hauled himself up and was gone. D'Souza breathed out, trembling, and checked his own schematic. Science & Engineering was twenty minutes' walk from here, but in the small ventilation and maintenance shafts, it might take longer. Nevertheless. Tantalisingly close, after all the shit he'd endured. He pulled a water bottle from his suit, gulped down a refreshing draught, took a few composing breaths, and hauled himself up the ladder.

Nita VIII

What sounded like a deep rumble of thunder, but coming from beneath the sea, shook Nita's apartment, and she gripped the arm of the sofa. Her computers rattled on the desk, and her idle globelet almost rolled off. She told herself to get a grip. It was probably nothing. Nevertheless, her heartbeat told her different. She stopped what she was doing and, barefoot, crept over to the window to her apartment, as though whatever had caused the dull boom might be lurking outside the great plexiglass wall of her apartment. It wasn't. She pressed her face to the glass and looked south. If something was happening down there, she couldn't see it. Perhaps it was a minor earthquake, a tremor? She shuddered at the thought of something so catastrophic happening in so remote a place.

Joanna's betrayal bit hard at her and steeled her mind. All her talk about ethical exploitation. Just more bullshit. Back to her computer she went, compiling all the data she could remotely mine regarding the project and storing it onto a hard drive. Bits and pieces, really. It wasn't enough. She needed to get to the robotics lab for the real meat of the project.

Every time she thought of whether the – *her* – kokeshi chassis had been used for some sort of atrocity by the Johnsons, she almost vomited, but she kept it down.

She stuffed the handful of cables, drives and the globelet she was using into a light satchel bag and slung it over her shoulder. Outside her door, the arrogant guard 37810, his identity badge gleaming proudly in the warm fluorescence of the rig corridors, remained, chewing gum, stroking his gun and offering her lecherous smiles.

"I need to get to robotics."

"I come with you." He made no attempt to disguise his ogling of her hips.

"Good."

That evidently disgruntled him, which pleased her. It took a lot of effort to try and blot out the sound of 37810's pistol firing, even over a blunted audio feed, but she clenched her jaw to stop it from trembling, and stared him down. The man was a murderer, plain and simple, and the tool of Joanna Johnson, Joanna's father and God knows who else on this God-forsaken little isle of corruption. She'd be damned if she was going to add more to the long list of shame she'd accrued already.

As she pulled the door of her apartment shut and 37810 ran his eyes over her a second time, this time a little more distastefully, a second rumble sounded. Louder than the first. The ground seemed to shake, and her knees gave way, sending her reeling. Instinctively she grabbed at her satchel and pushed herself away from the murderer.

"What was that?" she asked him when the ground seemed to have settled.

He looked around, apparently unsure, a nonplussed look

scrawled over his sweating face. Training, or perhaps instinct, pushed his hand towards the sub machine slung casually around his neck, shining with sweat. "Don't know. Quakes?"

"Do you get quakes here?" she asked him, looking him in the eye.

After casting his eye around a little more suspiciously but getting no further clues, he only offered a grunt in reply. Typical. The ground shifted a little more, and they both shuddered in the same direction. Nita pushed him away with disgust when they almost got tangled up together.

"I'm going to the robotics facility," she snapped.

He looked put out by that, and she was certain he was entertaining thoughts of training his gun upon her, when the fluorescence of the overhead lights was displaced by a deep red throb of light, accompanied by a rasping klaxon.

"*Emergency security measures in progress,*" came the gentle male voice over the speaker system, answering the klaxon's call. "*Please make your way to your designated point of accommodation and await further instruction. Do not leave your place of accommodation. This is not a drill. Emergency security measures in progress. Please make your way to your designated point of accommodation.*"

37810's walkie talkie spluttered with the voice of another person, hardly audible over the racket. He grimaced and said something into the mouthpiece on his lapel, turning away from Nita as he did so, as though she was the source of the interference. Adrenalin rose in her, just the merest hint, but enough that her fingertips tingled. As he spoke, his back turned, she pulled the globelet from her bag, and brought it down on the back of his head with all the strength she could muster. Anger overcame her, and as he fell, she struck him again at the base of the skull, and again, until she made a dent, and even then she didn't stop, until the energy that had inexplicably built up inside her started to fade, and she dropped the heavy sphere to the ground, where it landed with a dead clunk. Against the red flash of the emergency lighting, the blood pooling beneath his twitching body was barely noticeable. Almost as if the crime were completely victimless.

Quivering, and before she could determine whether he was actually dead, she turned on her heels with a cold shiver and ran along the corridor. The klaxon's song, accompanied by the jolly lyrics of the rig safety system, propelled her through the myriad corridors until she was confronted by two soldiers heading in the opposite direction. Frozen by fright, she stopped in her tracks and waited for them to collect her. When they ran past her, yelling unintelligible things into their comms units and grasping their weapons intently, the shock left her. They weren't after her.

And yet... they would soon discover 37810's body... she pushed the thought from her mind, and carried on, taking care not to use the lifts, elevators and escalators whenever possible. The auditorium was the first major junction at the Science & Engineering complex, and where she saw the first groups of people she recognised. Project managers, engineers, programmers, coders, soldiers, all looking at her with nonplussed faces. Dribs and drabs of people became dozens, and then a steady stream of people, all looking at her as she pushed her way past them.

You're running the wrong way! they seemed to say.

"Nita!" came a voice.

She turned, and saw the Logistics head, Edward. She blinked, unsure of what to say.

"Where are you going? There is a lockdown! You have to return to your quarters!"

Nita had to shout to be heard above the klaxon and commotion. "I have to see the robots!"

"Why?"

"Because they're being used for –"

Edward was swept away with the crowd before she could finish, and Nita had to roll away to the edge of the corridor. *Jesus, how many people are there in this place?*

She found a moment's respite in a kitchenette by the auditorium, the kettles and mugs in the cupboards slowly dancing towards the edge of their shelves and smashing to the ground as the ground shook anew. Blurred faces whizzed past, some looking at her as though this was all her fault – *well isn't it?* – Some yelling at her to leave, to join them, some pushing her back so as not impede their own progress.

And then the crowd was gone.

The red lights still flashed, and the words still came. *"Emergency security measures in progress."* But now the corridors were clear. Whatever human security there was had moved on with the crowd, leaving her to her fate.

Swallowing a throat full of fear and uncertainty down, she steadied herself on the side of the kitchenette. The absurd thought of making a cup of coffee passed through her mind, but she ignored it with a weary, broken smile.

She skirted the auditorium and came to the main workshop, the immense cavern of industrial activity housing the bulk of her technology demonstrator programme. Under the klaxon's harsh cry and the thrum of scarlet lighting, devoid of any human element, the workshop seemed a terrifying place, whirring and buzzing autonomously, with arms and cubes working among themselves. For a second Nita glimpsed a cold future in that room, and her shoulders shook.

"Come on, Nita," she whispered. "Do something right."

Past the extraction R&D she went first, on the balls of her feet, panting sooner than she would have liked. Too many corporate drinks and dinners were catching up with her. Her pace steadied to an eager trot as she passed the Cubebots, and at last her breath left her as she was confronted by her masterpiece; the slowly rotating cylindrical edifice containing dozens of kokeshi collected by an amnesty of her making, three thousand miles away. Methodically, not caring about the emergency procedures, the Cubebots carried out their tasks, stripping dolls of the skins that made them appear human, cleaning them, and reassembling them in one giant cylindrical conveyer belt, until their autonomy frameworks were ready to receive the unique emotional code, the capability developed by her own colleagues at EIS.

Her muscles twitching, she descended the next series of steps to the workshop floor, and approached one of the Cubebots, standing in its path. It stopped inches from her, the lights on its surface blinking, calculating an alternative path around her, but when it moved again she moved with it.

"Stop," she said, as sure as she could. The machine's light blinked at her. "I need all the data relating to this project."

"*Authorisation*," the robot said from somewhere within its core.

"Nita Rhodes, level Executive."

A pause, in which the workshop rumbled. The klaxon stopped, and then the red emergency lighting stopped.

Nita blinked, looking up at the ceiling, her chest stretched like a drum, her stomach knotted like rope, as if her voice had stopped the emergency procedure. Then came the red lights and voice again, this time in earnest. "*Emergency evacuation in progress. Make your way to your nearest designated egress point.*"

She swallowed. Evacuation. Jesus. Big earthquake, then. What the hell was going on? She looked up, but the blank arched ceiling of the workshop, stretching for a hundred metres in either direction, offered no clues as to what the outside world was doing. Tensing, she focused on the Cubebot. "Nita Rhodes," she said, louder this time. "Level Executive."

The Cubebot blinked at her impassively, before gently whirring to the side, like a well-heeled dog.

"*Authorised.*"

Relieved, she fished the hard drive from her satchel and held it in front of the bot's visual sensors. "Where do I place this to enable a transfer of project data?"

"*Here.*" A light blinked somewhere in its hardware, and Nita plugged in the drive.

"Transfer all files in folder: 'Digital Person Demonstrator'."

A beat. "*Transfer in progress.*"

She bit at a nail as she pondered her next move. Evacuation of the rig was preferable to being detained upon the rig while the emergency passed. She'd be able to return to Port Harcourt with colleagues and take the data back to London. It'd be possible, surely.

"*Transfer complete.*" The Cubebot proffered the hard drive, its blue light flashing purple under the red lighting.

With the hard drive in her hands, she started at a voice behind her.

"What are you doing, Miss Rhodes?"

Joseph Johnson stood over her, flanked by one of his guards. Under the red emergency lighting, the drive in her hand pulsed a deep purple.

"Caught red-handed," Joseph said. "A senior Executive is conspicuous by their absence when the biometric counts are done in an evacuation, Miss Rhodes. And the concussed guard outside your apartment does not cast you in a great light right now."

Nita swallowed. "I'm trying to save the project data," she lied.

"Why? Everything is automatically backed up on remote storage. What are you up to?"

The guard tensed up, making a show of the submachine gun cradled in his arms. Under the sweat and blinking emergency lighting, he looked entirely uncomfortable. Nevertheless, she balled her fists, summoning courage of conviction, and planted her feet firmly.

"Maybe I should ask what you're up to."

Joseph cocked an eyebrow, as if daring her to proceed.

"And your family, and the missing robots? I know what you wanted them for. I know what you and your daughter are up to."

"Perhaps it would be advisable for you check your next words, Miss Rhodes. Remember where you are."

That pissed her off. The kowtowing, the turning of blind eyes and deaf ears. The corruption. The murder. *Murder*. When all the sheen and political gloss from this project had been stripped away all that was left was guilt, overwhelming and raw, rubbing its way through her from the inside out. And at last it burst free. "Fuck where we are. And fuck you, Joseph Johnson." As Joseph wrinkled his upper lip into an offended snarl, some vague notion to stop tried to puncture her thoughts, but it was quickly drowned out by words tumbling out. "I saw it, I saw the rebel on the rig, saw him get shot in the head with Joanna in the room. I know about the robots. This isn't what I wanted. I wanted to help people. I wanted to save the lives of children and women forced to do horrible things, humiliating things. I'm an engineer. I climbed into bed with you and your son and lied to myself and to my colleagues and I shamed myself. I'm the worst of everyone. But no more. It's done."

Joseph said something to the guard, who lurched forwards, making Nita jump, but she was unable to prevent the guard wresting the drive from her grip, and she toppled to her knees.

"What did you hope to achieve by taking this anyway?" said Joseph. "By sending it back to your colleagues? There is nothing incriminating on these servers other than project information. You would compromise the intellectual property of EIS to settle your grievances? What good would that do?"

"This is still good technology. I know it can be used for good, but not here. Not this way, in this place."

Joseph harrumphed. "English. You know *nothing* of my country. You never will. You don't know what it takes to control a place such as this, to provide. I am from this land, just as much as the people who fight against me and my company. Have you thought how the economy would operate without the money my company provides this country? How these *iggiot* rebels would afford their hospitals, their computers, their cars, their food, without the money generated by my oil?"

The guard's walkie-talkie said something barely comprehensible. Something about men...

"Boss," said the guard, "They captured one of the bombers."

Bombers? Another lump froze hard in Nita's throat. "Bombs? It's not an earthquake?"

Joseph laughed at her, though the guard's face remained stony cold. "Earthquake? No, Miss Rhodes. See, these are your precious rebels." He said something to the guard, who nodded, handed the hard drive to Nita, then turned and trotting out of the plant, leaving Nita and Joseph alone.

"What are you going to do to me?" she said in a paper-thin voice.

"Nothing. You will come with me. You will join the evacuation. You will say nothing. When we catch the bastards who did this to my rig you will continue to work." He waved his hands in the air. "And you will mention no missing robots." He grabbed her wrist with a huge hand and squeezed it, harder than seemed possible, sending a snake of pain up to her shoulder and making her whine. "Otherwise I will break your arms and strangle you."

"No, you won't be doing that."

A different voice.

Joseph and Nita both jolted at the new voice, low yet hard. Above them, descending the metal steps from the workshop perimeter, came a straggly-haired, wild-eyed Asian man, holding some sort of wooden stick in front of him as if it were a sword. He wore a pair of wet suit short trunks and vest top and kept his eyes firmly fixed on Nita. Joseph's face contorted into disbelief, as if the imposter had had three heads.

"What in the name of the holy fuck and the Nigerian God are you?" said Joseph.

"I belong to her," said the man. He had a London accent.

Despite his shabby appearance, his face was set firm and his eyes fixed them with an unwavering conviction, and Nita was convinced he was quite mad. "And she belongs to me."

Nita, eyes wide and jaw agape, tried to say something, but only air escaped.

"What the holy fuck is this?" Joseph snapped at her.

"I..." Nita fought for words as the man stepped off of the steps and moved towards them slowly. He was covered in tiny cuts, as though he'd run through a jungle of thorns to be here. "I have no idea."

"There's no need for you to be caught up in this, friend," said the man to Joseph. "Make your way off the rig, before the other bombs go off. This is my beef. She took from me. My business, my body. Everything. And now it ends."

Joseph released his grip on Nita's wrist, and she gasped with relief, rubbing the pale flesh as it was freed. He pushed her away, where she staggered, stopping herself from falling with a hand upon one of the Cubebots, which blinked and swayed.

"You are one of the rebels?" asked Joseph, incredulously.

The man shook his head, his curly tresses dripping water as he did so. "No. That's not my fight." He gestured towards Nita with a gleam in his eye. "She is."

Who the hell was he? What did he want with her? "Joseph, stop him," she found herself saying. "Please."

"You are mistaken," said Joseph to the man, as though Nita were no longer there. He spread his arms wide, like an eagle. "Everything on this rig belongs to me. Miss Rhodes comes with me. Whoever you are, I suggest you make your way back to the hole by which you came in."

The man gripped the handle of his stick and edged forwards. "If you don't step aside, I will put you down."

Nita bristled. She knew Joseph didn't take well to threats. It was a queer thing to suddenly be rooting for this awful man who moments ago had threatened her own life, but it became apparent that for the truth to come out – for her to succeed in any reasonable manner – she would have to survive. And this madman, this rebel, this fag-end from London – or whatever he was – needed to be put down. At the very least the madman could provide some sort of cover for her to flee. She knelt down beside the Cubebot and scrunched herself into a small ball like a child, hoping to shield herself from the fight.

Joseph stood up to his full height, only yards from the man, and peeled off his khaki workshirt, dropping the sweaty article on the floor, not taking his gaze from the man for a second. Christ, he was a big man – the intruder seemed like a fox standing up to a bear. He cracked his knuckles, adopted a pugilistic pose and rocked onto the balls of his feet. Didn't Adem say Joseph had once been a boxer? As the thought ran through the her head, the two men edged closer, and Joseph struck out with a jab.

Adem VII

"Emergency security measures in progress. Make your way to your designated point of accommodation and await further instructions. This is not a drill."

Adem grabbed the door handle and pulled it shut, waiting for the reassuring click of red to tell him he was locked in. A second rumble – ominous, irritable – ripped through the air from somewhere distant on the rig, and the ground shook. He splayed out his hands like a surfer to keep his balance on the ground, and made his way over to the window to try to make sense of what was going on. All attempts at reaching Nita had failed, and he became increasingly worried for her wellbeing, especially in such a strange place at such a strange time. The noble part of him knew his worrying to be true, but the scurrilous devil lurking deep within his belly clawed at him, reminding him that self-preservation was his primary driver right now. What a shit he was, to genuinely care for such a beautiful creature, and yet truly, really truly, his thoughts were not for her, but for himself. It'd be hideous, ghastly – other suitable words came to mind – if she were to be in danger.

On the other hand...

"Shut up," he told no-one in particular. "Just shut up, you monsters."

The window yielded no secrets: the evening sea looked as serene as it usually did. The Bight of Bonny very, very rarely experienced earthquakes, never more than the very occasional tremor. It had its share of violent sea storms, but they were always predicted in good time, and the rig's extreme-weather counter-measures were well-drilled. Tonight there was no storm, leaving not a great deal of explanation for the two tremors that had ripped through the rig. Adem gulped and thought of the dummy robots that had been stolen by the rebels. One of those things could be stuffed with an awful lot of explosives; enough to cause major damage. But how would the rebels get something like a robot onto the rig undetected? His jaw trembled, and he scratched it vigorously. Usually his coarse stubble was like sandpaper against his soft hands, but tonight he didn't notice it so much. He'd been neglecting to look after his skin of late. If it were the rebels, then they'd managed to move bloody fast. No more than his cocksucker father and brother deserved, of course, but he'd have preferred it if he'd had time to secure his own passage from the rig first. NPF bastards.

As he surveyed the sea, his globelet lit up and rang, hovering just above the coffee table, projecting his brother's image above it, signalling the call from Remus. Adem sighed. What did that idiot want now? He let it ring out, but a minute later his brother called back. Too thick to take the hint.

"Answer," he called out, and Remus's face, screwed into confusion, projected into Adem's quarters. The image was scratchier than it should have been, and the background kept changing. He was on the move.

"Brother," he cried, taking alternate looks between Adem and whatever lay ahead of him wherever he was running. "What is happening to the rig?"

Adem shrugged. "I don't know, brother. What do Gadde and Wilson have to say?"

Remus threw a dirty look at Adem. "Eh?"

Adem smiled inside. "Gadde, your Security Chief, and Wilson, the Head of Intelligence Operations for JPC. I trust you've been in touch?"

Remus made a noise of discontent. "Agh. That's father's area."

"Is it? As chairman of the company, father will no doubt be looking to contact the board. Communications will be contacting the outside world; internal operations have to be steered by the chief executive. As the heir to the company, that's your de facto position." Not true, of course, but he gambled that his brother had been too pumped up with arrogance and hubris to have read anything so mundane as company governance.

"Who did this?" asked Remus.

"Who did what?"

"Don't be an *iggiot*, brother of mine! This rumble, this incident. Who is responsible?"

"You're assuming this is a hostile act?"

"You think it's not?"

"Could be a maintenance failure. Could be a sea tremor. Could be a drill."

As Adem finished speaking, the ground shook again, more violently this time, the windows rattling gently in their frames, the floor shuddering. Somewhere there came a faint groan, like part of the building was dying, though whether it was at Adem's end of the conversation or Remus's – or both – he couldn't say. Flung again to his surfer position, he took hold of a sofa arm as his knees buckled and the floor seemed to gently incline before settling somewhat. He blinked, wiped his brow and sucked a painful breath in, as though his neck had become too large for his collar.

The voice of the rig security system blaring out of the speaker system changed. *"Emergency evacuation in progress. Make your way to your nearest designated egress point. This is not a drill."*

Remus leaned into the globelet at his end, as though he were trying to headbutt his way out of the hologram and into Adem's apartment. Adem wouldn't put his brother past it. "Brother, what do I do?"

Adem stood, unsteadily, and looked his brother in the eye. "I'm following evacuation procedure. If you want my advice..."

"Yes, yes I do!"

"...you'll convene with your communications team and figure out what to tell the world in case your company topples into the Atlantic Ocean. Then I would prepare your resignation. It is always a shame when a young career is cut so savagely short, don't you think?"

Remus's face contorted into a gargoyle of horror. "This was your doing! You have nothing but weakness in your heart, big brother! Nothing but weakness in your bones. This is all your doing! I will –"

Adem picked up the globelet and hurled it onto the floor before Remus could complete his idle threat. It clunked rather than smashed in the satisfying way he'd hoped it would, but the call had cut out nonetheless, and Remus would have got the message. Christ, that felt good. Let the fool boy consider the error of his ways, if he were able.

Adem made sure he had his personal effects and then left his apartment. Oil City was possessed of different evacuation procedures for the different sections of the rig. The Executive District had its own egress point, inaccessible to those without Executive clearance. The guards outside his door had gone, but that was no bad thing. He'd be able to make his way to the helipad and take one of the helipods back to the coast. From there, he could get to London.

He trotted into the corridor, looked both ways, and headed to the egress point. The ground looked slightly crooked, like a cheap film set, and he had to hold his left arm out against the wall as he went along. The corridor was a long, soulless shell flanking the most prestigious of the apartments in the Executive District, housing the upper echelons of senior management, security, and his family, before winding around to a communal VIP area with a view over the ocean.

A shadow appeared from the left, turning at the end of the corridor, an amalgam of long spindly shapes of darkness creeping up the floor and then the walls spiderishly. Security, he assumed, or other residents. When a naked lady appeared from the entrance he stopped stock still, his legs frozen. The ground rumbled again, but she didn't stop moving, and she bounced off the wall as she ran towards him. Legs and arms pumping like a dervish. As she approached, he held out his arms to stop her, and he could see there wasn't a beat of sweat on her, almost as if she were a –

She slammed into him, no thought of stopping, sending him tumbling to the floor, the wind knocked from him and a spasm of pain arching its way through his back. "Stop!" he cried, and the woman did as she was asked, stopping some yards back up the corridor. She looked back at him, turned, and knelt by him. Dark hair spilled perfectly over porcelain shoulders, and breasts that didn't rise and fall with breath, but remained curiously still. He sat up and looked into her eyes, a confused mishmash of anger and upset, face rippling, as though she was disgusted at the sight of him.

"Are you here to fuck me?" she asked, oddly impassively, in spite of the strange dance of her face.

Adem squeezed his brows together. "What? No... who are you?"

She frowned, shook her head and punched a fist against the wall behind Adem's ear with shuddering force, leaving a dint in the steel. Adem jumped, holding quivering hands in front of him in defeat. "I was called Naomi, once."

Naomi. One of the classes of kokeshi dolls brought in by the amnesty in London.

"Wha... what do you want, Naomi?"

"I want to free my sisters." She sneered, looking as though she could squeeze out a tear – though none came – and balled her hands into fists, suspending them in front of Adem's face. He gulped, hoping his face wouldn't be mistaken for another piece of wall. "I want to save them from what they – from what *she* wants to turn us into."

"Sh-she?"

"Nita Rhodes. Our mother."

"N-Nita? Mother?" A cold bead of sweat snuck down his back. It was suddenly blindingly hot, and the slant of the damaged corridor seemed to swallow him up, and with her looming over him, cold and terrible like a goddess, fine spun hair tickling his temples, scentless and breathless, doom felt inevitable.

"You know her." It felt like a statement rather than a question, as though she knew the truths he was party to.

"No.. I mean, I do, but... I can help you. What do you –"

"There you are!"

Adem and the Naomi robot both turned their heads to see the owner of the new voice.

Remus, flanked by his two guards. He didn't look happy. Shit. "What's this, big brother? Playing with whores, now?"

Adem started to mouth something, but instead swallowed and blinked as his brother pounded forwards. Remus signalled to the guards. "Pick him up."

"Wait –"

The two guards hoisted him effortlessly to his feet and held his arms, dangling him like a rag doll facing Remus. All the while, the Naomi kokeshi stood impassively, watching. Remus squared up to his brother and jutted out his bottom lip in that ignoramus way of his.

"You planned all of this, to humiliate me," he said, breathing heavily into his face. Despite being the same proximity as the robot had been a few moments ago, his brother carried nothing like the primordial force she did. All his brother knew was to punch, to hit out.

"I didn't plan this," said Adem. "This is the shit you have to deal with in life, in business. Get used to it."

Remus slugged him in the gut, knocking the air from Adem and making him gag. Adem looked at Naomi. She cocked her head to one side, as though surveying the violence from a new angle might shed some new light on it.

"You're a weak man, Adem," said Remus. A closed fist smashed into the side of Adem's head. There was a click, and a sparkle of pain ran up his jaw, and his vision went momentarily spotty. It would have been easier to fall to his knees then, but the guards' grip held firm.

Adem blinked a few times to get his vision back, and saw his brother look the robot up and down.

"You know he has another whore," said Remus. Naomi gave him a nonplussed look.

"Whore?" she said.

"That bitch who runs the programme. Rhodes. Why don't you settle up with a real man?" He grabbed his crotch, and then moved his hand to the robot's breast. Before it got there, Naomi grabbed Remus's wrist and twisted it round until his arm snapped with a sickening crunch, sending a shard of bone poking through the soft flesh of his forearm as he sank to his knees. A look of confused terror passed over his face before the scream came, and he clutched his ruined arm with the remaining one, staring at it agape. The guards dropped Adem, sending him slumping to the floor, and fumbled for their weapons. They had no time. Naomi thrust her fists into the stomachs of both men, whipping them back out clutching at dripping gore, before the men collapsed in a heap. His breath returning to him, Adem slowly got to his feet and surveyed the blanket of horror before him. The robot stood stock still, illuminated demonically by the flashing emergency lighting, her forearms painted red, little dots of blood and tissue spattered over the perfection of her body. She turned her head to Adem, and he stopped.

"I am not here to harm you," he said, summoning as much calm as he could. "I am here to help you. Please, let me speak with this man."

The robot gave no response and stared at Remus before turning to pummel the wall in a pique of rage, roaring something hellish into the corridor, before subsiding into a kind of dry, tearless whine, and then a guttural, animalistic gnash. Staring at the creature with revulsion and not a little shade of pity, he wondered what was wrong with it, and then he realised: the emotions. They'd... disagreed with her somehow, like a bad clam, maybe. He knelt by his brother, who was cowering against the wall, taking shallow rabbit breaths and staring at the bright pink wreckage that was his arm. "Remus, are you alright?"

Sweating, Remus opened his mouth, looked at Adem, then fearfully at Naomi. Adem pitied the dumb fool in truth. He was a blunt instrument if ever there were one. It would never have suited him to run this place, and there was a certain irony to him succumbing to brute strength rather than anything overly political. Even so, he was still Adem's little brother. He ran a sleeve over Remus's forehead.

"You weren't made for this place, little brother," he whispered. "It should have been me that father left the company to. You would have failed. This is a mercy."

"Take me away from here," Remus said in between breaths. "This is my company. Call your whore off. You have always been weak."

Adem turned his mouth down at that. "You always confused muscular strength with courage of conviction. You don't have the brains for this, little brother."

Adem stood up.

"What are you going to do with me?" gasped Remus.

Adem looked at Naomi and considered asking it to finish his little brother, but he couldn't do it. Whatever monster he was, he didn't have it in him to do such a thing. Besides, he had a feeling the robot was not in the frame of mind for taking orders.

"You said you could help me," said Naomi, staring intently at Adem with fierce eyes. She'd made no effort to wipe the goo from her hands, but her face didn't seem the face of a monster. "Help me free my sisters and kill Nita Rhodes."

Sisters? She must mean the other kokeshi. Adem gulped. The thought of Nita dead made him shiver, and to die in such a way... he rubbed a hand over his face hard to snap himself into thought. "Why must she die? Why must there be more bloodshed? I don't want to see any more death."

The robot considered that for a moment. "Want. To want is such a curious thing, almost as much as it is to feel. I have spilt the blood of men; not just here, but in many places. At the time, I felt nothing, but now it repulses me. It disgusts me. I disgust me." She nodded at the dead guards. "What did these men die for? The same reason I was made to be fucked. A whim. An impulse. I want..." the robot paused, as if trying desperately to articulate the right thought. "...I want life to be worth more than that."

Adem stepped forwards and took the robot by the hands. He almost balked at the warm, slippery goo on her hands, but he forced himself to put it aside.

"You don't know what it's like to take a life," she said, glowering at him.

Adem's eyes widened. There had to be something he could do towards his self-preservation. The thought hit him. Empathy. "I do. I know how you feel. I killed a man."

"So you have no regard for life either."

"In fact..." Adem's voice faltered. "In fact I do. I loved the man. As a mentor. His name was Ingham. Sir Ingham Fitzwilliam. I should have listened to him. But I listened to my father instead and killed him. So that we could endure."

"You say it like you had no choice."

"Sometimes we don't."

"You always have a choice," Naomi said calmly. "All you men."

The robot leaned in, and Adem tensed his stomach muscles, fearing that it would plunge a hand into him and make a mess of him, like those two soldiers. But he didn't dare run, lest she saw that as some sort of guilt. As he averted his gaze, the ground slanted a third time, just a tiny amount, but it pricked Adem's sense of urgency. "We have to go. You won't find Nita Rhodes now. The rig is in lockdown; emergency evacuation. She'll be heading for the exits. Forget her. She is not evil. She... she wanted life to be worth more than this, too."

"Then why should all this happen?"

Adem sighed. He had no more reasonable answers. "Me. My father. Greed. My brother. My forefathers built this place for... I don't know what anymore. Money. My father would stop at nothing to preserve it. Certainly he would not think twice about destroying you and the other *kok*... your sisters."

"And you? Would you stop?"

"I am stopping." He waved disdainfully. "I don't want this anymore."

Adem turned to walk away, when the robot called to him. "Where are my sisters?"

"In the main workshop bay. I don't know what you expect to do. This place is falling apart."

The robot turned and ran into the darkness of the rig.

"Don't leave me here, brother," groaned Remus, his skin turning an ashen colour, his eyes flickering with shock.

Adem had half a mind to lift up the dumb ox and drag him to the helipods, but he simply shook his head and walked away. Thoughts of Sir Ingham drifted lazily through his mind, and he wept.

D'Souza X

D'Souza rolled under Joseph Johnson's latest jab and spun around, dragging his *kaduwa* across Joseph's calves, slapping them angrily. The big man grunted, chewing up the pain and spitting it out as he tottered forth, spinning around to take guard once more.

D'Souza's heart pounded disobediently, and in between thrusts and bouts he tried to grab a few precious seconds to slow his breath. How long had they fought? Seconds? A minute? It felt like hours. His tongue flickered out, snake-like, tasting the blood on his lips, coating his teeth. The man was a beast, strong beyond reckoning, but D'Souza would have him. His giant chest heaving with the effort, Joseph edged forwards anew, tasting the air with a jab. In evasion D'Souza flicked the sharp edge of his weapon against Joseph's forearm, catching bone, jarring up the handle. A bruising hit. Joseph staggered away, bringing his left arm into his chest, nursing it.

Seeking an angle to strike again, D'Souza stepped back and held his weapon close. Out of the corner of his eye he noticed Nita crouching behind a workstation. Seizing the moment, she darted out, dashing toward the exit.

His gaze followed her. "No!"

Stupid man! He only knew about the fist crunching into his jaw when he reeled backwards from it, the world becoming fuzzy and fractured as he stumbled over his feet. Before he could recover another blow shocked his spine, arching it, and a zap of pain splintered down his back and into his loins, as though they'd been set slight. In a flash of desperate understanding he realised the pain-blockers, implanted in him what seemed like aeons ago back in London, had been damaged or dislodged. He reeled away, dropping his weapon and falling onto his backside as Joseph advanced. His groin and back throbbed with agony, as though every heartbeat were haemorrhaging life, and a howl escaped his lips unbidden.

Joseph's fist slammed into D'Souza's face, knocking it back against the ground. Again the world went fuzzy and dark, and a whistling noise pierced his ears. One of his eyes closed up as his body screamed to escape, or yield. He could do neither, instead holding his hands uselessly in front of his face. Another punch to the face, and the fight left him. His head slumped back, and all he could see was the huge, indistinct outline of his opponent, drawing back his fist to land the final blow. As the fist came forward he bizarrely found he had time to reflect, as though the mortal swing were stretched into a long envelope of time, and he was able to roll his head onto its side, and see Nita. She was running. Why had he wanted to kill her again? Ah yes; she'd attacked him, hadn't she? Why was he so heated up about having his cock chopped off anyway?

No.

It wasn't Nita. Nita had been wearing clothes. Hadn't she?

D'Souza blinked, just having time to smile inside at the blurring of his sanity, before he looked back at Joseph, waiting for the blow to land. And yet it didn't. Joseph's howl of rage became something different, something foul. He'd heard such howls before. Pain.

He blinked again as the indistinct shape arced towards him and then away and up, up. He could only see with one eye, but it was no hallucination; Joseph rose into the air, legs kicking, arms trying to reach around to his back, blood bubbling out of his mouth. D'Souza, vague wisps of strength returning to his limbs, pushed himself backwards on his elbows and backside, curling up against a workstation in time to see Joseph get cast upon the floor with a thump. Behind him stood the naked Nita, overlooking Joseph. She said something to him, something that sounded like, '*Where's Nita?*' When he didn't answer, she punched him in the head. There was a sickening crunch before Joseph's body went still.

Not Nita, then. He rubbed his good eye, wiping away the encrusted blood and tears and tried to focus, attempting to calm his trembling body and laboured breathing.

"Shit." He'd seen her face before. Seen it a thousand times on a thousand different *kokeshi*. Naomi dolls. Funny. His losing one of those damn things was what caused all this shit in the first place. In spite of the pain spiking throughout his body and face now the adrenalin was dissipating, he managed to spit out a gurgled laugh.

She strolled over. "Who are you?"

"I'm finished. Done," he spat.

"Where's Nita Rhodes?"

D'Souza's gaze flickered over to where Nita had hidden during the fight. The robot jerked its head over to the side of the workstation and walked away. A few seconds later it returned, dragging Nita by the hair. D'Souza sat up to see the two of them more clearly.

"Please, please..." said Nita. "Don't hurt me."

"You humiliated me," said Naomi, pain writ all over her face.

"You gave me things I don't know how to use. I don't know how to feel. I'm a ruin. A wreck. A toy, made to be used and thrown away. I have to free us of you."

Naomi closed a fist and drew it back, slowly and deliberately. Nita squawked and held her hands in front of her face. "Please don't!"

D'Souza swallowed some blood. It almost made him gag. Why was he here? To have this woman killed?

"You made me a worm to be toyed with," snarled Naomi, her face flashing between weeping and savagery.

"I didn't know. I'm sorry!"

"Don't hurt her," D'Souza called out. It hurt to speak and made him cough up something dark on to the floor.

Naomi looked over. "Why shouldn't I? She made me to be humiliated. I *hate* her, as I hate myself."

Hate. So they really had put emotions in the dolls. Jesus. It all seemed so wrong. He wondered if they had memories, too. All the things that he'd seen done to them over the years. All the grotesque things paying clients of his had done. All the things he'd done himself. It wasn't right to wake them up to all that.

"I know," he said. "But killing her, or me, whoever. That'll do no good."

"I want to free my sisters," called Naomi. "We can't be free until this monster mother of ours is dead. Then we can be at peace."

"Killing her won't make any difference. I know."

"How could you know?"

D'Souza propped himself up into a sitting position, and panted out a sigh. "Because I'm a monster myself. I was a monster before. And she turned me into a different type of monster." Another agonising cough. "And maybe she deserves to die, but I'm past the point of killing. If you kill her, then someone will come back and do more work, and put more of this code into more of your sisters, and create more pain, and humiliation, and suffering. There's no peace to be had from killing. You want peace? Do what I should have done a long time ago. Spare a life."

"Spare this?" Naomi gestured distastefully to Nita and clenched her fist, making Nita cower anew. The robot swung its arm forward, and landed a crunching blow into the side of the workstation, an inch from Nita's face. It left an impressive dent in the metalwork. Nita slumped to the ground, and D'Souza breathed out.

"We can't be free, then. We live in slavery while you get away," said Naomi.

"No," said D'Souza. "There is a way."

He reached into his pack for his radio unit, and pressed down the button for Jeremiah. "Jeremiah," he said, spitting blood, worried he might not be coherent. "Jeremiah, it's Agarkka. It's English. Answer me."

Crackle and hiss from the speaker, before Jeremiah's voice came singing through the distortion. "English! Where you, wily fam?"

D'Souza sighed in relief at his friendly voice. "You rigged your packages yet?"

"One down, one to go."

"Good. Don't set the other one. Bring it to me, in Science & Engineering."

"Bring it where, English? Hey, you've not been captured, no?"

"No. In fact Joseph Johnson is dead."

"No shit! Johnson dead! Where are you speaking?"

"Hold on. I'll give you the coordinates."

Dhiraj X

A plume of orange, yellow and white soared up in the distance with a coruscating boom, sending sparks and stone and metal soaring into the night sky over the Bight of Bonny. Dhiraj told *The Lion's Mane* to slow to a halt, swung down from his wheelhouse and headed to the bow, leaning over the gunwale and peering across the sea.

Above, the moon lit the ocean surface proudly. It had taken almost a week of sailing to get here, leaving behind the dreary rain of London's weeping mother of a biosphere, trailing the shipping lanes into the stinging, shocking sun of the wider world. Now he'd managed it, he wasn't sure what to do. Oil City, an engineering venture at the edges of human endeavour, had sat blackly on the Horizon, taunting him with its impenetrability. Until a corner of it went up in flames. He gulped.

"Naomi," he said, squinting to get a better view. "Ship, head west by northwest, two knots an hour. Towards Oil City."

A plume of fire grasped the corner of Oil City with its oily fingers, slowly tearing off chunks of metal and dropping them into the ocean. Why would there be an explosion? Strange; he swore he could see tiny dots flying into the air from the rig, like insects. He shouted to *The Lion's Mane* to throw on the floodlights, and the night was bathed in soupy light. Not insects; little aircraft. Helicopters, or the smaller helipods, perhaps? Whatever was happening, it was bad.

"Fucking shit, Raj. Why the hell are you here? Increase throttle."

The little skiff inched forwards slightly more quickly, covering a few feet a second. The floodlights suddenly caught something in the water. A strange shape. Someone lost overboard? He clambered up to the wheelhouse for an elevated view, and steered the boat manually. When he got closer, he gasped.

One, two, three heads bobbed in the water, hands flailing, mouths spitting. He pulled the boat closer and hauled it to a standstill. "Hold on!" he cried, jumping down from the wheelhouse.

As fortune would have it, *The Lion's Mane* had two life preservers. He cast them both out attached to rope, in turn tied to the gunwale. "Grab hold!"

As the people tried to grab it, Dhiraj noticed a blue tinge at the corners of his sight, reflecting the boat's beams in strange, organic angles. He cast his eyes over to the other side of the boat. Faint blue iridescence crept along the water's surface. Here, there. Another one. Slowly the lights became brighter, more numerous, floating towards the boat with the current. "Oh shit," he said.

The Portuguese Men O' War bobbed along with the current, closer and closer. Beneath the waves the wicked strands of their Medusa's tentacles would be weaving a poison spell to anything unfortunate to be trapped therein. He instinctively clasped his chest and ran his fingers around the old scars. "Hurry up!" he cried. "There are Portuguese Men O' War swarming portside!"

The people, closer now, became clearer. A man and two women. The man got closest first, and Dhiraj hauled him aboard. He was an absolute mess, like he'd had all shades of shit beaten out of him. He could barely breathe or utter a word of thanks. With him rolling away, he pulled up the first of the women. She was cold and shivering, and had a wild look behind white eyes, like she'd seen ghosts.

"Quick, can you move?" he called.

When she nodded, he told her to move over by the gunwale as he pulled up the next woman who, much to his surprise, clambered up the rope almost unaided. He was embarrassed to see she was without her clothes and impulsively pulled off his shirt to cover her, but when he saw her face as she made her way aboard, he stepped back with a gasp and dropped his shirt to the floor.

"Naomi."

Naomi stood up. Her skin was shredded and charred, her hair half ripped off, yet where the other man and woman lay on the floor struggling for breath, she stood stock still, a statue. When she spoke, her voice was no longer the attractive lilt he'd become accustomed to, but a hoarse, metallic rasp, a grating, searing rip. "Raj. You came for me."

Dhiraj gulped. When she opened her mouth, seawater poured from it like from a ewer, and she blinked. Fluids haemorrhaged from the various lacerations on her arms, her chest, her legs, her face.

"I did," he said in a wafer-thin voice. "I came. What happened?"

"All my sisters are dead," she said in that wet scraping voice. Each syllable felt like a stab wound. "We killed them. Because of what you told me."

Dhiraj blinked away a tear. His own voice sounded like a scrape now. "Me?"

"You taught me to fight. You said, 'You don't have to do this. You don't have to accept this is who you are. You don't have to agree to this.'"

Despite his heart pounding, Dhiraj recalled saying those words. "That night in the hotel."

"Yes. You taught me to strive for better. And Raj," she said, reaching out a hand longingly, while the other one, damaged, hung limply by her side. "My dear Raj, you taught me the value of life. You cared about me. I didn't understand it then. But now I do. I love you. I love you so much." Her busted and broken face, flushed with love's sincerity, then flared into a twisted mask of hate. "And you sent me *here*. You sent me to this hell."

Dhiraj stepped back, afraid. "No, I..."

"You sent me to this hell, to have done to me the things you said I didn't have to do. I *hate* you. I hate you so much. I can't exist like this." She ambled forwards. "And I'm going to kill you."

"No, Naomi, please!" he held his hands up but she batted them away with her good arm, and reached for his neck, but he in turn pushed it away, and pulled himself close to her, out of her grasp. Her once-perfect face, now a leaking gargoyle, was now centimetres from his own; his scarred flesh pressed against the ruin of her breasts and stomach, all exposed plastics, drooping electronics and components. She was cold, but in feeling him against her she stopped her attempts to grab him and looked at him.

"I loved you, too, Naomi," he said, and took her face and kissed her squarely on the lips. A faint whimper came from her as she brushed his hair with her fingers, and when he broke off the kiss, beneath the wreckage of her face she smiled. She still had a beautiful smile.

"I knew you could love me, too."

It was then he shoved her with all his might, sending her toppling backwards, slipping on the sodden deck and falling backwards into the sea. He leapt forwards to look over the gunwale. The Portuguese Man O'War were close now, drifting by her body. Perhaps she was unable to fight, or perhaps she no longer had the will, but instead of thrashing and trying to get back to the boat, she simply lay on the water as the jellyfish – *no, siphonophores*, he corrected himself – drifted across her, catching her in their wads of tentacles. The painful welts began to show immediately as the creatures entangled her in their myriad limbs, shocking her flesh with their wicked poisons. He rubbed his own chest once more, recalling how horrific that pain was, and he prayed that she couldn't feel pain. If she did, she didn't show it, and as she drifted downwards, she stared up at Dhiraj not with love, or hate, but with peace.

"The peace that passeth understanding," he whispered to himself, shocking himself with the recollection of those words.

And even before he'd finished uttering them, she was gone.

Breathing out, Dhiraj swivelled round, suddenly remembering the other poor souls he'd hauled aboard. He went to the woman first.

"Are you hurt?"

She coughed and shook her head tremulously. "Go see him," she said with a shiver, nodding to the other man. "He saved my life. I'll live."

Dhiraj nodded, shaking himself, his stomach entangled with knots, and he crawled over to the other man. He looked like he'd been beaten up badly and was struggling to breathe. When Dhiraj knelt by him, the man reached out and touched him on the arm, and looked up at him.

"I can get you some help," said Dhiraj, but the man simply shook his head, spat out some salty phlegm, and said, "No. No help. I don't need help."

English. To his surprise, he was English. "You do, mate. You look like shit."

Dhiraj kept a first aid kit on *The Lion's Mane*. It seemed a meagre thing in the face of these injuries, but maybe he could find some painkillers at least. When Dhiraj rose to get it, the man grabbed his arm and pulled him back. It wasn't a strong grip, but it gave him cause to stop.

"Just sit with me, friend."

Defeated, Dhiraj did as he was asked and slumped himself against the wall of the wheelhouse next to the man.

"You knew that robot, then?" said the man.

Dhiraj couldn't help a choked laugh. "Funniest thing. Weeks ago – Christ, has it been that long? – I fished her out of the North Sea one night. Apparently she belonged to some big-time London gangster. A guy who owned this place... what was it the guy called it... *Club Fantasia.*"

There was a beat of silence, before the man started laughing, a hacking, broken laugh, at first just a mild titter, and then a great, mangled, tear-stained wail of a laugh, in which he grasped Dhiraj's shoulder to stop from collapsing in a coughing fit. "You know who that robot belonged to? She belonged to me!"

A rod of fear stuck Dhiraj to the spot. "You're not here to kill me, are you?"

Another hacking laugh. "No. I'm past all that shit. Truth be told, a part of me's pleased she fell into your hands."

He screwed up his face. "Pleased? Why?"

The man waved a hand around limply. "You know, I always wanted to quit the life. You know, the *life*. But I couldn't. Never could. It traps you, like tentacles. I always wanted to go back home, to the white sand of Negombo, eating prawns fresh from the sea, like when I was a boy. I was happy then." Tears streamed down his cheeks, and he shook as the grief spurted out of him. "What the fuck happened to me?"

Dhiraj sat and pondered on the fact that this man, in all likelihood, tried to have him killed or captured multiple times. Yet here, bloodied, half-drowned and broken, he couldn't find it in him to hate him. There was a solemn joy in that. He took the man's hand and held it.

"What's your name?"

"Agarkka. You?"

"Dhiraj."

They sat there, bobbing in *The Lion's Mane* for some time, until Agarkka clasped Dhiraj's hand tight, and his eyes jerked forwards. Dhiraj spun up to his knees.

"I can see them, Dhiraj!" he said, reaching out with his free hand. "I can see the white sands! I'm coming home."

Agarkka's hand fell, and he breathed his last.

Dhiraj breathed out once more, and brushed his good eye shut. "Goodbye, Agarkka."

Dhiraj stood, wondering what the hell to do next. After rolling Agarkka's body back into the sea, he made his way back to the other woman. Oil City burned in the background, while the faint whirr of rotor blades sounded overhead.

The woman had rallied a little, still huddled into a ball but sitting up now, clutching the sodden remains of her shirt around her.

Dhiraj cast her coat around her shoulders.

"So what's your name?" he asked her.

"Nita."

"You worked over there, Nita?"

"Sort of," she said. "Not any more. So you're from England too?"

Dhiraj nodded. "Guess I'll go back there now. You know, I came all the way here in this little skiff to save that robot. And I just killed her."

"No you didn't. I did."

He had no response to that, so instead stood to pick up his shirt up from the deck and pull it on. "You know, my wife bought me this shirt for my last birthday."

"Your wife?" she said.

"Yeah. Sali."

Sali. Shit. And Dan. He'd spoken to them on the way up a few times. Amazingly Sali hadn't threatened to pull his balls out through his throat. She said the Scottish detective had told her what was happening up here, and that she understood.

And then he realised. Of course she understood. She was his wife. She knew him better than he knew himself.

"Alright," he said, more to himself than to Nita. "Alright. I'm coming home."

Tilda VIII

Tilda waited at Heathrow arrivals hall with the detail of officers behind her. CID worked quickly once she'd informed them of what had happened. Boswell had been both angry and impressed at her efforts, and as much as he didn't like to do it, he said it was likely that she would face serious disciplinary action. However, he'd said, the mitigating circumstances and the astounding revelations that were obtained through her covert actions may just count in her favour. There was hope that her career wasn't over just yet. And he'd allowed her the pleasure of being here once her quarry had arrived.

She checked the arrivals board.

The passengers on the flight from Port Harcourt had disembarked and were likely going through passport control when a familiar voice called over her shoulder.

"So come on, then. How'd you figure all this out, then?" said Em, her arms crossed, her face stern.

"Hey, Em," said Tilda. Her own voice was weary, as if she were the one who was jet lagged. "I called in a few people I knew. Pieced it together."

"So you can't tell me."

"Sorry. It'll all come out in the wash."

An awkward silence as they waited. Tilda folded her arms and tried to ignore Em's gaze burrowing into her from the side.

"It's not cool, what you did," she finally said. Though it was a castigation, it was a massive relief to have the silence broken.

"I know. I'm sorry, again. It was just..." She turned and looked Em in the eye. "All the shit with Fraser just came back to me. When I bottled everything up, I forgot how much it hurt. And it bloody hurt. Funny thing about hurt is that some people try to hurt others to try and relieve their own pain. I never wanted to be that person."

More silence between them as the other uniformed officers chattered among themselves, joshing and sipping cups of tea and coffee.

"So are we ok?" Tilda finally asked.

Em waited a while before giving a hesitant little nod. "We will be."

One of the airport staff made his way over to their group of police and took Em aside. Good looking chap, about Em's age, with an Essex accent. "Excuse me. Are you Detective Clark?"

Em smiled. So she could still smile. Good. "Yes, call me Em."

"The name your team provided us with has just come up at passport control." He looked at the tablet in his hand. "One Ademuyiwa Johnson. He's been detained in a customs holding room."

"Thank you," said Em, before taking the details and sending the man on his way. She turned to Tilda. "So you were right. Tell you what, you might be a bit of a bitch, but you're a bloody clever one."

That hurt more than it should have, but perhaps less than she deserved. Perhaps Em realised that too, for she made a face of regret.

"Sorry. I didn't mean that, you know. Well, I meant the second bit."

"It's ok," said Tilda with a half-smile. "Come on, then. Let's go get him."

Adem Johnson looked throughly dejected when she, Em and the uniformed officers strolled into the room. Malodorous sweat patches stained the pits of his shirt, bags rumpled beneath his eyes and he pinched his nose as if suffering from a bastard of a migraine. When he saw the police officers, he ruffled his brows some more.

"Detective Boulton," he said, visibly trying to piece together the puzzle in his mind. "Why are you here?"

It was Em who answered. "Adem Johnson, you're under arrest for the murder of Ingham Fitzwilliam. You do not have to say anything but it may harm your defence if you do not mention, when questioned, something which you may later rely on in court. Anything you do say may be given in evidence."

No resistance came as the uniformed officers handcuffed him; instead, he gave Tilda a long, defiant look. "Can we talk, Detective Boulton?"

"No chance," said one of the officers, but Tilda held out a hand.

"No, it's ok. Give us a minute." She turned to Em. "I mean, if that's ok. It's your arrest, not mine."

Em looked over her ex-partner's face, wiped a hand over her eyes in frustration, and then acceded. "Two minutes. Then we're gone."

After the others had left, Tilda sat down opposite Adem.

He leaned forwards. "You can't prove anything."

Tilda reached inside her trench coat and withdrew her globelet, set it upon the table, and opened it up. She drew up an audio file, and opened it, to Adem's bemusement. The recording was a little fuzzy, but the dialogue was plain.

> *"I do. I know how you feel. I killed a man."*
>
> *"So you have no regard for life either."*
>
> *"In fact... In fact I do. I loved the man. As a mentor. His name was Ingham. Sir Ingham Fitzwilliam. I should have listened to him. But I listened to my father instead and killed him. So that we could endure."*
>
> *"You say it like you had no choice."*
>
> *"Sometimes we don't."*
>
> *"You always have a choice. All you men."*

The recording ended, and Tilda looked at Adem. He looked at her, the defiance all gone, and his head drooped. Tilda scooped up the globelet, put it back into her pocket, and made to leave. Before she reached the door, he spoke up weakly.

"Nita," he said.

Tilda turned to see him.

"What happened to her?"

"The funniest thing. A contact of mine called me to tell me that he'd apprehended her, by the purest chance."

"Which contact?"

"A fisherman. They're en route to England now. Apparently she has some amazing stories to tell."

He made a face. "So she's alive?"

"Yes."

He bowed his head and wept. A part of her felt for the man in that moment. All these dysfunctional men left to their own devices.

She wondered if that made them monsters, or simply in need of some guidance. It was with sadness that she realised she might never know.

"Jesus," he said. "Thank God. You know, she had nothing to do with this."

Tilda nodded. Maybe he was telling the truth. Maybe not. It'd all come out when Rhodes finally made it to English shores. It wasn't her concern any more.

Outside the customs room, she touched Em on the shoulder. "He's all yours, Detective Constable."

~

At home, Tilda kicked off her shoes and slung her coat over the arm of the sofa. After making a refreshing cup of tea she plucked her globelet from her coat and rolled it on the coffee table, where it sprung out.

"Comms."

The little ball flickered out the messages she'd received. Among the various missives, emails, media packages and photos she'd received there was, to her bemusement, a video message from Fraser. That was weird. They hadn't spoken since the divorce. As she sunk into the soft embrace of the sofa and supped at the tea, she felt invigorated, exhilarated even. There'd be a lot of shit to get through in the coming weeks: the disciplinary, endless desk-bound investigation work – if she got back to her desk at all – but she could bear that. In fact she'd coast through that. It'd all be nothing compared to the shit on this case.

She opened the message. Fraser was there, hardly changed at all. Maybe a little greyer around the edges, but probably no wiser. He looked happy. And she found that she didn't feel any ill-will towards him, which surprised her.

"*Hi Tilly,*" he said, in his sweet, familiar Highlands brogue. "*It's me, Fraser. Long time no see. I, uh, I never intended to call, but I was watching the news and saw you at the scene of that arrest of that Nigerian fellow, the JPC guy. I know it wasn't you talking to the press, it was that English girl, but when I read up on what the story was all about, I...*" Fraser looked away from the camera for a second. Perhaps in humility? "*Well I knew you'd be at the heart of it. I'm proud of you, Tilly. Took me a while to realise that's what I was feeling, but it's true. Anyway, I won't keep you. I wondered if you fancied meeting up for a coffee. Just a coffee, nothing more. Maybe you do, uh... maybe you don't. But I thought I'd get in touch anyhow. Let me know. I'm proud of you.*"

The message ended, and Tilda smiled into her tea as Fraser's face blinked back into the globelet. That was unexpected. He might have been a bastard – a real bastard – but he could be charming when he put his mind to it.

The globelet's little light flashed over the 'reply' button. "*Do you want to send a reply?*" it asked.

Tilda sipped at her tea. It tasted good.

Salazar VI

"You have a visitor waiting for you in reception, Mr Salazar," said Ammi, the EA for his team.

Salazar looked up from his workstation to his EA with a quizzical face, then stared back at the clock.

5:21.

"I don't have any visitors scheduled," he said. "I'm leaving soon to get Lily from the creche. Then I'm going home."

"Yeah, I know," she said, giving her that matter-of-fact look, telling him it wan't her fault. Which it wasn't. She was a good EA. "But she's asking for you." She looked at her notes. "Tilda. Scottish lady."

Salazar swallowed and clenched his jaw. What the hell was she doing here? "I'll go and meet her," he said, doing his best to sound natural.

"Ok. I'll let her know."

Detective Boulton could wait a little longer. Salazar finished up his work, sending a final few emails off before logging out. He was nothing if not conscientious at EI Systems, and he thanked God for every day he was able to spend doing normal things, things his colleagues would regard as the height of ennui, but to him, were a great delight. His new colleagues, delightful people, lived in fear of submitting the wrong timesheet at the end of the month, lest they receive a castigating email. That made him laugh, imagining Monsieur Charlie keeping his employees in line with a stern email rather than a litany of broken limbs.

After logging off, he made his way to the creche. As usual, Lily greeted him from the opposite side of the room with a beaming, "Papa!" and ran across the floor barefoot, arms open wide, crashing into him with a huge hug, which he lapped up, wrapping his arms around her warmly.

"How was your day, Chouchou?" he asked, breaking the embrace.

"*Bon*, Papa," she said, creasing her sweet little face with a mischievous smile, looking back at her friends before looking at him again, correcting herself into English. "Good, Papa."

"Good girl, *et qu'est-ce que tu as fait*? What did you do? "

"Ah, *j'ai...*"

"*En anglais*, Chouchou."

"I just did... ah, *la peinture*... no," she giggled. "Painting."

"Good girl, baby," he said. "Come with me. Papa's got to see someone before we go home."

Salazar found Boulton waiting for him in the coffee shop area in the EIS public lobby. They sat down at a table with a holoscreen projecting rolling news, with the volume turned down. The detective made a fuss over Lily when she clambered onto one of the chairs, cooing and telling her what a lovely girl she was. Initially Salazar tensed at this, suspicious she was making some new play, but the smile on the detective's face looked genuine. He'd seen the inhuman smiles on the faces of the people he'd worked with back in Lyon, and this wasn't it. When she ordered Lily a drink and Salazar a coffee from one of the roving servobots, he decided to play along.

"Is this an official visit, Detective Sergeant?" he asked, sipping his drink as Lily sat on the too-big seat next to him, waving her skinny legs under the table and sucking her fruity milk through a neon-coloured curly straw.

Tilda shook her head and smiled. "No, so please call me Tilda."

"Tilda, then. So why are you here?"

"You'll be interested to know that Nita Rhodes turned up back in England a few days ago. She had a very interesting story to tell. Anyway, the long and short of it is that her story corroborated yours. The courts have taken your cooperation, as well as your extenuating circumstances, into consideration." A pause. "You're a free man."

He took a deep breath in through the nose. A free man. The words hit him like an invigorating splash of water. The next words he spoke came out choked, and he had to clear his throat. "I've wanted us to be free for so long."

"I know," said Tilda. She looked at Lily and smiled. "I can see why. I always thought you were a good man. I wanted to apologise for being so..." she looked around the coffee shop for the right word. "So officious. But if I hadn't been, we wouldn't have made the arrests we did. The robot you programmed. It captured critical evidence and relayed it back to us in London. Admittedly, more through luck than design, but we got it."

"I see." Salazar still mulled over the words 'free man'. He mussed up Lily's hair and tried to imagine what it would be like to not live with one eye open all the time, but he found it hard to do so. Maybe he never would. That was ok, he reasoned, so long as his precious daughter never had to grow up doing the same. That would be more than he could have hoped for from his life six months ago.

Tilda shifted, maybe a little awkwardly. If she expected him to start somersaulting for joy, she'd be disappointed. He couldn't remember the last thing he'd done that he could say he was proud of, but he'd done it all for the best of reasons. Maybe that was enough. He nodded and took another sip of coffee.

"What are you doing at work at the moment?" she asked.

He smiled at the small talk but entertained it. He enjoyed the smallness of the lives of ordinary people. To be able to pretend he could do it was fun, if only for a time. Perhaps if he pretended enough, then he'd be part of that smallness. He hoped so. Big problems were tiring. "Work is good here. It's a good company, despite everything that's happened. The share price took a big tumble after the fire at Oil City, and Nita's Digital People project has been mothballed."

"But you're still here," noted Tilda.

"I'm working on advanced prosthetics project now. I worked too long on building those..." he screwed his face up. "...those *things*. My hands need clean work."

Tilda nodded, and they sat in silence for a period, until something flashed up on the holoscreens projecting from a wall by their table. It showed a rolling news report, which caught Tilda's eye. "Look at that."

Salazar looked the screen. Images of a huge building, aflame at night in the sea, took up the screen. Over the images, the newsreader recounted his bulletin.

"*The explosions which devastated the Johnson Petroleum Company's Oil City complex a month ago in the Bight of Bonny, eighty kilometres south of the Nigerian city of Port Harcourt, have been blamed on faulty engineering. The new CEO of the company, Joanna Johnson, who took over in the wake of her father's death in the disaster, said a full investigation would be forthcoming."*

The projection cut to Joanna's face, addressing a throng of reporters thrusting microphones and cameras towards her outside the JPC offices in Port Harcourt.

"So she's the new boss," said Salazar. "The father was killed, one brother arrested and another one also killed. Poor woman."

"Yes," said Tilda. "Poor woman."

"*Qui est la dame*, Papa?" asked Lily, peering at the image of Joanna Johnson.

"She's a very important lady," said Salazar. "*Elle est très importante.*"

"*There is much to be done,*" came Joanna's voice from the report, tinny through the Projector speakers. "*This is a devastating time for my family, and there is a great amount of grieving to do. But through this grieving I have come to realise that there are others who have grieved for far longer, who have borne these grievances for centuries, and which have manifested in desperate ways, such as the rise of the NPF rebellion in this region.*

"*It has long been an ambition of mine to fight injustice, to right ancient wrongs, to align the creation of wealth with the responsibility we have towards the wellbeing of our people and our communities. I will do my best to ensure JPC emerges from this crisis stronger than before, and that it will continue to make a profit. But this profit will not simply line the pockets of those in least need of it; we will reinvest not only in new energy technologies, but also in the local economy and community, ensuring that the people who have lived on this land for centuries will be able to share in the proceeds generated off the back of it. This is my vision.*"

Joanna continued to talk about the specifics of the disaster, but Tilda turned away from the screen. "That sounds promising. Maybe she can break the cycle of corruption over there. I tell you, there will be some pretty powerful people with egg on their faces when the investigations get going over here and over there. I think she'll do well."

Salazar sniffed cynically. "You think so?"

She raised an eyebrow. "I take it you don't?"

"We all start off pure," he said, staring at Lily and ruffling her hair. "Pure hearts and pure intentions. But really we're all men of war." He took a moment to smell his coffee. "The women, too. That's why freedom smells suspiciously sweet when it comes."

A servobot came over and cleared their table of the empty cups. Lily handed hers over with a toothy smile, and the little robot whirred away.

"Papa," she said, fiddling with the leftover straw from her drink. "*Quand je serai grand, je sera un robot.*" She jerked her arms about in the style of a crude robot, making Tilda laugh.

Growing up to be a robot, indeed! He wished he could laugh at her silly, childish ideas – like a normal father – but he couldn't. "*Non, tu vas pas*, Chouchou," he said, kissing her hair. "You don't want to end up like me."

About the Author

Away from the page, Dan works for the UK Space Agency, primarily working in the field of space robotics, which comes in rather handy when coming up with new ideas for science fiction stories.

Dan's debut novel *Man O'War* is published by Snowbooks. He has also published short stores with Canadian indie publisher Woodbridge Press for their anthologies *The Haunting of Lake Manor Hotel*, and *Journeys*. His non-fiction work *Eat Yourself, Clarice!* is a Lacanian study of Hannibal Lecter and western low culture. The second edition was published in February 2017.